NIGHTWALKER

by

SIDNEY FILSON

AN ONYX BOOK

NEW AMERICAN LIBRARY

A DIVISION OF PENGUIN BOOKS USA INC.

PUBLISHER'S NOTE

This book is a work of fiction. Names, characters, places, and incidents either are the product of the author's imagination or are used fictitiously, and any resemblance to actual persons, living or dead, events, or locales is entirely coincidental.

ONYX TRADEMARK REG. U.S. PAT. OFF. AND FOREIGN COUNTRIES
REGISTERED TRADEMARK—MARCA REGISTRADA
HECHO EN DRESDEN, TN, U.S.A.

SIGNET, SIGNET CLASSIC, MENTOR, ONYX, PLUME, MERIDIAN and NAL BOOKS are published by New American Library, a division of Penguin Books USA Inc., 1633 Broadway, New York, New York 10019

First Printing, December, 1989

1 2 3 4 5 6 7 8 9

PRINTED IN THE UNITED STATES OF AMERICA

HE TRAINED AND TRIGGERED HER AS A WOMAN AND A WEAPON

Khan. Six-feet-four of beautifully sculpted muscle. Torrentially tireless and superbly skilled in making love. Poetry in motion and death in action in the martial arts.

He could have any woman he wanted, and he had chosen Grey. He could make his students do anything he wanted, and he wanted Grey to do more and be more than any of them.

Now he was gone. And only Grey could follow in his footsteps and reach his heights . . . in a battle against evil where no blows were barred and only the most magnificent moves could win. . . .

NIGHTWALKER

To Peter Konecky

ACKNOWLEDGMENTS

To John Goldman, a journalist, my eternal thanks for years of reading, friendship, spelling lessons, blue penciling, and encouragement.

To Beverly Stowe, who took the time and trouble to argue over a "gold-slippered foot"; and Anne Saxon, who was my first editor on a gray Southampton morning.

To martial arts masters: Peter Urban, Frank Ruiz, William Chen, Owen Watson, Ron Van Clief, Hui Cambrelen, and Thomas Agero, my thanks for years of schooling. To Master Jason Lau, my everlasting gratitude for sharing secrets of the Nightwalker.

Thanks to these people in the world of books: Charles Hunt, who believed in the first place; Barbara Lowenstein, who sold; Sandi Gelles-Cole, who loved the martial arts and took me out of my time warp; Maureen Baron, who bought something different; Nina Reznick, Esq., who picked up the gauntlet when she didn't have to; and my editor, Jackie Cantor, who displayed the courage of her convictions.

To master storyteller Sidney Sheldon, heartfelt thanks for encouragement, friendship, expert advice, and taking the precious time to read my manuscript.

A most special thanks to my mother, Pearl Grant, for teaching me to love books and every night's bedtime story.

1

She knew exactly how she would kill him. It had taken her almost as long to plan that as the three years it had taken her to find him. It was not to be a clean, long-range sniper action, and the MAC-10 she cradled—complete with silencer, covered matte-black so no glint of the moon would expose her position—would not blaze to life for him. Nor would she cut his throat silently and leave him dead without knowing why. Her razor-sharp Fairbairn-Sykes commando knife would remain sheathed.

No, she had done too much research. His death would be a scenario of both shame and torture. A harmonious duality, within which he would be aware he was dying by *her* hand—a woman was bringing him final karma. She would break the rules of her kind for this one. She would have personal satisfaction.

She had already been there for hours and would lay in wait until she felt his presence. His *chi* would precede him, just as an approaching swimmer sends waves ahead. There was no limit to the time she could stay hidden. Her crouched, motionless body would not cramp, nor telegraph pain or hunger. She had entered a trancelike state in which all her psychic channels were open, her bodily functions under control. Nothing but the task mattered. She could wait days if necessary.

Then a slight breeze and fragrance of sweet plumeria blossoms wafted in the May night air. Her forebrain stayed fastened in the present reality of the kill. Subconsciously she permitted herself to let the scent set off memory associations and drifted to another flower-smelling spring of years ago . . .

1975, Long Island, New York

Ivy Day at St. Anne's, a Sacred Heart boarding academy for girls. The whole school was present, but today seniors were the stars. As a class, they planted ivy at the North Wall's base, while at a distance, the yearbook committee, comprised of undergraduate girls, argued over which senior would be "Most Beautiful." The undergraduates had narrowed their choice to two gorgeous best friends: Grey Coltrane, the school's best athlete, and Llana Dellagio, popular for her feisty humor and wit.

Llana was five-three, small and lithe, a dark-haired madonna with huge brown eyes, velvety olive-rose skin, and pearly teeth that flashed when she smiled.

Grey was almost five-seven, with masses of auburn hair flowing in burnished waves to her waist. High cheekbones, a straight-bridged nose, and well-defined lips, the bottom one slightly full, punctuated her face. But it was her eyes that were first noticed—a startling green, sloe-shaped, and fringed with long black lashes. Her face was a sensual statement the nuns at St. Anne's had done their level best to suppress from the moment they had had charge of her.

"A child such as this, cursed with so much worldly beauty, must be taught suppression of the libido for the sake of her immortal soul," the mother superior had warned teaching nuns when nine-year-old Grey had first arrived at St. Anne's.

But there was nothing the nuns could do about the gifts nature had bestowed upon the Coltrane girl. Even the loose-fitting St. Anne's uniform could not conceal curving lines of breast and hip that blossomed with the years.

"Can you believe graduation is in a few days?" asked Llana.

"Llana, let's do it," Grey urgently whispered. "Let's do it now. It's our last chance."

"I don't know, Grey—if we get caught . . ."

From down the line, Mary Beth, who had the longest hair at school, broke in, "Grey, what are you doing this summer?"

"I don't know, except wearing human clothes," Grey said, making a face at the navy blazer and gray skirt she had worn at St. Anne's for the past eight years. "I wish I could go to gymnastic camp in Vermont." She packed earth gently around her vine.

"My parents are taking me to Europe as a graduation present," Mary Beth said. Her thick blond braids touched the ground as she planted.

Llana sighed. "My aunt and uncle are coming for the summer from Italy, so Mama and I will spend it cooking." Then her brown eyes lit with devilment. "But, as a saving grace, they're bringing their son, who is rumored to be nineteen and super-gorgeous."

Mary Beth's blue eyes widened. "Llana, he's your first cousin, then. That's incestuous!"

"Adds more excitement that way!" Llana quickly retorted.

"Watch out for the sisters, talking like that. We can still get into trouble," Mary Beth said, then sighed herself. "I'll never get to meet any boys with my mother and father taking me everywhere. God! Paris with chaperones."

Marguerette Calhoun, all blazing red hair and freckles on white, white skin, said, "There's more to life than boys, you know!" She made a too-quick move and tore her ivy plant in two. Marguerette could hardly see and wore thick glasses.

"Of course there is—*men*," said Llana, her eyes snapping.

Marguerette raised her lens-covered eyes skyward. "And our blessed Lord who gave us all life."

Grey and Llana exchanged raised eyebrows. Everyone knew Marguerette was going to be a nun.

"God, Grey, your eyes are the color of the ivy. I wish mine were a different color."

"Llana, your eyes are beautiful! Like brown topaz. You look like a Keane painting, they're so big . . ."

"Gre-e-ey, Grey Coltrane, where are you?" Their mutual admiration society was interrupted. Sister Marie-Carol, black habit all aflutter, her round, rosy face all smiles, came up to them. She was the most loved of the teaching nuns.

"She never told Mother Superior," Llana said as the blue-eyed woman approached.

"I know," said Grey, then stood to hug the sister. "Oh Sister, I'm going to miss you so much. You're the real reason I'm graduating," she said, and shuddered at what would have happened if Sister Marie-Carol *had* reported her unbelievable transgression. Then, arms about each other, girl and nun paused for a moment, looking at the wall of ivy growing to the very top turrets of the Gothic school building, and as one remembered that incredible night seven years before . . .

It was 3 A.M. when Sister Marie-Carol, responding to a sixth sense, made an unexpected bed check and heard Llana Dellagio's voice. It drew her into the room. Llana, in her white nightgown, was halfway out the window.

"Don't. Please come back, you'll get caught, you'll get killed," Llana pleaded out the window. "Oh, Sister!" Llana's eyes rounded with horror as Sister Marie-Carol thrust her from the window and leaned out herself.

The nun craned her neck and peered upward. "Jesus, Mary, and Joseph," the nun said, crossing herself. For there, as naked as the day she was born, ascending the ivy, was ten-year-old Grey Coltrane.

"I told her not to, Sister," Llana wailed in the background. Sister's panic abated somewhat as she noted the monkey-like ease with which the Coltrane child moved upward and realized she was not witnessing a first. The nun darted downstairs and onto the lawn, where she watched the rest of the twenty-five-foot climb and prayed for the child's safety. She breathed a sigh of relief when finally the moon spotlighted the roundness of small white buttocks spilling over the top of the ivy. Sister Marie-Carol crossed herself as a rush of anger overtook her.

The nun flew up four stories of stone steps. Quietly she pulled open the door to the roof. There she found Grey Coltrane contemplating the moon. Sister Marie-Carol stood for a moment, transfixed by how natural the naked child appeared, bathed in silvery moonlight.

The nun was furious. How dare the child? This incredible violation meant expulsion from St. Anne's. Yet, touched by the scene before her, for an instant Sister remembered when she had been a free-spirited schoolgirl. Empathy welled within her for the loneliness Grey's solitary little figure bespoke. And, truthfully, great admiration for Grey's courageous climb. The nun's tender side won.

Still, the nun spoke sternly, breaking the young dreamer's trance. This was, after all, St. Anne's. "Grey, why have you done this? You could have been killed! What if the ivy had given way?"

Panic overcame the child. "Sister, Sister, please don't tell on me." Grey began crying. "It was just I dared myself. I'll never do it again. I'll do penance for hours and good works." The little girl attempted covering her nakedness with her arms and sobbed so hard she began gasping.

"I won't tell," said Sister. And she never did.

Now, seven years later, Sister looked at Grey with a twinkle in her eye. "There's a little graduation gift for you here." She waved and a red Ferrari convertible zoomed up the curved school drive and pulled to a gravel-crunching stop.

A mechanic in overalls stepped out and handed a flabbergasted Grey keys and an envelope. "Hap-happy graduation, Miss Coltrane," he stuttered, disconcerted by her beauty. "She's all tuned and ready to go."

Astounded, Grey war-whooped, gave a cheerleader's leap, then froze in disbelief.

The seniors completely forgot their ivy, which paled in comparison to the red Ferrari. They squealed in envy and excitement, inspecting the blockbuster present.

"Give me the keys," demanded Llana, "you're too paralyzed."

Grey numbly obeyed. Llana took quick charge and expertly lowered the top. Girls piled over the sides as nuns and lay teachers gathered and stood watching with the undergraduates.

"How could Mom and Daddy be so cool? I thought maybe a trip to Europe with Mom would be my present," Grey said to no one in particular as she opened the card. "Wha . . . ?" She was taken aback. "Happy Graduation. Love, Ed," the card read.

"Oh rats!" She looked hurriedly about to make sure no sharp-eared nun had heard—expletives being grounds for hours of on-knee penance at St. Anne's.

"What's the matter, kid?" Llana had given the driver's seat to Daisy Waller, who knew how to automatically wash the windshield and was doing so repeatedly.

"Oh, Llana, I can't keep this car. My parents will

make me return it for sure. My mother says,"—Grey pursed her lips in imitation—" 'Nice girls accept only flowers and candy from gentlemen.' " She paused and considered. "Then again, Ed doesn't really fall into the 'gentlemen' category. I mean, he's not a suitor. He's— he's kind of older-brotherish."

Llana was definitely confused. "What do you mean? Who's Ed?"

"Well, he and his parents do business with Daddy. I'm not really sure. They don't tell me much."

Llana interjected, "Like me. I'm not even allowed in the room when the men are talking. Sorry."

Grey continued. "Ed's like a blood relative. I call his parents Aunt and Uncle Fowler. We all spend holidays together, and Ed and his parents always give me presents. Ed usually gives me books about dogs and horses." She smiled with affection. "He's kind of like a big teddy bear. When I was little, everybody joked, 'Grey's going to marry Ed when she grows up.' Then Daddy would laugh and call it 'the merger.' " Grey stamped her foot. "God! The Fowlers have oodles and oodles of money. Why shouldn't Ed give me a car for graduation?" Just as she was assured that she had a solid argument to justify keeping the Ferrari, Sister Marie-Carol signaled Grey to come near and further perplexed her.

"You have permission to drive it home," the nun said, causing Grey to scream in delight. "All right, child. Now calm down and go to the sanctuary. Thank the Lord for your happiness, then clean your room and take your belongings."

"Thank you, Sister, thank you," Grey said. She ran back to Llana and whispered, "Meet me in my room. *Now* really is our last chance."

Llana nodded assent and Grey sprinted across the manicured lawn dotted with lilac bushes and through the massive oak and iron doors of the school.

Once inside the castle-like building, her whole demeanor changed. The shadowed, somber interior of St. Anne's did not lend itself to high spirits. She made her way, treading silently through the wide stone halls, now and then passing dark birds that were nuns either walking silently or on their knees scrubbing the flagstone floors.

In the chapel, she took a white lace veil from a pile,

put it on, crossed herself with holy water from the font, then went to her assigned pew, and knelt.

Funny, she thought. Just when my knees don't hurt anymore, I'm leaving. They were always red, though. When she had first come, her knees had bled. Everyone at St. Anne's prayed on bended knee for hours every day. Morning mass, between-mass prayers, night vespers . . . Then, last thing, just before retiring, the girls again put flesh to wood and thanked God for the day.

She looked around for the last time. Here and there nuns washed by the pale light of the stained-glass windows knelt in silent prayer.

"Thank you, God, for everything," she said. "And please allow me to keep my present."

She left the chapel and passed through the dark school halls and up giant stone steps to her room. Most of the population was outside. Upstairs was deserted.

Llana was waiting in Grey's trophy-filled room, a worried expression crossing her features. "God! What took you so long? If we get caught . . ."

"C'mon," Grey said, and pulled Llana by her hand down the student halls, past all the doorless rooms. She whispered, "Won't it be great to have privacy?"

"My brother says we don't have doors so we can't play with ourselves," Llana whispered back.

Grey covered her mouth to stifle her laughter.

They reached the nun's quarters, where no students were ever allowed. They passed quietly through rows of cells the sisters occupied. Grey and Llana peered with fascination into the wooden cubicles—each with a cot and one open shelf. No mirrors, rugs, pillows, and no partitioning curtains. The nuns had no privacy, either.

"We'll never have this chance again," Grey said. She darted into one of the cubicles and pulled the bed away from the wall. "Sure enough," she whispered. "Look, Llana."

There, hanging from the metal frame of the bed was a small, black cat-o-nine tails. The two girls touched the leather whip.

"Gives me the shivers," Llana whispered, pulling up her shoulders and making a face.

Many nights they had lain on their beds and listened to the *whtt-whtt-whtt* of leather on flesh as nuns scourged themselves. The brides of God made no sounds as they paid with pain for their transgressions. The practice of self-flagellation for religious discipline had been officially outlawed by the church long ago, but this order of Sacred Heart cloistered nuns lived as they had in the Dark Ages. And the hierarchy of the church looked the other way.

"I wonder what Sister Marie-Carol could ever do wrong to have to whip herself?" Grey said. She remembered a time when Sister Marie-Carol had had to beg food on her knees from the other nuns at meals. Grey had suffered watching her.

"Okay, you win this one. They're real whips," Llana said. "Now let's see the bathroom. Quick!"

Grey pushed the cot back in place. The girls peered out of the cell cautiously—nuns had a way of coming up on you silently, suddenly. They jumped out and hurried down the deserted hall toward the nun's bathrooms.

"See, I was right," said Llana, pointing to the rain-slicker-like garments hanging in rows over bathtubs. "Sisters undress under them so they don't see their bodies. Then they climb in the tub and spread them out so they can wash without seeing their own naked flesh."

The two girls broke into hysterical giggles.

Grey pulled herself together first. "You better get out of here now. I'll come down in a minute."

"What about Scarlett and Amber?" Llana asked.

"God! I forgot," said Grey.

Hidden in a bush on the school grounds were two plastic-wrapped, forbidden novels, *Gone With the Wind* and *Forever Amber*, ragged from rereadings. Llana and Grey idolized their heroines obsessively.

"We'll never get the books without being seen," Grey said. "Maybe some poor romance-starved student will stumble onto them and be saved from a life of total ignorance."

In her room, Grey packed a canvas bag, then dealt with her trophies. Each first-place trophy sparked a moment's recall as she placed it carefully in a cardboard box: uneven parallel bars, balance beam, vaulting (that one had cost a sprained wrist), rope climbing, lacrosse . . . She closed the box, which would be picked up on graduation day, and took one last look at the room. I will not miss you!

Back in the sunny warmth outside, Grey again became exuberant and trotted lightly across the lawn. She frightened some cardinals, they flew suddenly up, scarlet, brilliant against the cloudless blue sky.

She ran to the Ferrari, filled with girls. "Everybody out, gimme the keys," she ordered.

"Nuts. C'mon, Grey, take us for a ride. Please?" Mary Beth pleaded.

"Sisters would never let me. Besides, I have to get home now!" Grey said, thinking of how precarious her ownership of the magnificent vehicle was.

She slipped into the driver's seat, inhaling the fragrance of the black leather interior. "Mmmm, smells so good!" Wiggling against the leather's cushy softness, she started the ignition and drove slowly at first, shifting gears, trying the brakes; then, sure of the powerful machine and out of any nun's sight, she sped through the school's massive wrought iron gates doing eighty.

With her long auburn hair whipping, she drove down the Long Island Expressway, reveling in the Ferrari's performance while remembering her begging and pleading to get a driver's license last summer. Daddy had been afraid she'd get "wild" like a lot of Long Island kids who raced around in their parent's cars. As a matter of fact, it was Ed who had interceded, taught her to drive in one of the antique cars he collected. "That old dear," she said, suddenly realizing she was alone—in an environment of her own control. She had never been permitted to drive by herself.

"Things are going to be different now. I'm graduating. I'm becoming an adult. I'll be eighteen in September," she said to the complicated dashboard. "I'm going to meet a swashbuckling admirer and have romantic adventures like Amber St. Clair."

She rehearsed her arguments for keeping the Ferrari as she pulled off the main highway. There were more cars than usual around her dun-color, two-story, English Tudor home. But the driveway was clear and she parked the Ferrari and gave the steering wheel one last loving pat.

Sounds of people approaching catapulted her to the present. Brush snapped underfoot. She calculated six by the noise they made. She peered deep into the jungle, closing her Master eye, conserving the visual purple in its cones. If whoever was coming shone a light, she would not be blinded. Instead, when she opened that eye again, she would still be able to see, cat-like in the dark. They had no lights. They called each other "Bhra." Their singsong island voices cut the tropic air, "Good night to move da kine, Bhra. Trades blowing low, not to carry the scent."

"Yeah, Bhra! Da hippies smell dis bud, dey come out da hills, smoke des buds."

"I'll kill dem *haoles*. This *pakalolo* go mainlan'. Make big money."

She heard the thumps of heavy loads being dropped close by.

"Gimme whiskey," one of the men said.

The answer was a warning. "Dat plane gonna be quiet. You got to be sharp, see it."

"Dat plane be comin' when it comin'." The voice became a growl. "Gimme whiskey, Bhra."

Her weapons were already attached to her body. With one smooth, silent leap, she hung by one leg from a branch in camouflage fatigues, looking like but another bunch of leaves on the massive banyan tree. She looked down on them.

She was right—six. Samoans and Portuguese/Hawaiians, she guessed by their huge size. The moonlight glinted off their twelve-gauge shotguns. The men probably came down from Kula in open trucks with giant palm fronds trailing off the backs—covering loads of the best marijuana in the world. They would have ridden standing in the back, shotguns openly displayed. Dogs back there, too. They were supposedly in the mountains pruning palm trees and clearing roads for tourists' safety. It was a common sight on Maui and no one bothered those trucks—least of all the police.

The marijuana runners meant nothing to her; they were only an indication *he* was coming. Lust for his blood came strong. Feelings were dangerous. Feelings slowed reflexive action by milliseconds. She stopped them, swung into the tree's crotch, and crouched there, her mind fixed on the danger below.

Dawn came soon, punctuated by the sound of exploding bombs. Across the turquoise water to Kahoolawe, a small and mountainous island, the Navy tested demolitions. She peeled the black-matte cover from the MAC-10. Now the submachine gun, dull green like her garb, blended with the tree in the daylight.

The bomb explosion and dawn brought response from the men below her. "I like go shoot dos Navy. Bomb des islands, kill de fish."

Another one said, "Dat plane not comin' in daylight. We stuck here, Bhra, till night."

They all started talking. "I'm hungry."

"We take da truck, go Kihei, get food."

She knew it would be a long trip. This was Makena, the westernmost point of Maui, and a wild, deserted beach. There was no water or stores for miles.

"Bring more whiskey." One of the men called after those departing.

"Get beer, too."

She watched four of them make their way to a rusty blue Toyota pickup. They untied the yellow dogs from nearby trees and loaded them in the back. The Toyota pulled off, leaving a trail of red Maui dust behind.

She could clearly see large burlap bags and the two remaining men. One of them had a wide scar that ran from his eye to his top lip and stood whitely out. He pulled a pocket knife and chopped at one of the burlap bags.

"What you doing, Bhra?" the other said.

"Gonna smoke dis Kula bud. You got paper?" Scarface asked.

"Yeah, yeah. Too good for dem damn haoles anyway."

They rolled the marijuana, then reclosed the bag. The pungently sweet smell rose into the tree and reminded her of a time with Khan. The memory of him brought a pain she could hardly bear.

The man she nicknamed Scarface unfolded his massive body—he stood well over six feet. "Hey, Bhra. One fine *wahine* come da beach."

She looked where his giant brown hand pointed and saw an island girl walking down the deserted beach, carrying a basket of pink, white, and purple plumeria blossoms. Putting the basket down, she dropped her sarong and strolled into the calm water wearing only a tiny black bikini. Her long black hair, adorned with a red hibiscus, fell to the young roundness of her hips.

"I like get me dat, Bhra," Scarface said.

"Hey, Bhra, we got dis pakalolo. Dat big boss kill us, we make trouble here, before they get dis bud."

"I kill her, Bhra. She don't tell nothin' that way," Scarface bragged.

"You all talk, Bhra," his companion goaded.

The young girl turned and came back onto the beach. She spread her flowered sarong on the sand and sat on it, her legs wet from the water. The girl's sheet of shiny hair stirred in the wakening trade winds as she began stringing blossoms into leis.

The scar-faced giant moved quickly out of the jungle and onto the open beach. He was almost on top of the girl when she saw his shadow. With a start she turned. He scooped her up under one arm, carrying her like a sack of potatoes, one hand covering her mouth, hauling his bounty back to the other man. The whole abduction had taken but a minute.

The Nightwalker watched from her tree perch. She could see the girl's eyes rolling, wild with terror. Scarface tore her bathing suit with one hand, while his other stayed across her mouth. He ripped off the top. Small, brown-nippled breasts heaved with fear. His hand grabbed the girl's bikini bottom. She tried to push him away, frail brown arms like willows against the wind. Still, the girl's meager struggle hampered his progress. He let go of her mouth to use both hands, and his victim's hysterical cry pierced the air.

Scarface backhanded the screaming girl across the mouth. A loud crack echoed through the grove as he hit her. The girl went silent. Blood began seeping from the side of her mouth. He drew a knife and pulled the point across her throat. The girl moaned. Scarface put his hand over the blood trickling from the cut on her throat and rubbed his palms together. Then he showed his bloody hands to the girl and smiled. He brought the knife back toward her throat. But there was no need to threaten— any thought of struggle had left her. The girl lay glassy-eyed with shock, like an animal about to be sacrificed.

"Stick her, stick her," the other man said. His pants

were a puddle around his feet. He stroked himself, ready, waiting.

The Nightwalker watched from above. It is nothing to me. It does not involve my task.

But she could not separate herself from the scene below. She looked at the blood and the rape and the waiting man. Waiting, waiting. Like the men had waited for her.

Pinned to the ground, clothes being torn from her. A line of brown-uniformed soldiers waiting. Her own screams filling the air.

The memory broke her discipline. Chi rose inside her until it was an explosion.

Below her, the second man stood, bent forward in anticipation, watching Scarface plunging into the girl.

She knee-dropped onto the standing man's upper back, snapped vertebrae, rendering him immediately senseless.

Thrusting his body from her, she dropped farther onto Scarface's back just as he reached orgasm, and plunged her knife through his ribcage—into his heart. His body collapsed over his victim. The double take-out took but seconds. Withdrawing her blade, she sheathed it, grabbed Scarface by the arm, and hauled his dead weight off the girl. The other man lay unconscious. She looked at the naked, blood-soaked girl lying there in the foliage.

Suddenly she wanted to help this girl because of the way she had been rescued by Y Shin Sha from where she had been left for dead.

2

⎯⎯⎯⎯◦§◦⎯⎯⎯⎯

She knelt beside the still figure, inspecting the oozing cut on the girl's throat. It was only a deep scratch. Where Scarface's fist had struck, the girl's lip already swelled black and purple, but it would heal. In one motion she pulled a small vial from her fatigue leg pocket and opened it. A tiny pink pill lay in a bed of white powder. She sprinkled the powder, *Yunan Paiyao*, made from stones, on the bleeding cut and waited for it to act. The bleeding stopped almost immediately.

The Nightwalker ripped off her hood, not wanting to scare the girl, and long hair spilled around her. Placing the girl's head in her lap and shaking her gently, the Nightwalker used a soothing voice, "Pull your self together. You have to go. There are others coming back here and they will kill you."

Then, putting her hands on each side of the girl's temples, she let chi flow through her palms.

The dark almond eyes opened slowly, grew suddenly wide with fright. "Pele, Pele." The girl spoke the volcano goddess's name, the deity Hawaiians believe still walks the islands.

At first the Nightwalker did not understand. Then she remembered her face was streaked with camouflage. I must look like a wild apparition to the girl. She thinks I'm Pele. Well, that's all right, at least I don't have to explain my presence, she thought.

In a firm but gentle voice, the Nightwalker commanded "Go!" and sent one last surge of energy through her palms.

The girl responded. Robot-like at first, she rose and took a few tottering steps. Then, with a last look of disbelief at her rescuer, fear overtook her. She ran, naked and bloody onto the beach, where her flowered

sarong still lay. She snatched it up without breaking
stride and, still running, wrapped it around her body and
fled, sobbing down the beach.

Suddenly the magnitude of what she had done struck
home. Her mind raced. Had she jeopardized all? No.
Nothing is impossible, she thought. You taught me that,
Khan, my beloved Khan. I will have him for you no
matter what.

The men, one dead, one unconscious, had to be dealt
with immediately. Brush cover would not be good enough.
If others came back and brought the dogs close, the
bodies would be discovered. Again her training took
over. The unconscious man first. No more killing. He lay
facedown. She turned his head to the side, forced his
mouth open, and squeezed a few drops of a strong liquid
sedative on his tongue. He would remain unconscious for
at least twelve hours. She rolled his body onto its back
and began to haul.

An hour later, nothing but the marijuana bags remained. The drag marks were swept away by the large
cactus leaf she painstakingly retraced her path with. Putting her small, canvas-booted feet into Scarface's giant
sandals, she walked away from the burlap bags, then
backed up in the same footsteps, making even deeper
impressions, as they would be from Scarface's massive
weight. She changed to the other man's sandals, did the
same, moving quickly, accurately. Sweat poured from
her brow, blending with the green and black camouflage
streaks on her face. It was already in the eighties.

She regained her position in the banyan tree and surveyed the scene below. It was to her satisfaction. The
mail truck to Hana the next morning would come upon
the still unconscious man in the road. It would be all over
by then anyway. Scarface was her gift to the ocean, his
body jammed securely between some rocks. Shark fod-
der perhaps. She secured the two pairs of sandals on tree
limbs and settled down to wait.

Not a moment too soon. She heard the truck even
before she saw the cloud of dust it raised. Then the four
of them were around the bags.

"Dey cut the bag!" one said in disbelief. "Dey left this
pakalolo. Motherfuckers crazy. Dat man kill us if anything happen to this load."

Another man followed the sandal prints in the dirt and brush. "Dey went off. Dey stoned and went off," he said.

"Don't matter," another interjected. "More for us. Dey come back, we split their heads instead of the money." He laughed at his own cleverness and the others joined in.

It had worked. Then they became more concerned with the rising wind than the disappearance of their cohorts. It was ten already and the trade winds gusted. By eleven, they would hit forty miles an hour.

The remaining four guardians of the marijuana wrapped towels around their heads, Arab fashion, and crouched together with the burlap bags. It would be at least six before the winds quieted—seven thirty until it was dark enough for a plane to come.

The Nightwalker watched the ocean change from calm azure to choppy gray as the raging Maui wind whipped the water. The yellow dogs sought shelter under the truck. She smelled food on a gust of wind and began salivating. It had been two days since she had eaten. The men below her ate the food they brought for the others, drank, and talked. She felt her bladder call. Why hadn't she relieved herself when she had had the chance? Too late now. She pressed hard behind her ears with her forefingers. The urge to urinate receded with pressure-point application. She closed her eyes against the blowing, stinging sand as the wind reached its peak, and nestled deeper into the banyan tree's protective crotch. So many hours to wait until dark. "Go back," she heard Mother's voice in her memory. "The wait in ambush is the hardest. Go to another time."

She slowed her heartbeat and went . . .

1975, Long Island

Grey vaulted the steps of her home three at a time. Her green eyes blazing with excitement, she burst through the front door, shouting, "Mom, Mom, where are you?" Her voice echoed in the high-ceilinged entranceway. She quickly checked her image in the seven-foot gilt-framed English pier mirror facing the front door. "God, what a mess," she said, attempting to smooth her wind-blown hair.

Her mother emerged in a pastel-plaid golf dress and matching cashmere sweater, neat and calm, the way she always was. "Here I am, darling." From her manner, no one would never guess she hadn't seen Grey since Easter vacation. "What's the excitement?"

"Ed—a car." Grey pulled her mother across the flagstone floor toward the door.

"I know, darling, Daddy and I saw the auto before Ed had it sent to school for you. Of course, he asked our permission. It's a wonderful car. The good sisters must have been startled by the color."

Grey was incredulous. They were going to let her keep it! "Mom, the 'good sisters' are startled by anything that doesn't take place in the sanctuary."

"Ed is here—in the den."

Ed rose quickly from one of the blue and brown tweed sofas as they entered the den. Grey smiled at him, displaying her perfectly even white teeth. Ed's round tummy was so cute, she thought, and he was so predictable—always dressed the same: a banker's blue-striped suit with vest, the habitual cigarette glowing in the long holder he was never without. Ed looked like the Penguin on the *Batman* series, Grey thought, and his small, pointed nose locked the similarity in place.

"Grey, how lovely you look," he said.

How could anyone think her school uniform flattering? "Oh, Ed—thank you!"

They stood at quite a distance. He had something in his small, well-manicured hand, holding it like a hot potato. He certainly is acting strangely today, she thought.

Grace Coltrane spoke. "Sit down, you two. I'm going to see about some tea."

Grey plopped onto her father's brown leather chair with her legs stuck out, bobby sox and penny loafers foremost, heels pushing the cocoa carpet's deep pile. She would rather sit on the floor, but Mom would disapprove.

Ed stood over her, beads of sweat on his brow. He thrust his hand toward her. "We thought you might like this," he said.

Grey took the petite velvet jewel case. How nice, she thought, opening it, Ed's parents must have sent a graduation gift. Probably a charm for her bracelet. She loved Aunt and Uncle Fowler.

The diamond blazed up at her, so large it looked fake to her undiscerning eye. Ed, who meanwhile sank to his knee, took her hand. Removing the huge gem from its case, he slipped it on her finger while stammering, "I finally formally request your hand in marriage, Grey." He continued, ignoring the fact she didn't say yes and was frozen in disbelief, "I think July would be a lovely time for our wedding, don't you?"

Then the wood-paneled den was filled. Mommy and Daddy, Aunt and Uncle Fowler, Grandma, Uncle Edward and Aunt Elizabeth. The ring was on her finger and instead of tea, Clarissa the maid served champagne and caviar. Everyone was congratulating her.

Grey suddenly felt part of an eerie stillness, as if she were witnessing the scene from the eye of a raging hurricane. *This couldn't be happening.* She had never even had a date!

Hours had been spent talking about boys with her schoolmates, but in actuality, athletics had taken all her free time. There were twice-yearly St. Anne's dances attended by pimply faced, tweed-jacketed, prep school nerds, presided over by stern-faced nuns. The dances sent her back to the fantasy world of Scarlett and Amber. God, I've never kissed a boy! I can't marry Ed! This has to be a nightmare to wake from.

Only a combination of shock and thoroughly instilled good manners kept her silent. To maintain her self-control, she fixed her eyes on the terra-cotta plaques of the four seasons hanging over the sofas. She drank a lot of champagne and felt the weight of the diamond ring each time she raised her glass.

The family and Ed attributed her behavior to maidenly shyness, perfectly understandable on such a momentous occasion. The exception was Aunt Fowler, whose infinitely kind blue eyes returned again and again to the schoolgirl she saw fighting to hold back tears.

The tears came later, when Mother attempted tucking her into bed after Grey had thrown up twice. Grey sobbed in great, wracking sounds as tears rolled down her cheeks. "But he's so much older than me. He's ugly, he's . . . My God, Ed must be forty," she cried. "This is crazy!"

Mom sat down, pulling Grey against her. "There, there," she said, gently patting Grey's back. "Now, now, darling, you've had too much champagne and excitement. You've always told us how adorable Ed is, how much you love him."

"As a friend, not my husband," Grey wailed.

Mom slipped into her patient voice, the one she had used teaching Grey to read when she was five. "Friendship is the most important thing in a marriage. Daddy is my best friend," she said, "and Grey, you have background—strong heritage. Just because our families are transplanted to America is no reason to discontinue tradition. We marry people of equal breeding. Ed is the last of a great English family. You are your father's only offspring."

Grey pulled away. "Mom, this is ridiculous! I've never even had a boyfriend. Besides, I'm supposed to pick who I marry, not you and Daddy. Things are different in America."

Mom took a folded piece of newspaper from her pocket and showed it to Grey. "This is an article about the daughter of the famous evangelist, Billy Graham. Dr. Graham chose a husband for her when she was seventeen, and she accepted her father's plan for her. She came to love her husband very much after they were married. You see, Grey, parents do know best."

"Mom, that's the *National Enquirer*. I'm not allowed to read it, remember, not even in the supermarket?"

Grace Coltrane would not be sidetracked, "For once they've printed something worthwhile."

"Mom, I've never had a boyfriend," Grey wailed.

"Now, dear, don't be repetitious. You've already said that. Ed will make a wonderful husband. That's what's important. Passing fancies in a young girl's life are just that."

"But, Mom, I've never had a passing fancy."

"Then that's just a bit of heartbreak you've been spared," Mom quickly reasoned. "Ed will always love and respect you. Your children will have position in life."

"Children. Oh, my God!" Grey buried her head in the pillows. Loud sobs began again.

Mom stroked her hair, then stood up. "Shush. Go to sleep now. We'll talk in the morning. Then you'll be as happy as Daddy and I are. You'll see." She straightened the covers one last time and turned out the lights.

Grey stopped her sobs after a while and indulged in her miserable thoughts. The moonlight, as though to contribute to her depression, shone through the blinds and cast oblique prison bars on the ceiling.

Children with Ed? The big ring weighed heavily on her hand as she wiped away tears. Have a baby—me? The very thought of sex terrified her.

More tears. Her long fingers picked spasmodically at the striped quilt.

When she had been twelve and about to go off to summer camp, Mom had read her a book about the birds and the bees. "You may get your period while you're away and I want you to understand why," she explained. "When I was a little girl, nobody bothered to inform me. I got my period and thought I was shamefully sick and hid the bleeding. My mother finally found a bucket of bloody towels soaking in the basement and that's the way she found I was menstruating. Then she still never explained it to me, just showed me how to take care of myself."

Grey thought the whole thing sounded fascinating, and she felt sorry for the little girl Mom had been. She paid close attention to the clinical animal stories Mom read out of the big book. When Mom finished, Grey was thoroughly familiar with the mating habits of animals. "But what about people? Do Daddy and you . . . ?"

"Yes, darling, people make love."

"But you don't have to do that, you already have a baby, me!"

"Well," Mom paused, seemed to be reaching for words, then lapsed into her Grandmother Dillingham voice, complete with English accent. "Married people have sex for other reasons, too—because they love each other and that's a way of expressing it."

Grey had been horrified. Then she remembered the time she had run into Daddy when he was naked coming from the bathroom with that big dangle between his legs. Her mom and daddy doing that!

Thereafter, Grey had shunned her parents' bedroom. No more climbing into bed with them on eagerly awaited Sunday mornings while Daddy read the funnies and she felt so warm and cuddly between the two of them. *Before she knew what they did in that bed.* She still thought of Mom's biology lesson as the end of innocent childhood.

Now this! Was she to be initiated into womanhood by Ed? Where was her Rhett Butler? I'll tell Daddy in the morning, this can't be!

But the thought of an adult conversation with Daddy scared her as much as marrying Ed. She began crying again. All the years of "the merger" flashed through the champagne haze in her head, as did images of Ed and Daddy always off in corners talking business. She brooded upon how importantly Ed figured in major decisions to do with her young life. Like when she had been nine and had not wanted to leave public school to board at St. Anne's. Ed lectured on the attributes of an education at a Sacred Heart academy.

"Listen to Ed, he's got your best interests at heart," Daddy said. And off to the convent she went.

At twelve, armed with Mom's biology lesson, she was so excited about going to summer camp for the first time, all set to go and have splendid fun. Ed suggested she could have more fun staying at home. Daddy went right along with that, too! Daddy always agreed with Ed and made such a fuss over him.

"Oh God, please help me," she pleaded aloud. Grey pushed the covers back and climbed unsteadily out of bed. She crossed the carpet to the dormer window seat, where her dolls were neatly aligned as though waiting for her to come and play. She leaned way out the window, through the crisscrossed organdy curtains, and into the night. She took a few deep breaths, desperately trying to clear her head. Then she slipped out of her white batiste nightgown and let it fall to the window seat. Lightly, deftly, with the same prowess that had earned her a balance-beam trophy, she climbed onto the windowsill, then onto a branch of the giant oak that touched the house—moves so familiar she had no need to look for footing.

And there she crouched, ensconced in the oak tree, where lived her "tree spirit," and moonlight displayed her skin's whiteness against the blackened green of the leaves. She felt the bark's roughness with the bottoms of her feet. Her still-little-girl breasts responded to the slight chill in the air, and her nipples hardened.

So had she perched for years at night when the house was still. Her parents would have been horrified knowing their convent-bred daughter spent hours naked in the backyard tree, like an Indian waiting to pounce, pretending she was one.

And well might she have been, so comfortable did the girl appear—dark hair moving in the wind, daring lines of face highlighted by glancing moonlight.

But no matter how she looked, she lacked the self-confidence of an Indian waiting to pounce from a tree. The young beauty instead possessed the roaring insecurities of a modern-day teenager raised in the suppressive fashion of an era long gone; when female children passed from father to husband by the men's mutual agreement. Purposely held from maturity, she was emotionally years younger than her chronological age of seventeen.

Crouched on the limb, her female parts opened to the breeze, she felt the whispering caress of the wind there. "Virgin Mary, help me—I'm a virgin like you. Help me talk to Daddy tomorrow. I've been good. Make Daddy listen."

She would indeed need help in dealing with her father, whom she absolutely adored, whose blue eyes were distant except when he was authoritative (Daddy did the spanking). Otherwise, George Coltrane seemed embarrassed by his overly beautiful daughter. He had never played with her or kissed her, and only pretended to listen when she talked.

Their one shared activity had started when she was eight and he began her riding lessons. He had been a champion equestrian. "Heels down, back straight, light hands," he instructed, to her delight.

Little Grey loved her riding lessons. The surging power between her thighs, the feel of the saddle—that special tickle while she watched beloved Daddy's straight back as he rode ahead. She quickly became an excellent horsewoman.

But her great prowess, the ribbons she earned, made no difference. Daddy remained remote. She envied her schoolmates, whose fathers openly made a fuss over them. Her guess that Daddy had wanted a son became the key to her tomboyish enthusiasm for athletics.

Her thoughts brought her full circle to the realization:

Daddy always wanted this marriage. She had never said no to anyone in her life. The thought of taking a stand against her father crashed her into yet deeper despondency. Realizing the problem was beyond her at this time, she left the tree to seek nature's cure—sleep.

A plane engine broke the Nightwalker's reverie. She stretched her hands, honing them. Electricity collected in her fingers. She formed them into vibrating claws.

The man below her also heard the approaching plane and stirred in preparation to move the marijuana.

It was a balmy Maui night. A twin-engine Grumman landed on the now calm waters of Makena Beach. A man stepped onto its wing. Disappointment washed over her. The man, clearly outlined by moon and starlight, was taller, heavier than the black man she sought to kill. As a matter of fact, the man was a giant and she thought of Khan. She pushed away the image of her dead husband, his awesome strength, the litheness unusual in one so huge, and concentrated.

The four men hauled the pakalolo toward the shore. The big man on the plane's wing inflated a rubber boat, then began paddling soundlessly over the silver water toward the shoreline.

She scrutinized the waiting Grumman, its engine idling. A hand rested outside the pilot's window. It flashed small, pale, and delicate in the moonlight. Not him, either. Her prey was not on the scene.

The man in the raft reached the shoreline. Taking advantage of the activity, she slipped from the banyan tree. Moving silently through the deep sand, at the same time blending with the tall cactus while avoiding its dangerous spines, she wiped streaks of camouflage makeup from her face.

She knew it would be two weeks before this was again a pickup point. Instead of waiting, she calculated, she would try to find him elsewhere in these islands. Clear of the area, she finally emptied her bladder among the cactus.

The man who paddled the rubber raft toward shore hunted the same prey as the Nightwalker, although his plan of action was quite different from hers.

His included making an ass of his prey before ever

confronting him. He was not a marijuana dealer and had daringly swooped down in the twin-engine Grumman knowing Mikel Anton's plane was due anytime.

Making haste, he paddled rapidly to shore. "Move that load quick," he commanded the four marijuana runners, who jumped to his authoritative voice, wrongly assuming he was the pakalolo's proper next guardian.

Suddenly the big man thought he sensed a presence in the night. He looked sharply at an enormous banyan tree, back from shore. The feeling receded.

The raft, loaded to capacity, rode low in the water. "I'll be right back," he said and paddled to the Grumman. It had taken two men to put each sack on the raft. The big man easily swung them one by one aboard the plane, then headed once more for shore. When all but one burlap sack was in the raft it was again low in the water. "I'll be back for that one," he said to the four men and paddled quickly away.

From the air, as his adopted son piloted the Grumman upward, the big man watched the four marijuana runners dance and wave their arms in disbelief as Anton's plane landed on the water and the men realized they had given the product to the wrong person. There would be no money for them this night—only hell to pay.

In the cockpit fragrant with the richness of marijuana, the big man laughed aloud, but his eyes were steely as he spoke to the slight boy. "I left one for him." The boy's eyes were ancient as they locked with his.

Her trained eyes saw clearly in the night as she headed for Kihei. A gekko atop a cactus chirped a mating call. Blessed was the home with a gekko in the bedroom, believed Hawaiians.

Her weapons and gear were stowed in flowered sarongs ingeniously knotted into a backpack. her parched throat and the thought of sustenance drove her to a trot. Even jogging, it would take hours to reach food.

Dehydration attempted to slow her progress. She recognized the feeling of vertigo just as the terrain totally changed and she came alongside the Wailea golf course. The first light of dawn was breaking. The grass was rich green, manicured, and watered. Condos bordered the plush course. Japanese tourists appeared in motorized golf carts. It was five-thirty, and they meant to beat the heat and wind on the links. Of course, she chided herself, the hotels!

She ran faster now, not even feeling the weight of her backpack, and soon came to the luxurious Wailea Hotel. Cutting down its winding paved drive, bordered by red hibiscus bushes and plumeria trees of every color, she reached the hotel entrance, slowing to a walk as the bellhops and car parkers in front eyed her. Another beautiful hippie, probably down from Hana, they thought. "Hey, sister," one inquired, "can we help you?"

"Ladies' room?"

She followed the directing finger past pools of sacred carp and stone statues of Hawaiian deities, through an open-air lobby decorated with magnificent wool wall hangings, into the bathroom, where she gulped handfuls of cold water from the sink until pains in her stomach caused her to stop.

She looked in the mirror and saw why the boys at the front had looked at her strangely. Vestiges of leftover camouflage makeup dirtied her face; her long hair hung unkempt from the tie-dye head scarf and held bits of leaves.

She washed as best she could at the small sink, pulled her fingers through her thick hair, retied the scarf gypsy style under her hair, and hurried on her way.

At six fifteen the Nightwalker reached Paradise Fruit, a twenty-four-hour, open-air, natural food restaurant, market, and gathering place, where she quickly bought and ate three mangos. Needing to locate a drug trafficker to renew her search, she decided to hang out by the checkout counter when she saw Zig-Zag rolling papers for sale, figuring sooner or later a big fish would come her way in this land of marijuana lovers and growers.

Mauiites rise early and Paradise Fruit was already busy. Several people bought rolling papers, but none sparked any reaction from her.

At seven a new red Jaguar convertible crunched onto the pebbled parking area. Its tall redheaded owner jumped out and came directly to the checkout counter. "Two Zig-Zag, please," he said, smiling at the gorgeous hippie in camouflage pants and a black bikini top, leaning against the papaya bin.

In the eighties, Maui seemed to harbor the last of the world's hippies. Fifty-year-old relics of Woodstock lived in the mountains on natural food farms, their graying hair still braided and beaded. The more youthful hippies, from all over the world, cruised everywhere, living on the beaches, sharing crash pads, having babies . . . They chanted Hare Krishna, strung beads, painted the sunsets, and smoked as much Maui Wowie as they could get their hands on.

She smiled back, noting white powder residue at his nostrils, two dried blood spots on his shirt. "Where are you headed?" she said in a velvety voice, looking at him with her emerald eyes.

"Kula, wanna ride?"

"Yeah," she said, and sauntered to the XKE, where she took off her backpack and slid neatly into the passenger's seat. She watched him expectantly from the car as he paid for his rolling papers.

"Can you roll?" he asked as they drove past the Kamole beaches: One, Two and Three, shallow turquoise bays where humpback whales play and mate every winter.

"Sure," she said, accepting the pack of papers and small film can he proferred. So predictable, she thought, opening the can. Perfect green and tan buds were packed inside it. "Mmmmm," she sniffed, "smells great, Kula bud?"

"Yeah, da kine," he said, thinking she was easily the most beautiful woman he'd ever seen, at the same time trying to pull his act together after an exhausting night with an unwilling blond condo owner from L.A. who had turned "willing" as a result of his batting her around a little. Feeling the effects of champagne and cocaine recede and a hangover coming in for a three-point landing in his head, he reached into the glove compartment for his sunglasses.

"Headache?" she asked.

"How did you know?"

"It's in your aura," she said.

Oh boy, was she a hippie! He hoped she wasn't too nuts. Some of these Mauiites were pretty bent out of shape—too much LSD in their carrot juice. He checked her out again from the corner of his eye. God, she was a beauty! "What's in your knapsack?" he asked to make conversation, and her sarong pack *was* bulging, looking heavy on her lap.

"A machine gun, knives, explosives, things like that," she said in a teasing voice, picking at her camouflage pants. "And a silk dinner dress," she added in a suddenly sultry voice. Raising her black lashes, she blasted him full power with her sloe eyes and handed him a neatly rolled joint.

"I suppose you're a healer?" he said, taking the joint. All these hippies thought they could cure anything—especially cancer.

"Yes. Want me to take your headache?"

"Sure," he said. Then her palm was cool on his forehead. When she took her hand away a few seconds later, the headache was better—gone, he realized. Must have been the aspirin I took in L.A.'s bathroom. "Wow, you're a real miracle worker," he said, lighting the joint.

The red XKE sped smoothly along, the sun bright now over the mountains at their right; the sea sparkling, calm turquoise at their left.

"I couldn't refuse you a ride, you know. You might have been Pele," the man said, referring to the legend that the goddess of the volcano traveled Hawaiian roads, particularly Maui's, in the guise of a hitchhiker. It was terrible if you passed her by, a curse on you and yours.

"Do you really believe," she asked, "the hitchhiking woman suddenly disappears from the car, next to the driver? The men making these claims come from all walks of life—lawyers, doctors, salesmen and surfers—and they always describe her differently with the exception that she's always about thirty-five years old?" She waited, her eyes fixed on him, for his answer.

He pulled on the joint. "I don't know," he said, just to say something.

"Living in these islands changes people's perception of things. The Big Island—Halemaumau churning red-hot lava, shooting liquid gold five hundred feet to the fire pit's rim. Awesome! I believe Halemaumau *is* Pele's home and she really exists," his green-eyed passenger said fervently, confirming his belief she was hippie dippie.

The Jaguar turned onto the Haleakala Highway, heading up-country toward Kula. As they climbed above sea level, the temperature dropped. Pine trees replaced palms.

Mansions and lush grass farms formed the panorama. Cattle and horses grazed contentedly.

Many of these mansions and farms belonged to the marijuana rich, she knew, evaluating the Jaguar's owner again: pitted skin, moist nostrils attesting to his recent cocaine snorting, skinned knuckles on his right hand. She guessed the blood on his shirt was someone else's. He was perfectly relaxed with her, taking for granted she was a resident because she knew Pele's legend. Good, the Nightwalker thought, and innocently asked, "What do you do on Maui?"

"I'm retired," he said, "from the New York stock market. I just enjoy myself now."

Sure! He couldn't be older than thirty-eight at the most. Perfect. He was live. "Great bud," she said, pretending to drift off on a marijuana cloud. "Can I buy a little bit from you?"

"I'll give you some. Where are you going in Kula?"

"Nowhere special. Just hanging out."

"You can hang out at my house."

"Super. Thanks."

He drove faster now, thinking how easy it was to take a hippie home.

They cruised high into the mountains and after passing a protea farm, fields of exotic furry flowers grown primarily on Maui, they turned off the highway onto a winding dirt road until he stopped the Jaguar at an isolated, unique, four-level wooden house built into the mountainside.

She followed him around a red wooden deck to the back of the house, where the deck became huge. There was the inevitable hot tub bubbling away and a breathtaking view of Maui and the ocean. A few cows grazed peacefully in lush grass right under the deck.

She leaned on the redwood railing, thinking how Kula could almost be the mountains of Vermont, so clear and crisp the air. But there was a difference: the subtropical Hawaiian sun cut sharply through the cool air. Exactly this combination, plus the world's richest soil, made this area's marijuana so prized.

He came very close and said, "How about a hot tub?" while brushing against her arm. Another great thing about hippies, they took their clothes off in a second!

"Wow, that sounds great!" she said with enthusiasm. "Can I have some herbal tea and another smoke first?" She smiled, her exotic eyes full of promise.

"Sure, sure thing, herbal tea," he said, leading her into the glassed-in living room, opening all the sliding doors so the room became part of the surrounding deck.

He reached under the sand-colored Brazilian leather couch and pulled forth a shoe box containing at least a pound of perfect buds. He began cleaning some.

"Let me do that," she said, "I love to clean grass."

She crushed buds on the box's cover and, tipping it back and forth, expertly rolled seeds into her hand. She spoke of Kula's high-quality grass. "When I get my house here," she said in a wistful voice. "I'm going to grow the best pakalolo and hide it from Green Harvest."

"How would you do that?" he asked, further assured she was local. Operation Green Harvest was police foraying in helicopters, often lassoing twenty-five-foot marijuana plants. It was not uncommon to see airborne pakalolo. Locals knew the score; tourists never imagined what was happening.

"Oh, I'd plant in heavy forest. I love to see pakalolo growing. I have friends in Canada who grow the biggest plants you've ever seen," she said, laying out the challenge.

"No, they don't," he said. "Come on."

She followed him outside and up a green hill and then into a cluster of pine trees, where he led her proudly to a few tall and lush pakalolo plants nearly ready for harvest, but not enough to support his lifestyle. This was a personal patch. "Too bad you don't have more," she said, following him wide-eyed around the marijuana as he pulled off overlong leaves and lovingly patted at full kolas. "I have friends in New York who buy really big."

He looked at her closely. His partner was two peaks up with acres of plants. They needed a New York connection. He thought of how many times he had made great contacts through smoke groupies like this one. They traveled around, crashing here and there, connecting dealers and buyers, living off commissions and free smoke— sleeping with dealers.

"What kind of big?"

"Ten thousand pounds every couple of months," she answered with a dazzling smile.

"Let's have that herbal tea," he said. "We can talk in the hot tub."

Back at the house, he found Sleepy Time tea for beautiful hippie and concocted himself a pitcher of heavy-on-the-vodka Bloody Marys. He got tight, talked too much, and broke open his hard-drug stash. He offered her cocaine and Quaaludes while staring at her black bra top. "Hot tub time," he said, wondering what color her nipples were. He looked from her breasts into her eyes that were suddenly jade stone. Then, catlike, her pupils narrowed. The redhead felt a tug of fear, but discounting the premonition, he grabbed a tempting breast and suggested she suck his dick. She pushed his hand away and said she'd think about his offer. He jumped her on the couch, throwing all his body weight on her, and slapped her across the face with one hand and ripped her bra with the other.

The drug trafficker awoke hours later and found himself hog-tied. While struggling with ropes, which would take him two days to get off, he brought into focus the chain of events that had left him like this. God, she had hit him hard!

He remembered as he struggled against his bonds that she had knocked him back—across the living room couch, out onto the deck. After that, and the last thing he remembered, she jumped on him, making a horrible hissing sound.

I wonder what she stole? I'm lucky, he thought, worrying his wrists against the hemp's burn, the weirdo didn't kill me! A Manson type. Can't even call the police once I'm free, he wryly conjectured. No matter what she had taken, a drug dealer needed to stay low-key. I've been had. For a moment, remembering the conversation in the car, he even wondered if she might have been Pele.

When the Nightwalker was well away from the four-level house, she sat in a field reading the black leather phone book she had taken. Loose-lipped fool, she thought, flipping pages. While bragging, he had mentioned several names. First names. Conveniently, people were listed by first names. "Ritchie" she found. He said that was the "man" in Kula. Well, she'd just have to visit Ritchie.

The face of the black man she sought was suddenly

before her. Hate filled her, boiled inside. Quickly she replaced his image with another, whispering, "Khan, Khan, I love you." She needed release.

She rose, beginning a strange war dance. It started with snapping, grabbing, and striking movements of her graceful hands and then incorporated her whole body. She whirled in circles, leapt, kicked, stretched, reached, and made movements that had no names. This way did she maintain her training, and it was both beautiful and terrifying. She began glowing. Those who made her what she was appeared in her mind's eye. *I feel you, Mother. I feel you, Y Shin Sha.*

When she finished, the glow about her faded.

She picked up the phone book and began the long climb upward toward ever richer land. She had missed Anton once again! Well, her three years of research were not for naught. She knew Anton was in Hawaii, and she would kill him here—it was fitting.

As she climbed toward clouds stationed like smoke puffs interrupted by mountain peaks, she saw not the surrounding beauty, only images of the man she would torture to death and the man she loved, interchanging with each other. Back and forth, the two images clicked incessantly inside her head as though powered by an out-of-control slide projector. Love, hate, love, hate, love, hate . . .

Madness threatened to consume her. As dictated by Mother and Y Shin Sha, the Nightwalker left present reality, and retreated to a time very unlike now, when she had not controlled her destiny.

3

1975, Long Island

Grey never had the talk with her father. She was basking in his approval for the first time in her life. Daddy was happy about the impending marriage and paying lots of attention to her, talking and joking, buddy-buddy. He swept her off her feet with his joviality. She didn't want to marry Ed, she thought, but then again marriage was glamorous and grown-up, and if Daddy thought it was right . . .

Graduation was to come. Grey drove to St. Anne's every day. The (by now she knew the details) ten-carat, blue/white pear-shaped diamond made her a celebrity, but she wondered if her classmates would have been so delighted if they saw Ed.

"I want to see a picture of Ed," Llana demanded in a whisper as they passed classes.

Grey adeptly changed the subject, managing to avoid Llana's questions, which proved no easy task. As Grey's best friend, Llana felt she had the right to know all. But, luckily, monitored by ever watchful nuns and busy every minute these last days at St. Anne's, there was scant time for talk.

A little person who had taken up residence in Grey's head since she had stopped confiding in Llana spoke: "You don't want to marry Ed."

One side of her listened to that little person, the other side loved being made a fuss over. The ring was spectacular. Every movement of her hand displayed the diamond's fiery flashes. Sometimes she told the little person she would return it to Ed. "He'll understand. Ed is my friend—he'll explain it to Daddy."

Grey was voted the most beautiful and Llana the most

popular. Their pictures contrasted side-by-side in the year-book. Grey, the strong-boned exotic; Llana, a doe-eyed pixie. Well trained by the nuns, humbly unaware of her striking looks, Grey said, "Llana's prettier."

Grey finally came to terms with the fact she really didn't want to marry Ed when the engagement announcement appeared in *The New York Times*. Her graduation picture looked back at her from the social section. The write-up was extensive. She read it over and over, her background, her family—and Ed's. Daddy beamed over the article and over Grey.

After graduation, which, thank God, Ed did not attend, her school days were immediately replaced by daily trips to Manhattan. The bridal registry at Tiffany made Grey feel grown up and important. She and Mom spent hours before finally settling on Royal Doulton china, so finely made that when the saleslady held a fluted plate to a lamp, the light shone through.

Her silver, handcrafted by Tuttle of Boston, was the only American sterling bearing a hallmark—initals of the current president. "When the chief executive leaves office, the mold is destroyed. That means your silver will be a collector's item," the saleswoman explained. "As each new president takes office, you should purchase at least one teaspoon with his hallmark."

She selected crystal. "Baccarat, of course," Mom said, Grey learned about tumbler sizes and champagne glasses and brandy snifters. Marriage was going to be fun.

"Not to Ed," said the little voice in her head.

Mom bought her a pink leather box filled with blank index cards in alphabetical compartments. "You list gift and sender, that way you'll breeze through your thank-you notes after the wedding," Mother lectured. It was a cute box.

Wedding preparations became an exciting game. The entire playroom was turned over to white damask-covered rented tables displaying gifts. Each time the doorbell rang, it was another marvelous present. There were already thirty-six place settings of Royal Doulton; a silver unicorn head by Roberto Estevez, mounted on a base of black ebony; a wine basket of sterling silver from Bucallati with a scroll-leaf design.

There was a case of Chateau d'Yquem 1975, Ed's

favorite present. A Pratesi white silk quilt with matching silk sheets and pillowcases was delivered by Rolls Royce. They were displayed next to a six-piece set of matching Louis Vuitton luggage, including a steamer trunk that opened into a traveling closet and set of drawers. Mom and Aunt Fowler entertained friends among the gifts while Clarissa served tea and sherry.

A fifteen-thousand-dollar gold vermeil English biscuit box circa 1865, in the shape of a drum, arrived from Bulgari. Grey knew its cost because Daddy had to get the biscuit box's value for insurance purposes. He was taking extra coverage while the presents were in the house. Alone one day with her presents, Grey lifted the biscuit box. The precious metal was warm and smooth to her fingertips. She saw her own green eye's reflected in the gold. Her eyes seemed to ask the question in the back of her mind. "What will my wedding night be like?" the seventeen-year-old whispered.

The tables in the playroom were soon loaded. Grey took to running downstairs and switching on the overhead lights so all the crystal and gold and silver would sparkle just for her.

European relatives of the Fowlers sent a full silver tea set and tray, made by A. Mazzucate & Figli (whoever they were), valued at eighty-five thousand dollars! Daddy hired around-the-clock security guards to satisfy the nervous insurance company. There was always a man in uniform sitting with the gifts.

Fittings at Bergdorfs began. Gray's wedding gown was a Dior original. It was traditional ecru made of seemingly weightless gossamer silk. "Oh mademoiselle, how magnificent you are," the fitters and salesladies exalted, exclaiming how exquisite she was in her gown. Grey had to agree as she gazed at herself in the many mirrors of the rose-carpeted fitting room. The dress did accent her blossoming breasts, her tiny waist, and fell to the floor like a froth. The lace for Grey's veil, so fine the green of her uptilted eyes was only slightly diminished through it, was handmade in a French convent. The ladies fussed and fussed over her.

Little did she know that later, in a gossip session, those same ladies would refer to Grey as the "virgin sacrifice." The Fowler family had long been delights of Bergdorf's

charge account department. The salesladies certainly knew
Ed Fowler, for many a woman had come to Bergdorf
after Ed's by-phone-permission to be outfitted. Certainly
not in the bridal department, but then the matronly ladies of Bergdorf's did not confine their gossip to floors.
He had sometimes accompanied the receivers of his favors. "Eddy" they called him. But they were nothing like
the beautiful child they now dressed.

Grey's bridesmaids' squeals resounded through the dressing rooms as they tried on rainbows that were their
floor-length gowns, off-the-shoulder watered silk with flowing organdy sashes exactly one tint lighter than the dress
itself.

"I'm stuffing socks in my front," Llana whispered one
fitting day.

Grey picked her bridesmaids' gifts, gold lockets engraved with the wedding date and "Love always, Grey."
For Llana, her maid of honor, a wide gold bracelet
similarly engraved.

The month of June passed like a week.

Aunt Fowler took Grey shopping. Unlike Mom, who
was a bit too plump for haute couture, her future mother-
in-law was fashionably slim, looking much younger than her
sixty-five years. "Let's not go to Bergdorf, you must be
tired of that store." Aunt Fowler smiled and crinkled her
blue eyes. "Let's be adventuresome and go to Bendel's."
Mom considered Bendel "too far out."

At Bendel's, Aunt Fowler seemed determined to outfit
Grey for life. "But, Aunt Fowler," Grey said of the red
leather boots with wine snakeskin cuffs around their tops,
"they don't go with anything I have." They had already
purchased twelve pairs of shoes and boots.

"They will, dear. Not to worry. This is only a start.
Let's go to Madison Avenue."

Aunt Fowler's chauffeured limousine waited outside
each establishment with growing piles of packages. Aunt
Fowler waxed ever more enthusiastic. It was a delight to
dress Grey's perfect size six figure. She had a daughter
of her own, but nature had not been so kind, and Jennifer's squarish body was a secret but keen disappointment
to her fashion-conscious mother.

Liza Minnelli was in the next fitting room at Halston,
and Grey caught a glimpse of her. Then Halston himself,

just as delighted with Grey as Aunt Fowler, personally supervised Grey's selections. One dinner suit was pink silk jersey. Its jacket had padded shoulders and lapels covered in tiny sparkling bugle beads. "You look like a young Rita Hayworth," said Aunt Fowler. They departed Halston with six outfits.

They whizzed to Betsy, Bunky & Nini, where they "picked up" flowered gingham sundresses—adorable at four hundred dollars each.

Grey tried to be polite and not pay attention to the cost of things as Mom instructed. But the way Aunt Fowler spent money was astounding. It seemed the American Express card was a wonderful thing to have.

Norma Kamali was the next stop. Grey was decked in a scanty bikini, a jumpsuit made from a parachute and a white silk pantsuit with a matching vest.

Among Julie's exquisite handmade clothes, Grey was drawn like a magnet to a work of art titled; "Minnehaha's Wedding Dress," white chamois-leather beaded in intricate swirls and turquoise flowers with fringes instead of sleeves. Once inside the butter-soft chamois, Grey stared into the mirror.

"We'll certainly take that!" said cheery Aunt Fowler, pulling Grey from a beautiful daydream wherein she waited for handsome Hiawatha. "Enough shopping for today, let's go eat something sinful."

In busy Serendipity they ordered fancy Alaskan crab salads and huge ice cream sundaes topped with bittersweet chocolate flowers. They commented on the chic Manhattanite's clothes, makeup, and hairdos. *Aunt Fowler was so much fun.*

"Tell her you don't want to marry Ed," the little voice said. And at that moment Grey nearly bared her heart. Then the thought of explaining—how Ed wasn't Rhett Butler—seemed an awful thing to do, something that would terribly hurt dear Aunt Fowler. Grey pictured Daddy's smiling face. It's going to be all right, she told herself, and the moment passed.

Grey fell asleep on the drive home and tottered groggily to bed. Aunt Fowler, with the stamina of a racehorse, stayed to chat with Mom about the wedding.

It was to be a huge affair. Six hundred guests at the church followed by dinner and reception at the country club. The politics of seating family and friends at times loomed an unsurmountable task.

Grey and Mom poured through Amy Vanderbilt's book of etiquette. Invitations were addressed and stamped until Grey had writer's cramp.

The flowers took forever to decide. Grey's bouquet was to be white: baby's breath, roses, and gardenias. The bridesmaids would carry mixes of pastels. The church was to have baskets and baskets of flowers. There were dinner and reception tables to decorate. Daddy gasped when he saw the bill.

"This would all be wonderful if it weren't Ed you're marrying," said the little person inside her head when she cried at night in bed, scared and caught up in the wedding like a leaf carried by a river current.

Contributing to her ambivalence, during the flurry of excitement over the wedding Ed was wonderful. He and Grey had twice weekly "dates." He first took her to Le Cirque. "We'll have to be careful, they could lose their liquor license by serving you," he laughed.

Ed was delighted by her youth and beauty. She wore the pink Halston suit which made her abundance of auburn hair seem more red. Pearl and diamond earrings, a gift from Ed, flashed on her ears. The beads on her lapels sparkled, and the diamond on her finger caught fire from surrounding light. No patron in Le Cirque could keep from admiring the extraordinarily beautiful girl so richly adorned.

Ed kissed her hand in cavalier fashion and presented another fabulous gift every time he came to pick her up. Each offering was embraced by a silk-lined velvet case with Harry Winston's name prominently embroidered inside. Grey's favorite was a wide, ruby-studded gold cuff bracelet with matching earrings.

Grey had never really sampled liquor before. An occasional sip of wine from Daddy's glass on a celebration day or communion wine was the extent of her imbibing. Now she accepted the happy haze that came with a cocktail before dinner and the champagne flowing through their meals. The haze diminished the importance of Ed's tummy.

That really didn't matter, a tipsy Grey reasoned, even as she noted Ed's belly pushing at the edge of the table.

They'd do lots of jogging and things like that after they were married and he'd be in great shape.

The alcohol also blunted the edge of Ed's caustic jokes. When he pointed out someone who was gay, Grey felt terribly sophisticated and thought how shocked the nuns at St. Anne's would be.

Absolutely everyone seemed to know Ed. He was bowed and scraped to—and so was she.

They became known as a New York couple. But there was a bittersweet side to celebrity. One night, just before they entered Lutèce, the captain glanced at the reservation book. With horror he read, "Beauty and the Beast." He quickly erased the offending notation and penciled "Edward Fowler, table for two," in its place. The captain then stormed off to find the literary culprit.

That same night at Lutèce, Grey glanced up and noticed a faraway look in Ed's eyes which she attributed to business preoccupation and concerned herself with the *pâté de foie gras*, which was delicious beyond description. But at that moment, Ed was reminiscing about their very first meeting . . .

He had started planning it all when he first saw her. Or rather, when she first cast her beautiful eyes on him: Twelve years ago, Grey's father was in dire straits, begging for a loan. Five-year-old Grey was with George Coltrane when he cornered Ed and Ed Fowler, Sr., at the club.

Coltrane came from good bloodlines. There had been dealings between their two families in England, and the tradition of doing business in America continued. A stockbroker, Coltrane had nowhere near the inordinate wealth of the Fowlers, but his breeding counted for much. They were members of the same New York social club, a last bastion against Jews and any other minority that dared to consider itself on a par with pure Anglo-Americans. Coltrane looked the gentleman; tall, slim, handsomely distinguished. He had achieved fame as a horseman during his Harvard years, competing in the Olympics—even taking a bronze in the open-jumping class.

Coltrane was a proud man, and Ed knew he had to be desperate to press Ed, Sr., for the loan. He was right. A Mafia threat had panicked Coltrane into throwing pride to the wind. Whatever stupid motive prompted Coltrane to invest seventy-five thousand in a fly-by-night stock in the first place was beyond Ed. But to have done so without the cash to back his purchase, and then, when the stock fell, to compound the stupidity by borrowing from a loan shark, made Coltrane in Ed's opinion a fool.

By the time Grey's father had come begging, he owed over one hundred and fifty thousand dollars with compounding interest skyrocketing each day. Two goons had visited a few days before. They administered a light beating and promised to return and cut Coltrane's balls off if he didn't come up with the money in a week. Coltrane's home was already heavily mortgaged, he said.

In the club's lounge, Ed listened to the story, wondering what the hell Coltrane had learned at Harvard. Ed, Sr., refused to grant the loan, believing no man should gamble or truck with the mob.

Following Coltrane from the lounge, Ed offered the loan himself. At thirty-four he had his own fortune left him by Grandmother Fowler. Ed did not offer to bail Coltrane out because he was sympathetic or generous—it was because of Grey.

Ed had not paid much attention to little Grey at first. Then, during the conversation, she bumped her head against the edge of the table. Drops of blood from a tiny cut on her forehead scared her, and she began crying. Mrs. Coltrane was playing bridge. Impatiently, in the middle of his plea, Coltrane asked Ed to take her to the locker room for attention. It was quiet in that area, and no women were about, so Ed picked the five-year-old up and took her to the bathroom, where he dabbed the small cut with his handkerchief and comforted her. Grey's tears soon ceased and she threw her little arms around Ed and kissed his cheek. "Now carry me back to my daddy, please." But once there, she refused to be put down. Ed sat with Grey on his lap for the rest of the conversation, her arms about his neck, the sweet, child smell of her in his nostrils.

Examining the five-year-old closely, Ed saw she was unusually beautiful—her coloring striking. Womanhood could only mean an advance in loveliness. She cried when her father prepared to leave, saying, "No, I want to stay with Ed."

No female had ever (no matter what her age) said they wanted to stay with him and meant it.

"What are you thinking about Ed?" Grey asked.

"Just daydreaming of you, my darling," Ed answered across the flickering candlelight.

Another night, in the Russian Tea Room after the theater, they sat next to Jackie Onassis and her sister, Lee Radizwell, and had caviar and iced vodka. Grey was so ecstatic over the meeting that she woke her mother when she got home.

Grey began to relax. After all, this was her Ed, the same person she had loved for years, and he was acting Rhett Butlerish, even if he didn't look the part. Each "date" ended soothingly, with no attempts at lovemaking. Ed returned her to Long Island and parted with another kiss of her hand. He was fun and great company. He was a dear.

Then came the parties. Aunt and Uncle Fowler—she'd never be able to call them "Mother and Father"—gave them an engagement dinner at the Sherry Netherland Hotel.

Grey wore a red silk Balenciaga gown with a daring décolletage. The roundness of her still budding breasts teased the scarlet silk. Her heavy auburn hair, coiffed by Cinandre in intricate twists, held three strategically placed diamond clips that caught the light from the overhead chandeliers each time she moved. Because her hair was pulled away from her face, her features appeared even more startling, her black eyelashes an even more luxuriant frame for her green cat's eyes. She dazzled the assemblage with her beauty and charm.

Daddy told her she looked beautiful, and Mom kept looking at her with tears in her eyes. Ed sat by her side, puffed with pride and happiness. His conversation was charming, his jokes making everyone at their table laugh— Grey thought him wonderfully clever. She did give a moment's thought to the fact no one her age was present, not even near her seventeen years. But the Dom Perignon kept flowing and she soon forgot about age. Strolling violinists entertained the five tables of guests, and the toasting went on all during the six-course dinner.

Uncle Fowler announced a surprise after the chocolate soufflé. "We wish to show our gift to the lucky couple," he said. Grey, Ed, and sixty guests were taken to a floor of the "Sherry"—sixteen rooms. "We thought this would be a suitable in-town apartment," Uncle Fowler said.

Grey was thunderstruck. How would she ever fill all that space? Mom had never even let her pick her own room color! Marriage began looking more and more like freedom to her, a chance to exercise her own judgment. She wandered the rooms, picturing this one a French salon, that one in an English motif. "These will be servant's quarters," Aunt Fowler said of two rooms and a bath off the huge kitchen and pantry.

A *Post* columnist who was forced to wait on the sidewalk outside wrote up the affair the next day. Grey was an "Ava Gardner-type beauty" and Ed "one of the world's most eligible bachelors," the column said.

That Saturday, as Grey and her parents brunched on kippers and eggs in the morning room, a heated confrontation developed because Llana was to give her a wedding shower and George Coltrane was first hearing of it. "No," he said, muttering "Mafia" under his breath. And that was supposed to be it. He expected to hear no further on the subject.

"I won't hurt Llana's feelings," Grey suddenly said, speaking to her own surprise, becoming quietly courageous as she defended someone she dearly loved. "She's sent out invitations. She's my maid of honor."

Grey had never been allowed to visit the fabled stone-walled fortress that was Llana's Long Island home. Mr. Dellagio—ever the smiling, well-mannered gentleman when Grey saw him at school affairs—was reputed to be a powerful Mafia chieftain. Grey had no idea whether the tales had any basis in truth, and she could care less.

Llana, as lovely as she was miniature, had shared Grey's girlish dreams, secrets, sports—everything—from the time they had first met at St. Anne's. But only at St. Anne's. The two friends were never allowed together away from school.

Llana was the only girl in an Italian Catholic family of seven. Llana, dark eyes snapping, often told Grey of the never-ending supervision. "The *boys* get to do whatever they want, go anywhere, drive . . . The *boys* have freedom and I have to stay with Mama in the kitchen. You don't know how lucky you are away from school. You have athletics and dance lessons and the country club. For me, St. Anne's is freedom compared to home."

And that was the extent of Grey's knowledge as to her best friend's home life. Certainly Llana was kept in a void concerning her family's affairs. If her father was a gangster, it was clear Llana Dellagio knew nothing about it.

For the first time in her life, Grey got her way. She spoke to Ed. Ed spoke to Daddy. She was granted her shower.

The day of the shower, Ed kindly sent his car and driver. The Bentley squired Grey and her mother to the Dellagio estate, which really did have massive stone walls around it. Robert, the chauffeur, stopped in front of tall wrought iron gates and spoke into a box mounted on a post. The grilled gates opened and the silver Bentley rolled along a tree-lined drive. Llana and Mrs. Dellagio were on the steps of a two-winged, three-story, red brick Georgian house awaiting their arrival. Behind them, scores of girls in pretty pastel dresses decorated the front porch's chairs and banisters. Like a scene from *Gone With the Wind*, Grey thought.

Llana ran down the steps to hug her. "Grey, you look beautiful," she said, approving of Grey's butter-cup-yellow, eyelet sundress, a matching yellow ribbon catching back cascades of loose ringlets and her feet encased in yellow Capezio slippers.

"So do you," Grey replied, admiring Llana's white sundress with a green fleur-de-lis design. A wide green patent-leather belt encircled her tiny waist, and Llana's shiny black hair was braided into a coronet framing her madonna's face and held in place by green fleur-de-lis barrettes. Llana's Capezios were white.

While Mrs. Coltrane and Mrs. Dellagio went inside to the coolness of the big house, thirty girls, the whole senior class of St. Anne's, dutifully followed Llana and Grey on flower-bordered stone paths to the back of the house.

"The Dobermans are kenneled, so we can go everywhere," Llana announced, pointing to a wooden structure. Menacing barks came from within as the girls passed close by.

Grey heard music. They came fully around the back of

the house, and there was a five-piece band on the manicured half acre of lawn.

Behind the musicians in tuxedos was a giant pink-and-white-striped circus tent. Attached to the tent's roof, hundreds of pink and silver balloons strained at their strings as though reaching for the bright blue sky.

"Surprise," Llana yelled.

"Fantastic," Grey said in awe, throwing her arms around Llana as the other girls gleefully clapped hands at the fairy-tale setting.

Just then male laughter was heard from behind some high hedges.

"Who's that?" Grey asked.

"The boccie court is back there. It's *for men only*," Llana said, making a face, then led the girls inside the tent to food-laden tables and piles of presents for Grey. Waiters were everywhere. One table held a lovely pink punch afloat with flowers.

"My brother poured gin in there," Llana whispered.

Grey and Llana giggled as Mary Beth downed her first cup of pink punch, then dipped for another.

Grey opened presents for what seemed like hours, then cut the huge "Congratulations, Grey" cake and gave a piece to each girl. While her mother, relatives, and Mrs. Dellagio were seated at a table, engrossed in conversation, and the rest of the girls, bright butterflies in their summer frocks, danced with each other to Elvis and "Don't Be Cruel," Llana whispered, "Let's sneak away from here."

"Won't they miss us?"

"Not our mothers, look at them," Llana said.

The two women were deep in conversation as a waiter refilled their punch cups.

"And certainly not our classmates," Llana added. "They're only looking for my brothers anyway."

They watched and nudged each other as the girls jitterbugged on the lawn. Each couple managed to make close passes at the hedge hiding "men."

"Except for Marguerette," Grey observed. "She's not dancing and she's the only girl not wearing Capezios." You could tell Marguerette was going to be a nun. Her plain beige cotton dress had sleeves, a high neckline, and did not even hint at a body contour underneath. She looked with disdain at her dancing classmates through her thick glasses. A passing waiter offered her a cup of punch which she accepted.

"Maybe she'll get drunk and loosen up," Llana said. "Come on, we're outta here."

With Llana in the lead, the two girls cut around the back of the tent, ran across the lawn, and into the big house.

"Hello, Miss Llana," a burly man sitting in a chair near the bottom of a wide staircase said. "Having a good time?"

"Yes, Anthony, thank you," Llana said, leading Grey up the stairs.

"Who's that?" Grey asked, at the same time drinking in her surroundings. The stairwell had flocked wallpaper hung with family portraits in ornate frames. "Anthony, he takes care of the house," Llana said, climbing ahead.

"Butler?"

"Kind of."

They were on the second floor, a long burgundy-carpeted, wood-paneled hall with many closed doors. "Bedrooms," Llana said, and led Grey to the very last door. "Mine."

She opened the door to a pink-ruffled shrine to Elvis Presley and teddy bears. Posters of Elvis in leather outfits were on the walls. Teddy bears perched in a rocking chair, on the bed, and in a group on the pink carpet.

Llana opened a closet door. "Look what I hid here." She produced a silver ice bucket holding an open bottle of champagne. "It's Tattinger. I got it from Papa's wine cellar," Llana said, offering it to Grey.

"Llana, you think of everything." Grey took a gulp of champagne and passed the bottle back. "This room is gorgeous! Thank you for this beautiful shower. God, you must have been planning for weeks."

Llana gulped champagne. "Actually, what I've been planning for weeks is how to get alone with my cousin," she said.

"What's he like?" Grey asked, staring at Elvis.

"He seethes with sex. He's gorgeous—the most gorgeous man I've ever seen. Black hair, huge brown puppy dog eyes, muscles, big white teeth. I get the shivers everytime I see him. He's right there behind that hedge, too!" Llana said pointing out the window.

"Can we sneak and look?" Grey asked, fascinated.

"Never happen. Forget it," Llana said, becoming serious. "I'm only allowed on the boccie court when Mama sends me with refreshments."

"What's boccie?" Grey asked as she stood at the window and swigged more champagne.

"Some stupid game men play forever on the grass, rolling balls. I think they just use it as an excuse to talk, drink, and smoke cigars."

Grey plopped onto Llana's bed and her dress flew up.

"My God, Grey, you're wearing garters!" Llana exclaimed, seeing the back of Grey's exposed thighs.

"Yes, aren't they cute?" Grey said. She turned over and hiked up her white crinoline petticoat, exposing a gauzy, flower-embroidered white garter belt. Her bikini panties were white satin and they had flowers on them, too.

"Sexy!" Llana said. "God, I'm still in Lollipops. Bet Ed's gonna love those." She squinted her eyes and peered closely at her best friend. "Or has he already looked?" she said wickedly, then pouted. "I haven't even seen a picture of Ed yet and he wasn't at graduation."

Grey's voice was strange. "You'll meet him at wedding rehearsal. God, Llana, your braids are too perfect, like a crown on your head. Who did them?"

"Mama. Your curls are perfect, too. You look like Scarlett. Who did them?"

"A hairdresser who came to the house this morning," Grey said, gulping more champagne. "Do you really like them?"

"Grey, you're changing the subject! Talk to me about Ed. God, Grey! You're almost not a virgin. You're getting married!" Llana said in abject admiration. Her silky skin was flushed tawny from champagne. She took Grey's hand and touched the flashing diamond ring. "I've never even seen a boy's thing," Llana said. "Mama stands in the hall at night if I leave my bedroom to go to the bathroom. She's afraid I'll see one of my brothers naked. And now that my cousin's here, it's even worse. I'm surprised they don't lock me in a chastity belt. God,

Grey! You're going to do 'it.' I'd do anything to change places with you!"

Llana's dark eyes widened as it dawned on her something was terribly wrong. "Grey, you are avoiding all the subjects you normally love to talk about. And you won't look me in the face." Llana touched Grey's cheek, turning her best friend's face to her, and saw Grey was doing her utmost to hold back tears. "Come on, Cochisa, spill it," Llana demanded.

That did it for Grey. "Cochisa" was Llana's dumb endearment for her, picked on that day years ago when the two girls had made shallow cuts on their wrists, swapped blood, and sworn oaths of allegiance for life.

Grey broke down. She began crying and then couldn't stop talking. All the words she had kept even from herself spilled out. "He's twenty-nine years older than me," she sobbed. "He's forty-six! He's ugly! He sweats and smokes and coughs nonstop. He's got millions and millions of dollars and I can't stop it. It's too late!"

Llana could not believe her ears. Grey Coltrane, the most beautiful girl in the world. The fairy-tale princess in the middle of the fairy-tale life. How could this be? She hugged her, rocking her back and forth like a baby. "Shush, shush, there, there. We'll do something. We'll run away. That's it. We can hitchhike to California and get jobs as waitresses."

But even as she said them, Llana knew they were just words. Grey was lost, a victim like herself. Caught in their parents' web. She tried to soothe her friend. "Think of all the freedom marriage and a fortune will bring." Then they cried together.

By the time they finished another bottle of champagne, the two girls came full circle to the mutual conclusion Grey *was* the luckiest girl in the world and had nothing to worry about, but rather everything to look forward to. "Look at Jack Palance, he's really ugly and I'd marry him in a minute," Llana said, patting Grey's curls in place in preparation for their return to the party.

A mail truck stopped alongside the Nightwalker. "Aloha, wanna ride, sister?" the driver asked.

"*Mahalo*. I'm going to Ritchie's house," she said.

"Sure, got mail for him, too. C'mon."

The mailman drove up-country past the Thompson Ranch on one side and a spectacular sea view of the islands: Molokai, Molokini, Lanai, Kahoolawe, and the Maui countryside on the other. He gossiped on about Ritchie—how wealthy, how very charitable, sponsoring an island softball team, leading a Boy Scout troop. "Ritchie own the biggest restaurant and nightclub on the island, too," the mailman said in thick island pidgin.

Only in Hawaii, the Nightwalker mused a while later as she waved good-bye to the mailman with the thick handful of mail he gave her for Ritchie.

She sat, a short time afterward, concealed by trees, near the dirt road leading to Ritchie's house and read all of Ritchie's mail.

Finished, a small, reflective sigh escaped her. Then her demeanor completely changed and she got busy, dug a hole in the ground, wrapped her heavy weapons, explosives, and the black phone book in one sarong, and buried the bundle. Slipping out of her camouflage pants and white T-shirt, she wound another of the long, flowered sarongs about her until it was a sari with a piece to either cover her head or serve as a shawl about her shoulders. From the remaining sarong she took a mirror and a small green case. Propping the mirror against a tree and looking into it, she braided her hip-length hair until it was a thick rope hanging over one shoulder.

Her hair, pulled away from her left side that way, exposed what at first looked like a tattoo but was in actuality a brand burned deep into the nape of her neck.

Opening the green case, using the theatrical makeup she painted a red spot on her forehead and lined her eyes with kohl.

Ritchie, a pleasant-looking man in his fifties, gray-haired and easy to smile, opened the door and found himself looking into ageless emerald eyes.

The owner of the startling eyes spoke. "I've come to dance at the club," she said. "Do you have any bells? I'm a Sufi dancer, but I've lost my bells."

"Lillian, come meet the good luck who just knocked on our door," Ritchie called into the house, beckoning in the beautiful visitor.

Ritchie, whose fortune stemmed from a thriving marijuana business, lived with Lillian, who was involved in all his endeavors and kept the books for the restaurant and nightclub. The two warmly welcomed the gorgeous sufi dancer and invited her to stay with them. Other than hula practitioners, live entertainers were hard to find in the islands, and the club, the busiest on Maui, was known for its dance shows. It was also a hot spot for Maui's fast crowd, many of whom were aware of Ritchie's extracurricular activities or directly involved in them. It was "in" to be friends with Ritchie and Lillian, invitations to their home and parties were savored, and anyone they adopted was instantly accepted among their groupies.

"What's your sign?" Lillian began, immediately curious about the exotic Sufi dancer who radiated sensuality, looked as though she stepped from the *Bhagavad-Gita* itself, and was a roaring success her first night at the club. It was Friday.

Disco music played over the sound system. The club was packed and loud. Suddenly the music and lights were cut and the Sufi dancer appeared unannounced on the small, brightly lit stage. Ritchie had found bells. The Sufi dancer, draped in gauze, wore them about her ankles and on her wrists and tinkling from her long rope of hair. She began uniquely dancing, making her own music, and even drunks got quiet. Her movements were at once classical, skillfully provocative, curiously strong and perfectly rhythmic. Her gauzy costume parted now and then, revealing flashes of svelte waist, sensuously rounded hips, and belly. Continuing her swaying, sybaritic performance, she danced from the stage into the audience, encouraging the mesmerized patrons to follow her, which they did Pied Piper fashion. Adding the sounds of brass finger cymbals to her bells, the Sufi dancer intensified the beat, leading her followers through the club until they reached a dancing frenzy. Just when they were enjoying themselves most, she bowed and retreated to her dressing room.

The patrons paused a beat, absorbing the surprise of her sudden departure, then their applause and yelling was deafening, but the beauty did not appear for an encore.

The club buzzed. A million questions were thrown at Lillian. Where did she come from? Who is she? Is she married?

Lillian, who prided herself on knowing everyone's inside story, was profoundly embarrassed not to be up on her own houseguest's history. So her inquisitiveness made her seek the dancer's company between performances.

The beautiful dancer, who moved more gracefully than anyone Lillian had ever seen, was keeping to herself, not flirting with any of the handsome men begging entrance to her dressing room. "Come outside for a walk," Lillian invited and was pleased when her invitation was accepted. But once under the magic Maui night sky, she found herself, instead of learning about the mysterious beauty as she intended, talking about her own life. And after the dancer's suggestion that they smoke a joint together, she started talking about her relationship with Ritchie.

Lillian hadn't had a confidante for so long, and there was something about the way the Sufi dancer really listened, concentrated on every word, that made her want to tell all. She found herself focusing on the enigmatically embossed circle on the Sufi dancer's neck and rambling on and on . . . By the second day of the Sufi dancer's stay, Lillian had confided everything personal, and much about the pakalolo business.

The Nightwalker worked at Ritchie's club four nights. She spent much of her time between shows with Lillian, and seeing that, those who curried Lillian's favor were also anxious to have "talks" with the gorgeous, mysterious dancer. And like Lillian, they found themselves confiding more than they ever intended.

The Nightwalker concentrated on Ritchie and Lillian's friends she pegged as drug dealers. Without seeming to, she overheard important conversations, plans for meetings, and encouraged incessant talkers to smoke strong bud and further loosen their lips. And then she was gone, a beautiful, jingling memory.

A few days later on Hotel Street in Honolulu, wearing a white-blond wig, the Nightwalker sat in the Swing Club among the whores, pimps, and sailors. Several CINPAC ships were in Pearl Harbor and twenty thousand sailors on leave presently cruised Honolulu. A great majority of them converged on Hotel Street, where they drank, fought, and fucked. The Swing Club was the center of action. Two tables away, to her right, were Ritchie and two other men.

She sat by herself near the live jazz band and waited for *him* to show. Each time a sailor approached, she said, "I'm waiting for my man, he's at the bar." She looked like a whore, most sailors didn't want to get their throat cut by an angered pimp, so they drifted off. She stayed on guard—anything could happen in this place.

With no fear of Ritchie recognizing her, the Nightwalker observed Ritchie and his companions looking anxiously around. The blond wig, heavy, blue eye makeup, bright red lipstick, and the skintight, strapless leopard dress she wore were far from her Sufi dancer's trappings on Maui a few days before.

Ritchie and his friends had obviously not counted on the fleet being in when they made their meet. They craned their necks, peering through milling bodies for the "Merc," Mikel Anton.

The Nightwalker's hands sweated. Her prey was surely coming! He would be paid off here in the Swing Club and given his next assignment—and she would follow him.

Then, after three years, there Mikel Anton stood.

Agonizing memories assaulted her. Her hands clutched her barren middle that had held life until him. Waves of shock and hate tore her as the former Marine sat down with Ritchie. Stifling the scream threatening to come keening from her, she went to the table next to his and sat on a sailor's lap.

"Hey, where's your room, baby? How much for safe sex?" the delighted sailor said.

"Easy, sailor, I wanna drink. Handsome guy like you don't mind buyin' a lady a drink first, do ya?"

As the sailor cut his way through the crowd toward the bar, she sat in his chair and leaned back, her sharp ears overhearing conversation at Ritchie's table.

Ritchie also saw the Merc as soon as he entered the Swing Club. Even if he hadn't known the man's military background, it was obvious. The handsome, massive black had an air of authoritative command. Even boozed-up sailors made a path as Anton walked, muscles bulging against knife-pressed khaki shirt and pants, toward Ritchie's table.

Ritchie viewed the approaching man with mixed emotions. On the one hand, he was proud it was he who found Anton and put him in charge of the dangerous business of actually moving tons of grass, making sure there were no rip-offs when it came that treacherous time to exchange product for money.

On the other hand, Ritchie was scared to death of the bastard. Right away the crazy Merc had established his authority in Hawaii by blowing away two local guys who tried to rip him off. He dumped their bodies in the cane fields of the Big Island, where most of Ritchie's grass was grown, and acquired a statewide reputation because of the incident. There was a saying in the islands, "Look left on Maui and they know about it on Oahu." It was true, gossip was inter-island and Anton was firmly established as a force to be reckoned with in the Hawaiian islands.

There were other things about the black mercenary disturbing Ritchie. The man was always stoned on pot. He functioned anyway—no doubt about that, but it bothered Ritchie that the man didn't stay straight ever, not even to conduct business.

And he had a penchant for very young girls. Before Ritchie had known how violent the man could get, he had turned him onto a friend who arranged a tryst with a fifteen-year-old girl. Feedback was swift and shocking. The Merc had hurt the girl, almost killing her when he found out she wasn't a virgin! Ritchie never said anything to the Merc, but he did not arrange any more sexual encounters. Let him do his own dirty work, Ritchie thought.

In a far corner of the Swing Club, a very big man was flopped across a table as though drunk. Because of his posture, his enormous size was disguised, as was his interest in Ritchie's table. He peered from beneath a straw hat and watched, his vision somewhat obscured by the stir a blatant blond hooker was causing at a table next to Ritchie's. She had been sitting on one sailor's lap, but now she was alone and other sailors lined up trying to get to her.

Across the room, Ritchie could hardly believe his ears as he found out the Merc—his superman—had been ripped off and that he and his partners were down a half million bucks! Anton had let it happen *three times*. Three times the Merc said some son of a bitch discovered pickup points and got there first.

As his highly distressed partners questioned the Merc,

Ritchie further evaluated the situation, deciding the Merc wasn't ripping them off. The man had worked for them for two years, had a great thing going, a percentage of the product he moved. If he pulled a rip-off, it would be a giant one and he would be gone—no, this was real and from the Merc's anger and vehement promises to reap revenge upon the perpetrator, Ritchie saw it had become a personal vendetta. His gut feeling was to go along with the Merc's plan to set a trap at his next pickup.

Snatches of conversation the Nightwalker heard were enough. Haleakala Crater on Maui—the next pickup point. She would be there, and there she would take Anton's life. Bit by bit she would kill him, using the art at which he considered himself a master.

Then what? she suddenly thought. Would she be happy? *Happy.* A foreign word, its meaning forgotten. For years every waking thought had been revenge. And now revenge almost upon her, the vendetta almost finished—there was only emptiness.

Her prey was leaving the next table. She left also, much to the consternation of the young sailor who finally returned with a drink for her.

On Hotel Street, she tailed Anton as discreetly as possible, considering her getup and the fact that every sailor she passed (and two evil-looking transvestites) propositioned her. Anton paused in the doorway of a Vietnamese food shop and spoke, in Vietnamese, to a woman who quickly produced a sorry-looking girl of about twelve. The woman pushed the girl toward the Merc, extolling her virtues. He made to walk away, but turned when something the woman said caused him to perk up in interest. The Nightwalker saw what captured Anton's fancy when the woman pushed a young boy toward him and a smile broke on his face.

She followed him and the boy by cab to the Waikiki Banyan on Oahu Avenue and managed to ride the crowded elevator with them. Holding the door for a moment after they got off, she dashed out in time to obtain the apartment number they entered.

Downstairs in a ladies' room, she cleaned her face of garish makeup and removed the blond wig. Taking a gauzy, loose-fitting garment from her handbag, she slipped it over the sleazy leopard whore's dress, converting herself into a conservatively dressed tourist.

At the front desk she requested the apartment her prey and the boy had entered. "Sorry, ma'am, that condominium's booked for the week."

"I'm so disappointed. My husband and I honeymooned in that very apartment." A hint of a tear appeared in her eye as though a terrible tragedy had befallen that husband.

The desk clerk, mesmerized by her, came to the rescue. "It's off-season, I've got rooms on either side of it you can have."

Once checked into the one-bedroom condo, she pushed a small suction cup to the bathroom tile and inserted its connecting plug into her ears. The listening device was a sounding board into the next apartment if the bathrooms were back to back. She was in luck, they were.

The Nightwalker monitored the sounds of Anton ravaging the boy, which, if possible, made her hate him even more, then a one-sided telephone call which let her know he would be there another four days. She would have liked to drop an infinity transmitter into his phone. For now this would have to do—this primitive eavesdropping device which meant she would have to listen without being able to leave her station.

During that four-day period of mostly silence while she kept surveillance on the man she would kill, there were hours and hours also to kill and she used them to rehash the events that brought her to this point of no return.

As Mother taught, she separated her conscious and subconscious and drifted—as Y Shin Sha taught; she stayed ready to kill or leap from danger in a millisecond. Back she went, back, back . . .

1975, Long Island

Suddenly it was the night before the wedding. At the rehearsal, Grey faced the shock on her bridesmaids' faces as they first beheld Ed. Only Llana concealed her antipathy. Bless her, ever loyal, she made an effort to boost Grey's spirits. "He's so distinguished. Why he looks like a-a . . ." Llana searched for a complimentary metaphor. "Diplomat. And he's so funny!"

But the other bridesmaids avoided Grey's eyes and

were off in pews whispering. She could well imagine the sort of things they said, and she doubted they still envied her ring, her car, and her future.

Now, in a panic, she lay in bed. This is my last night here. Her eyes traveled over the ribbons and trophies that decorated her bedroom—over the bookshelves. Albert Payson Terhune's *Lad of Sunnybank*, *Bruce*, and *Wolf*—the collie stories she so loved. *Black Beauty*, *Sea Star*, *Skilled Horsemanship*, *How To Play Tennis* . . . Nothing to prepare herself for her new life to begin tomorrow. She was not going to play a game, nor be with horses or dogs. She was to marry Ed Fowler. "Mary, sweet mother of God, please help me."

4

Grey moved slowly on the purple carpet stretching before her. She dragged her back foot a bit, the way she had practiced at rehearsal, and kept time to the overpowering crescendos of Mendelsohn's "Wedding March" played by the church organ.

Slowly she moved past baskets of flowers at the end of every pew, past her bridesmaids, stationed like lovely flowers themselves, waiting for her to walk by before falling into the procession. Two of her small cousins tugged at the train of her gown, struggling to keep up with their silken burden.

Looking ahead, through the mist of her veil to the dais, Aunt and Uncle Fowler, Mom, Ed, his best man, and Llana, awaited her arrival. She looked at Ed as though seeing him for the first time.

I'm walking the last mile, Grey thought, holding on to her father's strong arm.

Ed came halfway down the steps of the dais to meet them. Daddy lifted a corner of Grey's veil, kissed her on the cheek, then took her hand, and gave it to Ed.

Walking up the steps to face Father Bondy in his white robes, feeling the heat of Ed's hand, anxiety overtook her. No, no, no! This is wrong. Father Bondy began praying and Grey prayed also, for a miracle, a rescue from the bondage about to be cemented.

But her prayers were not answered and the ceremony commenced. With her mind racing, Ed's figure a blur next to her, hardly hearing the priest's words, she felt doom weigh on her heart like a heavy stone. I'm seventeen and I'm losing the rest of my life, she thought. In order not to cry it aloud, she focused on those about her.

Daddy looked so pleased. Llana *had* stuffed socks in her bodice. The little boy who was the ring bearer shook the purple cushion he held. Both Mom and Aunt Fowler were crying. Uncle Fowler caught Grey's eye, smiled, touched the flower in his lapel. Llana's eyes were wide, liquid . . . A pinching lace garter on Grey's thigh reminded her this was not a dream.

Father Bondy stopped speaking. There was an instant while everyone waited for her to say "I do" when Grey fantasied turning, running down the aisle away from it all. "I do," she said, and her voice was small, as though it belonged to someone else.

Through tears Grey saw the simple band slip onto her finger. Ed lifted her veil and kissed her on the lips. My husband is kissing me, she thought. Oh God, it's done. Then they prayed as man and wife.

Walking back down the aisle, holding Ed's arm, Grey stepped quickly, keeping up with his excited pace, barely seeing the watching guests through mist-filled eyes. Ed rushed her through the open doors of the church into bright sunlight and a waiting limousine.

It was a short journey to the country club. Only time enough for Ed to fill crystal goblets with champagne from the Lincoln Continental teakwood bar, toast his new bride, and gently place his wedding present about her neck.

"There is no beauty to match yours, my darling wife. These diamonds pale before your splendor," he said.

Grey looked at the long, delicate chain of perfect diamonds glittering on her breast. Her hand touched the six-row pearl and diamond Queen Ann choker he had given her the week before. "Oh, Ed—"

"No," he stopped her words with kiss. "No thanks, my dear." He gazed at the vision of loveliness beside him. The lace veil framed Grey's face like a gossamer cloud. "It is I who am thankful," he said.

Seeing the love so plainly written on his face, guilt assailed her for what she felt. Torn by conflicting emotions, Grey fixed her eyes on the diamond chain for the rest of the ride and Ed was pleased at her admiration of them.

When she exited the limo at the country club, flash-bulbs of waiting society photograghers popped in her face. People will think I've wed for wealth, she suddenly thought. Why have I wed? Why? She hurried alongside

Ed through the club's oak and iron doors, escaping the prying lenses.

Inside the spacious reception room with its turquoise and yellow Persian carpet, the wedding party formed a line. Grey greeted six hundred people, and heard congratulations six hundred times. Happiness prevailed. Ed's laugh rang at her side. Hiding her despair behind a smile, Grey pumped hands and returned hugs and kisses.

Lester Lanin began the music while waiters wheeled in endless tables of splendidly displayed delicacies. Champagne corks popped everywhere and everyone was talking to Grey at once. Periodically her cousin Emily kissed her, leaving blood-red lipstick imprints which Mom immediately wiped with her hankie.

Then the guests made a giant circle, and Ed and Grey danced in the middle to "Oh, How They Danced on the Night They Were Wed." All the guests applauded.

Grey danced with what seemed like every man there, including her father, and drank champagne between the dances. Every now and then, as she and Ed danced, someone cut in and said something cute like "Come on Ed, give a guy a break—you've got her for the rest of your life." She cringed inside, pasting a stupid smile more tightly on her face because she didn't know what else to do.

Llana danced by with a handsome, rusty-haired young man. She saw Grey and winked. Decorating the dance floor in their pastel gowns and organdy hats, the bridesmaids were having a wonderful time, and their girlish laughter tinkled here and there like bells above the music. After the reception, the guests were ushered into the club's red-carpeted formal dining room.

At the raised table, with her back to the silver-striped wallpaper, Grey only toyed with her food, fed instead by despondency. She looked at the sea of heads below. Her wedding guests, a multicolored blur. Witness to the tragedy that has befallen me, she thought. Yet another bottle of Tattinger came into her peripheral vision as the waiter refilled her glass. She felt Ed take her hand and press it under the table. Turning her face toward his, looking at him, she was struck by panic. For a moment it was hard to get a breath. Her chest heaved, Ed's eyes dropped, noting the movement. Oh my God, she thought, feeling his gaze on her bodice, his hand clutching hers under the table, he's my *husband*.

Just then, to the delight of the guests, a six-tiered wedding cake was wheeled into the center of the dining room.

With Ed at her side, she cut the first slice while contemplating the couple on the cake. Dark and handsome atop the white icing, the groom was like Rhett Butler. With a sinking heart she dutifully fed Ed from the first slice and everyone applauded again. Waiters began serving wedding cake while more waiters appeared with flaming trays of brandied ice cream, while more champagne dulled her senses.

The music began again and more dancing. After an hour Mom whispered it was time for Grey to change into her going-away outfit.

In the club's locker room, the bridesmaids and Llana dressed her in a white linen suit with faint blue pencil stripes, black-and-white spectator pumps, and gold jewelry. Mom pinned her own sapphire and gold antique watch on Grey's lapel, then carefully placed the pearls and diamonds Grey had worn in their cases, and left to supervise the placement of the suitcases in the limousine. The bridesmaids scurried out for the throwing of the bouquet, and she and Llana were left alone.

They hugged, both trying not to cry again.

"Well, kid, here I go into never-never land," Grey said.

"Grey, I love you so much," was all Llana could say before running out the door.

Emerging from the dressing room, Grey stood at the top of the stairs. At the foot the bridesmaids and the single women waited to catch her bouquet. She saw Llana's rusty-haired dance partner cutting through the guests toward Llana. I wonder whose cousin he is, thought Grey. Then she and Llana made eye contact, just as they had when they had played basketball at St. Anne's. Grey easily lobbed her bouquet to Llana, who leapt high in the air and caught it. Blowing Llana a last kiss to much applause, Grey came down the stairs to where Ed, in his traditional blue stripes, waited.

Together, through the smiling crowd, they went into the late afternoon sun to the waiting limousine and her wedding night.

As they drove to what Ed called the "little hideaway" in Syosset, the champagne that had dulled Grey's senses began wearing off. Depression and fear came rushing back.

As if reading her thoughts, Ed broke open another bottle of Tattinger from the bar as they sped along the Long Island Expressway. "Here, darling, drink. I want to toast our first chance to be alone," he said, filling a crystal flute. She could see the bald spot at the top of his head.

She tossed the champagne down quickly, welcoming its obliterating glow. She smiled because she didn't know what else to do.

She was giddy from drink when the car finally pulled into a driveway. Ed instructed the chauffeur to take their luggage inside and to return for them at six the next morning— destination Kennedy Airport. Taking her hand, he whispered, "Come with me, darling."

Could he feel her trembling? she wondered.

"I have a little surprise for you," he said.

It was just dusk as he led her around the large two-story white wooden-frame house. This was the first time Grey had seen this rustic estate. Heretofore she had only seen Ed at her home or his parents' palatial Southampton residence.

A swimming pool came into view, and beyond it was a large building. "That used to be a horse stable, but I converted it for my hobby," he said, referring to his passion for antique cars. Inside the former stable, they walked a wide cement center aisle, passing stall after stall, each housing a gleaming vintage auto. "These are my Mercedes-Benz. That's a 300SL gull-wing coupé. I'm quite proud of that one. And this," Ed said as they passed in front of a huge automobile, "is a 500K Sports Tourer. It weighs three tons, was built in the thirties, and has the most beautiful coach work Mercedes ever produced."

As they progressed along the aisle, Ed waxed prouder. "This is a 1927 Swallow Austin. Ah, next are my Jaguars." He paused in front of a stall. "This beauty is the one off three-and-a-half-liter S.S. 100 fixed-head coupé. It was exhibited at the 1938 Carls Court Show." He took her hand as they neared the end of the building. "This stall, my dear, I kept authentic."

Grey gasped, for lying in fresh straw was a black foal with a white star on its forehead. Above the stall was a brass nameplate reading "DARKCHILD."

"Oh, Ed, you remembered," she whispered. *Scarlett Hill* was her favorite horse story, and she had often told him of her fantasy of owning a horse by that name, colored and marked as in the story.

Staring at the foal, an exact replica of the fictional horse, Grey realized Ed remembered every word she ever said to him. A wave of filial caring overwhelmed her as she realized her own father, so remote, did not know nearly as much about her as the man who stood next to her, beaming at her pleasure.

Grey threw her arms around him and kissed him. Then, still resplendent in her white suit and gold jewelry, she ran into the straw-filled stall and embraced the precious young thing. Looking up, her arms full of colt, she said, "I love you, Ed." And at that moment, she did.

An hour later, only the light from the slightly ajar bathroom door illuminated the bedroom. Grey, in a blue silk gown and panties, sat propped against oversize satin pillows in a king-sized bed. Terrified, she waited for her husband to consummate their marriage. Desperately she sought to ease her mind by drinking in her surroundings.

They were each to have their own quarters in all of their dwellings. "So much more civilized that way," Ed had explained.

French paintings of eras long past decorated the blue satin damask-covered walls. Women in ornate, tight-waisted long dresses lounged in parks and gardens. Grey's favorite color was blue, and the room was a study in it. Teal, cobalt, aqua, and sky blended beautifully. Even the gold-trimmed, delicately carved French writing desk against the window was lacquered blue. Yes, Ed had certainly been thoughtful when he decorated his bride's quarters in this house, she thought.

I wonder if I should take off my panties or if he's supposed to do it? The little person inside her head who she thought left, spoke. *You'll soon find out, Mrs. Fowler.* "Sweet Mary, mother of God!" she murmured.

She remembered in detached horror the time she was ten and witnessed an act of sex: at a riding stable, while

waiting for her father after a lesson, a stallion broke
through the side of a barn, mad to reach a mare in heat,
tethered nearby. The crazed stallion mounted the mare
in his frenzy, screaming and tearing the mare's neck
bloody with his sharp hoofs. Grey had watched, fascinated and frightened as the stallion plunged his huge
organ into the mare.

A cough interrupted her thoughts. Jesus, Mary, and
Joseph, he's coming. She smelled Ed's cigarette preceding him.

He pushed the door open. "Darling, I can hardly see
you in there," he said, carrying a silver tray bearing a
champagne bucket and glasses. Placing the tray on the
nighttable, he filled the fluted goblets to their rims. His
hands shook and he spilled some champagne as he handed
it to her. "To my lovely bride."

Grey sipped slowly, putting off the inevitable, his ner-
vousness elevating her level of anxiety. He smoked and
drank, perching on the edge of her bed. He chatted
about the wedding, the food, the music . . . He was
wearing a satin robe with a silk ascot and velvet slippers
with crests. Watching with horror, Grey saw the slippers
drop from his feet onto the carpet. "Well, let's see how
comfortable your bed is, my dear." He stood and removed his robe.

Grey's eyes were cast down. She caught sight of a
pendulous white belly as he climbed onto the bed, and
she closed her eyes tightly. He kissed her. The smells of
tobacco and toothpaste assaulted Grey's senses. Thrusting, his broad tongue invaded her mouth—probing, probing, probing.

With quick motions Ed pulled her nightie up and her
panties down. She lay exposed and cringing, trying not to
scream.

Taking his mouth off hers, he began kissing her body.
His wet mouth moved down her torso.

She thought of *Darkchild*, then Father Bondy's words:
love, honor, and obey.

She felt something at her crotch. Oh God, no! It was
his mouth and he was slobbering over her. He muttered
and rubbed his face against her soft, young female parts.
It felt like sandpaper. Grey moaned in pain. Ed took her
sounds for ardor and pressed on with his lovemaking. He

raised his head from between her legs and squirmed up the bed, falling heavily upon her. His huge belly pounded and pushed her. Then he started to cough. He was sweating profusely and she was all wet from it. Reaching down between her legs, he tried to stuff himself inside her. Grey felt something soft rubbing against her vagina. He continued fumbling between her legs, his fingernails scratching at her.

For the better part of an hour, Ed tried to enter her. Just when Grey thought he would have a heart attack and she would die with him, suffocated from his massive weight, he stopped. Without a word he padded off to the bathroom and she heard the shower.

Grey pulled down her sweat-soaked nightie, retrieved her panties, wiped his sweat from her face with a tissue. She prayed for her mind to be still.

He returned, the robe again covering his middle, his ascot back in place. One hand held the familiar cigarette holder. He poured more champagne. Sitting on the bed next to her he said, "Darling, I'm sorry. I've been under some stress . . ."

She interrupted him. "I understand, Ed, no matter." she could not bear to discuss what had happened, positive within her emotional insecurity and lack of sexual experience that his failure was her fault for not loving him as she should.

"It will get better, I promise. I'll be more relaxed in Italy and Paris. Certainly in Paris. It's the city of love, you know," he laughed. "And besides, darling," he patted her hand, "we have a lifetime to make love." He kissed her cheek and then padded off again, his slippers making little sucking sounds as they stuck to his heels with each step. The door closed behind him.

When she thought enough time had passed for him to be asleep, she stole out of the house and crossed the lawn to the stable. Only when Darkchild was in her arms did she let loose a stream of tears for her lost life. As if he understood her torment, the baby horse nuzzled her with his velvet muzzle, and through his soft, flaring nostrils, blew warm breaths on her cheek. A bond was born as the distraught seventeen-year-old shared the sorrows of her wedding night with the young animal. It was hours before Grey reluctantly let go of the colt and returned to the house.

While his teenage bride reflected on the rest of her life with him, Ed was also awake. In his sparsely furnished bedroom, so austere in comparison to his bride's quarters, the forty-six year-old man who now looked fifty-six poured himself a glass of champagne and walked into the adjacent sitting room. Lowering himself into the green armchair that was Grandmother Fowler's, he placed the champagne glass on the spindly legged English side table. His bathrobe fell open as he lit a cigarette. He averted his eyes from his flaccid penis just visible under the folds of his stomach. Next time. Next time.

Ed gazed at the walls. Pictures of Grey everywhere, Grey at five, at eight, at twelve, Grey on horseback, in her St. Anne's uniform . . . Hundreds of pictures of his darling, his wife!

His right hand drifted lazily to fondle his scrotum. He gazed at pictures of Grey and thought about *the book*.

He had found it in London, while browsing in a musty Chelsea bookstore. From the moment he had taken it off the shelf, he had been riveted by its contents. In great detail the book examined Arab sexual customs—especially the marriage practices of sheiks. What was on page seventy-four caused him to experience an immediate erection—a phenomenon less and less prevalent over the years.

The book said it not uncommon for a wealthy sheik to wed a child as young as four. From the beginning, the baby-wife was trained in his sexual preferences, taught to administer oral sex until she grew old enough to make penetration possible. Kept in a harem, away from all other males, her only life was the sheik. He was father, lover—lord. Ed bought the book.

Now, in his sitting room, he stroked his penis and imagined the delights of easing a girl child onto his erect member. Oh, how delicious it would be, how tight she would be. He concentrated on a picture of Grey in a bathing suit when she was six. He pulled harder and faster at himself. How she would squeal, how she would wiggle, so little that he could totally control her, hold her by her waist and pump her up and down on his cock, up and down, up and down; turn her around so he could watch her petite buttocks as his cock went in and out of her, in and out, in and out . . .

With a sudden surge, he came.

Ed fell back onto the chair and waited for his heart to quiet, then he walked on shaky legs to the bedroom, where he poured himself a glass of red wine. Ed *always* took his Seconal with a vintage Lafitte-Rothschild. The enormous amounts he drank gave him insomnia and the nightly sleeping pill was the only way he could sleep. His hand shook and he had to sit on the bed as he took it. Sighing, contemplating the peace sleep would bring, he stretched out on the single trundle bed, also inherited from Grandmother Fowler. Lighting one last cigarette before the pill took effect, he considered silver-framed miniature pictures of Grey covering the nightstand. At fourteen, she posed in a leotard on a balance beam, arms gracefully spread, sternum thrust high, legs stretched taut, displaying their curved definition.

His mind drifted to when he had first seen her. Spurred by her five-year-old affection, he had gotten the idea—based on the book—and bailed her father out. Up to that point Edward Fowler had been a dismal failure when it came to affairs of the heart.

There had been a spur-of-the-moment elopement to an exquisite, impoverished White Russian of royal lineage —Ed met her on holiday, celebrating college graduation in Paris. He was twenty-one, she was twenty-four and turned out be a secret morphine addict whose only need of him was money for drugs. At first, hopefully in love, Ed toured the world, putting her through this cure and that. Finally disillusioned, he arranged a steady supply of drugs for her and fell into his own alcohol addiction. She died of an overdose in Marrakesh in the third year of their marriage. Ed did not mourn her passing, the incident was well-concealed by the publicity-shy Fowlers, and few knew Ed was ever married.

After that, it was fortune hunters and hookers, a mistress here and there. Ed knew they were around for the money, aware he was neither handsome or finely built.

Then he found the book, then Grey appeared with her father and perched trustingly on his lap. Ed swore then he would have her, had to have her. He was no Arab potentate, but he did the next closest thing.

Coltrane, of course, accepted the money to pay his debt and over the years, much, much more. Ed made it clear Grey's father need never return the hundred and fifty thousand dollars. By Ed's contrivance, investments from the vast Fowler holdings filtered steadily through Coltrane's office, and Fowler business associates were recommended to Coltrane, whose reputation as an astute financial consultant grew, and even *The Wall Street Journal* published an article on his escalating career.

Through it all, Ed managed monitoring Grey's upbringing, carefully supervising her education, even her reading matter, stocking her bookshelves with dog and horse stories. No novels or women's lib (God forbid!) materials for her. He would have been distraught if he had known of her time spent with her two precious romantic novels. It was his plan to keep her as childlike as possible. A soft-spoken comment—"I don't think television is good for children, do you?"—put an end to her television.

He ended her public school education after she had a pajama party for her fourth-grade classmates, seriously panicking him, who remembered his sister's pajama party. The girls had gotten drunk on her father's one-fifty-one-proof rum and put Vaseline on the bottoms of their feet and slid on the playroom floor. Then they got *naked* and tried on each other's clothes.

Ed and his boyfriends were outside the house that summer night, peeping through windows and playing "circle jerk" while the nymphets changed clothes. A couple of his sister's little friends knew the boys were outside the windows and prolonged titillating poses accordingly. That remembrance in mind, Ed patrolled the night of Grey's pajama party like a police dog on duty, not going home until the Coltrane house was quiet and all the girls asleep. Ed suggested the Sacred Heart school. Two weeks later, she was in a convent.

From his position on the trundle bed, Ed picked up a picture of nine-year-old Grey with a lacrosse stick. Yes, that pajama party was the reason Grey became a boarding student at St. Anne's. He was no Catholic, but nuns knew how to keep a girl under wraps. Ed's suggestion to George Coltrane about the Sacred Heart school quickly became reality.

He selected another picture, Grey and Jane, her country club tennis instructor. Ed stopped twelve-year-old Grey's departure for coed summer camp by arranging a

Coltrane family membership at a grand country club and Grey's endless athletic lessons—with women instructors. During the summers also—hours of classical ballet.

Coltrane and Ed never discussed Ed's unnatural attachment to Grey. George Coltrane would never make waves—he loved a life of luxury, and Ed was marvelous at dangling ever more tempting carrots before him. Grace Coltrane followed her husband's child-rearing suggestions, never dreaming they were Ed's, knowing nothing of the unspoken pact acknowledged by both men, or of her husband's financial affairs.

With Ed's careful nurturing, the two families grew close. In the process Ed's parents and sister Jennifer came to dearly love the enchanting child. "Aunt and Uncle Fowler" thought their childless son's love for Grey merely parental and charming. They laughed along with the Coltranes when Grey solemnly announced at the age of eight, "I shall marry only Ed when I grow up."

There was a sticky period. Ed had to convince his father Coltrane had indeed legitimately paid his debt to the mob and seen the error of the whole incident.

Eight years later, the Fowlers were shocked he indeed wanted to marry her. But they soon got used to the idea. It was obvious their boy loved Grey deeply. They could overlook the twenty-nine years age difference, wanting Ed's happiness. Grey's breeding was unquestionable, her beauty breathtaking. The prospect of grandchildren was delightful. The Fowlers gave their approval.

Persuading Grey's mother took longer. The prodigious age difference between Ed and Grey concerned her. But George Coltrane, undaunted in his championing of the union, convinced Grace of the wonderful life Grey would have, marrying into an eminent, wealthy family who already loved her and was equally adored in return. Grace Coltrane finally felt secure in her consent, but did insist Grey not be told or formally proposed to until her high school graduation.

Ed congratulated himself on it all as the Seconal cloud descended. Ah, yes, he had done it perfectly, even seeing to it Grey learned no foreign languages, studying only Latin at St. Anne's until she could read Cicero in the original. She would have no need to communicate with anyone but him. Yes, he had perfectly plotted to have a love that would be the envy of all other men.

And now, finally, he was her husband. His last thought before the Seconal overtook him was of how achingly lovely she had been in her white suit, surrounded by straw, hugging his gift colt and looking up at him with adoring eyes.

In her room, Grey also had a last thought before she fell exhausted and tormented to sleep. Unlike Ed's beautiful vision, hers was practical, having its own macabre humor. *I'm still a virgin.*

The screams of a child prostitute being beaten echoed through her earphones, pulling the Nightwalker from the past of a still innocent young girl to the present debauchery taking place in the next condominium.

For the past two days, Anton had been in constant touch with the Vietnamese woman from Hotel Street. There had been a steady stream of young boys, young girls, drugs . . . And now, a boy and a girl—whom he was whipping. The Nightwalker listened as the man directed the boy to sodomize the girl.

Finally satiated after hours of depravity, he sent the children away. The Nightwalker listened to him make two phone calls, booking a shooting lane at the Honolulu Gun Club and arranging an iron-pumping session with massage to follow at the twenty-four-hour International Fitness Club. Then he too left.

For the first time in two days she pulled the listening device from her ears. Letting out a great sigh, she stood in the bathroom and stretched, arching back and elongating her body like a cat after a nap. Then she walked into the living room and, sliding open the glass door, went onto the six-by-ten lanai.

The Honolulu night sky was magic. She faced cloud-capped mountains lit by the moon. With the sunrise, rainbows would peek through those clouds. House lights in Manoa Valley and scattered up the mountainsides were jewels in the velvet night.

She spoke softy to her dead husband as though he were alive. "No wonder you love it here, my darling. Hawaii *is* the most beautiful place in the world. I will have him for you soon, my love. It is close. In two days I will have him in my hands. I will begin with a digital joint, my darling, and snap it quickly before I go onto the next. Yes, my love, he will dangle like a puppet broken at each joint, watching helplessly as a *woman* breaks the next." For a moment Khan's exotically handsome face hung in the night air before her. Every woman who had seen him had wanted him, but he had been hers. She blinked and his image vanished.

I need food, exercise, but first, to search his condominium. Leaping lightly to the railing, she was about to jump the five feet to the next railing when a shadow flashed from his condo. There was someone in there! Dropping back onto her lanai, she hurried into the bathroom and once again listened at the wall.

Sure enough, drawers being pulled open, sounds of searching. I am not the only one who watches Anton. *But no one will kill him before me.* She waited impatiently for the searcher to finish and leave; then leaping from lanai to lanai, the Nightwalker entered the mercenary's condo.

Signs of his erotomania were everywhere. Bits of tinfoil with residues of cocaine, a dildo, a whip, packets of marijuana.

Cold pizza lay half eaten in cardboard boxes. Wrappers from candy bars and empty, bent beer cans littered the living room carpet. She opened drawers. Nothing. She searched the refrigerator and freezer. Nothing. She went to the telephone and unscrewed the mouthpiece. An infinity transmitter was planted there!

Screwing the phone's mouthpiece back, she thought of what this meant. *Whoever had placed the infinity transmitter could hear her now.* With an infinity transmitter the telephone is a live microphone even when on the hook. Any sound in the apartment would be picked up. Had the person who just searched placed the device? Would the listener complicate her kill? Was it simply Ritchie and his partners double-checking their man's loyalty? The law?

Too many questions to seek answers now. She needed food. There was nothing in this apartment to tell her more than she already knew from two days of listening.

She headed into the Honolulu night.

A big man by the name of Charles Halehana entered an

apartment on Pau Street in Honolulu, where he had left the boy with instructions to monitor the infinity transmitter he'd dropped on Anton's phone. He had himself just ransacked the condo and found nothing of interest. What the boy told him as he came in the door captured his immediate attention.

"There was someone in there as soon as you left. Whoever it was searched, too—and it sounded like they took apart the phone."

Halehana reflected on the last two years spent tracking Anton. There had been a few times when he thought someone else might be on the same path.

The first time he had that feeling was at an antiterrorist training camp in rural Georgia, a gathering place for mercenaries, ex-special forces men, and rich men playing at war. Anton had recently trained there. Using the influence of mutual military acquaintances, Halehana got permission from the retired Green Beret colonel who ran the camp to go over records. Anton's photograph was the only one missing from his group.

Anton had trained with a class of ten and was voted the "most aggressive" by his instructors. By querying the instructors, Halehana also came up with the information that Anton had landed a job with two of his classmates, billionaire industrialists just come from digging for oil in China, on their way to Chile. Anton was to oversee a gold-mining operation for them.

While he was going through the camp's records, Halehana took a look at the class immediately following Anton's. It caught his attention because that group included the only woman ever to be allowed in the camp, a free-lance photojournalist whom the crafty colonel said he allowed in only because he thought the publicity would bring needed business. The unique aspect of a woman training as a mercenary was to sell the story.

When Halehana asked about her, the instructors at the camp were free with vignettes of her adventuresome ten days among forty men. She was a raven-haired beauty, they said. Besides getting her story, she had kept up with the men, qualifying with them at the end of the course. That was no piece of cake, as the training was the real thing, culminating with a shotgun stress course run under live fire. The big man also noted on her records that she displayed a flair for electronic surveillance, held her own in hand-to-hand combat class, and had excelled in evasive driving. *Her picture was gone also—along with her personal data.*

The second time Halehana had thought someone else was tracking Anton was six months later. Anton was back in the U.S. finished with his job in Chile, this time surfacing at an exclusive shooting camp in Alabama, where, for two thousand a week, men spent six hours a day firing everything from Uzis to .44 Magnums. That's where Anton met Ritchie, who later offered him permanent employment. Halehana got there two weeks after Anton left and one week after a woman, supposedly the blond editor of a gun magazine from New York, had been there and left. Too coincidental. Another female in another male bastion? He investigated further. She inquired after Anton, excelled at gunmanship, "had a Weaver stance like a statue," the gun instructor there said, and somehow managed permission to see the camp's files.

When next the big man was in New York, he went to the gun magazine's offices. The editor was blond, but short and cute, nothing like the tall, ravishingly beautiful woman described to him at the shooting camp.

Another time the big man had just missed Anton, who was shortly head of security at New Orleans' oldest, finest bordello until he savagely beat the house's biggest money maker, putting her out of business for months. Anton left town before the mob could find and kill him, gone from his rented apartment in New Orleans by the time the big man got there. Halehana had entered and searched that apartment and found planted there active, up-to-date, hard-to-purchase, electronic surveillance equipment.

Now, when the boy said someone just searched the Merc's condo and took the phone apart—he got that feeling again. Of course, the incidents could have no relationship. Many could be after the mercenary. God knew he had made enough enemies to last a lifetime.

Halehana broke from his reflections and looked at the boy. His hard eyes became gentle. They had never discussed what had been done to the boy and they never would. Nor had they discussed why the big man hunted Anton, although those reasons linked the man and the boy together as nothing else could.

Charles Halehana, who could easily pass for a *hapahaole* (part white) Hawaiian, loved his adopted son, and the boy worshiped this huge, handsome man who had rescued him from a life of rejection. But for both of them, the greatest love was the thought of Mikel Anton dead.

Whoever had just searched Anton's condo could be looking to rip off drugs. It could be someone connected to the prostitutes or a drug dealer—that was an old story, sell to a mark, then rob him, anything was possible—but the big man trusted his instincts, and they said a woman was tracking Anton. In the colonel's camp a brunette, in the shooting camp a blond . . . Tricky sister, whoever she was. He just hoped she didn't get in the way of his kill.

The boy handed him a piece of paper listing Anton's calls and appointments. "I told you to write in English," the man said. "Read this to me. Speak English."

The boy read haltingly. When he finished, the big man patted his shoulder approvingly. "We'll get you a job in the Secret Service yet," he said. It was hard to get the boy to smile, and failing now, he turned his attention back to Anton's appointments. His man had a busy evening ahead. Halehana ordered food for the boy and headed into the Honolulu night.

Mikel Anton went into McDonald's on Kalakaua Avenue and ordered three hamburgers, two orders of french fries, and two cokes. As he ate, the huge black· man thought about the case lying next to him on the seat, containing his current favorite revolver—a fast-cocking .357 Magnum Colt Python. He planned using it on the motherfucker trying to destroy his career.

He was boiling mad. In his life as a mercenary, this was the only job he ever wanted to keep. It was permanent. He didn't want to bust balls anymore looking for the next hookup. Besides a great salary and a percentage of product, he steadily stole a few pounds of grass each time he moved a load. Nothing big enough for the fools employing him to notice, but enough to make a difference in the numbered bank account he kept in Switzerland.

Besides, he liked Hawaii, a permissive society in contrast to foreign regimes like stinking Taiwan, where he had stuck for years, practically running the military. Hawaiian hustlers were unsophisticated in comparison to him with his keenly developed military skills, and he was able to terrorize and control them at will . . . He had killed a few times in Hawaii—men who tried to rip him off, an old whore who laughed at him. Now he would kill this bastard who thought himself so slick. *He had been made a fool of—three times.* Never again.

Assuming an insider was involved in the rip-offs, he planned his next marijuana deal at the Haleakala Crater on Maui carefully. Not only would he be there loaded for bear with his Magnum, he would ring the area with locals, complete with shotguns and dogs. Whoever the motherfucker was, he would get his at Haleakala Crater.

Anton left McDonald's, smoked a joint on Waikiki Beach, stopped at one of the ABC stores that were everywhere, and bought several packages of chocolate-covered macadamia nuts. He then headed to the Honolulu Gun Club, anxious to get his practice session over and on to the International Fitness Club, where he could work on maintaining his massive physique and stare at himself in the mirrors.

The Nightwalker strolled Waikiki Beach, barefoot in a T-shirt and shorts. Her hair was loose and over her shoulder, and she carried one of her sarongs knotted into a pouch. In it were her sandals and a .380 Walther PPK/S automatic, which she had just liberated from the hole where she had buried it six months before in Kapoliani Park.

The sand was silk between her toes, the moon lit the sea silver, Hawaiian love songs drifted in the night air as she walked by hotel after hotel. Words of an old song came to her mind. "Starry, starry night . . ." The story of Vincent Van Gogh and how he suffered for his art. Japanese honeymooners strolled by hand in hand. Hawaii was the perfect place for lovers.

I'm going to kill him and it will be over and then what? She thought of the Master she had sought to teach her the art with which she would kill Anton. That Master had said, "When two tigers fight, one is crippled and the other dead." But the ancient adage did not apply to her, nor would she suffer like Van Gogh for her art, she thought. She was too finely trained ever to doubt her ability. *No, he will be dead and I will be whole and then what?* Putting the question she could not answer away, she focused her mind on the immediate.

Her stomach was full, now she must further prepare for those parts of her body that would contact his. She paused on a cement platform near the beach holding chained surfboards, where she was totally hidden. Taking off her sarong shoulder bag, the Nightwalker dropped onto her fingertips and began to do an exercise that looked a combination of push-ups and yoga. Up and down, back and forward, each complete push-up had nine movements. Her body never touched the cement, only her fingertips and feet made contact. On and on she continued. When she had counted one hundred and her sweat formed a pool beneath her, she stopped and stood, and one by one, cracked each of her fingers at each joint. Now they were strengthened, honed, stretched.

Still in the shadows of the surfboards, she began violently snapping her hands in prearranged patterns, movements thrusting forward either her fingers, wrists, or palms. A faint light appeared about her hands, and then she commenced the deadly dance that incorporated her whole body.

I feel you, Mother, I feel you Y Shin Sha, she mentally acknowledged those who made her different. Now the Nightwalker's whole body glowed. She moved for hours and when she finally stopped, the glow about her faded.

She picked up her sarong bag, heading for the Ala Moana Shopping Center, where she would purchase leotard and tights, proper attire for the International Fitness Club.

Passing more honeymooners on the beach, her mind drifted back to the honeymoon of the still innocent, seventeen-year-old Mrs. Fowler.

5

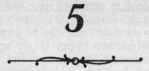

Normally, the checking-in rituals at Kennedy Airport would have fascinated Grey, who had never flown before. She certainly would have been pleased by the admiring glances she received, wearing a white cotton sailor's blouse, backflap edged with blue stripes, an easy white skirt with big pockets, white Louis Jourdan shoes, and gold accessories.

But it was not a normal day for Grey. She was Mrs. Edward Fowler now, and the excitement of new experiences and new clothes paled next to the overwhelming depression encompassing her after her disastrous wedding night.

She and Ed were in the red-carpeted skyclub, awaiting their flight. Twenty minutes until boarding time. Music played softly in the background. In comfortable blue armchairs, fellow first-class passengers drank coffee, orange juice, and munched on hot Danish served by smiling airline stewards.

Ed broke into her thoughts. "I think I'll have a little drink. I don't like flying very much, you know." And he trotted to the bar on the other side of the lounge which an attendant opened just for him. It was seven-thirty in the morning.

By the time they boarded the 747, Ed was tipsy and laughing at nothing. He ordered a drink from the first stewardess who passed.

Grey selected a *Time* magazine. She tried to read, to escape into world news, but Ed would have none of that. He wanted to talk to his bride. And that's exactly what he did—without cease—all the way to Italy.

He did not carry on a conversation, but rather delivered a soliloquy. Babbling, joking, burping, coughing, smoking constantly, consuming uncountable glasses of wine. Changing the filter in his cigarette holder each time he took a new cigarette, he mumbled something about filtering out the tars. Brow mopping and squeezing her hand at intervals left him never still.

Shrinking against the window, wishing she could escape through it, she was a bundle of raw nerve ends, Then he announced they were on their honeymoon, dispelling speculations she was his daughter, and ordered champagne for the first-class cabin. Achingly embarrassed by his behavior, adopting a if-I-pretend-it's-not-happening-no-one-else-will-notice attitude, she smiled at him just as though he were really amusing her.

She attempted thinking of Darkchild. Oh how she loved him! Ed had promised the colt would be returned to its mother and flown to Grey as soon as he was old enough. Nothing worked—Ed broke into her every thought.

Her only escape became the bathroom. She made numerous trips up the aisle, climbing over him to get out of her seat, and was further mortified by sympathetic glances from passengers and flight attendants. At one point she locked herself in the tiny bathroom and jogged in place. A discreet knock at the door interrupted her, and an apologetic voice asked, "Mrs. Fowler, are you all right? Your husband is asking after you." Shamefaced, Grey returned to her seat.

Relief came after eight hours when the plane landed. She supported him through customs, for he could barely stand. "There's my man Friday," Ed slurred, pointing to a short, swarthy man waiting outside the custom gate.

She pretended not to see the servant's surprise when Ed introduced her as "Signora Fowler." The servant spoke no English, but bowed and smiled pleasantly at her. He eased Ed into the back seat of a station wagon next to Grey and loaded their luggage. Judging Friday smoothly handling Ed's inebriation, she surmised he had seen her employer in this state before, and it dawned on her that Ed was not drunk because he was upset by flying or by their wedding night, as she had originally assumed, but was showing his real self: a part of him she had never seen in the controlled circumstances of their prior meetings.

Ed immediately fell asleep and his snores were the

background for the journey through verdant Italian farm-land. There were few cars on the roads they traveled, horses and wagons more common.

She had little stomach for sightseeing. During the two hours it took to reach Saubaudia, she tried quieting her inner panic and applying logic to her plight. That didn't work at all. She spent her time holding back tears, trying to quell the awful anxiety threatening to burst from her.

Finally the station wagon pulled through some iron gates and came to a halt in the circular drive of a sprawl-ing three-story stone building.

"Well, well, home again," said Ed, who awakened smiling, miraculously seeming to have sobered. "Come, darling, you must see our little country home."

"Signore, Signore," cried a group of people running toward them.

Ed proudly made the introductions. The gardener, the cook brought from Rome when Ed was in residence, the fisherman who would catch seafood for their table each day, and lastly Maria, Friday's wife and keeper of the keys, which she wore permanently dangling from her ample, apron-covered waist. "Friday and Maria live in year-round. Since I'm rarely here, they consider this their home," Ed said.

The newly introduced assemblage made a terrific fuss over Ed, who beamed with pontifical pride, the lord of the manor being welcomed home. Led by short, stocky Maria, the servants formally acknowledged Grey. When Ed presented "Signora Fowler" to them, the housekeeper examined the young, nubile beauty, and for a fleeting moment Maria's black eyebrows, nearly meeting over her nose, bushed in a frown at the rings on Grey's fingers. Her employer had brought women here before, play-mates. But a wife threatened the world she had made here for herself. Then smiling at Grey, she nodded a greeting and turned her attention back to Ed.

Grey noted the housekeeper's frown. Resentful of me? But that was the least of the seventeen-year-old's wor-ries. Like a puppy after its master, she followed Ed for the grand tour.

It was an enormous seaside villa, and each room was tiled in a different motif. "The tiles are handmade in local factories—the main industry of the area, my dear,"

Ed explained. Magnificent pictorial rugs decorated the tile floors in every room. He was proud of them. "Hand-woven of silk and wool by monks at a nearby monastery."

He squired Grey to her bedroom and sitting room with glass walls that made the sea just beyond the villa a mural. In her bathroom suite, white tiles were painted with glowing flowers. Here an orchid, there a rose or daffodil. Next to the flowered toilet was another bowl, also flowered, faucets inside it. He noted her confused glance and was amused. "That's a bidet, my dear. European women are known for superior cleanliness. You sit on it. The water sprays upward. You adjust it to wash your outside, or"—he leaned over the bidet, turning on the water, making the spray shoot high—"intensify the stream to shoot inside you." He was laughing, quite enjoying the moment. Embarrassed, she walked around a tiled wall and saw the bathtub was a sunken pool with a center island of white orchids stretching toward the sun streaming through a partial glass ceiling. Faucets and taps were cast bronze tulips.

Ed touched a switch panel. "Heat lamp, sunlamp, lights simulating day or night for your makeup, my dear, not that you need any," he said, showing the steam bath and Finnish sauna that completed her floral spa. "You look at home, my darling, a flower among flowers."

He pulled her along. "This house is quite a scandal in the neighborhood because we have eight bars, six in the main house, two at the pool house," he said. "This is a plebeian, Catholic countryside, and alcohol is the wine the church serves at communion." They passed through three living rooms, a huge dining room, a library, and eight bedrooms, each with its own sitting room and bath.

The vast kitchen, floored in terra cotta, had two refrigerators, two stoves, and an enormous stainless steel expresso machine Ed boasted "makes fifty cups at one time. We might like to do a bit of entertaining, my dear," he said, proudly pointing out adjoining servants quarters as lovely as the rest of the house.

In back of the stone manor they walked down stone steps through formal gardens to a six-room guest house, companion to an Olympic-size swimming pool. Just twenty feet beyond, ocean waves crashed in the sunlight. The water in the pool looked so calm, so inviting. "I think I'll take a swim," she said.

"Good idea—a swim." As he leaned close, she smelled wine on his breath. "Then we can try sneaking past the servants for a rendezvous."

Suddenly she was terrified. Trying to push the fear away, she sprinted up the hill in her high heels.

Her luggage was already unpacked, her clothes neatly arranged in closets and drawers. Quickly changing into a bathing suit, she ran barefoot to the pool, thinking, "If I can just get in the water, at least that's familiar territory."

At poolside, she saw two black and tan Doberman pinschers. Petting them, she said, "Where did you come from, beauties?"

"They patrol the grounds," Ed said, coming up quietly behind her, caressing her bare shoulder.

She dove for sanctuary, cutting the water cleanly, and her heart nearly stopped. The water was like ice! She struck for surface warmth.

Ed was laughing. "I forgot to tell you it's the world's coldest pool," he said. "The only thing colder is the ocean."

Grey, determining not to let him have his joke, swam nonstop in the icy water for forty minutes, ignoring the cold, pounding free-style, until therapy of movement calmed her enough to climb out and face her impatiently waiting husband. "It's not so cold," she said, smiling sweetly, thinking to fix him and his humor.

His comeback ruined her small victory. "Why don't we go inside? Besides, darling, you haven't properly inspected my quarters. I'll meet you upstairs," he said, turning on his heels, heading toward the main house.

In her suite, the open terrace doors and panoramic view made it seem part of the sea. But nature's beauty was lost on her; the ugliness that was her marriage waited. In a terrycloth beach robe she reluctantly mounted the stairs to her husband's quarters. Passing Maria, on her knees cleaning the stairs, Grey felt the housekeeper's eyes on her back and panicked. I can't run away. I have no money. Ed has my passport. Why don't I just tell him he can't touch me? Am I such a coward? God, why is this happening to me?

Ed awaited her with delighted anticipation. "There

you are, my darling. Come here." He was propped in bed, robe on, cigarette lit, wineglass by his side.

"Ed, we have to talk."

"Later, my darling. We have the rest of our lives to talk. Now is the time for love!" he said and grabbed her arm with surprising strength, pulling her to the bed. Grey attempted to break away, but he rolled on her, tearing open her robe. His sheer mass pinned her like a mounted butterfly. He began kissing her breasts with loud, sucking noises. His weight was suffocating.

"Please, I can't breathe," she gasped.

Through his alcohol haze Ed heard only "please." He got properly atop her, holding himself with one hand and focused all his attention on getting inside her. Her noises grew in volume. His attempts failed. "Maybe if I turn her over . . ." he thought. He couldn't breathe now; blood was rushing to his head. Suddenly he was dizzy, his heart was pounding, and he couldn't stop coughing. Managing a tender kiss on her cheek, he labored off to the bathroom.

She bolted to her room, where she closed the door and cried on the bed until no tears were left. Then she picked up the phone. After an interminable wait she finally reached an operator who spoke English. "Sorry, Signora, all circuits are busy. I'll ring you as soon as your call can be placed." The operator hung up. Grey heard a a second click. Someone in the house was listening!

During lunch by the pool, she somehow managed to keep her composure. She did not mention she knew someone had listened when she used the phone.

Friday stood by, one rigidly bent arm draped with a linen napkin. "I've spent a lot of time training him to serve," Ed said between mouthfuls. "Taste the wine, my dear, it's delightful with the fish." He smiled, liberally buttering freshly baked bread.

Her only relief from all-engulfing depression was Friday's comedy of errors. As a waiter, he was a pitiable figure. When should he approach the table to clear or pour wine? How long should he fuss at the ashtray and silver before backing away and reassuming his watchful waiter's stance? A wrong move from Friday brought raised eyebrows, dour glances from Ed, and poor Friday quickly retreated backward, abjectly confused. She pretended not to notice the Laurel and Hardy scene, but found herself pleased with Ed's frustration.

Her husband's concerns seemed more and more petty as she came to really know him. How did I ever find him adorable, she asked herself as he expounded on the glories of a rare Chateau d'Yquem accompanying crisp pears and brie for dessert. Then a flashing memory came—herself as a little girl on Sunday, waiting in delighted anticipation for Ed to come, her Ed who would have toys and books and jokes and make life exciting. Guiltily she acknowledged how very adorable she had found him for many years.

"By the way, darling, when you do reach your parents, I want to speak to them. They're my parents now, too." He reached across the table, taking her hand. "We'll do everything together from now on," he said with a smile.

It was Ed listening on the phone. The little person inside her head spoke up. Are you going to tell your mother what's going on with him monitoring?

After lunch, he led her to a garage and a Ferrari. "This is a classic, my dear, no longer manufactured. A limited edition even when it was built."

They covered the local roads at breakneck speed in the black convertible. "No speed limit here," he yelled over the engine's throaty roar.

Saubaudia was uninteresting. Lookalike farms, the land fertile and flat. "This was Mussolini's summer home, you know," he volunteered.

The distraught seventeen-year-old could not have cared less. She wondered why he even had a home here, but rather than start him on yet another long-winded tale, she kept her silence. They took turns driving and returned after three hours.

Dinner was four courses in the dining room, accompanied by four wines. Ed had evidently coached Friday in the interim, and the servant seemed less confused.

Grey fussed over the little cup of expresso at the end of the meal. "Delicious," she said, since Ed was so proud of his expresso machine, "a perfect end to the day. I think I'll read for a while and go to sleep. I'm so tired."

Dutifully kissing him, she beat a hasty retreat to her room, hoping her call would go through. Worried sick about him listening, she finally fell into exhausted sleep.

Breakfast brought bad news. "I spoke to your parents last night, darling," Ed said, too brightly. "I didn't want to wake you. They're so happy we're having a wonderful time. I promised we'd call from Paris."

She wandered through the day, hardly realizing what she did, what she ate. Life had become a miserable blur.

She suffered the cold, awful reality of the marriage, the physically repulsive nightmare she was living. And when she looked at a *lifetime*, the situation was utterly hopeless.

That night, awakened by far-off voices, she pulled on a robe and felt her way downstairs in the dark, intending to raid the refrigerator. There was a faint light in the big kitchen, the sounds came from the servants just outside the open door.

She opened a refrigerator. Empty. She looked in the other refrigerator, also barren—not even a stick of butter. Judging by the meals served three times a day, there had to be leftovers. She opened a cupboard. Not even a cracker. Walking toward the door, she saw Maria hand a package to a strange woman and pocket money. Maria selling leftovers!

Just then, hearing Grey's stirrings, Maria rushed into the kitchen babbling Italian, wringing her hands in her apron, obviously upset her domain was invaded.

"May I have some coffee and food?" Grey said.

Maria said nothing, only looking with blank eyes at Grey, who tried sign language to no avail, although she was positive the woman understood perfectly. Then Maria began a loud, hysterical yelling. "Signore, Signore," and ran pell-mell upstairs toward Ed's room.

Grey found it hard to believe she would actually wake Ed, but she did, and Ed came, bleary-eyed, in his satin robe to the kitchen. "What is it, darling?" he asked in a raspy voice.

"Oh, Ed, I'm so sorry you were disturbed. I just wanted a snack."

"That's perfectly all right, darling. I was just dreaming of you," Ed said, smiling at her. He spoke to Maria in commanding tones and pattered away, his leather slippers sticking, as usual, to his heels with each step.

Oh Lord, why couldn't he just have stayed my beloved friend? She retreated to her room.

After a few minutes Maria arrived with a tray of coffee, cheese, and fruit. I could expose her petty thievery, Grey thought. But Ed only comes here once a year and he thinks the couple so wonderful, why should I? It will be terrible enough for him when he finds out I'm leaving.

So she smiled sweetly. "Gracia, Signora," she said.

The incident was but a break in her depression. The black feeling of helplessness came back. There had never been a divorce in her family; something spoken of with pride by her parents. The nuns had taught divorce was a sin—marriage a lifetime bond. Her parents condoned her marriage. How would they react when she told them?

Lying in bed, gazing at the star-filled sky, for a brief moment she considered suicide as an alternative to the scandal she was sure to cause. Suddenly she pictured the sweet foal in the stall on Long Island. The love she felt then for Darkchild made her want to live, to be part of a future seeing him grow.

The next morning before Ed awakened, she took the Ferrari and raced along Saubaudia's nearly deserted roads. The speed thrilled her and, alone in the car, she laughed out loud, pretending she was winning the Grand Prix. She had a close call, nearly missing a truck by inches.

The next three days, she stayed away from the villa as much as possible. Avoiding Ed became a game she played too well for her husband. The fourth morning the car was gone.

"I've sent it to Rome for repairs. Besides, I'm jealous of the car. I want you with me."

The swimming pool became her next refuge. She remained in the icy water for hours while Ed sat in the shaded cabana, drinking. The times she joined him, his drunken ramblings went on and on. When she couldn't stand anymore, she dove in the pool again.

He had a fit at her new escape. I wonder if he'll drain it for repairs, she thought, desperately trying to retain sanity with humor. She found a plastic float in the cabana and took to lying on it, mid-pool with magazines. He watched for hours, finally taking up a book himself.

But the pool made other things worse. Hours of daily swimming made her already curvy body spectacular. She was solid as a rock, lithe and supple. The hot Italian sun bronzed her, bringing out tiny freckles across her nose and golden highlights in her auburn hair. Ed called her "Little Pesca" and waxed ever more amorous, although he was still not able to consummate their marriage. She remained a virgin.

After she made another unsuccessful attempt to call home, he announced the phones were out of order. Sure enough, the line was dead when next she tried. He said it was not unusual in so rural an area.

The housekeeper seemed to be everywhere, lurking with curious eyes, and Grey thought the woman recognized her desperate plight and was enjoying it.

For Maria's benefit, Grey took to skipping and cheerfully whistling as though she hadn't a care in the world. Ed, delighted in her exuberance, attributed it to her joy in their marriage.

Grey's boredom and misery took another turn—baiting Maria with the Dobermans. Grey had been bringing them to her room at night, where she played with them and shared her bed. Adoring her, the dogs followed her everywhere.

Maria discovered dog hairs on the bedspread and ranted at Friday. A pen appeared outside the villa. At sunset, the dogs were locked in under Maria's stern supervision. Grey simply unlocked the pen after dinner and took her friends to her room.

By day the pool game with Ed, by night the dog game with Maria. What have I come to? I have to get out of here before I go crazy, she thought one morning after being in Saubaudia for two weeks.

As though he could read her mind, Ed surprised her at lunch. "You need some city life, darling. Let's go to Rome in the morning."

She jumped from her seat. "That's a wonderful idea. I'll starting packing now." She ran to her room, excited at the thought of calling home and winning her freedom.

Ed, thrilled to see Grey so perky, threw himself into departure preparations. At dinner he told interesting stories about Romans, their amusing habits—like pinching females on the fanny along the streets—their wonderful culture.

She laughed at his jokes and got a little tipsy with him. She was looking forward to Rome, for her years of Latin and Roman history made it already seem familiar. Then, blessing of all blessings, he went off to sleep without asking her to come upstairs.

The next morning, servants gathered in front of the villa for good-byes. The Dobermans were there, too. Grey gave each dog a big hug and kiss, which they adoringly returned by lapping her face as Maria watched with open disapproval. Grey rose from the Dobermans and placed a dog-wet kiss on the horrified housekeeper's cheek. "Good-bye, Maria," she said, smiling.

Later, on the flight to Rome, she laughed aloud, recalling the look on Maria's face.

Ed, thinking she was enjoying the long tale he was spinning, squeezed her hand lovingly.

The temperature in Rome was ninety-five degrees. They were out of season, Ed said on a walking tour of the steaming streets, explaining why there were so many closed shops.

A restaurant where Grey saw young people gathered attracted her eye. "Oh, let's eat there," she suggested.

"Not for us, my dear, not the sort of people we want to socialize with," Ed countered, then choose a gloomy, deserted restaurant instead.

Grey attempted calling her parents from her suite, which adjoined Ed's, as soon as she was alone. She was thwarted by the hotel operator. "Signore Fowler left instructions to be rung before any long-distance calls are placed."

Grey clenched her fists in fury when she hung up the phone. Tears filled her eyes. "How dare he?" she raged aloud. Well, she'd end this farce in Paris. Ed said they would speak to her parents from Paris. I'll just tell Mom right out, with Ed there, that I have to come home! Then the little person inside her head said, "Why don't you tell him yourself? Why don't you pick up the phone, call his room, and tell him?" But that little person had more courage than she; confronting Ed was beyond her.

All those childhood years of thinking him so wonderful, loving him so—and now she . . . Unbidden came the phrase "hated him."

But one thing was certain, she could not tolerate this marriage. Amber St. Clair beat the black plague and Scarlett O'Hara schemed her way safely through the Civil

War. Grey Coltrane (she would never think of herself as "Fowler") would solve her problem, too, she swore.

That night, she stood in the open casement window of her bedroom, looking at a grass island in the street below, where, illuminated by a street lamp, a girl her age stood in a mini-skirt. A car stopped. The girl and the driver began a conversation. The car pulled away. Shortly, another halted. Again the girl approached the auto and more conversation ensued. This time, the girl in the mini-skirt got in and rode off. In a flash, another girl crossed the street, taking up the post. Even to Grey's unsophisticated eyes, it was plain her window overlooked a prostitute haunt.

She kept her station at the window for hours, watching young whores ply trade. Her own plight flooded her mind: at least they have their freedom, she thought. I've been bought—and I'm a prisoner.

Suddenly anxiety overtook her. She was weak at the knees and her sweat turned cold. She knelt in prayer. "Oh Mother Mary, blessed virgin, help me find strength in my time of need. Oh Lord, why have you visited me with this trial? It is my duty to be a good wife, and I know I promised you, God, that I would be. But what am I to do?"

Only momentarily on their fourth day in Rome, when she visited the Sistine Chapel, did her spirits soar. It took them two trips, however, to enter the Vatican.

The guard at the gate, who somehow managed not to sweat in his heavy red-and-yellow-striped uniform, eyed Grey's nipples clearly outlined by the soft material of her blue dress. He refused her admission, something to do with the dress code. Ed was flattered by the rejection.

Her stomach felt queasy. She only picked at food the last couple of days. Heat and Ed made an appetite-suppressing combination, and the strong expresso she had instead of breakfast was not agreeing with her.

The double trip was worth it. Even though her stomach was worse, nothing could detract from Michelangelo's genius, or the fact she was in the Vatican.

At one point, as they stood in front of the *Pieta*, she thought, I wonder if I can ask for sanctuary? I could become a nun—a better fate than continuing as Mrs. Edward Fowler.

"Come, darling, we're off to the seven hills of Rome," Ed said, booming with cheer. He told her of the gate situated on the highest hill, where she would be able to look through a keyhole and see all of Rome. "It's good luck," he said, "like kissing the Blarney Stone in Ireland."

Tired, her head and neck aching from staring at the Sistine Chapel's ceiling for so long, she climbed into another cab and motored into the sweltering noonday sun.

Instead of a cool breeze as she had hoped, the temperature rose with their ascent. The oven of a cab was small. Ed was jammed against her, constantly mopping his brow with a sweat-soaked handkerchief.

When they finally reached the tourist attraction, she wearily climbed from the cab to look through the keyhole. She bent down and nausea overtook her. She stood atop the seven hills of Rome and spewed expresso, then fell in a faint at her horrified husband's feet.

During the long ride back to the hotel, he was only able to half revive her.

Later, he paced his room, a glass of red wine in hand. The doctor assured him she'd be all right; heat prostration was common in August. He left her sleeping peacefully after the doctor's sedative. How beautiful she was in repose. His sleeping beauty. Nothing must happen to her, he thought in a panic. He was so happy now. Every time he saw the admiration she drew, pride filled him. His wife, his precious Grey. She had changed a bit, not quite as bubbly as before their marriage. Well, he reasoned, just part of growing up. Actually, as he thought of it, they had been having a bit of a dull time.

He remembered how many times he had refused her requests to stop at places attracting her eye. Places where children gathered. But, he chided himself, he should remember she was a child, what he desired, a child bride. He drank another glass of wine and continued pacing. The problem was, he feared contact with people her own age, even if she didn't speak the language. He had kept her from her parents by controlling her phone calls. He wanted her all to himself, but he also wanted her to be happy.

They'd go to Paris in the morning. No woman, whatever her age, could be unhappy in the shops of Paris. I'll buy her the most beautiful wardrobe in all of France, take her to the best restaurants. I'll call ahead to friends. After all, we're on our honeymoon. We should celebrate. I'll show her off to Paris society. Yes, Paris will cheer my darling.

While he planned ahead, Grey tossed and turned in a nightmare. She was in her room at home and the walls were closing in. She looked at the ceiling. Daddy and Ed were staring down at her—faces big and round, like huge balloons floating above. Then Mom joined them and her face was a balloon, too. They were all laughing down at her. She screamed in her sleep. Her screams mixed with the telephone's ring. It was Ed asking if she were well enough to travel to Paris.

In Honolulu, on Kapiolani Boulevard, the Nightwalker squared her shoulders, let go thoughts of Grey Coltrane, and entered the sensorial, musical world of the International Fitness Club.

Lionel Ritchie's latest album played in the plushly carpeted reception area, where she filled out a guest application handed to her by an astoundingly beautiful *hapa* (mixed blood) girl with straight black hair and slanted sapphire eyes.

The ladies' locker room, with Belinda Carlisle singing "Heaven on Earth," was peopled by such unusually attractive women, it was as though exotic Hawaiian flowers chose to take human form and dress in shiny tights. Her own spellbinding beauty let her easily blend in. She changed into a turquoise unitard and left the dressing room.

The club was crowded, the men as exotically handsome as the woman beautiful, creating a surrealistic atmosphere within which she moved toward her surveillance point. She passed glassed-in racquet ball courts with viewing bleachers, a restaurant, a lounge with pool table and a massive video screen showing a prize fight. Entering the main workout area, she climbed the stairs to a balcony overlooking a basketball court on one side and a vast sea of Nautilus machines and an iron-pumping area on the other.

On the balcony, giant speakers blasted Michael Jackson's "Bad," an aerobic class in full swing to its beat, men and women equally partaking enthusiastically. She joined the large class led by a petite Filipina beauty in pink-and-black-striped tights, moving easily though the snappy workout which soon ended. Immediately a jazz dance class began, led by Hawaii's dance master, Simeon Den. She followed the famous dancer in perfect sync to the Pointer Sisters and "Jump." Anyone noting would think her concentration lay solely with the shaven-headed hapa instructor.

But the Nightwalker's attention was on the floor below. She scanned the Nautilus machines. He was not there. Then she saw a doorway marked "POWER ROOM," but from her high vantage point could not see into it. She left the class, now moving to Billy Ocean's "Suddenly," and went down the stairs.

She stood in the doorway of the Power Room, where massive men grunted under massive weights, and saw him loading the squat bar. She watched calmly as he placed weight plate after weight plate on the Olympic bar, then lifted it easily with his back and did a set of fifteen full squats. A wide weight lifter's leather belt was pulled tight about his small waist. Each time he squatted, his powerful buttocks thrust toward her. She evaluated his performance as perfect, his huge, bulging quadriceps as magnificent. *My beloved enemy.* She stayed glued to her spot, watching the mercenary in fascination.

Anton stared hypnotically into the mirrored wall as he squatted, admiring the incredible peaks on his quads. The tiny cutout shirt he wore showed his delineated bulk to perfection, and his tiny soft cotton shorts exactly outlined his large phallus. Among powerful men, he felt the most powerful and loved his own gleaming black flesh. He decided he would lunge next. These lazy bastards probably never lunged, in his opinion the most difficult exercise, requiring the heart of a lion.

He finished his squats, dropping the load with disdain onto the rack, making as much noise as possible, clanging iron on iron, hoping one of the wimp faggots who worked at the club would dare tell him be careful of the equipment. He was spoiling for a fight. He scanned the large room, where at least thirty men were working out. No one took his eye-contact challenge. They're all afraid of me, he thought with pleasure, at the same time feeling his headache returning. He reached into his workout bag for another packet of chocolate-covered macadamia nuts.

He would exhaust himself further, then sleep. He thought back on his last days of drugs and debauchery, and realized he had achieved no sort of satisfaction. Satiation for him meant killing the motherfucker who had ripped him off. The Haleakala Crater pickup loomed foremost in his mind, and as he loaded another bar in preparation to lunge, only that encounter to come occupied his thinking.

In a far corner of the Power Room, Charles Halehana disguised his size, which easily equaled the merc's, by bending over almost double as he sat on a bench and curled twenty-five-pound dumbbells. He wore an oversized T-shirt, covering his own magnificently sculptured physique. Under the T-shirt his waist was wrapped and padded so that each time the shirt moved against his body, it seemed to outline a substantial beer belly. His adopted son had shaved the front portion of his head as though he were balding, and a five-day growth of beard darkened his face. For all intent and purposes, he looked like an out-of-shape fifty-year-old. Halehana was satisfied his disguise was complete when one of the Power Room attendants suggested he use the Nautilus machines outside. But he stayed, watching Anton's disgusting display of egomania. The big man curled the twenty-five-pound dumbbell as though he were having great difficulty and wondered to himself if he should let the boy kill Anton. If that would make the rest of the kid's life better or worse . . .

Turquoise-covered feminine legs caught his eye in the doorway. Racks of weights made it impossible for him to see the body's top, but the legs were terrific. From the positioning of her feet, he knew their owner was also watching Anton. Probably mesmerized, he thought, wondering how fast their owner would run from that doorway if she knew the true character of the man she stood and admired.

But he was wrong. The Nightwalker was at that moment utterly consumed by her prey's evil character, by the animal magnetism radiating from him like a call from the devil himself. A pulsating Isley Brothers song played. Anton moved with it. Perfect rhythm, too, she wryly thought, realizing she was getting very crazy. She forced herself away, her mind entering an even deeper state of agitation. Chi was building inside her, needing to be released.

She hurried back to the locker room, no longer noting the beauty of the people. She forced her thoughts to 1975 and Paris . . .

The penthouse on the Place Vendome was all antique charm. Even the elevator was a beautiful bird cage of delicate wrought iron. The view from the dormer windows was spectacular. But as Ed pointed out the giant statue of Napoleon in the Place Vendome, Grey looked for a phone.

He couldn't wait to show her bedroom, decorated white on white, luxurious beyond anything she ever imagined. Tiffany lamps provided touches of color, and a "Hunt of the Unicorn" tapestry rug covered the marble floor. But it was the painting over the marble fireplace that made her gasp. She crossed the room, drawn like a magnet to the Renoir hanging there.

"I had it taken from the vault for you, darling," he said. "It's a present. You must always be surrounded by lovely things," he said, making a courtly bow.

The speech was delivered with such sincerity, such love, tears came into her eyes and she was awash in guilt for what she planned. Then, much to her surprise Ed said, "Now, come, let's call your parents. You must be dying to speak with them. I'll just say hello and then be off for a while. I have some business at the bank downstairs, and I'm sure you and your mother will want to girl talk."

He spoke with the operator in his fluent French as she stood by, filled with anxiety. "They'll call you as soon as they can get through," he said, walking toward the door. "I'd better take care of my business before the bank closes. Just say hello for me, will you, darling?"

And he was gone. She wandered the apartment. She paused in Ed's bedroom. It was so plain. She opened his closet. Amazing. Ten suits, all exactly the same. He certainly was a creature of habit, she thought.

The phone rang. She jumped for it, her heart beating fast. The operator was placing the call. She heard the receiver being picked up. The German accent on the other end was Clarissa's. "They're away until tomorrow night," the servant said.

Grey started crying, then stopped, talking sternly to

herself. "Come on, Coltrane. They're coming back tomorrow. It's gonna be all right. Besides, is that any way
for a girl who just got a Renoir to act?"

Ed found her standing before the painting. How beautiful her profile, he thought. How lovely her throat's
graceful arc to collarbone. Renoir could have painted her
justly.

He didn't tell her he hadn't gone to the bank, but to
his doctor. Sometimes lately, he couldn't quite catch his
breath. But the doctor was reassuring: just cut down on
drinking and smoking and no attempts at sex for a while.
The last directive saddened him most. But Grey hadn't
been feeling so well herself. And besides, they had years
and years of lovemaking ahead.

The next morning, a uniformed maid appeared in Grey's
bedroom. The gray-haired servant, smiling warmly in
direct contrast to Maria from Saubaudia, placed a tray of
freshly baked croissants, orange marmalade, and steaming boullion on the nightstand, and marched into the
bathroom. Grey heard water running.

Sunlight streamed through the windows. Ed had gone
docilely off to sleep last night. Relaxing for the first time
during her honeymoon, Grey nibbled at the breakfast
tray, wiggling her toes against soft linen sheets and admiring her Renoir, then went into the bathroom, where a
bubble-filled tub awaited. The maid stood smiling as she
bathed, then draped her in towels, and escorted her back
to the bed. An expert massage followed and Grey gave
herself up to the pure luxury of being rubbed with sweet-
smelling oils.

"I thought you might enjoy Lilly's administrations."
Ed was in the doorway, smiling and chipper. "Ready for
shopping?"

It was off to Dior, Guy Laroche, and Balmain. The
couturiers were delighted with Grey's splendid figure and
Ed's bottomless pocketbook.

During lunch, at an outdoor café on the Left Bank, Ed
handed Grey a large flat velvet case. "A little something
to match your green eyes."

The emerald and diamond-net necklace and earrings
were worthy of an empress. People at nearby tables
stared. The huge diamond on Grey's finger, her youth
and beauty, contrasting with Ed's age and obvious

dissipation—and now flashing jewels in the case—were a riveting sight.

For the first time Grey wondered how much wealth her husband had. "Ed, can you afford presents like this? It must have cost an enormous amount."

"Don't you worry your pretty head about what we can afford."

"Aren't I too young for jewelry like this?"

"Silly, anyone would rather look at gems on you than an old dowager's wrinkled neck. We're invited to the Baron Rothschild's for dinner, and I want you to out-shine every woman there."

And she did. Her jewels, her blazing hair piled high by Alexandre, her exaggeratively simple white silk gown, made her the focal point for the baron and forty other guests at the table that night.

A silent focal point, for all she could do was smile at the French spoken by two men at her sides. She looked down the long table, lined with crystal, silver, china, flowers, and candelabra, at Ed, sitting between ruby-encumbered Baroness Rothschild and a duchess. Both women looked with open envy at her as Ed, beaming with pride, gestured in her direction. Two seats from Ed's was Rhett Butler come to life. Tall, dark, and handsome, he wore tuxedo and colors, as did the baron and other titled guests. Grey melted under his blue-eyed gaze. Earlier in the evening he had been introduced to her as Viscount Bugueot. Every woman at the table tried drawing his eye.

Nibbling lightly at the haute cuisine, remembering Scarlett was taught not to eat much at parties, she thought, I wish Llana were here to see this. She felt Rhett Butler's eyes on her. God, he's fascinating, she thought.

Then she noted with horror that Ed was drinking heavily. Many guests also were in their cups. It was a long dinner, following a reception, and they were on a fourth course of smoked salmon with capers. Each course was accompanied by a prized wine from the baron's cellar. A liveried waiter stood behind each guest and no glass was ever empty. Then, the overly madeup duchess sitting next to Ed knocked over her wine glass. The dutchess's place was quickly reset and a new glass filled. Grey watched the woman's ring-laden hand reached for it before the waiter could finish pouring.

The guests were unbending as they imbibed. A man was talking too loud and one woman's chiffon bodice came open. It looked as though her ponderous breasts would be fully exposed before the evening was over. Grey took but a sip of each new wine. Still, she felt a bit heady herself.

The gentleman on her right said something, and assuming he was complimenting the cuisine, she nodded pleasantly. His knee pressed hers. Shocked, she moved her chair a bit to the left. Rhett Butler smiled at her.

A between-course mint sherbet was served. Then an enormous rack of venison appeared and was carved.

The baron took that moment to stand and propose a toast to the newly married Fowlers. Grey would never forget the moment.

Tiny quails were served. She lost track of how many courses followed. Drinking more wine, she began laughing at nothing as the others seemed to be doing.

By the time after-dinner drinks and demitasses were served in an opulent salon hung with rare paintings, Ed was knocking things over and his laughter rang above the strains of the violin quartet. Grey escaped to an all-mirrored bathroom.

She stared at herself. Who was that beautiful creature staring back at her? Not Grey Coltrane, captain of the St. Anne's lacrosse team? Giddy, laughing, turning this way and that, she admired herself from all angles.

The strapless gown needed no underwiring to hold her breasts, rounding high above the silk bodice. Taking a deep breath, watching the soft fullness expand, she thought, so that's what they've all been looking at! Drawing air deeper, she saw she could make her diamond and emerald-drop necklace rise. Turning her back to the full-length mirror, craning her neck, she saw her hips and shapely rear were emphasized by her tiny waist and the four-inch heels on her Dior evening slippers.

Slowly she turned around and around. The crystal chandelier overhead sent light to her diamonds and they flashed answers with their own gleamings.

Totally engrossed in her image, Grey was startled by a knock at the door. Speaking in French-accented English, a deep male voice surprised her even more. "Are you all right, Madame Fowler?"

Grey opened the door. Rhett Butler was very tall. "Yes, I'm fine, thank you," she answered.

"Your husband was worried about you and I cannot blame him. You are magnificent." He kissed her hand. "Andre Bugueot, at your service, Madame," he said and offered his arm.

She walked with him back to the babble of conversation and music. Steering her toward her husband, he touched her bare back. Chills flashed her body. Their eyes met, his were clear, clear, blue. There was a moment when time stood still. Then a clammy hand on her arm and Ed's high pitched laughter brought her abruptly back to awful reality.

Somehow she managed getting Ed into their limousine. She convinced him to give their address instead of a nightclub he wanted to show her. Feeling like a neutral observer, she watched the chauffeur haul Ed to the iron gate of their building, then, glad for her athletic training, she half-carried Ed to their apartment, literally dumping him onto his bed. Running into the living room, she picked up the phone, tapping her foot anxiously as she requested her number.

This time the transatlantic call took but a minute. The familiar sound of her mother's voice filled her with relief. "Mom, Mom, I have to talk with you," Grey began.

"Are you by yourself?" her mother interrupted, sounding strained.

"Yes, Ed's asleep. Mom . . ."

Her mother interrupted again. "Darling, I'm so glad to have a chance to speak with you alone," Grace Coltrane said, fighting to keep her own composure. "I'm afraid you're going to have to break terrible news to Ed. The Fowlers were killed in a private plane crash this morning near Los Angeles, on their way to Palm Springs. You're going to have to come back home immediately!"

6

The trip back to America was horrible. Ed cried openly most of the way, leaving Grey to keep her composure as best she could—one of them had to. Only when she was finally in her mother's arms at Kennedy Airport did she give in to the grief she felt at the loss of beloved Aunt and Uncle Fowler.

Grace Coltrane barely hid her shock when she saw Ed. Completely unhinged, drunk and distraught, hardly able to stammer hello—he was a shadow of the man who had left on his honeymoon a month before. She attributed his condition to his parents' death. After all, under such circumstances, any behavior, no matter how bizarre, was understandable. Grey's appearance was perturbing as well: she was thinner, her pretty face showing signs of strain and worry. Ah, well, this is a horrible thing for us all, thought Grey's mother as she guided her daughter and son-in-law to the waiting limousine. Time will heal.

During the week of the wake and the funeral, Grey was loyally at Ed's side. He was never sober, nor did he eat, becoming disturbed if Grey was out of sight for even a moment.

They stayed at the Fowler estate in Southampton, where Ronald, the butler who had known Ed since childhood, accompanied him everywhere. Only in Ronald's presence did Ed respond rationally. He seemed comforted being treated as a child again by the man who had helped raise him. Grey and Ed's sister, Jennifer, accepted condolences from hundreds of friends, family, and business associates who came to pay their last respects.

When it was all over, the Fowlers laid to rest in the family's white marble mausoleum, Grey once again considered her marriage.

Dr. Harris, who arrived to attend Ed, advised her to

hire a male nurse. "Just for a few weeks," the kindly physician counseled, "until he can get over the shock of his parents' death, start eating again, cut down on the drinking." The doctor laid out in no uncertain terms the deterioration of Ed's health, especially the state of his heart.

If I leave him now, it will kill him. I will be responsible for Ed's death. She reasoned that in a while, when Ed overcame the trauma of his parents' death, it would be time enough to make her move. She put away thoughts of herself for the moment.

A month later, on September thirtieth, Grey celebrated her eighteenth birthday as Mrs. Edward Fowler, sharing her birthday cake with Ed, who still needed constant care, the nurse, her parents, and the servants in Southampton.

The day after, she went to supervise moving six-month-old Darkchild from Syosset. Wandering the house, she discovered the shrine to herself in Ed's sparsely furnished sitting room. She stared in amazement at hundreds of pictures of herself taken over the years, every wall and tabletop covered. She sat down in the room's only chair, continuing to look and saw an old book lying on the table. She picked it up, saw a page earmarked, and turned to it. With horror she read page seventy-four and its detailed descriptions of Arab shieks' baby wives' sexual training.

She suddenly understood it all: Ed's master plan, the premeditative planning of her life. "I hate you, I hate you," she cried alone in the memorial to her carefree youth that had been taken from her. Then she destroyed it. She tore the horrible book apart and demolished the pictures—throwing, ripping, stamping, all the while crying for the little girl Grey who was so used. She left the room looking as though a cyclone set down there.

Ed only partially returned to himself, and it was impossible for him to consider returning to Europe. Slowly he took up the reigns at the Fowler conglomerate's helm, making him one of the wealthiest, most powerful men in America. His failing health and the new business responsibilities thrust upon him created a heavy load. Grey, watching him labor and weaken, decided to stay a bit longer.

She never informed her mother of her marriage bed disaster. In Ed's condition there was no need to worry about sexual demands; he could barely get through each business day. She lived in a state of limbo, where Darkchild was her only joy.

Although there were other horses on the estate, polo ponies and pleasure mounts with attendants, Darkchild ran free on the hundred-acre grounds. Grey would not have him stabled, even when the head groom complained. "Mrs. Fowler, he's too wild! No one can touch him but you. Training him is going to be impossible."

Grey refused to listen. She might be a prisoner of circumstance, but Darkchild would be free as long as she had anything to do with it.

As though he knew freedom was a gift from Grey, the yearling waited outside the main house each morning. When Grey appeared, he shoved her pockets with his velvet black muzzle, demanding the apple she always had for him. Girl and yearling were a familiar sight on the estate.

From the servants' house, connected to the main house by an underground passageway, Cook and Ronald the butler watched one day as Darkchild and his mistress played in the grass. "It's good she's got that young horse, poor pretty Mrs. Fowler. A shame, tied down like she is," Cook said, preparing to go to the main house and start dinner. But it wouldn't be the same. Dinner with old Mr. and Mrs. Fowler had been an elegant affair every night. There was fine company and entertainment in the big house, and Cook was always called in at the end of the meal for compliments. Now evening meals were a somber scene. Cook watched Darkchild follow after Grey. "Acts more like a dog than a horse," she mumbled, tying on a white apron.

At dinner one night, Ed asked, "What are you going to do with Darkchild, my dear?"

"What do you mean?" Grey said, reaching the heart of the artichoke she was eating.

"One of the ground men told Ronald he's turning over garbage pails, and I understand he's making a nuisance of himself at the stable. He runs around the paddock, teasing the horses inside—flaunting his freedom." Ed laughed. "It sounds as though Darkchild is showing his hot Arab blood at a young age. I've sent for one of the finest horse trainers in the world for you, my dear. He'll stay as long as you like."

Under the tutelage of Shannon MacHenry, who arrived the next morning, Grey broke Darkchild to harness. The Scotsman had a rich brogue and unending equine knowledge. "You see, Missus," the soft-spoken, seventy-year-old horseman said, "there is nothing better for a growing colt than to romp, play, and race, but it's prudent to teach the youngster manners as early as possible. He's got to be obedient, raise his feet on command when the blacksmith comes. Good blacksmiths are few and far between and have no patience with bad-mannered horses."

On Shannon's advice, Darkchild spent time in the enclosed paddock with other young horses. "He's got to fight some with his fellows, even if it gets a bit rough. If a colt is kept to himself, he may become timid, horse-shy. Then you could never show him or race or stable him without a terrible time."

Grey loved the hours she spent with Shannon, and soon Darkchild was prancing in circles around her, hooked to the long leather lunge line she held, responding perfectly to every command. He would have five gaits when his training was finished, Shannon promised.

"Remember," he lectured, "proper training leaves a horse with fire as well as a good disposition." The trainer noted the sensitivity and intelligence the colt displayed beneath his arrogance. He privately bet the butler when "Let them rack" rang out in the show ring, the bonnie missus would be atop a winner. Ed Fowler had spared no expense when he had purchased Grey's wedding gift. Darkchild, out of Gaines Dainmark, the foundation sire of the American saddle horse, possessed stamina, beauty, and intelligence from Arab blood; sturdiness and adaptability due to Morgan blood; and fineness of line, greater size and speed from his Thoroughbred lineage. The primary requisite for a gaited horse is high, true action. Darkchild was a natural.

The only thing Grey looked forward to as the days of her life with Ed passed was the time when Darkchild would be old enough for her to mount.

She frequently rode to Manhattan with Ed, and while

he labored at business, she worked with decorators on the Sherry Netherland apartment. Filling those many rooms took a year, and during that time she came to know Ed's offices well.

Fowler Enterprises occupied four floors of the Seagrams Building on Park Avenue. Often she came early to meet Ed and wandered through the offices while waiting for him. The lawyers, accountants, brokers, and secretaries came to know the beautiful Mrs. Fowler, whose presence lit any room she entered. Out of curiosity, she began reading the Dow Jones printer and the employees were amazed at her astute questions. She came to understand how vast the Fowler holdings actually were. There were railroads, oil wells, international real estate, and a law firm, Fowler and Fowler, one of the largest in the world. Surprisingly, she found herself drawn to the excitement of the stock market or the news of a new well.

It was at the office she saw her father most, since George Coltrane was keeping close to his declining son-in-law.

In part, Ed came to assume the role of an adoring father. He completely abandoned any sexual advances and went back to treating Grey with parental affection. He was amused, then proud of her interest in the business, and invited her to meetings he thought she would enjoy.

The month of hell that was her honeymoon faded into a bad dream. Ed grew thinner and weaker than ever. He was plainly sick and Grey gave him comfort by her presence.

Desperate to tell the truth of her life to someone, anxious to have her best friend near, Grey called the Dellagio estate at Christmas, expecting Llana to be on vacation from Sacred Heart College.

"We have no daughter," Mrs. Dellagio informed Grey in a dead voice.

"What do you mean, Mrs. Dellagio? Where is Llana?"

"She ran away from college—with a man! We have no daughter," the woman shouted, then broke into tears and hung up.

Grey could find no further information about Llana, but those worries were interrupted by Ed's distraction with his sister. "Jennifer's going to marry that gigolo," he bitterly announced. "John Parish is nothing but a fortune hunter."

He was right, Jennifer was no beauty. Fiftyish, with the same penchant for alcohol as Ed, she was a female version of her brother, gravely voiced from too many cigarettes and jaded from a lifetime of overindulgence. It was obvious to everyone John was only after Jennifer for her money.

When they married, Ed refused to attend the wedding and became incensed when Jennifer prepared to hand her vast inheritance over to her much younger husband.

Privately Grey thought no harm in Jennifer buying companionship. But Ed began legal proceedings to prevent Jennifer from signing over her shares of Fowler Enterprises to John. The suit proved a further strain on Ed. Lawyers took up more and more of his time, and Grey spent more of hers with Darkchild.

The process of mounting came so naturally that the high-spirited yearling never realized what was happening. Grey, on Shannon's advice, took to putting her arm over Darkchild's back and resting her weight so a saddle and rider would not seem strange. The next step was putting on a saddle with a loose girth. Darkchild allowed it, although he quivered all over. "Easy, Darkchild, easy, my boy," Grey cooed, easing the saddle onto his back. As wearing it became familiar, she tightened the girth.

Grey mounted Darkchild for the first time when he was twenty months old and within an inch or two of his full height. Then the really hard work of training began.

Darkchild learned well and was broken to saddle. But on Grey's orders, he still ran loose on the property. If Grey went into Manhattan, Darkchild would wait near the front gates for the Bentley to return, then race it to the main house, and snort and paw at the gravel until Grey got out and touched him.

He was jealous of her moments away from him. Magda, a member of the Bolshoi before she defected to America, came two mornings a week and gave Grey ballet lessons. It was time of joy for Grey, frustration for Darkchild. Dancing to strains of *Swan Lake* and the *Nutcracker Suite*, Grey would laugh at Darkchild looking through the window. In the winter, his impatient snorts steamed the glass as he waited for her to finish dancing, and she finally had a wire screen put over the glass, preventing Darkchild from breaking it.

A year after Aunt and Uncle Fowler's death, Grey's only social life was with her mother, much of it decorating consultations over the Sherry Netherland apartment. One day, they stood in its finally completed library with serried ranks of beautiful books. Bound in calf, tooled in gold, many of the books were of great antiquity and in the Fowler family for generations. "Aunt Fowler would have loved it, don't you think?" Grey said, running her finger along a smoothly burnished shelf of Philippine mahogany. At intervals between the bookshelves were stationed early American bronzes: horses and long-horned cattle, a collection Uncle Fowler had amassed over many years.

"Yes, dear, she would have," Grace Coltrane replied, thinking Grey's voice plaintive and that it was not caused by a poignant memory of Aunt Fowler, but rather her daughter's melancholic existence.

"Let's lunch at Lutèce today, shall we?" she said, breaking the mood, pushing unbidden guilt for Grey's circumstances to the back of her mind. Guilt often visited Grey's mother nowadays when she compared her beautiful daughter's life to that of other young married women. They did not discuss Ed's health as he was much weaker and having difficulty working. There was no need to voice what was so evident.

For Grey, shopping, museum visits, and charity benefits attended with her mother were time-passing events she drifted through while longing for someone her age to share experiences with. Oh, Llana, where are you?

One Friday, after selecting just the right Chinese flowered silk at Schumacher for a chaise longue in one of the guest rooms, Grey and her mother lunched by the pond in the Four Seasons. After endive salad and shrimps in whiskey sauce, Grey went to meet Ed. Instead of her usual friendly greeting, Mary Ann, the receptionist was silent. "Tell Mr. Fowler I'm here, please," Grey requested.

Mary Ann burst into tears and pushed the private intercom button. Ed's secretary, Mrs. Waters, appeared. She, too, was crying. "He's been taken to Bellevue, Mrs. Fowler. The ambulance just left."

Accompanied by Ralph Daniels, Ed's senior lawyer, financial adviser, and confidant, Grey rushed to the hospital.

It had been a massive heart attack. Grey was horror-stricken when she saw Ed in the brightly lit intensive care unit, hooked to machines with electrodes, tubes, and needles. Displayed on a television screen over the bed, in uneven green spikes, was her husband's heartbeat.

She took his hand lying at his side, being careful not to disturb the intravenous needle. He looked awful, his skin pale, his eyes sunken. Feelings rushed at her: she was visited by hate for his manipulations of her life, then by love for the dear friend and caring human being he also was. "I'm here, it's going to be all right, you're going to get better," she said, knowing it wasn't true, offering up a silent prayer.

At the sound of her voice, his eyes opened. In a moment of clarity, he tried to speak. Grey could not hear and leaned close, her ear near his lips, and heard his faint whisper. "No one will ever harm you. You'll be safe always, taken care of. I've arranged it, my Grey," he gasped. The green line on the electrocardiogram wavered and went flat. His eyes closed, never to reopen. It had been a year and a half since the death of Aunt and Uncle Fowler, and Grey was nineteen-and-a-half years old.

The obituary filled three columns of *The New York Times* and ended: "He is survived by his wife, Grey Coltrane Fowler, and his sister, Jennifer Fowler Parish."

After the funeral service at church, just before Grey entered the long black limousine on her way to the cemetery, with her mother and Jennifer already inside, someone pulled her arm. Turning around, she was engulfed by Llana's hug. "Oh, Grey, I'm so sorry," Llana said, pushing a piece of paper into Grey's black-gloved hand. "It's my phone and address. When you can, call me. I'll be waiting."

As the limo pulled away, reaction to the sight of Llana hit too late for Grey to even speak to her friend she so longed for. But, spirit bolstered, she tucked the paper safely away in her purse.

The will was read the next day in the wood-paneled library of the Southampton estate, where folding chairs were placed. One windowed wall presented a view of the ocean. Waves rolled in, their foam caps meeting the fabled white sand dunes of the Hamptons. Backed by bookcases holding thousands of leather and gold-bound volumes, Ralph Daniels, executor of the will, sat at a magnificently carved rosewood and marble Italian desk. The light from a Tiffany lamp illuminated the document he held.

Daniels looked up as cousins Charles and Cora entered, completing the group of relatives clustered in the library.

Grey nodded to the cousins she vaguely remembered. Daniels was ready to read the will.

Despite air conditioning, Jennifer sweated on Grey's left. Her husband, John Parish, sat on her other side. Ed had hired private detectives to investigate Jennifer's husband and shown Grey a report indicating Parish had a penchant for hookers and "golden showers." Grey could not help but think of that every time she saw John.

As the reading began, John glanced sideways, peeking into Grey's black silk blouse, but was frustrated from a real look by her thick rope of pearls. Grey crossed her hands in her lap. She could almost hear John evaluating her wedding ring's worth.

"I, Edward Fowler, being of sound mind, do bequeath . . ."

The will was surprisingly brief, amazingly complete. Jennifer and the cousins were left tokens, Grey a vast fortune.

The reading finished, Grey looked up to find her father standing in front of her. "Well, Grey, that was quite an impressive document. Ed has made sure you'll never want for anything in your life."

"Yes, Daddy, he loved me very much."

"I will of course take over your financial affairs. You're much too young and inexperienced to handle these matters."

Grey stood with confidence. "No, Daddy, I have an entire firm of lawyers for that, thank you." And she turned away, leaving George Coltrane open-mouthed, staring after his suddenly matured daughter, just come into one of the world's great fortunes.

Llana Dellagio stepped from the limousine and stretched

her small, lithe self. The ride from Manhattan was over
two hours and the last leg of the journey, from the gates
of the vast estate to the main house, was, even to a girl
raised in luxury, an awesomely opulent sight.

Llana had gazed wonderstruck at a lake with swans,
rolling acres of manicured lawns, gardens, and an or-
chard. The limo cruised smoothly past horses being exer-
cised in a paddock near a stable. Positioned at small
roads leading off the main estate road were signs indicating the way to tennis courts, guest house, pool, and polo
field.

A gray-haired butler greeted Llana and led her inside
the four-story, sprawling stone mansion, equally mind-
boggling in its grandness. "Roger at your service," the
impeccably mannered man said, leading her to a second-
floor sea-view bedroom with ankle-deep apple-green velvet carpet and depositing her suitcase on a flowered silk
bench. "Millie will unpack for you, miss. Mrs. Fowler is
on the beach. Please make yourself at home."

Llana went out the beach side of the house. The sun
was high and it took a few moments for her eyes to
adjust to the bright gleam of the sand dunes and the
ocean's sapphirine sparkle.

Then she saw them—girl and horse, running side by
side, the yearling obviously adjusting his lope to her
pace. Both their manes streamed in the sun. Like a fairy
tale come to life or one of those incredible TV commer-
cials that could never really be, thought Llana. Her excitement mounted as Grey came closer. God, how I've
missed her.

And then Grey was right there. Llana laughed with joy
at the sight of those shocking green eyes and they were in
each other's arms, both of them crying and kissing and
hugging, when Llana suddenly felt a searing pain. Screaming, she grabbed her shoulder, "that goddamned horse
bit me!"

"Get, Darkchild," Grey commanded, spanking his flank
hard. Darkchild wheeled, snorted, and galloped off over
a dune. "I'm so sorry. Did he hurt you badly? Let me
see. He's so jealous of me, probably thought you were
going to hurt me."

The incident turned out to be only a scare, and, arms

about each other's waists, Grey and Llana followed the
black horse over the hill to the main house.

Many hours later, after dinner, Llana and Grey lounged
on a white sheepskin rug and pillows in front of a crackling fire. Grey had just finished the entire story of the
last year and a half, leaving out none of the gory details.
The telling brought a catharsis; she was drained but renewed. "Oh, Llana, I've missed you so."

"I've been nuts without you, too. But it's over now,
thank God. What are you going to do with yourself?"

"I don't know," Grey answered, "I really don't know
what to do with me."

"Well, first off, you need to get fucked."

"Llana!" Grey exclaimed and looked hurriedly around
to see if any servants were lurking nearby.

Llana persisted. "It's only the truth. Come on, Cochisa.
You're nineteen, been married and widowed, and don't
know what it is to get it on. You're still a virgin, for
God's sake," she continued with exasperation in her voice
"and the way you're living—you're sealed up here like a
mummy. This is a museum, not a place for you to meet
anyone. You have an apartment in New York. Move into
it. You can't spend the rest of your life holed up in
Southampton with a bunch of antiquated servants and a
horse." Llana stopped talking to allow the "houseboy,"
who was in his sixties, to place a tray of fruit, chocolate
truffles, and snifters of brandy on the floor next to them.
She continued when the servant left, "I know it's only
two months since Ed died, but life has to go on."

"Llana, I'm afraid," Grey said.

"Afraid of what?"

Grey stared ruminatively into the fire, as though the
answer lay in its flames. "Life, I guess," she finally said.

Llana put her arm around Grey. "I was, too. Remember, this is Llana, brought up like you. Convent, convent, convent. And at home . . ." She rolled her dark
eyes. "I wasn't even allowed to be alone with my own
brothers after I got my period."

"Llana, you're exaggerating!"

"It's the truth. After I became a 'woman,' my mother
moved my room to the far end of the hall, with her room
in between me and my brothers." Llana sipped brandy
and Grey saw the fire's reflection in her glass. "And you

know what," Llana continued, the brandy warming her, "I don't give a damn my parents don't speak to me anymore. If they had their way, I'd be locked in a convent as a nun for the rest of my life." Her pearly teeth flashed as she smiled. "As far as I'm concerned, meeting Dan at your wedding was a signal from God it was meant to be. I'm thrilled he's a 'no-good hippie artist,' as my father says and I live 'in sin.' " She squeezed Grey's hand. "I can't wait for you to meet Dan, you'll love him."

"I know. Your life sounds like an adventure."

"It is," Llana said, and bit into a chocolate truffle. "In more ways than one. My old man's a freak," she said with pride.

What an odd way to describe someone you love, Grey thought, but was stopped from asking for further details as Llana earnestly went on.

"I'm turned onto life because of Dan. That's what you need. I'm personally going to see you get a dose of fun. What the hell are best friends for?"

Llana stayed for two days of swimming and riding and talking. When last they rode together, Grey bareback astride Darkchild and Llana on a Fowler mount, Grey said, "Tell me more about Dan."

"He's an artist with a future. His canvases are selling and galleries are beginning to take notice," Llana said proudly.

"Tell me more about *Dan*. And how did he come to be at my wedding?"

"He's originally from Long Island, too," Llana said, opening buttons on her checked blouse. The day was getting hotter and she welcomed the ocean breeze. "He comes from a family of lawyers and was supposed to be one, too. But he didn't fit the family mold—like me," she said, smiling. "He dropped out of law school and sold silver flatware door-to-door and actually made enough to put himself through art school. His father refused to pay for that kind of education. His father thinks all artists are homosexuals. Dan's from an Italian family, too— Northern Italian, that's where he gets his light hair. And at your wedding he was Ed's third cousin's escort. A fellow art student, nothing serious, just friends."

Later, Llana, her size-four figure overencumbered by

Grey's size-six Guy Laroche gown, turned around and around in Grey's mirrored dressing room. Clothes were strewn everywhere, covering petit point benches and scattered on the white carpet. "God, Grey, this stuff is worth a fortune, but most of it would do better for your mother. This is 1976. You need some Calvins."

"Calvins?"

"You've got to be kidding," Llana said, rolling her eyes. Then she saw Grey was serious. "Don't you watch TV?"

"Hardly ever."

"Grey, you've got to get out of here and start living. And why the hell are you wearing your beautiful hair that way?" Reaching up, Llana pulled the tortoise pins from her friend's sedate bun. A deluge of mahogany tresses spilled onto her naked shoulders. Between dresses, the clean-lined perfection of her nude body seemed endlessly reflected by the many mirrors.

Jesus, thought Llana, she is magnificent. Looking at Grey, naked like that, she wished Dan were there to see. For some reason, Grey's still being a virgin was titilating. For a flashing moment, Llana wished she were a man, the first one to have Grey.

They poured over Grey's jewels, scattering them like the clothes. Grey insisted Llana take a heavy gold and ruby cuff bracelet as a present. "But this is worth a fortune," Llana protested as she snapped the bracelet on, watching the rubies sparkle, the gold gleam.

"I want you to have it. I love you."

In the present, back in the Honolulu night on Kapiolani Boulevard, outside the International Fitness Club, the Nightwalker's seething mind proved past reflections did not quell her rage at having been once more in such close proximity to Mikel Anton.

I know everything about you. Scattered facts of his life gleaned from the last three years of relentless research, played across her consciousness as did self-disgust at the perverse attraction for him that had overtaken her in the club. He had boxed in his teens. In Marine basics he had loved hand-to-hand combat sessions, where first he was the student, but soon even the best instructors didn't want to take him on. After basics, he was stationed in Okinawa.

Off duty, the rest of the men in his company drank and went to whorehouses. Not Mikel, he frequented the martial-art fighting schools, learning from Okinawan masters, loving the structured violence. He kept it up all through his military tour. In Vietnam he belonged to a military police karate club. After the service, he was with the Chicago police department for a short time. Anton made more collars than any rookie cop in the history of the department. He also busted more heads, put more alleged perpetrators in the hospital than any cop on record. But the department brass didn't appreciate his enthusiasm, and Anton was finally brought up on charges of excessive violence. His psychological/sexual profile declared he had told an examining police psychologist he couldn't hold his come . . . He was removed from street duty and assigned to teach hand-to-hand combat at the police academy.

Getting a grip on the horrible dementia that had almost overtaken her in the International Fitness Club, the Nightwalker waited for Anton to reappear on the street. Then she followed his massive back through Honolulu's streets toward the condo, where she would once again listen at the bathroom wall. One hand drifting to the deep brand on her neck, her fingers tracing its design, she thought there were few days before his Haleakala Crater pickup. She must monitor him carefully, in case he changed his plans.

Her plans included listening to him and going over, step-by-step, the events bringing her to this fork in life, to relive it just once again . . .

1976, Southampton

After Grey waved good-bye to Llana, she stood watching Darkchild devour his evening apple and thought about her only friend's advice. Llana certainly was happy—and changed. How mortally shocked the sisters at St. Anne's would be to hear Llana, so beautifully angelic with her great innocent eyes one moment, cursing like a drill sergeant the next.

Grey laughed aloud. Darkchild threw his head back and whinnied at the unexpected sound. She fed him another apple and watched as he chomped contentedly.

"Good boy, beautiful baby, how'd you like to live in the Big Apple?" Then a solemn thought struck her. "Oh Lord help us, you're going to have to learn what the inside of a stable looks like!"

Stabling Darkchild would not be simple. He had been in the Southampton stable before, but only to irritate. To the chagrin of the grooms, he would gallop through, as though laughing at the other horses in stalls. The stable opened at both ends, which allowed Darkchild to make his teasing runs and escape.

But this day was different. Darkchild by now allowed Shannon to touch, lead, and to saddle him—all necessary as others would care for him in a city stable. The yearling even allowed another of the grooms to handle him while Grey stood nearby. Now, for the first time, he was led into a large box stall and the door was closed, leaving Darkchild and Grey inside. "There, Darkchild, good boy, my Darkchild." Grey patted him soothingly.

"That's it, missus," Shannon said from the other side of the stall door and handed Grey a bucket of hot mash. "Now offer it, let him eat here, make it home."

Darkchild stuck his nose into the steaming bucket.

"Now, while he's eating," Shannon whispered, "ease out the door."

Grey moved from the fragrant, hay-smelling stall and closed the half gate. Darkchild raised his head from the bucket, a curious look in his eyes. But Grey was right there and that meant everything was all right. He went back to the mash.

"Good, missus. Good," Shannon said. "When he's finished, you'll take him out again. If he eats here everyday, this stall will come to mean good things to him."

So, with the door closed, Darkchild ate in the stall for a week. Then Grey began leaving him for a few minutes. Darkchild stayed quietly eating until she returned to take him out. It seemed everything was proceeding well, and it was decided Darkchild would spend his first night in the stall. Grey fed him, curried him down, and left at dusk.

An hour later Darkchild's shrill whinnies cut the air. "Shannon, I've got to get him out of there," Grey said.

"Not if you want to take him with you to New York," Shannon replied sternly.

Grey went guiltily off to bed with Darkchild's heart-rendering screams in her ears.

At dawn, Darkchild broke through the side of the stable, and all one thousand pounds of him waited as usual for Grey outside the main house.

"Now, missus, don't cry," Shannon said by the shattered stable later that morning. "There's no horse problem that can't be solved."

"But, Shannon," Grey said, wiping tears, viewing the devastation Darkchild had caused, "he'll hurt himself. He could break a leg if we put him back in tonight."

"He's a wild one, Mrs. Fowler, I've seen the likes before," said a groom who stood nearby. "Naturally vicious . . ."

Another stable man who was pulling loose boards away from the hole Darkchild had come through said, "What he needs is a good beating—straighten that renegade right out."

"Shut up, both of you, for what you know of horses," Shannon said vehemently.

"Does that mean we should hobble Darkchild?" Grey asked, looking at her horse grazing nearby as though nothing unusual had occurred.

"No, missus," Shannon said with a grin, "we're going to 'Ace' him."

That night, while Darkchild munched his mash, Shannon and Grey stood in the stall with the black yearling. "Now, missus," Shannon said, "spank him on the flank a bit."

Grey did and Darkchild continued to eat, loving the attention from his mistress. Then Shannon thrust the needle full into the horse's flank where Grey's hand had been.

"He never felt it, Shannon," Grey said with admiration. "What's the drug really called?"

"Acepromazine, missus. He'll soon be content to stay here or anywhere else in the world he might be," he said with a chuckle.

Soon Darkchild's eyes were half closed. Grey placed her sweater in the hay on Shannon's directions. "That'll leave your scent and make it even more pleasant for our high-spirited young fellow," Shannon said as he opened the stall door for her.

Darkchild, in a light stupor, hardly acknowledged his beloved mistress's departure.

"Oh, Shannon, how long will we have to drug him?"

"Not long, missus. Two, maybe three nights, and he'll be stall broke."

To her relief, Shannon was correct. Four nights later, Darkchild was stabled without aid of the drug, and the stable's new side stayed intact.

There was no way Grey was going to live at the Sherry Netherland, another depressing reminder of her life with Ed. With Llana in tow, she looked at apartments until both their feet ached. At one vacancy in the Dakota, where John Lennon lived, Llana could not believe Grey was not familiar with Beatles music. She insisted they stop apartment hunting and buy Beatles tapes and a cassette player. They went to Central Park and listened. Chills ran up and down Grey's spine as she listened to George Harrison's "My Sweet Lord."

Llana watched Grey's pleasure, thinking how much fun it was going to be to turn Grey onto all the things she took for granted. She told Dan about Grey's naivete later that night. "I'm looking forward to knowing Grey," Dan said, expectation in his voice.

"When she's settled," Llana firmly replied.

Finally, two months later, Grey and Llana found an eight-room apartment on Fifth Avenue in the eighties, overlooking the Metropolitan Museum of Art and Central Park.

After heated negotiations with Charlie, owner of the stable in Central Park, Darkchild had *three* box stalls for himself. At first, no matter how much Grey offered for the enlarged space, Charlie refused. Only a visit from the world-famous Shannon MacHenry finally secured the extra stalls.

Magnanimously, Grey lent the Southampton estate to Ed's sister, Jennifer. After all, Jennifer had grown up there and Grey wanted none of the recollections the place held. She put the Sherry apartment up for sale and it immediately sold for 3.5 million dollars.

Occasionally Grey traveled to Ed's old offices, but as time passed, she found herself allowing Ralph Daniels greater control.

In June, Grey's mother came to see where her daughter was living. Before commuting from Long Island, she made sure to turn her diamond ring into her palm, hiding it from potential muggers. Grace Coltrane believed Manhattan's streets were too dangerous to walk. They had tea on the apartment's fifty-foot terrace and argued.

"You're living like a vagabond," her mother said, referring to the fact that only the terrace and bedroom were furnished.

"Oh, Mom, I'll get around to the rest. Don't worry."

"And that gangster's daughter living in sin is your only friend. Really, Grey, you must meet some of the better New York people if you insist on living here."

"Don't refer to Llana that way. And I don't want to meet anyone right now."

Grace continued as though Grey had not spoken. "There's no live-in help here. You're totally unchaperoned. Why is the name Coltrane on the door instead of Fowler?"

"I want to be alone and I want my own name on my own door!" Grey screamed.

A yelling match ensued, during which Grey accused her mother of ruining her life and never really loving her. Grace yelled back Grey had everything and it was all due to her parents' caring.

By time it was over, they were crying in each other's arms and Grey promised to attend a dinner party the next week for the Danish Ballet Company's benefit. Her mother handed her the invitation and seeing "Grey Coltrane Fowler" listed among the patrons, Grey realized the party was her mother's main reason for coming.

Grace Coltrane had the good sense to look a bit sheepish, but stood her ground. "Grey, you've got to meet the right people. How else will you find a husband?"

Grey was relieved to see her mother go. But as she closed the door, she realized her mother was right about one thing: the apartment needed furniture. She went to Bloomingdale's with Llana to furnish her living room. A television with a huge screen taking a whole wall, a giant navy velvet couch that could seat twenty and an enormous coffee table sculptured with the design of the Egyptian sun god Ra to fit the big semicircle the sofa made.

"It's going to look like a screening room," Llana giggled. "When are you coming to dinner? I want you to meet Dan."

"Llana, in a while. I just don't want to meet anyone yet."

Actually, Grey didn't want to meet any men. When she rode Darkchild in the park, she saw the way men looked at her. When she shopped with Llana, bold Manhattan men undressed her with their eyes. She wondered how she'd ever learn to relate.

"I promised Mom I'd go to a fancy benefit next week," Grey said, changing the subject. "Help me shop for a dress and I'll buy you one too."

"This shit is cut!" Anton's belligerent cry in her earphones forced the Nightwalker's attention to the present. Next door, he was purchasing cocaine again, complaining at its quality. Amazing. It was phenomenal to her that he hadn't just dropped dead, heart stopped, from the drugs he had consumed since checking into the condo.

"You don't want it?" the drug dealer said nonchalantly, his tone implying he was ready to go on his way.

Anton was infuriated by the scumbag's manner. I could kill him, he thought, staring into the small piece of tinfoil. The powder was dull. He stuck his finger into it. Licked it. Tasted the lactose cut, but also the tiniest sting of real cocaine. If he let this asshole go, he'd have to truck back out onto the street, look for another dealer. He had to stay by the phone, Ritchie was supposed to call. "How much?" he grudgingly asked.

There was satisfaction in the dealer's voice. When they're hooked, they're hooked, it said. "Two hundred," he muttered, jacking the price by another fifty to sock it to the black motherfucker.

Anton refolded the tinfoil, placing it on the nighttable, gave the man two hundred dollars, stared at him with reddened eyes, then watched him exit the mess of a bedroom. The door slammed as the dealer left the condo. Standing, Anton stripped and looked at himself in the mirror, admiring his blackness.

Mikel was coal black, his color a gift from his African father. "Descended from fucking kings," he said, angling his face toward the light so his keen bone structure was predominantly displayed. He hefted his heavy penis, thick, long . . . "Fucking royal," he said approvingly.

He snorted coke, returned to the mirror, ogling his body, his face—dissipation was written in his eyes. Lack of sleep, no big deal, he never slept anyway. There was a time he had kept records of how much he slept. Used to be important, now he didn't give a fuck. He needed a shave. What happened to discipline? "I'm a fucking Marine," he said at full volume, pulling his naked body to full attention, his huge chest expanded to maximum. "Let's go! Keep going! There *is* nothing else!" he chanted, "I ran Taiwan, the whole fucking country," he yelled, catapulting his drugged mind into the past. Across town, a quaking boy who also listened was pulled by the chanting to that same time frame.

1981, Taiwan

The entire populace of the island was kept in check by the regular army. Two years since Mikel Anton's gung-ho background got him hired by the dictator, President Chiang. The title of commander came with the job as did high authority. The mercenary's duties included training elite forces and monitoring native insurgency. In some ways, Anton was second only to Chiang. He had his own efficient spy network and his personal stoolies were seeded through society, zealously watching for T.I.M (Taiwan Independent Movement) activities. Anton kept a tight cap on things, going to villages personally, selecting recruits for his special forces, seeing, always keeping the "feel" of the people, snaring new stoolies—terrorizing.

Now, in his command tent in a mountain camp, Anton glanced approvingly at a framed slogan on the khaki tent wall. LET'S GO! KEEP GOING! THERE *IS* NOTHING ELSE! He had dreamed it. Many things appeared to him when he slept. A chronic insominiac, Anton obsessively recorded his slumber in a black notebook upon rising each morning. He was averaging three hours a night, lately nightmare-filled—a repeated scenario in which one character emerged from his dream and came to life in his tent. Anton shook off the thought. Impossible. Not real. *I only deal in realities.* he suddenly shouted, "Let's go! Keep going. There *is* nothing else!" and strode naked to a full-length mirror. His two hundred and seventy-five pounds vibrated the wooden plank floor, striking terror into the breast of Yu, the nine-year-old, eighty-pound orderly scrubbing it on his knees.

In the mirror, Anton preened, gazing with unabashed admiration, silently extolling his virtues: athlete, crack soldier, skilled trainer of men—lacing his hands by the fingers, he cracked his joints—killer.

He expanded and admired his muscle-roped chest. "Contains the heart of a lion," he yelled, then stretched and flexed, venerating his bulkly deltoids. Turning his back to the mirror, he craned his head over his shoulder, idolizing his superbly developed traepzius muscle. He loved the way his back tapered into a sleekly narrowed waist, forming the classic V so sought after by weight lifters.

Commander Anton's aide, Yu, saw the familiar egomanical display from the corner of his eye. Fearing and despising the too-perfect monster with no heart who fate had made his master, the boy scrubbed the already spotless floor with a wire brush. Yu was not alone in his feelings. Proud of their heritage, the Chinese soldiers detested being under this American black, now washing the ebony sculpture that was his body. No man should have a form like that; men were meant to be small and yellow, the boy thought. And no man was meant to have a sex like that, as big as an animal's. Yu knew the size of the swine's organ. It was savagely rammed into his anal canal on horror-filled nights when Anton wakened from nightmares and snatched the sleeping boy. Yu bled each time from his split rectum for days after.

The first vicious rape had happened soon after the boy was conscripted, at age eight, from a nearby village to be the commander's orderly—ripped from his mother's clutching arms and screaming pleas. The last sight of his mother, after a soldier kicked her to silence, was of her lying vomiting in the dirt.

Repeatedly assaulted by Anton, the boy never knew when it would happen or if Anton even remembered. The beast never referred to the incidents. But by Buddha, the boy would forget neither the pain nor the shame. He looked into no man's eyes. How many in the camp heard his screams at night and speculated on their cause? Bitter hatred burned inside the nine-year-old boy whose life was an interminable nightmare, servant to the devil himself! But he did a perfect job as such. Otherwise, he would raise the wrath of this black demon who demanded absolute perfection.

"Let's go! Keep going! There *is* nothing else!" Anton chanted and washed from a basin, congratulating himself yet again on the slogan. Words with meaning. He took no note of Yu's presence, considering the boy no more than part of the woodwork. He hated them all as much as they hated him. Slanty-eyed Chinks. Babbling crazy language. He longed for the sight of a proper Marine.

He dressed in full combat regalia. The steaming jungle heat made no difference to him. His fatigues were camouflage printed, Ripstop poplin, tucked into U.S. special forces boots, designed specifically for mountain operations. He welcomed the familiar grip of the leather sweatband lining his Canadian special forces beret, set at the proper jaunty angle. The green beret made his high cheekbones appear even more prominent.

He selected his weapons for the day, knife first. Even in this nuclear age, the edged weapon was irreplaceable for the silent kill. He taught the gooks that the soldier with the knife was the one who conquers. He was never without a blade, although there was no feeling quite like killing with one's bare hands.

He took up a U.S. Marine Raider stiletto, a favorite, admiring its deadly beauty and balance, slid the razor-sharp knife into a sheath at his waist, and considered his extensive handgun collection. He choose a small, lightweight, matte blue .45 Detonics. The Combat Master, Mark VL. Squinting down its adjustable sights, he admired the unique, three-dot lineup for rapid target acquisition.

Fully attired and armed, every button gleaming, every seam pressed rigid, Anton executed a perfect about-face, and strode, his back ramrod straight, from the command tent. Spit and polish all the way!

Inside the tent, upon Anton's departure, Yu breathed normally again. The commander's exit left a void, the boy spat derisively in it, then hurriedly wiped his gob of spittle lest the monster change his mind and return.

Outside, Anton took no notice of nature's magnificent scenario. A beginning sunrise, mountain peaks with tops hidden in white clouds, and lush green surroundings bored him to tears.

Crossing the parade grounds, his steps raised puffs of dust, daring to settle on his boots, marring Yu's mirror shine. Contemptuously, Anton looked to troops at attention in khaki fatigues and combat boots awaiting his inspection by dawn's first light, thinking how he got the goddamned skinny little bastards out of fucking pajamas and into clothes fit for men!

His enforcers, the biggest of them, fell in behind him as he walked past lines of soldiers. Three times he pointed out infractions. Two for uniforms, one for a dirty weapon. Each time the offender was methodically beaten unconscious with billy clubs by the enforcers. The hollow sound of wood striking skulls resounded in the quiet dawn. The commander stood at parade rest, watching with detached approval. There would be no excuses, no mercy given, no letup—ever.

"Let's go. Keep going. There *is* nothing else," Anton yelled into the mirror in the Waikiki condo and reached for the blow.

Across town, on Pau Street, Charles Halehana and the boy listening to the infinity transmitter heard the yelled slogan. The boy was shaking all over. I should let him make the kill, Halehana mused, noting how ashen the kid's face was. "I would like to be closer to him," he said. "I wonder if the condo next door is empty? I'll rent it if it is." He prepared to leave the apartment.

The boy looked worried. He was terrified of the confrontation to come. As much as he wanted Anton dead, he feared to lose this man he loved.

The Nightwalker, in the condo Charles Halehana was preparing to go toward, also heard the shouted slogan. Through the wall she heard Anton sniff more cocaine, and then the familiar theme music of CNN News, the only station Anton watched, filled her earphones. She relaxed, knowing he would wait for Ritchie's call.

Manhattan, 1976

Andre Bugueot could not believe his luck. Not only had his business trip to New York been a success, but the dinner party he was dressing for would bring him contact with Grey Coltrane Fowler. He ran his finger over the engraved print of the invitation. What did he care for the Danish Ballet? He had never forgotten meeting *her*. How could he? That startling beauty, draped with a fortune in jewels—the old drunk of a husband. And now she was widowed and rich, rich, rich! What a catch! Everything a man could want in one beautiful package. I wonder if she's still an innocent?

Andre, who had dedicated his life to the pursuit of rich and beautiful women, had immediately recognized Grey's lack of sophistication. It didn't take much to determine she must have been frustrated with Ed as a husband.

As he adjusted his bow tie, Andre wondered if she had lovers. Then he remembered her response to his touch in Paris. It was electric, and she had attempted to conceal her reaction. Not the way of a trollop. No, she was too young to have figured out how to have her cake and eat it, too.

He examined his carefully crafted image. It was plain to see why columnists adored him. Andre Bugueot, tall, dark and handsome; titled and always perfectly turned out. His two marriages and divorces plus numerous affairs with daughters of international society were gossip column grist. The more worried parents warned their daughters of Andre, the more likely the object of his affection was to fall under his spell.

"I hope someone has told her what a bastard I am," he said aloud.

7

The gown was black—Givenchy, a startlingly simple toga hooking over one shoulder, looking like a million dollars. With it she wore a wide, hammered gold necklace set with black onyx and circular diamonds.

At Elizabeth Arden, with Llana watching enthusiastically, Paavo finished Grey's coiffure. Her blazing hair was held high, with gold and black cloisonné clips Paavo proclaimed "would kiss the lights," then cascaded in twisting curls. "You are a Roman empress tonight," Paavo said, stepping back to view his artistry.

Grey and Llana had been at Arden's for hours. Now they hurried downstairs and out the red door onto Fifth Avenue, where the doorman assisted Grey into a waiting limo as Llana excitedly gave last minute instructions. "Don't forget—mingle! Don't be shy." As the long silver Mercedes pulled off, Llana, dressed in a white linen suit, stood waving and smiling on the sidewalk.

The benefit was at the Carlyle. The many hours Grace Coltrane had spent phoning friends in excitement over Grey's reentry into New York society proved fruitful. A terrific fuss was made over Grey. She was introduced to art patrons, some who were at her wedding, and others who knew her identity though Grey never met them.

After cocktails, hundreds of guests were ushered into the dining room, where Grey found her nameplate at a round table set with Limoge china and a centerpiece of American Beauty roses. On her right sat the Danish Ballet's blond lead dancer, wearing a flame velvet jacket and floppy silk bow tie. The dancer, whose name already escaped her, glaringly stood out amid the room of tuxedoed men. During small talk Grey confessed she had never seen him perform. Insulted, the haughty dancer turned his attention to a white-haired dowager dripping with diamonds on his left.

Oh dear, I should have lied. I'm not doing very well.

The gentlemen on her left began a conversation. He was a publisher—a slim, fortyish man who was quite nice. They were discussing George Bernard Shaw's plays, a conversation Grey thought her mother would highly approve, when a French-accented voice broke in. "Excuse me, I am Madame Fowler's escort and was detained. My apologies, sir."

The waiter who accompanied the Frenchman led the publisher, openly miffed at being removed from the most beautiful and eligible woman in the room, to another table.

"*Pardon, madame.* I know that was extremely rude. My only excuse. I had to sit next to you. Your beauty is a magnet that drew me across the room. Do you remember me?"

His hair was dark waves. "Yes, of course," Grey said, "at Baron Rothschild's in Paris. I'm sorry, I don't recall your name."

How droll, he thought, to be so truthful.

"Andre Bugueot at your service, madame." And looking deep into her eyes, he kissed her hand.

Late the next afternoon there was still no answer to Grey's telephone. Llana had not heard from Grey, whom she normally spoke with several times a day. "After all," Llana said anxiously to Dan, hanging up the phone, "I'm the only friend she has in New York." Llana was deeply concerned about Grey, who she felt needed her protection and guidance.

Dan looked at Llana wearing an ecru silk teddy, its fine lace trim lightly brushing her smooth, tawny thigh as she moved. "Stop worrying about Grey and come sit on my cock and tell me again about her pretty body," he said.

Eight-foot-wide bridle paths wind through Central Park's vast acreage. Skillfully placed foliage blocks the sight of skyscrapers for long stretches, negating the surrounding city, and equestrians can imagine themselves in the countryside. To Grey it was paradise. For, cantering alongside her, on a rented roan gelding, was Andre Bugueot.

Peripherally, she admired her noble companion, sitting his horse as though born to the saddle. His white-shirted back erect, Andre's long legs, encased in mustard-yellow

britches and high black boots, gripped the roan with easy
perfection.

In a white Lacoste shirt, rust jodhpurs over brown
jodhpur boots, mahogany hair floating free in the smooth
motion of Darkchild's canter, Grey was wide awake despite lack of sleep. After last night's dinner, Andre had
introduced her to New York nightlife.

First to Le Jardine, a disco on West 43rd. Thousands
of tiny pastel feathers dropped on dancers gyrating to
ear-shattering music. "I don't know how," she confessed
as Andre prepared to lead her onto the dance floor.

She has the candor of a child, he thought. "Not to
mind, I will teach you when we are alone," he said.

I wonder when that will be, she caught herself thinking.

So they stayed at the bar with drinks, watching the
revelers, then went to an after-hours casino.

The illegal casino was situated behind a record shop on
Second Avenue in the eighties, and from the facade she'd
have never known it was there. Andre assured her the
interior would be as elegant as any casino on the Riviera.
He was correct, there were professional tables under
crystal chandeliers with elite clientele at the games. Grey
and Andre blended perfectly in their formal dress.

They shot craps and played blackjack while sipping
champagne. Others patrons stared openly, and Grey,
catching their dual reflection in a gold-flecked mirror,
understood why. She saw Andre looking into the glass
with the same approval. He turned to her and smiled.
"We are a perfect match, are we not?"

She could only shyly agree, feeling a blush.

At the poker table, just after he draped her Russian
sable stole on the chair behind her, a burly man in a
tuxedo offered something in a small bowl. Andre refused.

"What was that?" Grey asked.

"Nothing to be concerned with—cocaine, an accompa-
niment to New York night life for some."

"Oh, that," Grey said offhandedly, trying to be blase,
turning her attention back to her potential full house.

At six they went to the Brasserie. Entering the restaurant, popular with New York's stay-up-all-night-crowd,
they were "on stage" at the stair top. Seeing open admiration from people seated below, Grey was again reminded of what a stunning couple they made.

Over eggs Benedict, Grey told Andre about Darkchild, which prompted him to suggest they ride and brunch.

"I'd love to," Grey said immediately.

The experienced women Andre knew would make a man wait to see them again—play the coy game. But to his surprise, he found her childlike innocence quite charming. He dropped her off with a hand kiss at seven-thirty.

For Grey, it was an enchanted evening and the nineteen-year-old secretly thanked her mother for forcing her to the benefit. Andre did not get drunk or even tipsy. He did not smoke. He was movie star handsome, and each time he touched her hand or draped her sable about her shoulders, Grey had felt chills and electric charges in private places.

She glanced to Andre, cantering his horse in sync with Darkchild. He smiled.

"Hungry, Grey?" he asked in his smooth voice.

She nodded yes and smiled back.

"Come on, then," he said, galloping ahead.

Head high, eyes rolling, Darkchild caught up. Rarely partnered with another horse, he was uneasy. Grey kept a tight rein, preventing him from leaving Andre's mount in the wind. At Tavern on the Green they tied the horses where they could see them during brunch in the garden.

Andre, as though understanding what she'd been through in living with an alcoholic, requested tomato juice for them instead of the Bloody Marys Ed certainly would have ordered. Stop thinking of Ed, for God's sake, Grey chided herself.

Talking and laughing, they ate deliciously light vegetable souffles, browned and crispy on top. Andre ordered apples for the horses and later, feeding them, he said, "Why don't you go home, nap, and join me for dinner and theater tonight?"

Grey was overdressed for the Village Gate in dangling pearl and ruby earrings and off-the-shoulder white chiffon, but not for Andre, who, as though anticipating her color scheme, was resplendent in a white silk suit accenting his Riviera tan. Everyone at the long wooden shared table stared as they sat to watch an exciting revue of gospel-trained black performers. Grey's palms ached with clapping.

After, at Le Sans Coulette, a French country-style

restaurant, the appetizer—a basket of raw vegetables, racks of assorted sausages, ceramic crocks of pâté, dressing, and bread—covered their entire table. Grey could only laugh when the waiter came for their choice of entrees. But Andre, confident of both their appetites, ordered duck to follow.

Sipping Dom Perignon, they talked about the show. While Andre delivered a soliloquy on black music, Grey noticed the way his beard was beginning to peek through his sculptured jaw, and how strong his hands were. He had long, square-tipped fingers . . .

They finished the evening at a Midtown jazz club, listening to a quartet, and then a twenty-four-hour record store, where Andre bought jazz, gospel, and soul albums. "I hope you think of this evening when you play them," he said, looking directly with his clear blue eyes into hers.

"I'll get a record player now. Thank you, Andre," Grey said, taking the albums.

It was 5 A.M. when he kissed her hand and dropped her at her door. For the second night in a row, she'd been in wonderland.

Grey was still asleep at noon when the buzzer rang, summoning her to the intercom. "Delivery."

While two extremely efficient workmen installed a stereo record player in its own polished mahogany cabinet and two matching large speakers, Grey read the accompanying card. "Thank you for a wonderful evening. Andre."

Grey Coltrane had found her Rhett Butler.

Seething, Llana arrived unannounced eight days later, ringing the intercom, until Grey, who was gambling again until five, answered in a bleary voice and invited her upstairs.

Llana had her Italian up. "How could you?" she said, her beautiful features accusingly arranged.

"How could I what?"

In answer, Llana thrust a copy of the *Daily News*, turned to the society column, under Grey's nose.

"Oh, nice shot," Grey said, smiling, looking at a photo of herself and Andre brunching at Tavern on the Green. Yawning, brushing her heavy hair from her face, she wondered when it had been taken. Riding and brunching with Andre had become a daily occurrence. She looked at Llana's face. "Why are you angry?"

"Nice shot!" Slapping her hand against Andre's picture, Llana exclaimed, "This guy is the world's worst! Don't you know? He's a fortune hunter. Read what the paper says."

"Coffee," Grey said, heading for the kitchen in a short white silk pajama coat, reading aloud. "Grey Coltrane Fowler, this year's best catch, being wined and dined by international playboy Viscount Andre Bugueot. Could it mean wedding bells again for Andre? And if so, would this be number three, or is it four? This columnist can't keep track. What does he have? Other men must be dying for his secret." Depositing the newspaper on the kitchen counter, she plugged in the preset coffee machine and watched as it instantly, aromatically began its task.

"Grey, don't you see? He marries rich women, gets a pocketful, and he's onto the next. You don't need him."

"I'm having a wonderful time. He hasn't even kissed me," Grey said, pouring coffee into a flowered mug, adding a spoon of raw honey. And even as she said it, wondering when he would kiss her. She wanted him to, very much.

"Sure," Llana said with great sarcasm, paying no attention to the coffee Grey prepared for her, "and you're falling, hook, line, and sinker. That's the oldest game in the world. He's baiting you—he's so practiced. Oh, baby, please don't go for it."

Grey bridled. "You're wrong. Andre's probably been misjudged. I hate gossip!" Then in a complete turnabout, she hugged Llana. "Please, let's not argue. C'mon, have breakfast with me and we'll go shopping."

Llana's tirade began again later as Dan stood, hammer in hand, before a twelve-foot-long abstract he had just hung on the red brick wall. As he stepped back and contemplated his work, the sunlight, muted through the dusty glass skylight, made his longish sandy hair glow red.

"She's going to get hurt, Dan! He's got her. She won't hear a word against him. I mean, she wouldn't even come here to dinner, and now she's out on the town every night with him and he's out for the kill!"

Dan, realizing there was nothing he or Llana could do,

decided on distraction. Stepping naked from his one-piece overalls, he began stroking himself. "Take your clothes off."

Llana, watching him grow hard, obliged.

That same night, Andre kissed Grey. Her first romantic kiss: soft, sweet, gentle. And sitting there, on her big blue couch, she felt an unbidden moistness between her legs.

He pulled his mouth slowly from hers. Taking her face in his hands, so all she could see was him, he said, "I love you, Grey."

Then, holding her, he told her about his former too-fast life and the mistakes he had made in his relationships.

Grey wanted Andre Bugueot more than anything she had ever wanted in her life. Telling him she didn't care about his past, she explained having a pretty bad one herself with Ed.

While they talked, his hand massaged her neck lightly, and she had to stop from moving along with it. His cologne was a light, spicy scent. She thought she would explode with desire.

Then he said, "I must go to Paris tomorrow."

Oh no, don't leave me now, she thought with a sinking heart. Oh God, is there a woman waiting in Paris?

"But I shall return next week. Will you be here for me, *cherie*?"

"Yes, Andre," she said, relief washing over her.

She waited for his return with tingling expectations. Lying in bed, touching herself, she wondered what having him make love to her would be like, visualizing his hard body on top of hers. She wished she had confessed her virginity to him.

She talked over her chastity with Darkchild, her only confidant now since she and Llana had agreed not to discuss Andre in order to keep peace between them. "Oh, Darkchild, he thinks I'm a sophisticated lady, and I'm doing my best to act like one, but I don't feel the part."

She certainly couldn't discuss Andre with her parents, who came especially to New York to talk about her foolishness and his terrible reputation. She didn't even want to think about the horrible argument they had.

Jennifer called. "Congratulations. He's fascinating. Gorgeous hunk!" She waited for gossip.

Telling her former sister-in-law someone was at the door, Grey promised to call back and never did.

Two columnists called, asking if she intended to marry Andre. Wondering how they obtained her unlisted number, she stammered "no comment" both times, then turned off her phone, and did not turn it back on until the day Andre was due.

In the meantime, to soothe Llana's rightfully hurt feelings, Grey agreed to come to dinner and properly meet Dan. It was he who answered the door. Grey presented him with an armload of yellow roses and profuse apologies for not coming sooner while looking curiously at the man she had seen once before at her wedding, who so had rapturously captured Llana. Ruggedly handsome, keen-featured with penetrating eyes and lightish hair, Dan was barefoot in a white T-shirt and billowy black cotton pants tied at the ankles. He kissed her on the cheek. "You're here now and that's what's important. Take off your shoes and let us entertain you."

Grey slipped out of her heels, at the same time feeling his strong magnetism.

"What a wonderful way to live," she said, hugging Llana, drinking in the surroundings. "I've never been in an artist's loft." She immediately inspected Dan's works, covering long expenses of brick walls. The paintings, amazingly versatile, ranged from Op to a portrait style akin to old Flemish masters. Additional canvases were piled on the wide, varnished wooden plank floor or leaned against walls. As she admired a portrait of Llana, keenly capturing a familiar impish glint in her dark eyes, Dan stood at her side and she noticed how erect he held his muscular body. "I'd love to paint you sometime, Grey," he said, offering a hot cup of sake. "This is going to be an Oriental evening."

Following his example, she drank with one motion. Her insides warmed. "I'd consider that a great compliment. Your paintings are brilliant," she said, smiling, glad she came.

Llana, in faded skinny jeans and a white T-shirt stretched taut across her bouncy breasts, said, "Come on, Grey, let me show you the rest of our digs." She led Grey up a wooden ladder to a room-sized sleeping platform, underneath which were closets and a bathroom. From the king-sized bed through a low railing, the two women could see the entire loft, one floor-through expanse, with the underside of the bedroom the only enclosed area. Sitting on the bed's dove-gray comforter with Llana, Grey said, "It's so clever, you've created different rooms even though there's no walls."

"Dan decorated," Llana said proudly, pushing her bare toes into the velvety silver carpet.

Grey leaned close to Llana. "I know what you mean now. God, he's talented—and so good-looking," she whispered.

Llana wiggled in delight. "And he's a ten!" She ducked the pillow Grey threw.

They drank more sake, Grey and Llana lounging on a white pillow couch. Dan, sitting cross-legged on the white shag carpet, announced he was off to get dinner. And like a coiled spring slowly pulled straight, he rose in one fluid movement, then turned, walking with powerful grace toward the door. The motions of a trained dancer, or maybe a gymnast, Grey thought.

"Dan moves beautifully," she said when he left.. "Lithe, like a cat."

Llana smiled. "That's from karate. He practices every day. It's his next love after painting."

"I don't know anything about karate," Grey said.

"I really don't, either. Dan never lets me go there. Says it's no place for a woman." Llana twinkled. "He moves like that in bed, too."

Grey laughed. "You're obsessed. You know, I feel terribly *avant garde*. I'm in a real artist's loft, being entertained by the artist and his model."

"Grey, I know I promised, but please, let's talk about your lover," Llana said, abruptly changing the subject.

"He's not my lover, and you did promise."

"You mean you're still intact?" Llana said incredulously.

"Llana, that's a really weird way to put it, and I don't want to talk about Andre!"

Reaching and touching Grey's cheek with one finger, Llana said, "Okay, just be careful, huh? You're playing with the big boys now."

Dan returned and they ate sashimi, sushi, chicken teriyaki,and marinated raw vegetables with ivory chopsticks at a low table on brocaded floor pillows. Lights

were muted and a very un-Japanese Dvorak violin con-
certo played in the background. During dinner Llana
leaned against Dan and he kissed her forehead. Watching
the tender moment, Grey longed for Andre.

After dinner, Dan placed a gilt-covered oversize book
on the table. "I got it at auction today, international art.
The color plates are magnificent," he said, sitting between Grey and Llana, slowly turning pages.

Grey and Llana looked at the book's unique collection
while Dan commented. Turning to a Japanese print that
hung in a Danish museum, he asked Grey and Llana
what they thought. Grey carefully examined the page,
her long hair spilling over it as she bent forward.

A beautiful Japanese woman dressed in elegant ki-
mono sat in a cloth swing held by two men who stood on
either side. A hole in the bottom of the swing allowed
the giant penis of a richly dressed man lying underneath
to penetrate the woman, whose head was thrown back.
Her expression combined fear and ecstasy.

Flushing with embarrassment, Grey said, "It's—it's very
nice." Oh, God. Why didn't I say something clever?

Llana had much more to say. "Notice the way she's
totally controlled. After all, there's three men there. The
master fucking her, two servants moving the swing and
watching. God, it's stimulating!"

Dan's arm was around Llana's shoulder. From the
corner of her eye Grey saw his hand brush Llana's breast,
a momentary caress as they gazed at the print. Grey was
suddenly surprised by her own unexpected titillating reaction to the pornographic picture and the overseen intimate moment between Dan and Llana.

"Llana, you're so astute," Grey said, laughing, breaking the poignant mood at the table. "It was a great
dinner—and wonderful meeting you, Dan. Your paintings are terrific. Super dinner."

Grey kissed and thanked her way out and went home
and touched herself, thinking of Andre and those pictures and Dan's hand on Llana's breast.

"Fucking whore," Anton screamed, slamming the phone,
jarring the Nightwalker next door. A Chinese madam
had told him he was sick, not to phone again. He took a
one and one, wishing he had her to torture. The coke

rushed into his brain. His thoughts shot back to when he had tortured one of those stinking gook females during an interrogation session. He had been the Marine officer in charge of MPs, and she had been an NVA agent. No one could get her to cooperate. Except Anton. She talked under his hands . . .

The pleasurable memory calmed him and he returned to requesting child prostitutes by phone, allowing the Nightwalker her own retrospections.

Andre returned to New York with a diamond ring in a lovely, lacy setting and proposed to Grey in a horse and carriage he hired for the evening. They just came from *Chorus Line*, and Grey was still under the musical's spell.

The horse's hooves were the only sound as the carriage turned into Central Park. He placed the ring on her finger and told her it was his mother's. "I beg you to be my wife."

There was no hesitation on her part, acquiescence being the only proper way to deal with Prince Charming. "Yes, Andre." Her heart filled with joy of love and being wanted.

Later in her apartment, she sipped champagne for courage and somehow managed to tell him she was a virgin.

"I thought that," he said, giving her another sweet, soft lip caress that made little contractions happen to her. Looking into her eyes, placing his hand over her breast, as though he could see right through the red silk evening jacket she wore, his fingers found her nipple's thrust. Her whole body vibrated. He leaned forward and kissed her again. She moaned, feeling her legs weaken and begin to part. He took his lips from hers.

"You will be mine on our wedding night, *cherie*. I shall be the only man you ever know and our life together will be perfect."

Kissing her once again, he returned to his suite at the Waldorf Towers, where a highly imaginative lady of the night smoked Maui Wowie with him and pleasantly reduced the stiff erection Grey had given rise to.

"She's going to marry him," Jennifer said, lying in bed, staring at her husband's nakedness while he combed his hair. His hard buttocks stood whitely out against his deep tan.

"So what do you care?" John Parish said, just to say something when she talked. His back was turned so that he didn't have to look at her in a mauve organdy pegnoir trimmed in dyed-to-match ostrich feathers.

He heard her pull on a cigarette and sip the drink always at her side. He wondered how much longer it would take to drink and smoke herself to death as her brother had. Then she said something that suddenly gripped his attention.

"We're almost out of money."

That was crazy. He knew there should be millions available since Ed had died in the midst of the lawsuit contesting Jennifer's inheritance and Grey had agreed to release the funds.

Jennifer continued, "Grey is letting me have the money with no contest, Ralph Daniels is working out the details. Grey only has final papers to sign. But I think Bugueot is going to get to the pen and checkbook first. He may not be so generous." Jennifer's worried voice was a rasp.

John Parish was at Fowler and Fowler the same day.

"Mr. Parish, you do not seem to understand," Ralph Daniels said, "I am in Mrs. Fowler's employ, and I would breach client confidentiality were I to continue this conversation. Mrs. Fowler's personal affairs are just that."

But after Parish left, Ralph Daniels worried. Was Grey to be bilked of everything by an international fortune hunter? He requested an appointment with her, intending advising her of the conversation, and also of the not-so-veiled offer of a bribe Parish had hinted at to speed things up.

It was always a pleasure to see Grey Coltrane Fowler, Ralph Daniels thought later that week. She sat across from him, her beauty delightful, dressed simply in a brown cashmere sweater and skirt, her only jewelry a wide gold bangle bracelet. She no longer wore the blaze of a Fowler diamond. He hoped she kept her jewels safely. Then she lifted her other hand and the gray-haired lawyer saw the new diamond. "May I offer my congratulations, Mrs. Fowler, on your impending marriage," he said, thinking whoever Bugueot was, he made Grey happy. What a change from the introverted, bun-wearing, newly widowed woman he had dealt with. Now she sparkled. Her tipped-up green eyes gleamed. Her hair was loose, floating around her pretty face when she smiled and threw her head a little to the side. "Thank you, Mr. Daniels."

He told her of Parish's visit, leaving nothing out and silently waited to hear from her.

"First off, yes, I want Jennifer to have the money left to her with no contest and no stipulation on how she spends it," Grey said adamantly. "And thank you for telling me all. Maybe I do need to talk to a fair-minded person about these accusations against Viscount Bugueot."

After Grey left, Daniels thought over their conversation. She was smart. She'd be all right. He merely advised her not to sign any financial agreements without his looking at them. She promptly defended Bugueot. "I'm sure that won't ever be an issue. There could be no possible reason for it. Andre has homes around the world. He's a wealthy man in his own right. We have never even discussed my financial situation." She glanced at the engagement ring on her finger, its square-cut, blue/white stone at least eight carats. "Our relationship is based on love and trust," she said finally, absolute faith shining brightly in her eyes.

They went full steam ahead with the wedding plans. Two parties had already been given them by Andre's terribly sophisticated famous friends. Grey did not like the way beautiful women constantly kissed her tall, handsome, titled fiance, calling him "darling." But she did like the way he totally ignored them after perfunctory greetings and spent all his time with her, seeing to her every want, making sure she was happy and feeling loved. And when they were alone, he sexually teased her to a fever pitch until she thought she would die of desire. Then, laughing softly, he would promise her the coming delights of their wedding night.

Llana saw through it all when she met Andre at a party. The Frenchman kissed her hand. "What a pleasure it is to finally meet Grey's best friend," he said in his smooth voice. For a brief moment they exchanged cool, calculating looks. This beautiful little dark one is my enemy, Andre sensed immediately, feeling her eyes on him as he shook Dan's hand. The two men judged each other's power. He bears me no goodwill either, Andre thought as the artist gripped his hand, realizing the calluses he felt were not from holding a paint brush.

Llana saw how hot Grey was for Andre at that party, how she blushed and dropped her eyes when the Frenchman pinned her with his gaze, and how unbelievably beautiful the two of them were side by side. Scarlett O'Hara and Rhett Butler come to life. Llana knew nothing was going to stop the wedding.

Well, baby, Llana thought, watching Grey, in a black silk dress, purring under Andre's hand, I hope you have a great wedding night. Because with Ande Bugueot as your husband, you're going to suffer.

As Llana watched from across the room, a blond goddess of a woman, Talia, approached the engaged couple. Descended from Norwegian nobility, born in Lapland, she was twenty-one years old, six feet tall with great slanted blue eyes and was making quite a name in films. "My congratulations to you both," Talia said, looking only into Andre's eyes.

Another one of Andre's overly beautiful friends, Grey thought, realizing she would have to get used to these jet-set children of the world who knew him so well. When the ice queen left, Grey said, "She's the most beautiful woman I've ever seen."

"No, my cherie. In a room full of beautiful women *you* are the shining star."

Grey didn't know if her mother and father were coming to the wedding, nor did Andre promise his family's presence. She was marrying him, that's all that mattered. The nuptials were to be in two weeks at Andre's friend's town house, and life continued a whirlwind. Andre took her out day and night, showing Grey how to enjoy her young life.

In jeans, at the Lone Star Café they drank beer and danced on a sawdust-covered floor to live country music. At the Roxy, he bought her a glittering short-skirted outfit and they roller-skated to disco. They weekended at his friend's Saratoga estate and shot skeet. To her surprise, she turned out to be a natural with a shotgun.

Their pictures were constantly in the papers. She became used to having her photo taken everywhere they went.

She was happy all the time now, finally going to live her fairy-tale life. She and Andre were obviously made for each other. She dreamed every night of making love to him. She was ready—God, she was ready! Now the thought of children brought her joy. How beautiful they would be.

Six days before the wedding, Andre initiated a legal discussion. At first, Grey was not sure she was hearing correctly. They sat over drinks in the Plaza Hotel's Oak Room. Outside the picture window in the gathering dusk, couples in hansom cabs passed.

"What legal arrangements, Andre? Why should we have to go to France *before* the wedding to see a lawyer?"

"The pre-nuptial agreement must be signed, cherie." His voice was matter-of-fact.

Strange, she thought, you can actually feel the pain when your heart is breaking. "Pre-nuptial agreement? I don't understand, transfer my funds to France? Aren't we living in New York, too?"

He spoke to her as though she were a child, holding her hand, caressing it. "Yes, *cherie.* We shall maintain a home here also. But traditionally a French husband handles financial matters. So you see, it is better we take care of such business in my country."

His voice was soothing, but suddenly his handsome face looked satanic. "Besides, darling, I wouldn't want your lovely mind bothered by such trivialities. We will have a champagne flight to Paris, take care of the agreement, dance the night away, and be back *tout de suite.*"

At nine the next morning—red-eyed from tears and lack of sleep, Grey was in Ralph Daniels' office. As gently as he could, the elderly lawyer explained what Bugueot really had in mind—total control of all Grey's assets, including Fowler Enterprises itself. "And," Daniels added sorrowfully, "should you divorce under European laws, you could easily be left penniless. I'm sorry, Mrs. Fowler. I realize the pain this is causing—but you should not do this."

In total distress Grey looked across the massive desk at him. "I would like you to contact Viscount Bugueot immediately. If this marriage cannot go ahead without my signing papers, I want you to inform the viscount I cannot marry him under the circumstances." As distraught as she was, even as she said the words, there was a glimmer of hope in her heart Andre would accept. After all, he does love me.

Beautiful heiress, Grey Coltrane Fowler, and dashing international charmer, Viscount Andre Bugueot, call off nuptials, read the headline. Within the story, Contessa Nubea Bogavich, described as a long-time Fowler family confidante, was quoted as saying, "The young heiress just couldn't put up with his womanizing." Grey had never heard of the woman in her life. She used the *Star* gossip column to line the bottom of the wrought iron bird cage housing her newly acquired giant cockatoo. "Shit on that," she said in a good imitation of Llana and started to cry again.

In the following days, Bugueot regretted his rashness. She probably would have given me everthing, he thought, looking at the returned engagement ring. He tossed it in the air and caught it with a quick swipe. I should have known she was different. Underneath her childish candor and innocence was a discerning mind. And backbone. Too bad, he mused. She would have made a fitting wife, more than the others. He would have even considered a child. He almost would have begged forgiveness if he thought it would make a difference. But he knew she would never trust him again.

He thought of her gorgeous rounded derriere spread over her magnificent stallion's withers. She would have been delicious. Another serious mistake. He should have taken her—then she would have been putty in his hands. Well, he regretfully considered, with not a little bit of jealousy, there'd be a man there *bientôt*. She was too ripe and ready and rich to be alone. He found himself hoping she'd find real happiness. In a perverse way he was proud of her for escaping him. Andre was really not the bastard he was reputed to be. It was just that drafty castles and ropes of polo ponies cost a fortune to maintain.

Adieu cherie, enfant richesse, my beautiful Grey.

He called for a bellman to pick up his Gucci luggage in the thirty-second-floor Waldorf Tower suite. He was off to London. Bonnie Prince Charles, who was not yet married, attracted lovely young things from wealthy families. Andre was not above picking up the castoffs of future kings.

8

Grey vacillated between reliving the near delirium of Andre's touch and bouts of profound weeping. "Oh God, what's wrong with me?" she said one day, scrutinizing her face in the mirror. "I do look like Prince Valiant," she said, thinking back to when she had been ten, despising a new haircut—too short—as if someone had put the proverbial bowl on her head and cut around it. With her hair that awful way, accenting her strong cheekbones, little Grey was convinced she could double for the comic strip knight.

Now, at nineteen, her heavy sheet of auburn hair hung below her waist. Dropping her blue and white pajama top, she stood naked before the mirror and further inspected herself. Clearly she did not look like Prince Valiant. Whether Andre had stirred her womanliness, or nature in its own time, her hips were evidently rounder, her breasts fuller. Her beauty escaped her. "I'm only going to be wanted for my money," she said, turning from the glass, cloaked only in depression.

The responsibility of her horse forced her to face everyday reality. She decided to teach Darkchild to jump, finish decorating her apartment, begin ballet again, and through literature educate herself to life.

As part of this planned discipline, designed to save her sanity, she swore she would never think of Andre Bugueot again and would end forever the stupid fantasy of finding Rhett Butler.

Grey named the cockatoo Jose for no special reason, then decorated the kitchen around him. Tropical birds and flowers adorned tiles covering the walls and countertops. A wrought iron glass-topped table with chairs upholstered in a green bamboo print coordinated with the bird cage. She positioned Jose's six-foot-tall cage in the sunniest corner—in front of the twenty-foot glass wall opening onto a huge greenery-filled terrace. She surrounded his roomy cage with flowering tropical plants. "That should make you feel at home," she said to the bird.

But Jose was not appreciative and turned out to be alarmingly noisy and possessed of a truly nasty disposition. He shrieked piercingly at the slightest provocation, including the rising and setting of the sun, and no matter how sweetly his mistress coaxed, he would not allow her to touch him. Instead, the big white bird puffed his scarlet crest and hissed—terrifyingly beautiful in defiant anger—even when Grey offered treats.

She mirrored an empty room, installed a ballet barre, and arranged private instruction with the Carnegie Institute of Dance three afternoons a week.

Steady on her regime, she created a reading room with a white wool shag carpet, a soft blue leather chair opening into a lounger, and floor-to-ceiling bookcases. She bought a little wooden ladder for reaching high shelves and a great circular globe of a lamp. At Brentano's on Fifth Avenue she began filling her shelves. She purposely ignored the screening room that was her living room, wherein stood the stereo reminding her of Andre, and when she was home, she stayed with her books and read and read.

Charlie, the owner of the Central Park Stable, recommended a trainer renowned for his preparation of Olympic jumpers. At outlandish fees, Jack Brian agreed to work with Darkchild—much to the arrogant stallion's distaste—for now his headstrong impulsiveness had to be curbed. Although Grey put her foot down at using a martingale, that cruel device preventing horses from throwing their heads back in freedom, she knew he must be brought under control.

"He is like you, my *cherie*, who throws and tosses her head like a pony," Andre had said of Darkchild's feisty temperament. "In you it is adorable. In this horse it is dangerous and shows he is too strong-willed." Andre thought Darkchild worthy of an Arab sheik, but personally would not leave him with so much spirit.

Above all, she reminded herself, *I am not going to think of Andre.*

It took months, during which she was at the stable by five thirty every morning, to quiet Darkchild. At first, sighting the indoor ring's hurdle, the stallion was overexcited and galloped into the gate instead of over it. There was real danger for Grey and she was thrown twice.

On Brian's advice, thick rubber reins were substituted for the leather ones, and a stronger bit was employed. Then, using all her strength on the easier-to-grip reins, Grey turned Darkchild's head sideways as he cantered toward the jump. That way the mighty black stallion could see the barrier only at the last moment when she let his head go forward.

The day finally came when Darkchild, head held straight, cantered evenly to the jump like the well-bred gentleman he was and sailed smoothly over.

After that, Darkchild progressed rapidly, taking ever higher obstacles on the slightest knee pressure from her. She'd be up in the stirrups, forward over his neck, saying, "Hup, baby, hup," in his ear. How she loved experiencing the mighty stallion's awesome strength as he surged into the air, then delicately touched ground again as though aware of his precious cargo. During those moments she truly felt she and Darkchild were one.

Darkchild was approaching the seven-foot mark when Jack Brian said, "You'll take a ribbon," referring to an upcoming horse show in Darien, Connecticut. The world's record that year was seven-foot-five.

Grey, feeling guilty abut Darkchild's underground stall, spent hours in the park every day riding and jogging alongside him in addition to his lessons. She became a well-known figure to those who frequented the park.

In the autumn, Grey and Darkchild, walking next to each other at dusk, were suddenly surrounded by a youth gang. "Tits and ass," sneered a leather-jacketed boy about sixteen.

"I want some of what you got in them fancy pants, Mommy," said another boy in a dungaree jacket. Staring at the crotch of Grey's jodphurs, he began unwinding a bicycle chain from around his waist.

"Let's all fuck her, then go horseback riding," said the leader.

Another boy pulled a pair of wooden *nunchakus* from under a red satin jacket emblazoned "SAVAGE GHOSTS" and began whipping the sticks around with frightening proficiency.

The gang leader laughed. "Go ahead, Bruce Lee," he said with approval and drew a knife. Grinning, he began tossing the knife from one hand to the other and moving slowly toward Grey.

Like salivating coyotes zoning in for the kill, the gang of eight were closing a circle around Grey and Darkchild. The wide bridle path was deserted now—no police. Grey found herself frozen with fear, beyond speech or action.

Not Darkchild! Smelling Grey's fear, the stallion ran at the knife-wielding leader and trampled him underfoot. Then Darkchild wheeled sharply, confronting the boy with the chain. He reared and screamed, slashing the air with his hoofs. The boy dropped the chain and ran. Still screaming in fury, Darkchild gave him but a moment's chase, then, like a whirling dervish, the giant stallion wheeled again and in a cloud of dust galloped to deal with the others, who at this point wanted nothing to do with the black demon from hell. One boy screamed in pain as Darkchild kicked him solidly in the chest.

A few moments later, after the injured dragged off or were pulled away by other members of the gang, Darkchild was left pawing the ground, raising swirls of dirt, and blowing air loudly through anger-distended nostrils.

Grey began sobbing uncontrollably. Darkchild moved to her. She buried her forehead in his neck, feeling heaving excitement inside him and the warm foam sweat his passionate defense of her had raised. As her composure slowly returned, she thanked God, then spoke to her defender. "You love me, Darkchild, thank you." At least her horse could be trusted, she thought bitterly.

Later, she marveled at the delicacy of Darkchild's ankles as she brushed them. What a contrast to his thick stallion's neck, his powerful breadth of muscular chest . . . She curried him until he gleamed, thinking what marvelous creatures God created. She buckled a blanket over him, then carefully picked his hoofs clean of dirt. She talked in a low, soothing voice all the time she worked. Darkchild, loving the attention, answered with soft snorts of pleasure.

Leaving the roomy triple stall, Grey went to the feed room at the other end of the stable and filled a bucket with ground cornmeal and oats. She poured in rich blackstrap molasses, then mixed it all with very hot water, and brought it back up the aisle. It was peaceful in the big stable now. Attendants and owners were bedding down the horses. She moved through the wide aisle, her black boots making no sound, muffled by the fine dirt underneath. She was totally unaware of the two men who watched her from above in the second-floor office of the stable.

"She doesn't talk much, does she?" Conners, who rented space for a dappled mare, asked.

"Just to the horse," Charlie, the stable owner, replied, then rudely turned his swivel chair away from the big glass window overlooking his "barn." Conners got the idea and left. "Nosy mick bastard," Charlie muttered aloud after his office door closed.

Turning his chair back to the window, where he could see every movement below, Charlie watched the Coltrane girl walk down the aisle, steaming bucket in hand. One by one, every male horse owner was in his office, sniffing around like a bunch of dogs in heat, making bullshit conversation so they could ask about her.

Charlie, who hadn't seen his home turf in the Blue Ridge Mountains for forty years, still thought like a mountain man and fought the same way. I'll horsewhip the first bastard who bothers that filly. He felt sorry for her, pretty head all down like a whipped puppy. Well, she'd get over it. She was real young. People were just like horses—time made them forget hurts.

He had seen the fancy frog down there, making a fuss over her. The frog could ride, too, Charlie grudgingly admitted. Everybody in the stable knew the story by now. It was all in the papers. He had personally chased reporters from the premises a couple of times.

Reaching to the wooden cupboard above his desk, he slid open a door revealing an intercom system. Charlie listened into the stalls when he was alone. It was his place—he'd do what he wanted. That he was invading his clients' privacy never entered his mind.

He listened to six, belonging to Fredrik Gruber, who'd gotten tanked once and beaten his horse. Charlie'd told

Gruber he'd throw him out if it happened again. It was quiet. A lot of things happened in a stable in Manhattan. There were a hundred horses, and some of them had weird owners. Charlie squinted through the glass. There she came back up the aisle with that crazy mash she concocted for her wild heathen of a horse. Actually, Charlie had great admiration for Darkchild, the most valuable piece of horseflesh in his barn. Shit! Couldn't anybody but her really care for that one anyway. The stable attendants were afraid to go in the stall—damn horse wouldn't allow it. Had one hell of a good aim on his kicks, too. Chuckling aloud, Charlie reached a wrinkled hand into his desk drawer for the bottle and took a swig of whiskey.

Most said it was too much horse for the girl. But old Charlie knew different. He'd gone quietly into the ring one night when he'd assumed everyone was gone. And there she was: like an Indian, grabbing the big horse's mane, jumping up onto his back and off again.

Charlie watched her return to the stall and pour the mash into the feed trough. Then he saw the slick Cuban with the two five-gaiters across from her triple stall go over there. Charlie opened the intercom just to make sure the Cuban didn't bother her.

"A beautiful animal, señorita. But don't you think he should be gelded?"

Charlie observed the stupid asshole then standing there proudly, like he'd said something great.

Grey hugged Darkchild by the neck. "I'll see you that way first!"

Charlie laughed out loud and smacked his knee as the Cuban retreated. She had spunk, stuck up for hers. The spick might be right about gelding, though. Darkchild was over sixteen hands. A giant, probably weighed twelve hundred pounds or thereabouts. There was going to be hell when a mare went into heat around him.

In the stall below, Grey finished pouring from the bucket. Darkchild gave his "thank you" neigh, pushed her side with his nose, then sank his head contentedly into the warm mash. She draped her arm over his neck and watched him eat, thinking of how he saved her from those horrible boys . . . God only knew what they would have done to her.

In the following days, she seriously considered moving. But where? Where do I even want to go? She just didn't know. Nothing seemed to really matter except Darkchild.

She finished a best-selling novel. Its heroine's problems included being wrongly jailed for homicide and losing custody of her only child—all for love of a man. Maybe women aren't meant to be happy, she mused. She began another novel.

Grey and Llana spoke every day They made small talk, and Llana patiently waited to no avail for Grey to discuss Andre and the disaster. One day Llana spoke of the Japanese print they had examined with Dan. The evening seemed ages ago to Grey. "That picture was certainly disconcerting," she said.

"You know, Grey," Llana replied, "sex is fun. Meeting another man would take away the pain."

"Maybe so, I'm just not ready for that kind of fun," Grey replied, remembering her excitement just watching Andre's strong body.

Llana began suggesting going to this place or that. Grey refused. Her pain was a lonely thing, her life filled with introspection. She read a mystery novel, a spy thriller. The tape recorder was in the kitchen and played Beatles tapes while she ate alone. She bought and read piles of slick magazines. She danced.

Jose bit her finger to the bone while she was cleaning his cage one day. She hardly reacted to the attack and the pain, almost as though it were her fate now to be hurt.

"Grey, why don't I come by?" Llana said.

"I just want to be alone for a while."

"You're nineteen. You can't be a recluse! Holiday season is coming. Your birthday is coming. *You've got to go to parties. Everyone* in New York goes to parties from Thanksgiving to Christmas!"

The last thing Grey wanted to consider were the holidays, which she had planned to spend as Andre's wife in Paris.

During one call, Llana rambled on about Dan and his blossoming career. "He's having a show at a top gallery on Madison Avenue. I'm sending you an invitation."

On another call, Llana said, "I met Dan's karate instructor finally. What a hunk! A Vietnam war hero, too!

Varsity sexy. I spent hours there. All the men are super gorgeous. You've got to come to the dojo over the holidays. They're having a party—a big one."

"No thank you."

Ralph Daniels phoned. "Mrs. Fowler, the taxes have soared on the Saubaudia property. Unless you have a fondness for the estate, I would suggest selling."

Memories flooded back. The horrible time in Saubaudia with her drunken husband—the lurking housekeeper, Maria.

"Yes, sell. But there's a couple of dogs I'd like to keep. Could you please arrange to send them to Jennifer Parish in Southampton?" She hung up the kitchen phone and switched on her tape recorder. "Lucy in the Sky with Diamonds" filled the room. She made a mug of coffee laced with cinnamon and honey. Her glass wall showed a cold, gray Manhattan. She sat in the contrasting warm, cheery kitchen in front of Jose's cage, and dialed Jennifer in Southampton. Jennifer answered immediately.

"Do me a favor, please," Grey said after the opening amenities. "There'll be two Dobermans arriving soon. Give them the run of the place and some love?"

"Sure, sweetie," Jennifer's raspy voice replied. "Why don't you come here for the holidays?"

"No thanks, Jennifer," Grey said. "I have plans already." (To read down through the pile of old best-sellers the clerk at Brentano's, to whom she'd confessed the literary abyss of her past life, had sent over.)

"Oh well, too bad, sweetie," Jennifer replied. "John and I would have loved to see you, but your doggie friends will be just fine. They can run with the horses and live in the big house."

Since Grey had released her inheritance, Jennifer—always fond of Grey—now adored her. She called regularly, genuinely concerned over the unhappiness she knew Grey's broken engagement brought.

Llana phoned. "Grey, did you see the *Enquirer*? I think you should sue!"

Under the headline "Poor Little Rich Girls" was a picture of Grey next to photos of the two Carolines, Rainier and Kennedy. "How awful," she said, tossing the paper into the trash basket near the newsstand, not wanting to be further depressed by reading the story. Little did she know that odd moment when a name becomes, by strange alchemy and virtually overnight, a household word, had happened. Grey Coltrane Fowler was news.

She read *Tai Pan*, then *Hawaii*.

Grey's mother began making tries at social life again. Grace Coltrane, already concerned with Grey's introverted behavior, seemed to know she could alienate her distant daughter forever, and there were no "I told you so's." Never mentioning Andre, she merely suggested lunches and came from Long Island to sit with Grey at Lutèce and the Colony, discussing trivia and greeting an occasional acquaintance.

A plethora of invitations appeared in Grey's mailbox, running the gamut from society galas to rock concerts. She attended none. Ballet, Darkchild, and reading were enough.

As the weeks passed, Llana nagged and nagged her about the still faraway party at Dan's karate dojo. "Please, we said you'd come. Please, Grey?"

"I'll think about it, Llana," Grey finally said, just to have peace. She had no intention of going.

She spent her twentieth birthday with Darkchild. At home, she turned off her phone and did not answer the buzzer from downstairs, which rang and rang. She thought about Andre and wept.

Llana finally caught her at the stable. The sight of Llana was like a breath of fresh air, making Grey wonder why she kept away this person she loved so much. "You're coming with me," Llana said, and would not take no for an answer. She cabbed Grey to a fashionable new hair salon, a unisex shop frequented by rock 'n' rollers. An hour later, Grey's heavy one-length tresses were transformed into gleaming rows of curls swinging in pretty patterns as she moved her head. "It'll curl if you let it dry naturally. If you want it straight, blow dry it," the "in" hairdresser counseled.

"It's a shag," Llana announced, pleased to see Grey taking an interest in herself. "Now we need to 'Mary Quant' you."

The makeup artist, who sported henna red hair and purple liner circling blue eyes, was named Debbie. She was funny, a little fat, very friendly, and spoke in a thick Cockney accent. "You don't need much paint, luv,"

Debbie said, sizing up Grey's gorgeous face and already high coloring. "Nature's been good to you." She taught Grey how to use kohl in her eyes and play up her beautiful features. "You put a little yellow close to your nose, on your eyelid, and it's going to make your green eyes greener."

Llana squired her next to an enormous rock 'n' roll club in the Village, where they were seated at a table on a large balcony overlooking the stage. Grey watched in amazement as Tina Turner, clad in jagged leopard skins that parted to show her muscular thighs, sang "Proud Mary" and rubbed the microphone up and down with her crotch in rhythm to her song.

Mick and Bianca Jagger, accompanied by Lenny Holzer and his wife, "Baby Jane," came upstairs. Someone was already seated at their table, but bouncers closed in on the patron who didn't want to relinquish the prized table. He was roughly hustled out and the intruder's date meekly followed.

Grey watched the melee in fascination, then turned her attention back to the stage, wondering *how* Ike Turner could remain so calm at his guitar while his wife publicly made love to a piece of steel. The music was blaring and Tina was now executing full squats as she sang. Sylvester Stallone waved to Mick Jagger from another table, and during the course of the concert a fan approached Jagger with a copy of the Rolling Stones' newest album, *Fool to Cry*, and the superstar signed it with a flourish.

When the performance was over, Llana whisked Grey to La Louisiana on Lexington Avenue for a fabulous French Creole dinner. Afterward, Llana dropped her in a cab, and whether it was her a new hair style and makeup, the outrageous club they visited, or just Llana's caring, Grey was renewed. "I love you, Llana. I'm a new person," she said, kissing Llana, happy as a lark with Grey's revitalization.

Two days later, as her ballet instructor was leaving, Llana invaded Grey's apartment. "I haven't been here since you furnished more rooms," she said, walking into the kitchen. "I love it. Jose is scary, though," Llana said, noting the profusion of Beatles tapes scattered on the counters, including the very latest "Got to Get You into My Life." Continuing her inspection, Llana paused, amazed, in the doorway of the room where Grey spent most of her time. "What the hell?" she said, looking at the books and magazines scattered everywhere on the carpet. A lounger and a lamp were the only furnishings in the huge space.

"My reading room."

"Grey, you're not becoming a female Howard Hughes, are you?" Llana blurted.

Laughing, hugging Llana, Grey said, "No, I am not becoming a female Howard Hughes. Let's go to the movies."

"Okay," Llana said, then heartened by Grey's cheery demeanor, a familiar and mischievous twinkle lit her soft eyes. "Grey, about that Christmas party . . ."

"Yes, I'll go," Grey said, her sloe eyes holding their own twinkle.

They went to a double feature at the Waverly theatre in the Village and, armed with popcorn, soda, and candy, viewed the young Yul Brynner, first in *Moses,* then *The King and I.* "He is the most exotically handsome man ever," Grey said, after the films.

"You won't think that after you see Khan!" Llana said.

"Khan?"

"Dan's karate instructor. Remember—the Christmas party?"

"Oh, I forgot."

"Stop teasing, come hell or high water, you're going to that party!"

Grey's period came the morning of the party. Being athletic, she suffered no real pain, but felt the way women do that first day. Calling the garage, she ordered her Mercedes 280SE coupé to be ready at nine.

The Mercedes was a recent purchase. Her red Ferrari, with its highly tuned, twelve-cylinder engine proved impractical for city use, and Grey was drawn into the Park Avenue Mercedes showroom by the coupe's spectacular British-racing-green metallic finish.

What shall I wear to the party? she wondered at seven, lying in a bubbly tub laced with Jungle Gardinia bath oil.

She decided on red—for Christmas. The dress was short, simple, and silk. She slipped into gold-flecked

Dior pantyhose and delicate gold-strapped sandals. Ballet muscles flexing her calves, she pirouetted in the mirror.

Vigorously she brushed her layered hair, which looked even better as the cut "relaxed," and then applied gold to her eyelids and kohl to her eyes, à la Debbie. Finally, clipping on a wide gold bangle bracelet, pulling on a full-length Nutrea cape trimmed with coon tails, she gave herself a last inspection. "I will not be introverted," she promised her image, with Llana's lecture on party behavior in mind, "I am going to have *fun* and meet people."

The phone rang, its bell startlingly loud. The Nightwalker did not answer, thinking the ringing a mistake. Next door, Anton was crashing around, talking to his TV set, something about "tell the motherfuckers." She left her listening post at the tile wall in the bathroom and walked to her TV set. Switching it on to CNN—the channel Anton was watching—leaving the volume off, she positioned the set for viewing while returning to her earplugs at the bathroom wall. On TV, a mercenary caught gun-running to a banana republic was testifying before a congressional committee, sparking Anton's comments.

A knock on her condo door surprised her. When she did not answer, the knocking continued for a bit, then she heard sounds of a key in the door. Turning on the shower, wrapping a towel quickly around her head and another about her naked body, she stuck her head around the partition separating the bedroom from the living room just in time to see a man in a Waikiki Banyan uniform entering. Sighting her, hearing water running, the embarrassed hotel employee stuttered, "Sorry, ma'am. We called from downstairs, there was no answer. Will you be keeping the room? There's someone who wants it."

"Oh, yes, I will be staying. I'll call the front desk in a few minutes. Thank you."

Downstairs at the front desk, the big man waited impatiently and was finally disappointed at not being able to secure the condo next to Anton's. Slipping the clerk a discreet twenty, he was informed with a wink that a beautiful woman was there and not definite as to how long she would be staying. He was still at the desk when her call came, and he heard the desk man insist she come downstairs and sign another American Express form. In typical Hawaiian style, the first one was lost. Seeing him still there, the desk man said, "There's another room on that floor available if you want it."

The big man agreed, signing "Charles Halehana" on the register, slipped the bellhop another twenty in lieu of identification and paid cash for the room. As he turned to go back to Pau Street and collect the boy and his things, the clerk said, "You ought to stay a few minutes and grab an eyeful when she comes to sign. The guy gave her the room in the first place says she's a widow—here because of honeymoon memories. She's gorgeous and never goes out and doesn't let the maids in. Must be lonely." But then something about the big man's seriousness stopped the clerk's gregariousness aimed at angling another twenty. The clerk looked again at the register. Halehana was an Hawaiian name, the man in front of him could be part Polynesian. He certainly was big enough. Only Halehana had no belly. A prominent middle was as much a source of pride to an Hawaiian as great height. This man's faded, open aloha shirt, although common attire for a local, exposed a rock-hard stomach and a tight waist. Definitely not a product of poi and pork. The clerk stopped his patter. The woman he spoke of came to the front desk just as Halehana's huge form moved from view around a stone wall hung with paintings of banyan trees in the lobby.

The Nightwalker was irritated at being taken from surveillance by this trivia. She asked the desk man to hurry, handing him her credit card, at the same time noting the massive back of the man she glimpsed in retreat. As big as Khan's . . . The memory hurt, and the pain stayed with her. She left the clerk's prying eyes, returning to surveillance of Anton, who was still next door, still talking to the TV, waiting for his call, and almost out of cocaine.

Manhattan, 1976

The delicious scent of leather greeted her as she slipped into her new Mercedes coupé and pulled smoothly onto Fifth Avenue.

It took a long time to drive to Soho. She was caught in

an endless stream of traffic cruising at a snail's pace by the giant Christmas tree at Rockefeller Center. Stores were open late and tourists filled the sidewalks, blocking intersections.

During the bumper-to-bumper journey, Grey again reminded herself she was off on an adventure and going to have *fun*. Her musing ended abruptly at Fifth and Fortieth, where she was stopped for the light. The Mercedes began rocking and voices around the car were shouting at her. "Holy shit!" "What a piece of ass!" "Hey, rich girl, how about some?" A group of young blacks were all over the car, banging and rocking it. She sat terrified, no policeman in sight. Panicked, she stepped on the gas, careening through the red light, across the intersection, narrowly missing a Chevrolet. She drove many blocks before her heart quieted.

Dan and Llana were waiting. If Grey had had any doubts as to her appearance, they were quickly assuaged by the gleam in Dan's eyes and Llana's compliments as Dan slid into the front bucket seat and Llana cuddled on his lap. Grey told them about her second street gang experience. "You're becoming a real New Yorker," Dan said, "and just think, you haven't been mugged yet."

"I can pass on that one." Following the artist's directions, she realized she was seeing Dan for the first time since dinner at the loft. She was acutely aware of his intensity as he sat holding Llana. Grey switched on WBLS and the stereo speakers poured Rod Stewart's "Tonight's the Night."

Llana lit a joint. The pungently sweet smell of marijuana filled the car.

"What's that?" Grey asked.

"Pot," Llana said.

"But that's illegal!" Grey said.

"Grey, this is New York City, the seventies. Everybody smokes grass. Hey, break down. It's Christmas, we're going to a party." Her hand ran over the smoothly polished cherry wood dashboard. "When did you get this gorgeous car?" she said, passing the joint to Grey.

"Last week, and no thanks."

"You'll get a contact high just from being in the car," Llana said.

For some reason or other, that struck Grey's funny

bone, and she began laughing. Dan and Llana did, too, and they all giggled at nothing until Grey asked where they were going anyway.

"Avenue B and 6th Street," Dan said. "The College of the Streets."

"That's a strange name for a karate school," Grey said.

"The school is within the college. It's only one of the programs offered there."

"Well, this will certainly be my first party in a karate school."

"It's called a *dojo* and the party's not there. It's upstairs in Khan's quarters."

"Tell me about this Khan. What's so special about him?"

"For starters, he's a real martial arts master, a teacher *par excellence*. His students worship him. He's presently the world's karate champion—*nulli secundus*," Dan said.

" 'Second to none.' I haven't heard that since St. Anne's," Grey said.

"He lived through hell in Vietnam," Dan continued, hot on his subject, "the only member of his special forces team to survive. He was wounded, a POW, tortured, imprisoned like an animal. Got the Bronze Star, Purple Heart . . . After enduring all that, he came here, saved the College of the Streets from going under, which wasn't easy, and saved uncountable kids from the streets and narcotics addiction . . ." Dan interrupted his instructor's biography. "Here we are," he announced, waving his hand. "Welcome to the ghetto."

They were on a city block of potholes decorated by rusted skeletons of long dead cars. Open garbage pails spilled their contents onto the cold, deserted street and sidewalks. In front of a seedy-looking building on the corner, a man in a torn overcoat, unmindful of anyone watching, urinated against the wall. The sparkling green Mercedes stood out glaringly on the street.

They entered the building by a side door. Faint sounds of far-off, pulsating Latin music wafted to them as they stood in a dirty entranceway. Graffiti was everywhere. Dan pressed the elevator button, but no light came on and there was no sound of machinery working. "Sorry," he said penitently. "The elevator doesn't work, we have to walk."

"What floor is the party?" Grey asked, looking askance at her surroundings.

"Seventh and eighth," Dan said, leading the way up long, dirty, smelly stair flights in the old building. Many of the narrow slate steps were broken. Grey and Llana, hobbled by high heels, picked their footing carefully.

The music grew louder as they climbed and by the time they reached the eighth floor, Dan shouted over its din, "When we go inside, stay on this floor and I'll find sensei." He opened a door, the volume of music increased tenfold, and Dan was swallowed up by darkness.

Llana took Grey's hand and pulled her through the door. Her heart racing from the climb, Grey could only see dimly glowing lights providing the barest of illumination. It took a moment for her eyes to adjust; then she saw wall-to-wall people, most of them dancing. There was a profusion of young men with rolled-up T-shirt sleeves displaying bulging muscles and girls in tight jeans. The majority were Hispanic, black, and Chinese.

I should have worn my jeans, Grey thought as Llana tugged her through the crowd to a table loaded with bottles of Gallo wine and paper cups. Permeating the air were smells of cheap perfume and incense mixed with whiffs of marijuana and odors of perspiration. Tito Puente rhythms blasted.

Perfectly comfortable amid the tightly packed, gyrating assemblage, Llana poured drinks, then guided Grey to the kitchen lit only by one flickering candle. The volume of music was the tiniest bit less loud there, and they stood in the corner watching four rough-looking young men on the other side of the kitchen. They were clustered around a fifth, sitting on top of the stove, staring into space.

"He's been there for hours without moving," one of the young men shouted.

"That's okay, man. He's just doing his thing. The Sunshine is heavy. He'll be cool," another yelled in answer.

The burners must be cutting into him, Grey thought, fascinated by the tableau. She wondered whatever "Sunshine" was.

Llana spoke into Grey's ear. "Wait until you see Khan.

Dan says he's a priest of the martial arts, too, and"—she broke into a grin—"he's reputed to be the best lover in the world. You should fuck him and lose your virginity tonight!"

For some reason the lascivious expression on Llana's face reminded Grey of Sister Marie-Carol, which was ridiculous. But there wasn't any sense in attempting conversation over the music, so Grey just stuck her tongue out at Llana's attempt to shock her.

They left the kitchen, Grey wondering why they had gone there in the first place. Llana began dancing in place by herself, and immediately a cute Chinese boy joined her. Llana dropped her coat to the floor, suddenly sexy in a backless gold lamé halter and black flared skirt. A black velvet ribbon caught her dark, shiny hair at the nape of her neck and big sparkly earrings like Christmas tree decorations dangled from her ears. She danced really well.

Grey shrugged from her heavy fur cape and, holding it over her arm, watched dancers like birds in mating rituals, undulating to a steamy salsa beat. Close to her, a darkly handsome, muscular man said, "*Vaya, Mommy*," to his partner.

"*Suave, Poppy, sauve,*," the languid-eyed Latin beauty answered, giving an extra flick of her hip.

Turning, Grey was attracted by a spotlighted wall niche, wherein a curved sword rested on wooden pegs, its bright blade gleaming. Grey touched it. Suddenly a strange hissing sound caused her to look to her side and its source. What she saw made her catch a breath.

Moving toward Grey was a man so unusually attractive, it was as though he was a figment of her imagination stepping out of a book—not like Rhett Butler out of an antebellum novel; this man looked catapulted from an *Arabian Nights* tale.

He was a six-foot-four, spectacularly handsome Eurasian with bulging muscles pushing a white Chinese jacket. His gold-skinned, exotic face was accented by wide, slanting eyes, slashing cheekbones, and sensuous lips parted in a smile. As he walked through the crowd, people bowed to him making the unfamiliar sounds Grey had heard. "*Ossss*, Sensei."

He walked directly to her. "One should never touch a

sword's blade," he said in a deep bass voice. She pulled her hand back from the sword quickly, as though from a white-hot flame. Mesmerized by his approach, she hadn't realized her finger still rested on it. "Oh, sorry."

Dan's pride-filled voice introduced the towering man. "Grey, this is Khan, my *sensei*."

"Let's go where it's quiet," Khan said, offering Grey his arm. Llana winked, *I told you so*.

Grey, Dan, and Llana walked with Khan, whose bearing was unmistakably of one used to command. Wending their way through the crowd, Grey felt Khan's rock-hard bicep pushing against her shoulder. Many men and a few of the women bowed, giving hissing tribute. "Osss, Sensei."

Khan's hand was an electric connection on her arm. She wryly observed he could have his pick of women there. Many of them flirted outrageously with him, casting hard, appraising looks at her.

They passed through two more packed rooms, then Khan opened a doorway, and they went through to a suddenly quiet room where the four faced a six-foot ladder. Khan made a sweeping gesture, indicating Grey go up it first.

Aware of her short skirt, struggling to keep her aplomb, Grey skittered up the narrow ladder sideways, holding her legs as closely together as possible, all the while feeling Khan's eyes on her. Reaching the top of the ladder and a platform, she used her St. Anne's acrobatic skills and made a quick jumping turn, plunking into a sitting position with her legs dangling over the edge. She looked at the floor. Khan grinned.

She felt a rising blush and turned her head away as if inspecting the candlelit loft with its king-sized futon. She saw a complicated stereo system, TV, phone. The hot flush receded. She turned back in time to catch Dan goosing a laughing Llana up the ladder.

Khan chose not to climb. Placing one hand on the loft's edge, he sprang in a single, panther-like leap, landing in a seated position next to Grey, forcing her to admire his effortlessness. Seeing Dan's teacher, she remembered how impressed she had been with his own fluid movements.

Tossing shoes to the floor, the four moved onto the futon against two walls: one of built-in cabinets, another curtained. Llana immediately posed like a sexy Vargas girl in a candlelit corner, Dan and Khan sat cross-legged and Grey pulled her legs under her. She was not very comfortable, and her discomfort was magnified by Khan's gaze.

From his jacket pocket Dan pulled a silver flask. Khan smiled at Grey. Smiling back, she thought how right Llana was. Once seen, Khan's unique and alluringly handsome face could never be forgotten.

"Sensei, Sensei, they can't find Bobby," a voice said. there were sounds of scurrying feet on the ladder, then a head appeared. It was a wild-eyed kid, maybe sixteen.

"Get me Ralph," Khan snapped.

"Osss, Sensei," the head disappeared.

In a flash another head appeared. This time it was a calm-eyed Filipino. "Yes, Sensei."

"Is there Sunshine here?"

"Yes, Sensei,"

"I thought so," Khan said. "Go find Bobby. Make sure he's okay. Get rid of the acid heads. And this room is off-limits. Understand?"

"Yes, Sensei." the second head bowed. "Osss," and vanished.

By now the flask was coming her way. Grey already felt high—and confused. Llana's look as she handed her the flask said, *This is a party.* Llana winked. Taking the flask and swigging, Grey immediately began coughing. Tears filled her eyes at the unexpectedly strong brandy. She coughed harder.

"First drink?" Khan said teasingly, then laughed, throwing his head back as he did, flashing big white teeth.

The next time the flask passed, she managed not to choke.

Khan and Dan were discussing martial arts, using words in foreign languages Grey and Llana did not understand. Dan, hanging on Khan's every word, was plainly awed.

There are two good-looking, sexy men across the bed from you, Coltrane. Grey almost exclaimed aloud, so thoroughly did the unbidden thought surprise her. She was suddenly, dizzily high.

Llana, who needed to be the center of attention, began changing poses. She hiked her skirt high, exposing black lace garter straps with red ribbons. Turning toward her, then looking at Grey, Dan said, "Two gorgeous women. Right, Sensei?"

Could she have heard correctly? Was she being discussed as though not there? She was highly insulted and fully intended to protest. But the brandy whirled in her head and she suddenly felt complimented instead and began giggling.

Reaching over to Llana, Dan pulled her easily to him. Clearly he was used to moving her. Putting one hand up her skirt, his intense eyes pinning her, he said, "You need to be quieted down, little girl."

Fixing her eyes on him, she began shuddering.

Mortified, Grey pulled back farther into a corner.

Llana moaned.

Khan watched.

"We're going to make love, Sensei," Dan announced, "and come back later." He bowed his head. "Osss."

The next thing Grey knew, they were gone, leaving the atmosphere permeated with their lust.

A wave of fear engulfed her. She was in this man's *bed.* He was some kind of cult leader; everyone around her was stoned or weird, and her best friend had turned into a sex maniac, purposely setting the scene for God only knew what. I could scream bloody murder and no one would even hear me over the din outside, she thought. Paranoia threatened to overtake her. Feeling her eyes widening, she spoke to relieve the moment. "Sorry about Llana and Dan . . ."

Khan chuckled. "Artistic, sensualistic free thinkers, rambunctious tonight. Have you looked at the roof?" he asked, just like a normal person and drew the curtain, disclosing a picture window overlooking the roof of the floor below. More party goers danced to a five-piece conga band, whose players sweated over tall drums. On another section of the large roof was a garden and next to that were fenced runs leading from a tar-roofed structure. In the runs, medium-sized dogs watched the dancers.

"It's so big! Who do those dogs belong to? What grows in that garden?"

"The dogs are mine. In the summer that's my vegetable garden," he said.

"How neat. I would never expect dogs and a garden on top of a building."

"I'm glad you like my roof, Grey." His voice was deep, rich.

She liked the way he said her name.

He reached behind her and she jumped. "Nervous, aren't you?" he said and his full lips spread, revealing his perfect teeth again. "Would you like some wine?"

Without waiting for an answer, he withdrew a bottle from a small refrigerator built into the cabinet behind her and took glasses from another. Grey was suddenly reminded of Hugh Hefner, who, she read, ran his empire from a huge bed and a control panel of buttons. She laughed aloud, again shocking herself.

"I'll take that for yes," he said, opening the bottle. He handed her a glass of wine in the candlelight, watching with his wide, slanted eyes as she drank.

They remained near the window for a few minutes, watching the scene below. As he turned his head to the side while drinking, Grey saw, high on the back of his head, a bun of hair bound with leather.

"What's that?" she asked, pointing.

"A war lock."

"A war lock?" she said increduously.

"It denotes me as a warrior."

"Why?"

"Because I am one," he said matter-of-factly.

"How so?"

"Because my father was one, and his father was one, and his father before him was one."

How romantic, she thought, going to ask more when she forgot her question. Was the wine making her feel so relaxed now? She found her shyness slipping away and she remembered her next question. "Would you mind if I asked more?"

"Ask away." He smiled again.

"Your father, mother, from . . . ?" She hesitated, not quite sure how to ask his nationality.

"Father Mongolian, mother Russian," he volunteered easily, evidently used to the inquiry.

"Sunshine, Bobby?"

He looked at her sharply. "Sunshine is LSD. Bobby is a kid who's got a problem with it."

God, he's handsome. "Why does everybody bow to you?"

"They are my students, their courtesy is traditional."

His white cotton jacket's frog closings were not all hooked, and as he shifted, the jacket fell disconcertingly open, revealing deeply sculpted muscles. She saw in the flickering candlelight he had no hair on his chest.

"Are you a priest?" she asked, pulling her eyes back to his face, remembering Llana's statement.

"Yes."

"But you're a fighter, aren't you?"

"Martial arts were originally conceived by holy men. Monks."

Her curiosity liberated, she continued. "But isn't karate like boxing except you use feet? I mean, what's holy about that?"

He answered with a teacher's patience. "In martial arts we strive toward physical and spiritual union—a oneness. Through this way one seeks perfection."

"Do martial arts priests marry?" she blurted.

He turned toward her. In the candlelight his skin was bronze gold. "Seldom, but it is allowed. Few women are understanding enough to stand by such a man's side," he said, smiling.

Concentrating on what he said was difficult, so flabbergasting his beauty, she thought, noting how his long, upturned eyelashes cast shadows on his pronounced cheekbones.

Embarrassed by her scrutiny of him, hoping he hadn't noticed her staring, she looked around again. On the wall, a picture frame held a khaki cloth patch, a skull wearing a beret, crossbones underneath it, and the initials "MACSOG."

"What's that?" she asked, indicating the patch, thinking it macabre.

"An organization's symbol. MACSOG stands for Military Assistance Command Vietnam Studies and Observation Group. SOG was an acronym used by those involved."

"What did SOG study and observe?"

"Its basic mission was conducting covert operations in denied areas of Vietnam, Laos, and Cambodia. By military definition: Joint Unconventional Warfare Task Force."

"What exactly did it do?" she asked, trying to understand the seemingly unfathomable.

"Guerrilla warfare, subversion, sabotage, escape and

evasion, black and gray psychological operations. Stuff like that."

"Oh. I take it that's your patch."

"Yes, I was a SEAL, part of a SOG team working with Nungs."

"Nungs?"

"A Thai tribe of Chinese origin—tiny, tiny people who live in Vietnam. Some of the world's greatest fighters, despite their size. Nungs were teamed with our men to teach jungle warfare and how to live in trees."

"Did you live in trees?"

"Yes," he said too-quietly, changing the mood, making her realize she had struck the wrong subject for small talk. She tried bringing the conversation to the present.

"Why do all the people around you look so . . ." she searched for words explaining the unique intensity displayed by Dan and many others she had seen tonight, but mostly by Khan.

"Because they are tough, centered, aware motherfuckers," he said, smiling.

Her shock at his words was negated by his beautiful mouth.

Putting his hand on the back of her head, bringing her face to his, he kissed her. His lips were soft, so soft . . .

She jerked suddenly away, to his amusement. Laughing, taking her arm, he pulled her to him again, this time kissing her commandingly. Frightened, she pulled away again and smoothed her hair. "I better go home now," she said, thinking no matter what Llana tried to maneuver, this was hardly the grand seduction she imagined—that sacred time she would lose her virginity. Feeling a tiny cramp, she was reminded she had her period. Neither was this barbarian her cup of tea, she thought, even if he was the handsomest man she had ever seen.

He took her arm again, attempting another kiss.

"Let me go or you're no gentleman," she said adamantly.

He found that uproariously funny. When he finished laughing, he ran his finger from her temple down her long hair. He gave it a gentle tug. "I'm letting you go, but say you'll come back."

Come back? For what? she thought. Really! She smoothed her now wrinkled dress to no avail and ripped her gold stockings going down the ladder. By the time she had crawled around the floor in the near dark, locating her shoes and cape, she was wet with perspiration.

He led her through the crowded party, passing girls with expressions plainly saying they envied her time alone with him, assuming much by her disheveled state.

The music, disco now, was even louder, if possible, than before. Reaching the top of the stairs in the hallway, just as she started to go down them, Khan spun her around like she was a rag doll. His incredibly soft lips were again on hers. There was a millisecond of melting on her part, then she pushed hard at him as he towered over her. Chuckling at her show of strength, he let her go, raising his huge hands in a submissive gesture. She ran down the stairs.

"Come back soon, please," he called in his deep voice. His strong laughter followed her down the stairs.

Llana called the day after the party. "Grey, isn't Khan the most gorgeous man you ever saw?"

"Yes, Llana."

"Well?"

"Well, what?" It was fun to tease her.

"Tell. You've got to tell! Did you? Did you do it? Are you seeing him again?" she demanded.

Shifting the phone to her other ear, Grey said, "Llana, he's an animal—a pagan!"

"I know," Llana sighed. "Isn't it wonderful?"

Grey laughed, buckling the belt of her khaki safari suit as she held the phone between her ear and her shoulder. "You are nuts, too! I did not appreciate your leaving me alone. Listen, I'll have to talk to you later, I'm due at the tennis matches."

Taking great satisfaction in leaving Llana's raging curiosity unsatisfied, Grey rushed to Madison Square Garden to meet her mother and see a match between Billie Jean King and newcomer Evonne Goolagong.

During the second set, Grey's mother pointed out a square-jawed, blond man of about twenty-five, wearing a tweed jacket. "Now, that's what I call handsome," she said.

Grey suddenly pictured Khan. Compared with him, Mom's choice lost hands down. In her mind, Grey replayed the martial arts master's effortless leap to his loft, and now that she thought about it, his silent landing had been amazing for his great size. But crude wasn't even the word for his behavior. She mentally compared last night's party with Baron Rothschild's Paris dinner party when she first had met Andre. Then she pictured Andre, armed with a dueling saber, facing Khan with his great curved sword he didn't want anyone to touch. The imagined confrontation was so incongruous, she giggled aloud.

Hearing the laughter, Grace Coltrane smoothed her wool skirt over her lap and glanced at her daughter, glad she was able to have fun again. At the right moment she would suggest Grey meet the son of a golfing companion. He was charming, wealthy, of Grey's social class. After all, Grey was twenty now, and like any mother, she wanted to see her daughter safely married.

In the following days, Grey thought about Khan's mouth a million times—the way his lips spread over his teeth when he smiled. She had trouble reading, for the image of his mouth continually superimposed itself atop all-at-once stale words. She tried to visualize the martial arts master's whole face again, his unusual skin color. The picture wouldn't come. One afternoon, it suddenly became very important to see him in person.

Ordering the Mercedes from the garage, she dressed in jeans, boots, a cashmere sweater, and a fringed leather jacket and drove to the building where she had met Khan.

Everything looked different during the day. The karate school was on the ground floor and people were crowded around, looking in its large picture window. Hearing intense screams coming from the school, she thought maybe she shouldn't have come even as she approached the door painted with red Oriental characters. Hesitating only a moment, she opened it and stepped into another world.

It was a huge dojo, floor-through, white-walled, and spotlessly clean. The main workout area, cordoned off by a low wooden railing, held about a hundred students. Sitting on benches behind the railing were a few silent spectators. Joining them, she sat on a bench. Across the room, cordoned off by another low railing, was an office area with an unoccupied desk and a few chairs.

The hundred students, in precise rows atop a straw-tatami-matted floor, were males of varying ages in white *gis* and colored belts denoting their ranks. Two good-looking black belts, a blond man and a tough-looking, dark-haired woman, led front-kicking students across the room. Heavy canvas gi pants made snapping sounds as they kicked, and the air smelled of their sweat.

In a far corner Grey spied a kneeling student. Behind him a huge Japanese battle flag, red rising sun and red rays on a white ground, covered the wall from floor to ceiling. Looking closer at the kneeling student, whose hands lay palms up in his lap, she saw, to her shock, blood mixed with perspiration on his face. The bleeding student in front of the battle flag looked straight ahead.

"*Zen mukso saza*," yelled the female black belt in a voice worthy of a master sergeant. Instantly, as one, the hundred students dropped into a kneeling position, their hands resting in their laps, still as statues.

Then Grey saw Khan, wearing a dark blue *hakama,* the skirt of the swordsman. Naked from the waist up, he wielded a sword before a back, mirrored wall. The Eurasian's massive, chiseled torso gleamed with sweat. Muscular ropes across his back and arms undulated as, whirling, he cut and parried the air so swiftly that Grey saw only a steel blur while hearing the singing blade in the otherwise silent dojo.

She watched, fascinated. With one smooth movement he thrust the sword into a long scabbard hung at his left side. The sword sheath made a decisive click.

He walked across the tatami and through the kneeling ranks of students, who touched the mat with their foreheads as he passed, to the visitor's area where she sat. "So you came back," he said.

"I just happened to be down this way and thought I'd like to see what karate is about," she lied, immediately regretting the words, which rang stupid and empty.

"Come," he said, "be my guest. One can learn much from observation."

Following him to the office area, she sat in the chair he indicated. Draping a gi jacket over his wet shoulders, he sat at his desk and watched the students. Pulling her eyes from his mouth, she looked again to the workout area, where the students were now throwing punches followed by front kicks while moving rapidly across the mat. They began a deep, guttural screaming, causing her to start.

"Why are they shouting like that?" she asked him.

"It's a *kyii*, a yell of spirit. It's also a weapon to strike confusion and terror into an opponent's heart. The kyii also releases the practitioner's own fear."

Deliberately keeping her eyes from his face in order to concentrate, she looked at the bleeding student who remained kneeling in front of the battle flag. "Why doesn't someone help that man?"

"It is his time to help himself," Khan answered.

"What happened to him?"

"He bobbed when he should have weaved."

She was about to say how cruel and unfeeling his attitude was when the school door opened and an Oriental girl wearing a blue Mandarin jacket and pants entered. She stood in front of Khan's desk and bowed to him with a graceful little dip of her head. She was very pretty.

"Sensei, I seek instruction but have no money," she said, smiling. "But I know where I can get you some beautiful fresh apples in return for your teachings."

He smiled as well. "I don't need apples."

"Then other fruits can be offered as exchange."

He was amused and said offhandedly to her, "Can you do a split?"

The little Oriental beauty bowed again, acceptance in her bearing. "Yes, Sensei," she said, her almond eyes fixed on him. Grey got the feeling it wasn't karate she came for and the "other fruits" were of her body. She was suddenly jealous.

Khan addressed the class, raising his voice until it rang through the dojo. "Watch this," he said to the class. The students stopped in their tracks and stood at attention.

He motioned to the girl, who slipped off her shoes, bowed, and stepped onto the tatami, where she fell into a perfect ballet split with ease. Her arms made graceful arcs over her head.

He spoke again. "That's what I want from you guys, real stretching."

The Chinese girl rose effortlessly.

He addressed the woman black belt. "Tell her where to get a gi." Then he turned to Grey. "Come with me," he said, leading her onto the street, to an entrance at the building's side that she recognized from the party.

Once inside, he inserted a key. The elevator began a whirring sound. So Sensei doesn't walk the steps, she thought, riding silently with him in the small car, terribly aware of his power and huge size in the close proximity. She was titillated and frightened by him at the same time. Not knowing where to rest her eyes, she focused on the fringes of her suede jacket.

The elevator opened onto the roof they had viewed at the party. He guided her to a parapet and they looked over, her small hands resting on the ledge next to his. She saw for the first time his knuckles were distorted, rising high from his large, powerful hands.

In the clear, cold January day, the tops of buildings for blocks round were easily visible. Some of the roofs held pigeon coops and laundry lines. Children played on others.

"New York's a living city up here," she said.

He looked at her curiously. "You've never been up top?"

"First time," she said, smiling at him.

It was a warm genuine smile, and it took him aback. He looked deep into her green sloe eyes, unsure for a moment. He was used to hard women—he didn't know how to treat her.

He continued looking at her, though he knew it made her uncomfortable. He was fully aware of how frightened she had been alone with him the night of the party—like a fly caught in a spider web. He had taken special notice of her because of her neat turn at the top of his ladder. He admired natural athletic ability when he saw it. Other than that, she was just another beautiful face and body. There were so many of them—and they always pursued him, like she had by returning today. Her innocent, open face was probably an act, he thought.

Unable to withstand his scrutiny, she looked away from him, over the roofs again. Strong profile, good bones, he thought, then remembered her rounded, gold-sparkle-covered legs moving up his ladder. It amused him, as had her discomfort. Pointing to a sparkling green Mercedes on the street below, she said, "Is my car safe here?" obviously just to make conversation, uncomfortable at his silent examination of her.

He remembered Dan telling him she was rich. He

looked at her manicured fingernails, her expensive cowboy boots. She was slumming, he decided.

"The money that cost could be put to a lot better use,"
he said.

Wondering what she had said wrong, not understanding his tone, captured by the bold planes of his face, the
slant of his eyes, she asked, "What do you mean by
that?" and saw that his skin had a pinkness to it.

He didn't answer, just looked over the roof, seemingly
absorbed in his own thoughts. Then he said, "So you
came here to learn about karate?"

Her words didn't seem empty now. What she had seen
in the dojo was foreign and fascinating. "I'd like to, it's a
brand-new concept for me, warrior's skills . . . What's a
SEAL?"

"What?"

"When I was in your loft, you said you were a SEAL
teamed with tiny Nungs."

"For a while, yes. You don't forget much, do you?"
He smiled, evidently admiring that quality. "SEALS are
Navy Special Forces. SEAL stands for Sea, Air, and
Land. They fight in all those elements."

"How did you come to be a SEAL?"

"My father was involved in creating the original concept, along with President Kennedy," he said proudly.
"SEALS use unconventional Ninja training methods."
Seeing her confusion, he clarified patiently. "Ninjas were
the assassins of the ancient emperors of Japan. They
practiced psychic martial arts and were masters of stealth
and death."

"Are you still friendly with the Nungs you met in
Vietnam?"

"They're all dead," he said flatly.

Remembering Dan saying Khan had been wounded
and a prisoner of war, she sought to lighten the conversation, thought of how gorgeous he had been in the dojo
with his flashing sword. "You were wonderful with your
sword," she said. "Do you teach that also?"

"No."

"Why?"

"I am a student of the sword myself."

"Who teaches you?"

"Right now, a skilled friend and a Japanese master."

"What do you mean by 'right now'?"

He scrutinized her, determining if her questioning was backed by genuine interest. Deciding it was, he spoke of things he normally didn't. "Probably sounds like a fairy tale, but I want to find a classical master in the ancient way and become a disciple myself."

"Where do such masters exist?"

"Deep in Red China. Okinawa. But I seek a particular master—a woman."

She could not imagine this giant under a woman's tutelage. "I don't understand. Aren't you already an expert?

"In karate—a Japanese martial art. I wish to learn the Chinese arts, particularly the way of the Chinese sword. You see, the Chinese originated the martial arts."

"Tell me about this woman, please," she said, fascinated by these things she never heard of or imagined and this startlingly handsome and talented man.

He had already surprised himself by sharing so much with this stranger. Life until now had not made him a trusting person. He changed the subject. "Let me show you my dogs," he said.

Grey followed him to the wooden, tar-roofed house. Inside was his "pack," twelve long-haired, mixed-breed dogs, each with its own spotlessly clean straw-bottomed bin. The dogs lazed, tongues lolling and tails wagging, as Khan walked through, petting and naming each animal. "Hey, Kyiii, pretty Mitsake, that's a good Tshiro." He paused by a black and white dog with light blue eyes that was bigger than the others. "This is my number one, my Kyoshi," he said, opening the bin, grabbing the big dog's neck and tussling with him.

"They're beautiful," she said. "I love blue-eyed dogs. Husky and shepherd aren't they? How long have you been crossing the two breeds?"

Khan gave her another appraising look. "Yes, husky-shepherd. Twenty generations down. You like them?"

"Very much."

"They'll kill you if I give the command. They're trained to protect the top of the building. They patrol here when I let them out. Anyone coming up the wrong way is taking their life in their hands."

The beautiful dogs suddenly became ominous. Khan

took hold of her arm, and she felt the strength of his grip as he pulled her close. She was very aware of all the dogs around her, watching. "I have to go. I have an appointment," she said, again frightened by him.

He thrust her away. "Go then, come back when you have more time," he said, his words quick and short.

"You don't have to be so—"

Before her sentence was finished, he turned and left the tar-roofed structure. She followed to the elevator. He silently towered over her head and did not speak, even when they got to the street. He stopped short of her car and calmly watched as she climbed in.

In the rearview mirror, she saw him smiling as she pulled away. Then she remembered the Oriental beauty with her "fruits," who she was sure still waited in his school.

A few days later, in her new shell-pink bedroom, Grey sang along with the Beatles singing, "Yellow Submarine" on her tape recorder. She had changed the room's color scheme last week, deciding she was in a blue rut.

On the mirrored top of her dressing table, next to a vermeil clock, lay a photo album opened to a particularly cruel picture of Edward Fowler, cut from a gossip column about Grey. There was also a picture of Andre in polo garb. In retrospect, Andre looked plastic as she stood near the table.

The room's many pink-finished mirrors reflected her wearing only panties. She dropped into a perfect split on the rose-bordered Aubusson rug and arced her arms gracefully over her head in better form than the Oriental girl in Khan's dojo.

Gazing at her full, pink-nippled breasts pulled high by her raised arms, Grey thought of the men pictured on her dressing table. How each touched her breasts: Ed's loathsome, sweaty grapplings, Andre's teasing pinches. *I wonder what Khan's touch is like?* Caressing herself where she pictured his hand, feeling deep stirrings, she admitted she *needed* to satisfy them.

Later that week, for want of something better to do after Darkchild's workout, she went to see Debbie. The makeup artist worked diligently for an hour, then said, "Take a look, luv, you're right splendid."

Debbie had lined Grey's eyes to seem even more tilted and worked her blazing auburn hair into an intricate French braid secured with flowered pins. The effect complemented the floral-printed white cashmere skirt and sweater she wore.

"I hope you're off to something special, luv, you look smashing," the cockney artist said. "You should show off."

Liberating her car from a nearby garage, Grey drove around, checking her image in the rearview mirror, pleased with Debbie's artistry. She ended up on the lower East Side, in front of Khan's karate school.

Through the glass window she saw the wild-eyed boy who had climbed the ladder at the party. Once he saw her in the Mercedes, he began talking on an intercom. He came outside.

"Sensei says to come upstairs," the boy said through her open car window.

She followed him up the familiar stair flights, glad her buff suede boots were low-heeled. She took her ranch mink jacket off on the fourth-floor landing. By time they reached the seventh floor, she was sorry for wearing a cashmere skirt and sweater.

There had been a drastic change since the party on the seventh floor. Hanging white sheets, billowing from hidden fans, were everywhere, creating an ethereal atmosphere. Unfamiliar instruments played Oriental music. The wild-eyed boy saw Grey's questioning look. "For the party," he said. The two continued through the gently moving hangings until they met Khan. He was dressed in white, accenting his gold skin. She drank in the sight of him while his electricity sprang at her. Shivers ran along her spine.

"Welcome back," Khan said. "How about a tour of tonight's party preparations? That is," he smiled, and teased, referring to her last abrupt departure, "if you've got more time today." She nodded yes and he continued pleasantly, "The entire building is decorated. Each floor represents an element of nature, done by a different Manhattan department store. This floor is "water" by Bergdorf Goodman. We're supported by grants and donations, and this is our yearly fund-raiser."

She waved a hand at the hangings, aware that her

sweater clung invitingly as she moved. "It does remind me of water! So does the music. What is it?"

"Japanese temple music. Each floor has its own sounds. Some will have live bands. There'll be Latin, soul, and pop for the more conservative folks." He smiled again and she absolutely melted, resisting a temptation to touch him and see if his skin was as soft as it looked.

"That sounds like quite an undertaking. Who's footing the bills for all this?" she said, then was immediately sorry. The question sounded patronizing.

He took umbrage, speaking bitterly. "The rich. It's a tax write-off and they get to ease their social conscience, like the fancy decorators from the department stores."

Just then one of the sheets was moved aside. Grey was suddenly face-to-face with a striking blond whose icy blue eyes held hatred. In a flash the sheet moved back and the face was gone.

Khan, looking elsewhere, completely missed the inter-play, and Grey had no time to give her imagination reign, for Khan now opened the hall door. Surrounded by plentiful graffiti, she followed him downstairs.

Opening the door to the sixth floor, Khan said, "Wel-come to 'Earth' by Bloomingdale's."

The floor was rich sod. More sheets, painted with clever green and brown strokes, created an illusionary forest. An unseen tape played chirping birds, and here and there bright glimmers of light, in good imitation of the sun, peeked through. The smell of real earth under-foot further authenticated the scene.

In a voice as rich and soft as the loam, Kham said, "Take off your boots, there's more."

She saw he was barefoot. Removing her boots and socks, she followed his broad back, soft earth caressing her bare feet. They came to a place where real trees, bushes, and lush grass surrounded a pond built from moss-covered rocks. It was fed by a gurgling waterfall, and the rocks were high enough for Grey to lean on her elbows and look down at floating water lilies. "Oh, how beautiful. Like a fairy fey place. I could expect to meet a leprechaun here," she said, enchanted by the romantic setting, terribly aware of Khan in back of her.

She was astounded to feel his hands lightly touch her breasts from behind. Then he kissed her neck softly. She dropped her mink jacket in surprise, at the same time reminded she had imagined his hands just where they were.

She turned to him. The magnificent Eurasian kissed her, and all the games between them were suddenly over. Her unleashed desire startled her and she sank into the ecstasy of him, opening her mouth to his tongue. With his mouth drinking hers, he slowly undressed her and gently laid her down. Then standing naked himself, he looked at her lying there. "You are very beautiful," he said.

From her prone position, his large, rigid penis was formidable, the trunk of his huge body rising from it. His eyes burned into hers. Answering the unspoken question there, she opened her arms, beckoning, longing to be his.

Then he was beside her and her only awareness was the unexpected doeskin softness of his flesh, the thrill of his powerful hands, touching, searching, moving her so easily. His lips were gentle on her nipples, neck, and belly, covering her with soft kisses. He nipped her big toe, the inside of her knee, the soft inside of her thigh. then his fingers were at her pussy lips and he softly stroked her there. Ecstatic sounds escaped her. "Say you want me," he said.

"I want you," she heard herself say in a breathless whisper.

His mouth sought hers once more and suddenly the big hardness of him was inside her. His initial thrust hurt her so much, she screamed in pain.

"Open your eyes, look at me."

She did as he commanded and found herself controlled by the rhythm of his constant stroking. His wide, slanted eyes pinned hers.

"Am I your first man?"

Grey could only lie in waves of exquisite sensation as he thrust and pulled. An unbidden moan escaped her.

He thrust deeper. "Answer my question," he said.

"Yes, yes. My first man," she gasped.

"Say, I'm fucking Khan. Say it! Look at me!"

She opened her eyes that kept closing. "I'm fucking Khan," she moaned.

Their faces were side by side. "Say, I'm coming!" He smiled, then he thrust, pounding, demanding, so it was wonderful to feel. "Say, I'm coming, Khan," he whispered in her ear.

But she could only scream.

He took her time after time. When she thought she could bear no more, he took her again.

His lovemaking was like music, ever changing keys. He was gentle, softly stroking, coaxing, his soft lips teasing, then suddenly he was again demanding, hard, plummeting the very depths of her passion.

When he reached for her yet again, she said, "Please, I'm so sore, please."

He moved her to him. "Come here, woman." And this time, with his fingers probing, teasing, thrusting, he made her frantically beg him to be inside her.

Finally, when he was satiated, she cuddled in the circle of his arm, adoring his exotic face as he lay with eyes closed in repose.

She was all woman now, spirit truly touched by the earth-shaking revelations her body had revealed. I want nothing more in life than to stay in his arms, she thought. There were no words to describe the intensity of her feelings.

"Khan, Khan, where are you?" a cloyingly sweet female voice called. Somehow Grey knew it belonged to the blond.

Khan gently extracted his arm from under her, sat up, and began pulling on his clothes. In what seemed to her an absentminded manner, he said, "Why don't you come to the party tonight? You'll have a good time."

The words thrust a knife into her heart. She had just given her precious virginity while another woman waited in the wings? He was acting like this was an everyday occurrence.

Aghast at how lightly she was taken, how callously he now addressed her, she was ashamed of her nakedness. Grabbing her dirt-covered clothes, she saw blood on her white skirt. Shaking earth from her mink jacket, she said, "No, thank you. I'm busy tonight." The words were spoken coldly to cancel the terrible hurt she felt.

"Too bad, I'll have someone take you downstairs," he said nicely.

"I can find my own way, thank you," she snapped imperiously.

He spun her around, his grip hurting her arm. "Listen, Miss Attitude, you came here to get fucked and that's what happened. You sought to use me, and now you're royalty or something? Nobody uses me. Understand, you—you piece of fluff?"

She started crying. "I am not a piece of fluff!"

"Rich girl, what did you do today?" He was yelling and his eyes were ice-cold. She felt like the bone in her arm would crack under the pressure of his fingers.

She sobbed out her answer. "I rode my horse. I had a ballet lesson. I had a pedicure and a manicure and a makeup session, then I came here." It sounded awful, even to her.

He pushed her away, hard.

She grabbed her arm where he had hurt her, rubbing a rapidly spreading bruise.

"That's probably the same shit you were doing while I was in the Mekong Delta, you piece of fluff!"

He was louder and louder. She was very afraid of his tirade and, thinking to calm him, asked, "The delta?"

This only incensed him more. "Why, you stupid . . . You don't even know what I'm talking about! I lived in hell so rich bitches like you could ride around in Mercedes!"

She began sobbing again, but her tears meant nothing to him, only a sign of weakness which was more grounds for despising her. She finished pulling on her clothes, grabbed her mink jacket, and ran, hoping she would not meet the blond beauty who waited somewhere behind the decorations. At least that was granted.

She cried all the way home in the car while the smell of Khan and earth mingled in her nostrils and the soreness of where he had been constantly reminded her of what had happened. Her mind raced with confusion and self-accusation. Maybe that woman was a decorator from a department store. He did invite me to the party and I did go there to show off, get fucked, just like he said. But he could have been more . . . more what? Caring? I hate him! And even while she wept and cursed his name, the sensations he had aroused revisited her.

"I want a young one!" Anton yelled into the phone.

Ritchie still hadn't called. He was out of drugs and couldn't cruise Waikiki for more until his boss called. So, after informing the front desk to break into his calls if anyone tried to reach him, Anton dialed the Vietnamese woman on Hotel Street and when her phone didn't answer, he began calling the extensive escort services listings in the yellow pages. Demandingly he placed orders for young boys and girls, which by law the escort services could not fill. One by one he was refused. "Fuck you!" he yelled as this one followed suit, banging down the receiver.

Across town on Pau Street, Charles Halehana disconnected the equipment monitoring the infinity transmitter in Anton's condo and hurriedly packed it, the last of his things to go. His adopted son waited downstairs in a cab. It would only take a few minutes to get to the Waikiki Banyan and get everything set up again.

The Nightwalker, listening to Anton harass escort services, thought for a moment of the infinity transmitter she had discovered when she searched Anton's condo. Why had it been there? Police? If Anton was busted for his drug dealing with Ritchie, she would not be able to carry out her blueprint for his death. No one must have her prey! She decided to enter the condo again as soon as Anton left, and remove the transmitter. She listened, hoping Ritchie's call would come soon.

9

Grey, in a red jogging suit and sneakers, watched Herbert hook a VCR to her wall-sized TV, wishing the Brentano's clerk would hurry. She held two films he suggested in lieu of books on Vietnam: *Apocalypse Now* and an NBC documentary. Llana was on her way and the young clerk was deliberately slow in order to stay around. Grey was well aware of his passionate crush. Indeed, it was impossible not to notice, since he lapsed into spasms everytime she spoke to him. "Are you finished yet, Herbert?"

He jumped to his feet as though stung by a bee. "Yes, Miss Coltrane," he gulped, staring adoringly. In awe of his best customer's fame and beauty, he began nervously swallowing and his tie jiggled in cadence with his Adam's apple. "Is-is there anything else?"

She smiled. "Just the bill, please."

He watched in fascination as she wrote a check without blinking or bothering to check figures. "It's two decks in one. You can play three-quarter and half-inch tapes on this hookup *and* edit," he said to justify the astronomically priced VCR.

"Thank you, Herbert. You're a real friend, and this was a wonderful idea," she said, planting a sisterly kiss on his cheek.

He exited on cloud nine. She closed the door behind his plaid-jacketed back, wishing for a flash Khan harbored half the feeling for her as the salesman from Brentano's.

"I hate him!" she said vehemently, pushing up her sleeves, looking at purple outlines of Khan's fingers on her forearms. The bruises proved it was not a sexual fantasy in which Conan the Barbarian had come to life and taken her virginity. "He's a savage. I hate him." *A savage you begged to take you again.* She moaned aloud, remembering the hardness inside her, throbbing ecstasy too much to bear.

She walked into the kitchen, where her glass wall showed the lights of tall buildings across the park on Central Park West. She turned on the popcorn machine, watched popcorn fill a blue ceramic bowl, and thought how Khan had taken her to unbelievable heights of feeling, controlled her until she was lost in his massive power. Then she thought of his cold, vicious overview of her life. *Rich bitch. Piece of fluff.*

"There is no meaning to my existence. I am not contributing to the human race," she said, then jumped as Jose screamed a non-answer at her from *atop* his wrought iron cage. He had eaten through its bars with his terrible beak and had been out for two days, holding her at bay. "I'll deal with *you* another time," she said to the cockatoo, who hissed, puffing white feathers and red crest in answer.

Llana came armed with a pepperoni pizza, and the two friends settled on Grey's big couch to watch *Apocalypse Now* and the documentary.

Hours later, the blank screen's light played over Grey and Llana as they sat speechless in the aftermath of horrifying carnage and human despair. Finally, Llana, looking about sixteen with her hair in pigtails, broke the silence. "Why did you pick *those* films?"

"I'm just interested in the Vietnam war now," Grey said, too casually.

"Big switch from *Gone With the Wind*," Llana said, not believing Grey for a second. "You're up to something, but I haven't got time to grill you now. Anyway, Vietnam is one of Dan's favorite subjects, because of Khan."

Hearing his spoken name caused Grey to shiver.

"You two can be macabre over lunch tomorrow. Remember?" she said, reminding Grey it was Dan's last show day and Grey had invited Dan and Llana to lunch after she went by the gallery. "I'm going home and simply attempt to sleep without nightmares," Llana said, pulling on a navy sweatshirt. "Dan says a lot of Vietnam

vets are pretty nuts. No wonder. Jesus, Grey—those
films. I hope I get them out of my mind."

It was Grey who had nightmares—severed heads on
stakes, women and babies mowed down by bullets,
trenches stacked with bloody bodies. She awoke screaming, then fell back into fitful sleep, and this time dreamed
of lying in the circle of Khan's arm. It was not a good
night.

The next afternoon, at La Côte Basque's best table,
surrounded by marvelously realistic murals of the South
of France, Dan savored the moment. On his right, Llana
enjoyed *fruites de mer* and reveled in success. *All* Dan's
paintings had sold *and* received rave reviews from important art critics. Llana had been instrumental in arranging
the show and had proved a high-powered saleswoman as
well. He was very proud of her.

On his left sat his hostess, Grey Coltrane, who had
also became a patron by purchasing the work *Confrontation*: a vividly colored, monstrous, fire-breathing dragon
undulating down a sandy beach toward a slant-eyed barbarian with a sword, a raging sea as the background. The
savage warrior, whose muscular torso was naked above a
wide-studded leather belt, was unmistakably Khan, even
to the leather-braided war lock hanging to his powerful
shoulders. Looking at the mural-sized canvas, one knew
the swordsman would emerge the victor.

Dan thought it odd, Grey wanting *that* painting. Llana
had told him Grey didn't get on with Khan at the Christmas party, and *Confrontation* was a hard sell, being so
big and fierce. Dan had considered donating it to the
dojo—until Grey had produced her checkbook. And
now, at lunch, the ravishing Ms. Coltrane was making
inquiries about Khan and Vietnam. Strange . . .

The artist took another bite of succulent cold lobster
dressed with dilled mayonnaise, and prepared to answer
Grey's questions. Recently achieving *shodan ho* (prelim-
inary black belt rank), Dan had another year to go before realizing his goal of shodan (first-degree black belt),
which in Khan's system took five years. In Dan's four
fascinating years with Khan, there had been ample opportunity to learn about the man. Proudly he recounted
his first meeting with the teacher he venerated:

"A friend took me to the dojo for an interview, and

they sent us upstairs to see Khan. He was hanging by one hand over the street from a fire escape on the seventh floor, as comfortable as a monkey. It really freaked me out. He asked me about myself and why I wanted to study martial arts, all the while just hanging over the street by one hand . . ."

He saw the strange expression on Grey's face and offered an explanation. "He lived in trees for years. In the Nam, as a Special Forces SEAL—"

"Tell me, what are SEALs?"

"Navy high-IQ men, trained as superhuman killing machines—beyond Marines or Green Beret training or anything our armed forces ever conceived before. Their conception was President Kennedy's pet project. Then Khan was pulled into SOG. I'll go on if you're that keen," Dan said pointedly, hoping Grey would let him know the reasons behind her new interests.

But he was flabbergasted as Grey took a bite of trout and coolly said, "SOG was an acronym used by those involved. The organization was actually MACSOG."

Llana's interest returned to her endive and watercress salad and the famous theatrical couple seated at the table next to them. She was really confused by Grey's new and bizarre penchant for war.

"Tell me more about SOG, Dan," Grey said.

Dan raised his glass. "No gentleman could refuse a request from such a lovely lady," he said, sipping Dom Perignon, then going on. "SOG's actual history is mostly classified by our government." Again seeing confusion on Grey's face, he clarified: "In other words, men who were involved, like Khan, feel even *more* denied and lost than other Vietnam vets because their operations were under wraps and were not even admitted to—and still aren't.

"Khan was the only survivor of his eight-man team. The rest were actually burned to death by the Cong while Khan watched from a tree trap, where he was luckily caught. Unluckily the Cong found him two weeks later, even though he eventually escaped. He was also wounded —I don't know details, he doesn't talk about it.

"So when I met him four years ago, he was still jungle crazy. The College of the Streets needed someone who was crazier than the people they deal with. Most of the kids in the programs are former junkies, school dropouts, bullies—rough cases. Like the boys Khan named 'Romulus and Rebulus.' One's black, the other's white. Khan found them when they were twelve, living like stray cats in a condemned building. He took them for sons," Dan said. "Of course, first he had to kick their asses, because that's the only thing they understood. They're both A students now. All the kids in the dojo bring Khan their report cards, and there's hell to pay if their marks aren't top-notch."

As Dan spoke, Grey could not help but think again what a fine-looking man he was. His Mediterranean blood was evident by the slight swarthiness to his skin and sensual lips. He wore a finely cut black suit, a white silk shirt, and a white silk scarf about his neck. It was, strangely enough, the flowing scarf about his neck that made a strong statement of masculinity and played up his light sandy hair and penetrating brown eyes.

"What about the adults at the dojo? Where do they come from?" Grey asked, finishing the last almond sliver decorating her fish.

"Mostly former Vietnam vets—Marines, Army, special forces guys—also some cops. It's a potpourri. A few neighborhood people, some Soho artists like myself. It's a rough school, not like the uptown commercial dojos. They survive on long-term contract deals, go easy on the students, get the money, and call it martial arts. Khan is the real thing. You should see him fight. When Sensei lets his lock fly, they all shake."

"What do you mean?" Llana asked.

"He lets his war lock down when he fights."

"Like in my painting?" Grey asked.

"Just like that."

The arrival of the dessert cart put a halt to the conversation, and as lunch drew to a close, Dan again acknowledged his happiness. Besides the chocolate soufflé melting on his tongue, he relished the envious, admiring glances from other men in the restaurant. Feeling an urge to capture the two beautiful women at his table on canvas, he contemplated them. Llana's ruffled white silk collar against her rose-tawny skin, umber highlights in her raven-black hair. Grey's deluging auburn waves highlighted red and gold against her navy silk blouse . . . He also relished the fact that the money from his sales, plus excellent reviews, put him exactly where he wanted in his career. Life was more rewarding all the time.

Later that night, Dan and Llana mulled over Grey's strange behavior. It was after Dan's karate class and Llana was attempting to massage his aches away.

"Harder. Right there. Ahhh," he moaned.

Kneading away at his muscular back, she was mystified why anyone would want to do pushups until his muscles were about to rip apart. But karate was her man's hobby. No, she mentally corrected herself, his obsession. "Yes," she said. "Grey *is* acting suspiciously. Buying that painting. War movies. All those questions about Khan . . ." She ceased rubbing his broad back hard and began a light tickling with her long nails.

He turned over and pulled her to him. "Think she saw Khan again? What a couple they'd make! But Sensei would never be with one woman—he's got a harem of beauties chasing him. Besides, his wife is martial arts."

"They do come from two different planets," Llana said. "No way they could ever really relate. I just wanted her to have a diversion, forget about that French disaster she was engaged to. I thought if she had a fling with a real man, she'd know how lucky I am," she said with a little laugh, then softly attacked his left nipple with her lips.

"I could stand that for the rest of my life," Dan sighed. "Want to get married?"

She raised her head and looked at him with radiant eyes. "You talking about making me legit so my father and brothers can remove the contract on your life?" Her little nibbles once again moved down his body.

"Yeah, Mama. And we can establish peace in the family with a big Italian wedding. Ahhhh." Llana had found her ultimate target.

Pulling the Mercedes to a stop near an ivy-covered wall of St. Anne's, Grey was assaulted by memories. It seemed impossible that less than three years ago, she had been a student here. Walking into the school, dark halls flooding her with further remembrances, she made her way to the mother superior's office and her requested visit with Sister Marie-Carol.

"Grey, my child, how are you?" Sister's embrace was hearty and her round, rosy face looked from her habit with love.

It was Sister's patient ear that Grey sought, her peaceful visage to draw on, and once she began speaking, she could not stop telling of her useless life.

Sister Marie-Carol studied her former student pouring her heart out. She would always remember Grey as the naked child who had climbed the ivy and the most beautiful girl ever at St. Anne's. Now the nun's kind heart went out to the troubled twenty-year-old. Beauty certainly did not mean happiness. Nor, as the Bible said, did riches. And here was living proof! "In order to live a meaningful life, one must do the work of the Lord," Sister said.

Grey's eyes filled with sincerity. "Sister, I have been charitable," she said, thinking of the anonymous one hundred thousand dollars she had instructed Ralph Daniels to donate to the College of the Streets. "But it doesn't mean anything. I have too much. My life has no spiritual meaning. My days revolve around my own self-indulgence."

Sister's blue eyes twinkled and her dimple flashed. She took Grey's hand and patted it. "Trust the Lord, love will come and give your life meaning, my child. One that will allow you to give of yourself, share love, and receive in return the peace of mind you seek. Now, join me for prayers."

Afterward, as Grey sped toward New York on the Long Island Expressway, the cold February day took on a brighter cast. Just seeing Sister Marie-Carol had been uplifting and comforting. She switched on the radio. Music filled the Mercedes.

As she listened to the sultry voice of Billie Holiday, she was overcome with wanting Khan.

"What do you mean, there's no transportation?" Khan demanded.

"Sensei, the bus broke down again. The students will have to take the train to Bridgeport, and I'll start calling around for a car to take you."

"Never mind that. Call Dan. Tell him to give you the phone number of his friend with the green Mercedes."

* * *

She was reading when the phone rang at nine that night.

"Grey?"

She almost dropped the receiver. "Khan?" Her heart felt as though it were missing beats.

"Would you like to go to a karate tournament tomorrow?"

"That sounds interesting. Yes," she said.

"You're driving, then." It was a command.

So that's it. *He needs a ride.* I should just hang up! "Okay. Where to? What time?" she queried sweetly instead.

Grey was at the school promptly at 5 A.M., wearing a pretty sweater and jeans. She had spent a long time at her toilet.

The wild-eyed boy was waiting under the street lamp when she pulled up. He went inside and a moment later Khan appeared wearing a sheepskin jacket, jeans, and boots. The sight of him made her breath come faster. Rolling the window down, she felt the cold air wash her face. She smiled.

"Good morning," he said pleasantly, and walked around the car.

Not even a handshake, she thought as three students climbed into the Mercedes' small backseat and sat shoulder to shoulder with their canvas athletic bags on their laps. Grey turned politely around and smiled. "Good morning."

Two of them, grown men, returned the hello. The third, the wild-eyed boy, nodded. Khan slid into the front seat, gave directions in a staccato voice, and they were off to Bridgeport, Connecticut.

It was a mostly silent ride. Khan was deep in thought and the students were quiet in the back. Once Khan turned to the backseat, speaking to the wild-eyed boy. "Marcos, you crazy Puerto Rican, if you don't kick ass today, you face me tomorrow."

"Oss, Sensei," the boy replied.

So Marcos is his name, Grey thought, shocked by Khan's violent threat. Then she remembered Dan saying many of the kids only respected hard knocks. Privately she thought there must be a better way.

"NORTHEASTERN MARTIAL ARTS CHAMPIONSHIPS" read the coliseum's marquee on Bridgeport's outskirts. Inside, to

Grey's untrained eye, it seemed thousands of people in gis milled about with no purpose. She was guided to a high bleacher seat, a vantage point where she could clearly see everything transpiring.

The coliseum's entire floor was marked into white-taped rings. Each ring had five chairs at its edge, soon seating five judges. "*Kata,*" blared a loudspeaker. The rings filled with competitors arranged by belt color and who sat cross-legged on the floor. The exception was the women's ring, where white, green, purple, and brown belts crowded together. In one section of the vast arena, children occupied many rings, but most competitors were adult men.

"Sensei told me to answer your questions," Marcos said, having come up quietly behind her.

He does know I'm alive. She easily saw Khan, one of the biggest men present, in a white gi and black belt, seated in a judging chair. "What's going on?" she asked Marcos, now seated next to her.

"Kata. Martial arts form also known as 'Dance of Death.' "

Grey could see the whites of Marco's eyes all around his pupils. He looks as though he's in permanent shock, she thought. "What's that?"

Looking at her as though she were the dumbest person in the world, not savoring his role as Grey's guide, Marcos spoke by rote, as if reciting from text. "Kata—prearranged movements simulating one person fighting multiple opponents. Each move is either a kick, hand strike, block, hold break, sweep, or throw. Kata is done alone—into the air, classically performed according to rank and is passed down from ancient times. White belts are beginners and their katas will be simple, basic moves. The brown belts will be the most advanced you'll see now."

She glanced to his waist, where a twice-looped black belt was intricately knotted. "What about black belts?"

"They judge the underbelts and will compete later by themselves."

"What's a sweep?"

"When you take someone's legs out with yours. Tripping someone with precision."

She shrugged off her warm jacket and sat in her light yellow angora turtleneck sweater, jeans, and boots.

As kata commenced, Grey could see all the rings at once. It was obvious brown belts possessed greater expertise. They had better balance, stronger stances, more precise moves. Her own athletic background and dance enabled her to appreciate their forms. Many katas were theatrically interspersed with blood-curdling kyiis that rang across the coliseum.

Sympathetically, Grey watched white belts, new gis fitting badly, belts pulled too tight at their waists in contrast to the upperbelts, with obis low on their hips. The white belt neophytes forgot forms in mid-performance, wavered in stances, and mewed weak, ineffectual kyiis, embarrassed to give full vent to the karate cries.

Kata went on for hours. Grey mostly watched Khan, who judged purple belt men, drinking in his astounding handsomeness, reliving the ecstasy of him. Between contestants he laughed and joked with his fellow judges. But as purple belts performed before him, he was serious and never took his eyes from their kata. Grey wondered what the Oriental characters embroidered in black on the ridged collar of his gi jacket meant.

Finally, first-, second-, and third-place winners stood proudly in the center of each ring and were awarded trophies.

"Black belt form," the loudspeaker announced.

"Who judges black belts?" Grey asked Marcos.

"High-ranking black belts, masters, and grandmasters."

"Are you competing?" she asked.

"Sensei doesn't want me to do kata today," he said flatly.

"Do you always do what Sensei wants?" she said, smiling, teasing a little.

"Yes," the boy answered, not responding to her friendliness. He was watching Khan, who rose from his judging seat and went to sit cross-legged with thirty-five other black belts in the center ring.

Five masters took up the judges' chairs: three Orientals, a Caucasian, and a black man. Older than the black belts who waited before them, they were all in street clothes and uniformly carried the same air of utter confidence that distinguished Khan.

Grey spotted one woman black belt among the contestants and recognized her from Khan's dojo. "Will she be judged along with the men?"

"A black belt is a black belt," Marcos said dryly.

Khan rose and removed his gi jacket. His physique brought whistles and catcalls from the audience.

"Why did he take his jacket off?"

"He has to. He's going to do breathing kata."

Barefoot in gi pants and black belt, Khan walked assuredly to the ring's center, bowed to the master, and spoke. "He's announcing his name, rank, system, and kata," Marcos said.

Khan stood in a moment of meditation, his eyes closed. Overhead lights shone on his powerful torso. Shivers ran Grey's spine. Then he began, and to see Khan performing kata was to witness the love he possessed for martial arts. The giant Eurasian was poetry in motion, powerful and graceful at the same time; so the lethal moves took on an erotic quality, sparking yet another ecstatic shudder in her.

Suddenly he ceased kicking and leaping and low-floor sweeping and struck a solid stance. His kata changed dramatically. He began breathing in slow motion, mesmerizingly synchronized with hand movements. The breath he pulled in through his nose was a loud, long sound, like the sigh of the sea. And when breath whooshed from his mouth, it sounded like the roar of a crowd. The sonance of each breath filled the entire coliseum, and his finely delineated muscles expanded and contracted with the breaths.

Every eye was fastened on him. The entire audience was silent until Khan completed "Breath of Fire" kata.

Finally, running with sweat, he stopped still before the judges. A wave of applause rose from thousands of spectators and participants. "Khan, Khan, Khan," they chanted.

Korean master, Chung Kwo, whose downtown Atlanta dojo made a fortune by supplying students with easily earned black belts, evaluated Khan's performance. His expertise reminded Kwo of his own competitive days as a young man in Korea, when he had been idealistic—and poor. Not a generous man, Master Kwo gave Khan eight out of the possible ten.

"Why did he breathe that way?" Grey asked, under the spell of Khan's kata.

With eyes shining with pride at his instructor's performance, Marcos said, "To build *chi*, as the Chinese call it. *Ki*, as the Japanese say. It is intrinsic energy. Special power martial artists seek to develop."

She was far from understanding, but saw he was tired of questions. A little boy sitting next to her spilled his popcorn, and she watched yellow butter drip over her white leather cowboy boots and wondered if it would stain.

"Isn't he the most gorgeous?" a teenage girl, sitting in front of Grey on the bleachers, said to her companion, also a teen, staring at Khan, worship on her young face. A sinking feeling reminded Grey that Khan drew women's admiration—and returned it. She felt a sense of hopelessness about the day, watching him, standing six foot, four inches tall in the center ring, receiving his score from each judge. It was my car he wanted, not my company. She shifted her position on the hard bleacher and felt Marcos's eyes on her as she moved.

After a while Dan did kata. He came closer to Khan's expertise than anyone else, and Grey wished Llana were there to see how Dan captivated the audience.

The pretty, tough-looking brunette from Khan's dojo also gave a clean, strong performance. Moving with assurance her kyiis rang across the coliseum with passionate intensity.

There was no kata to rival Khan's and he placed first. His school took all awards, for Dan was second, the woman placed third. With the awarding of the trophies, the audience poured from the bleachers, congratulating winners, commiserating with losers. Picture-taking groups formed and proud parents photographed trophy-holding children, some hardly more than tots.

The admiring group around Khan was deep. Grey watched from the bleachers as the two teenagers who had sat in front of her offered him autograph books and giggled nervously as he smiled and signed.

Darned if I'll join his groupies. She was ready to go home after sitting on hard wood for hours.

"Hey, good-looking, how about some lunch?"

She glanced up at a tall, blond-haired black belt, standing next to her. Before she had a chance to speak, Marcos broke in, "Get lost. She belongs to Khan." The black belt melted away and Marcos returned to his silent brooding. *I belong to Khan?*

Khan climbed the bleachers to her side a few minutes later. "Watch this for me, Grey, while I change. Then we'll have some lunch," he said, smiling, placing his five-foot trophy at her side. The trophy had a metal man on top, doing kata.

"Sure," she said, suddenly infused with happiness, caressed by his charm. Picking up his trophy, feeling envious glances from nearby women, she held it and watched Khan's broad back retreat to the locker room, Marcos following at his heels like a faithful dog. She forgot how hard the bench was.

"Are you his new woman?" The question was a sneered demand, the bold voice belonged to the cocky female black belt holding her third-place trophy in the crook of her arm. The comely brunette stood too close, crowding Grey as she sat. "Well, are you?"

Khan's deep voice saved Grey from her disquieting questioner. "Get lost, Carol," he said, dressed in street clothes.

"Osss, Sensei." Carol bowed and moved away, throwing a dirty look over her shoulder at Grey.

Khan was smiling. "Carol trying to eat you up?"

"Maybe."

"Don't worry. The students are just jealous. They're not used to my having company at tournaments."

"Are we going back to New York now?"

"Back to New York?" he laughed. Her heart lurched. "The day has only just begun."

"There's more?"

"Wait and see," Khan said, taking her arm, walking her down the bleachers. Marcos followed, carrying the big trophy, and Grey found she was no longer weary or anxious and didn't really care what she did as long as it entailed staying near Khan.

Lunch was tuna sandwiches and cherry cokes at a nearby drugstore. Grey watched in amazement, along with the counter man, as Khan downed five sandwiches to her one.

"How do you like it so far?"

"Fascinating. The kata was beautiful. What happens now?"

"Breaking," he said, then saw her questioning look. "Just like it sounds," he said, teasing her a little.

"And after that?" she said, melting inside.

"Fighting."

"Is this a martial arts decathlon?" she said.

Khan looked at her sharply, again reminded the green-eyed beauty had a brain. She was waiting for an answer and smiling that disconcerting innocent smile. He kept looking for the chip on her shoulder—the rich bitch attitude he expected to surface, but hadn't as yet. He looked at her long, shagged hair spilling onto her yellow sweater where her breasts pointed skyward. As she sat on the stool next to him, her jeans were stretched tightly over her thighs. He remembered how she had screamed and moaned when he fucked her and how she had cried when he treated her cruelly. Embarrassed by his scrutiny, she swiveled on the stool, and he was again struck by the strength of character in her face, now in profile. He thought of how he had been her first man, and for a fleeting moment he considered what losing her virginity might have meant to her. "Today's contest will fall short of a decathlon. There's only three events. Let's go. You can see for yourself."

Once more ensconced on the bleachers, this time with Dan for company, Grey rapidly watched the breaking competition.

As a brown belt sliced through three boards with a spinning knife hand, Dan watched Grey. Who would ever have imagined *Grey* engrossed in a karate tournament? He saw her eyes following Khan, her hand caressing his trophy. He thought of how much unhappiness her past relationships had produced. It was hard to believe someone as magnificently beautiful and loving as Grey could not find happiness with anyone but a horse. But she was not ready for Khan! Oh, Llana, he thought, my naughty pixie, what have you wrought?

When Dan left, his replacement had a musical Jamaican accent and was quite gregarious. "My name is Ed. Sensei said I should sit with you," the pleasant-looking, tall black man with a purple belt said.

"What makes you want to study karate?" she asked.

"I'm a teacher in the New York City public school system. That's reason enough," Ed said with an easy smile. Then the black belts began breaking and Ed explained the techniques. Several black belts split four boards at one time. One contestant hit the pine boards incorrectly, bloodying his knuckles, then stood in obvious pain on the sidelines.

"Why didn't the boards break?"

"He lost confidence and pulled his punch at the last minute. Here comes Marcos. You'll enjoy this break," he said.

There was a flurry of activity. Four chairs were lined up in the center of the ring, then four men stood alongside them, and standing opposite each other, made arches by holding hands. Four more men stood at the end of their chain, supporting four boards.

"Whatever are they doing?"

"Marcos is famous for this. He's going to fly over the chairs, through the four-man arch, and break those boards in midair with a flying side kick."

And sure enough, whipcord thin, his crazy eyes even more enlarged, Marcos took a running start and with the loudest kyii heard so far, took flight. His left leg was extended, heel foremost, his right leg tucked neatly under him. Over the chairs he flew, through the hand arches and broke all four boards with his left heel. The coliseum broke into pandemonium.

"He'll win, won't he?" Grey said.

"Not necessarily. It's a spectacular break. But the judges seek more than theatrics."

A tall, heavily muscled black man broke five boards with a round kick. Then it was Khan's turn. He bowed to the judges, then approached the pile of boards and, yelling a mighty kyiii, punched downward, snapping six boards like tinder. Grey was stunned by his power.

Khan placed first, the round-kicking black man second, and Marcos finished third.

Khan came and sat next to Grey on the bleacher, a towel about his neck, his new trophy resting alongside the first. "You were wonderful," she said. "You went through those boards like they were butter!"

"Thank you," he said, his big, slanted eyes on her.

Marcos stood behind him, pummeling his shoulders, loosening him up for the next event.

"*Kumite*," blared the loudspeaker.

"I'm refereeing now. But I'll come back for you before I fight." And he was gone, back to the action-packed floor.

Ring protocol changed. Four referees stood in corners while a fifth judge, the "center sinban," stood with the fighters in the center. When he called "*ajami*" and dropped his arms, the fight began. When the center sinban called "*yami*," the contestants froze, awaiting a decision. Grey found the scoring simple to understand, since, if a judge saw a front kick connect, he would call "yami," name the technique "*Yoko geri*," then execute a front kick himself. The center sinban would then ask each judge's opinion, and a majority ruled.

"How's it going?" Dan asked, again at her side.

"The children are interesting," she replied, nodding toward six rings where little *karatekas* battled according to belt colors, displaying no fear, trading blows with Lilliputian ferocity.

"Their parents are hard to contend with. You watch, every time a referee makes a call, he has to argue with a gung-ho parent on the sidelines. That's why children's division outlasts all others."

"Why are the women not separated into rings by belt colors?"

"Sorry to say, the martial arts are sexist," Dan said. "The ladies are simply lumped together, as you can see. If there are enough female black belts, they'll create a separate division for them. If not, they'll just throw the black belts in with everyone else and match them as closely as possible by weight and expertise. That's what's happening today."

"Not fair."

"It's not, but male martial artists have not welcomed women. Maybe things will change someday, but for now it's a tough row for a lady to hoe."

"Tell me about Carol." The brunette black belt sat cross-legged on the floor waiting to compete, intently watching an ongoing match between two purple belt girls. One, a black girl, had a strong kyii and aggressive, hard kicks. Her blond opponent was no match for her and lost quickly.

Dan pointed to Khan's ring and they watched as Khan, who was the center sinban in the men's brown belt division, pulled two participants roughly apart and lectured them for not stopping when he called, "Yami." "Sometimes during sparring, tempers flare and fighters forget they're in a contest," Dan said. The chastised brown belts bowed to Khan, to each other, and squared off again.

"Carol's not your ordinary female," Dan said. "Her mother died in childbirth and she was raised by her father along with six brothers in a section of the Bronx where a kid fights everyday just to make it down the street. Carol didn't know she was a girl until she went to school. You'll see, she fights like a man. Her first match will be with the other black belt in the division."

Khan was finished judging brown belts and, towering over everyone, walked to different rings, watching the action.

Carol was now in the center of her ring, glaring with open disdain at her opponent, a preppy-looking blond who smiled with good sportsmanship. A piece of cake, Carol thought, bowing to the center Sinban, then to the preppy blond.

"Ajami", called the center sinban.

The blond was taken completely aback by Carol's ferocious attack, a gorgeous round kick to her solar plexus. The fresh-faced girl hit the floor, the air knocked out of her.

The referees called time and Carol knelt in the zen position, her back to her felled opponent, waiting for the judges' call.

"Why is Carol kneeling in that direction?"

"In compliance with *bushido*, the code of honor, not to witness your opponent's discomposure. If they weren't black belts, the judges would disqualify Carol for excessive contact, but she'll probably just get a warning."

Which she did, and the fight continued. By now all but the women's and children's divisions were done, and much of the crowd came onto the floor. Except for parents of children still battling, all the attention cen-

tered on the women's ring. The milling crowd was very
excited by the fighting women.

"Ajami."

Carol sprang forward, firing a solid reverse punch into
the blond's already tender solar plexus and at the same
time kicked her hard in the shins. The blond threw a
front kick, lacking power, as her only defense. Carol
easily dropped under the front kick and, spinning low,
extended a leg, sweeping the blond to the floor. The girl
landed on her behind with a loud thud, then flopped to
her back.

Ouch, thought Grey, as the judges awarded a point to
Carol.

It took but another moment for Carol to score the final
point, a well-timed side kick to the ribs, and she went
back to sitting cross-legged on the floor. By her demeanor one would never know she had just participated in a
fight.

"I see what you mean," Grey said, watching Carol pop
gum into her mouth and chew it.

"She'll end up fighting the black girl with the purple
belt," Dan said, pointing to the girl who had also beaten
a blond opponent in her first match.

"Is there a name for the way Carol put that girl on the
floor?"

"A dragon tail sweep."

Grey looked with concern to where an unconscious
brown belt was stretched out on the floor. "Why don't
they take him to a hospital?"

"See that man checking him out? That's Master Ote.
A martial arts medicine practitioner. He knows what he's
doing."

Sure enough, as Dan spoke, the prone fighter stirred
and with the help of the Oriental master got shakily to
his feet. Then she saw a bizarre sight. "*Why* is that man
sitting in that bucket?" The man she spoke of, in a white
gi, looked like a white cocktail napkin crumpled into an
old-fashioned glass after the party's over.

"Because he got kicked in the balls," Dan said, "and
that's a bucket of ice water he's in."

"My God! What is the purpose of all this violence?"

Dan looked at her strangely. "I guess everyone has his

or her reasons for participating in martial arts. You would
have to ask each person his motive."

"What's yours?"

"Beauty of form, excitement, challenge, discipline that
carries into my art, making my work easier to accomplish." Dan took a moment to contemplate. "But most of
all, it's Khan. He truly inspires me."

A girl with a green belt climbed the bleachers, a
blossoming shiner decorating her swollen face.

"Black belt kumite," said the loudspeaker.

"I have to go. I'm fighting," Dan said. As he rose to
leave, Marcos appeared. "Sensei says for you to come on
the floor. Bring the trophies."

Commanding little bugger, aren't you, Grey thought.
Picking up the heavy trophies, she followed him.

"You can see everything from here," Khan said. "Don't
let anyone shove you away. Be careful, sometimes the
fighters fly out of the ring." He sat her in a lone metal
chair at the perimeter of the black belt ring, and then
seated himself with the rest of the contestants inside it.

The contenders gathered with Khan looked frightening. A huge black man wore a black leather glove on one
hand. For some reason the glove made him more threatening than his size. Grey remembered the black man as
the second-place winner who had broken five boards with
his kick.

Dan pushed through the crowd and squatted by Grey's
side. A jump rope was looped about his neck, and he
dripped with perspiration.

"I don't know—this looks pretty insane," she said.

"That's putting it mildly. You're almost *in* the heavyweight division. You have the best seat in the house to
see Khan kick ass. See the guy with the glove? That's Big
John. He's going to try to annihilate Khan. Bad feelings,
been going on for years, since four of his students left to
train with Khan. This is the first time they're competing
in the same tournament. Should be interesting."

She was suddenly afraid for Khan. Thinking of him
hurt made her nauseous. Dan took note of her ashen
face.

"Don't worry," he said, rising, "Sensei can more than
take care of himself."

Dan faded away. Grey watched Khan interact with his

fellow black belts. He laughed with one, banged another on the back, hugged, even kissed a comrade. Positioned beside an Oriental, his face took on a more Caucasian caste. Then a blond man consulted with him and while their heads were positioned close together, she found herself wondering what Khan's Russian mother had looked like. Her reverie was interrupted by a piercing kyii. It was Big John, the huge black man with the glove, screaming, throwing furious kicks and punches to warm up. Her hand trembled where it rested on Khan's trophy.

Khan, nonplussed, dropped into a split, loosening his legs.

The black belt division came to life, the sparring began. The heavyweights moved slowly in comparison to lightweights who competed in a nearby ring. If lightweights seemed like cats, heavyweights were bulls.

Several times black belts were thrown from rings by well-placed kicks, and Grey jumped from her chair to avoid being hit. Grey, who had never been even at a boxing match, had nothing to compare with this violence. As the big men clashed, spectators moved closer and closer, crowding the ring, screaming for their favorites. Direct hits, even face blows, meaning disqualification in underbelt kumite, were ignored in this division. Here were black belts; they could take it.

Suddenly there was blood on the floor of the heavyweight ring. "Yami," the center sinban called, halting the action. The two contenders assumed zen kneeling positions, backs to each other. An Okinawan judge in a black business suit wiped blood from the shiny wooden floor. One of the kneeling black belts bled continuously from his nose, and his chest pumped with adrenaline as he waited to resume fighting. Moments later, the bleeding man delivered a hook kick with his heel into his opponent's lower stomach, scoring the winning point.

Then it was Khan's turn. He squared off against Big John.

"Grudge match," a man standing close to Grey's chair confided to a companion. "Should be hot stuff. *Black Belt Magazine* says they hate each other." "Twenty on the ugly jigaboo," his companion, a tall man, blood lust in his eyes, retorted. Grey shivered, equally repulsed and excited.

The center sinban, a Japanese eighth *dan*, a disciple of Japan's Master Yamaguchi, "The Cat," called, "Ajami."

Big John screamed, running at Khan with a mighty, lunging front kick. At two hundred and twenty-five pounds, his body was a massive moving force.

Neither the kyii nor the kick ruffled Khan's composure. Smiling, the giant Eurasian leapt lightly to the side and *in*. His braided war lock flew, lending a theatrical air to his already magnetic appearance. He threw a back fist, so controlled, it was but millimeters from the black man's cheek. "*Uraken uchi*," the judges collectively called.

Khan stood smiling as the judges made a point count. He looked to Grey, then blew her a kiss.

Big John was infuriated. To have been picked off so cleanly, to have felt the wind of Khan's fast-flying fist and never to have touched him tore at his gut. Then Khan blew a kiss at him also! Big John steamed. Khan laughed.

Khan's affectionate gesture toward Grey drew even more attention to the ravishing beauty flanked by the two tall first-place trophies, and the only person seated. She flushed, feeling curious eyes. "That must be his woman," someone said, and she heard.

I wish I were. She surprised herself with the thought, and it flowed on. *I wish I did belong to this wild man.* Then she had no time to think of such things. Khan was awarded first point and the match continued.

"Ajami."

Big John, determined not to make the same mistake, stalked this time. Waiting for a move from Khan to take advantage of, slit eyes fixed, black-gloved hand forward, he finally threw a vertical punch at Khan's face. Khan wasn't there to receive. A quick move put him at his opponent's side on his right foot, while his left, lightning fast, delivered; side kick/round kick/back kick, never touching the ground between kicks. All of the kicks found targets on Big John's body.

The judges debated which of the kicks to call as the winning point, finally deciding on the *yoko geri*, the side kick that had caught Big John in his ribs.

The spectators roared their approval. Khan raised his arms in triumph, then offered his hand to Big John, who walked away, refusing the handshake. The spectators booed after him.

The elimination progressed. Khan had four more matches, all of which he won. Twice he opened by powerfully sweeping his opponent's legs. After crashing to the floor, the shocked men were putty in Khan's hands and feet. He initiated another bout with *kensetsu geri*, a shin kick so paralyzing its receiver stood like a statue and Khan scored on him at will.

Grey was incredulous. The man seemed more than human. No one could touch him, so complete was his control and understanding of the space around him. Now, realizing he was in no danger of being hurt, she watched in fascination.

After winning the heavyweight division and having a total of ten matches there, Khan faced the middleweight division winner for the grand championship. The middleweight champ, a one-hundred-sixty-five-pound, orthodox Jewish black belt wearing a religious cap pinned to his hair, gave Khan a good fight, but against Khan's six-foot-four, two-hundred-ten-pounds was out-reached and out-powered. Khan scored the winning point by leaping (something heavyweights rarely do) into a flying, spinning reverse crescent kick stopping milimeters from the middleweight's head; and it seemed for a moment that Khan was suspended there with his heel next to the man's temple.

Whistles, cheers, and loud applause continued as Khan was awarded two more trophies; one for the heavyweight championship, then a six-foot trophy proclaiming him Northeastern Martial Arts Champion for the third year in a row. That trophy was so big, Grey wondered how it would fit in the car.

Then Khan was beside her, one arm about her, making a place where she was secure, protected from the jostling throng. She looked up into his face, and in the midst of the noisy, puching, congratulating crowd, Grey Coltrane was at peace.

Which must have shown on her face. "No time for daydreaming," Khan said into her ear. "I want to see Carol." And within his protective arm, he walked her to the women's division, which was winding down.

True to Dan's prediction, the only two contestants left

after eliminations were Carol and the purple belt black girl.

"Why is she only a purple belt if she's so good?" Grey asked as the two women prepared to spar.

"She may have held a black belt in a different system and be working up the ranks under a new instructor," Khan explained. "When a black belt from another system comes to me, I require he put on a white belt and start from scratch. Or, her instructor may have busted her, taken her rank away."

"How can you tell what system a person belongs to?"

"By the patch on their gi."

Of course, how stupid of me, she thought. After a whole day of looking at thousands of people in gis, she first noticed the patches over their hearts. She looked at Khan's chest, and saw his patch the same red and white one Carol now carried into battle.

The black girl, taller and heavier than Carol, screamed and kicked her way forward. Front kick/front kick/round kick. Carol sidestepped the first two, but was neatly picked off by the last. "*Mawashi geri*," the judges agreed. Carol's eye, where the round kick struck, began to swell and darken.

"Ajami." Now Carol made the rush, screaming kyii, closing distance with a spinning back kick/round kick, followed by a hand combination: reverse punch/back fist. The judges called a back fist to the purple belt's head, making the score one to one. The next point would determine the women's championship. Both women appeared fearsomely determined. Khan's face was expressionless and Grey could not tell what he thought.

"Ajami!" Mutually respectful, the two opponents were careful. There was no rush this time, but stalking, throwing calculated techniques. Carol flurried hand blows. The purple belt successfully blocked, countering with her own rain of kicks and punches. Carol avoided, dropped, and attempted a spinning dragon tail sweep. What had won Carol a match earlier in the day nearly lost her one now. The black girl jumped over Carol's spinning extended leg, throwing a fast round kick to Carol's head. Carol was fast, too, ducking the kick, coming up jab/right cross/back fist. But the black avoided all the hand techniques.

The center sinban squared the women off again as the excited crowd threatened to overrun the ring's perimeters.

Carol's eye was swollen completely shut. She focused her good eye on her opponent, who also dripped with rivers of sweat.

"*Think*, Linda Lee," a black man with a gi and black obi screamed from the sidelines.

"That's her instructor," Khan offered.

"How come you don't coach Carol?" Grey asked in sympathy for the wounded black belt.

"I did that when I trained her."

God, he can be so cold, Grey thought as the match resumed.

Linda Lee, figuring Carol's closed eye gave her an advantage, attacked on that side. Front kick/crescent kick/spinning ridge hand. But Carol's timing was not affected by her injury; she avoided and countered with a clean reverse punch to Linda Lee's ribs.

"Yami." The judges conferred as Carol and Linda Lee, chests heaving, sweat running, kept their eyes on each other.

"Not enough," the center sinban announced, and the two squared off again.

Carol threw a fake front kick. As the purple belt moved to block it, Carol's real reason for moving, a shin kick, found its mark. Even though the judge didn't call it, the kensetsu geri served its purpose. Linda Lee was visibly shaken, her mind on her painful shin.

"Yami." Carol backed up instead of advancing, confusing Linda Lee, then she hit the floor, employing an acrobatic roll carrying her past and behind Linda Lee, then jumped to her feet and side kicked Linda Lee neatly in the ribs as the black girl turned to face her. It was Carol's match.

The crowd went wild. Carol and Linda Lee embraced and walked off, their arms draped about each other, their fight a prelude to friendship built on respect. Carol carried her big trophy in the crook of her free arm.

In letting out a long breath, Grey realized how tense she had been during the fight, and for that matter, the whole very long day.

"Let's get out of here," Khan said. The children's division was still going on as they exited.

In contrast to the morning trip, Khan was jovial on the drive to Manhattan, talking and joking with the students in the backseat, who held his grand championship trophy stretched across their collective laps and out the window. They reached the College of the Streets at eight and just as Grey thought of food, Khan said, "We'll have dinner as soon as I put the trophies away."

In the dojo, she watched as he added his newest acquisitions to the mountain of trophies already there. Most of the students had returned and were gathered for an after-tournament lecture from Khan. Carol held ice to her eye, but made no protest as Khan assigned her hundreds of knuckle push-ups. She was still pumping them out as Khan and Grey walked out the door.

Grey was aghast. "Why does she have to do push-ups? She won and she's hurt!"

"She's not supposed to get hit. Besides, circulation is healing. You let me handle my students. Okay?"

"Okay."

10

Worn plastic-topped tables decorated the pizza parlor's black-and-white tiled floor. Khan seated Grey, then spoke with the owner. Observing, she determined Khan was asking for credit. Watching the Eurasian champion walk toward her, two beer mugs in hand, she wondered how many ten-dollar entry fees he had paid for young students that day.

"I was thinking," she said, broaching the subject delicately, "you're the grand champion, so why don't you let me treat you to a winner's dinner? We could grab some great seafood at Oscar's or terrific steaks at the Palm." By the expression on his face, she knew she had put her foot in her mouth again.

"What's the matter—not fancy enough for you?"

"No, no, it's just fine."

And it was. Khan introduced Tony, the owner, who went great lengths preparing a delicious, colorful antipasto.

Grey finished a spicy piece of Genoa salami topped with pimento and helped herself to an eggplant-stuffed mushroom cap. "Tell me about the woman master now?" she asked Khan.

He laughed. "Got a memory like an elephant, don't you?"

I remember your hands on me. I remember you inside me.

"When Chiang Kai-shek fled mainland China with his defeated Mandarin army, he raped the country of its treasures on the way to the sea, then descended on the island of Taiwan, also known as Formosa. It is said among martial artists he also stole the greatest martial arts treasure of China. A woman master—a Wing Chun nun—also a great healer and psychic. It is said she escaped from Chiang Kai-shek and is hidden somewhere in the mountains of Taiwan. I would like to find her."

So he's a dreamer, too. "Is there any proof of her existence?"

"Not really, I just have a gut feeling about the whole thing," he said, digging into a steaming plate of sauce-covered pasta and meatballs. "Anyway, there are classical masters on Taiwan. I will go there someday."

She was fascinated. "What is a Wing Chun nun?"

"What you're asking for is a history of martial arts, which will take many tellings, my pretty. But"—he smiled his magical way—"right now I want to find out more about you and as soon as we eat, I want to see where you live." He held her with his glance.

Delicious tingles began under his scrutiny. She shifted in her chair, ducking her head toward her food to hide a hot blush. Twisting spaghetti between fork and spoon, eating became a task to finish before being alone with Khan.

He made no small talk as the Mercedes sped toward uptown Manhattan. Glancing to his stone profile, she wondered what he was thinking. She drove into the garage of her building, where the attendant gazed with unabashed curiosity at Khan's war lock, which was still down. The next day, the attendant would be the center of attention, reiterating to his beer buddies how Grey Coltrane Fowler brought home "Attila the Hun."

Leading Khan through the foyer with its polished stone floor, black lacquered chests, and mirrors, into the living room, she asked, "Would you like a drink?" He took off his sheepskin jacket and as she reached for it, a loud shriek sounded in the not-too-distant background.

"What is that?"

"Jose," she said sheepishly as he headed for the sound.

With much amusement he viewed the devastation the giant cockatoo, now defiantly perched atop the refrigerator, had created. Toppled and broken glasses and pottery, half-eaten plants, droppings . . . "Why isn't he in his cage?" he asked.

"He ate one, I can't get him in the new one."

"Why?"

"He's too fierce," she said as he approached Jose.

Fixing fiery red eyes on him in anticipation of what was

to come, Jose raised his red crest and his feathers expanded to their fullest. He screamed a challenge.

"Be careful," she warned. "He bit the maintenance man's hand through a leather glove."

Yelling, leaping, Khan took Jose by surprise, covering Jose's beak and eyes with one hand and grabbed the cockatoo's feet with the other. Khan whisked Jose, wings violently beating the air, into the cage and latched it. "Now I want to see the rest of this place."

In the doorway of an otherwise empty room, Grey watched him viewing Dan's *Confrontation* for the first time. The oil of Khan facing the dragon took up an entire wall. She waited for his comment. He made none, turned on his heels, and proceeded to the next room.

"What's this?" He asked, looking around the dark ballet studio.

"For ballet lessons."

"When do you take them?"

"Afternoons."

"Dance for me," he commanded, tossing her a pair of pink satin toe shoes that were lying on the floor.

"These clothes. I have to—"

"Take them off," he said, seating himself in a wooden chair.

In lacy underwear she danced on *pointe*. Strains of *Swan Lake* filled the room, and the mirrored walls reflected the moonlight coming in the windows, playing over her. Leaning his arms on the chair back, he let the gracefully dancing silver apparition enchant him.

When the music stopped, the spell was broken. Embarrassed by her scanty apparel, robbed of *Swan Lake*'s protective cover, she sank, like a resting swan covering her body with her wings, to a low, sweeping bow.

Scooping her up in his powerful arms, he carried her through the barely lit apartment into the bedroom, where he laid her on the bed and looked at her in the gentle glow of the heavily shaded lamp while he removed his clothes. She was beautiful, and her legs seemed endless in the tiny bikini panties. As she moved, her breasts strained against the silky wisp holding them. He removed it and she moaned. Sinking to her pink nipple, he felt her body trembling with his sucking lips and moved them downward along her smooth belly to her silky mound, where his fingers parted her nether lips and his softly sucking mouth and flicking tongue took her clitoris. He knew by the pumping of her hips that she was ready for him. "Not yet," he said over her moans and guided her hand between his thighs. "Stroke me," he said, feeling her take gentle hold of his hard penis, covering her fingers with his, showing her how to move her hand on his shaft.

By the time he entered her, she was aflood, and her flowing juices blended with his as he sank deep inside her, burying himself to the hilt while she called his name, then God's. He rode high within her, causing feelings so intense for both of them it seemed they were part of another dimension, and then the whole world shrank to a sphere only Grey and Khan and sensation inhabited.

Hours later, when they should have been exhausted and were instead exhilarated, she knelt on the carpet between his legs as he sat on the edge of the bed. One of her hands was on each of his knees. She looked with awe at the naked Adonis before her. "Khan, teach me karate, please?"

It was absolutely the last thing he expected her to say, and he laughed a denial. "It's not for *you*. Not my way."

"Try me." The dim light in the bedroom played on the high rise of her breasts.

"It's a commitment to a way of life that is opposed to everything you are," he said, a muscular arm swinging wide at the plush, richly furnished room. "You'd be no more than a slave in my dojo."

"Let me try."

"It means pain, humility. As a white belt you'd have to scrub floors, polish trophies, bow to me!"

"Osss, Sensei," she said, bowing her head.

As he looked at her, she gave the proper martial arts courtesy, proving she picked up things quickly. Her ballet performance had shown how she could stretch, something martial artists worked at diligently. The fact she was already stretched and trained to form meant a lot. But then again, he mused as he looked at the statue she was, naked on her knees, thick hair tumbling forward onto her sloping breasts, waiting for his answer, he had trained dancers before. They progressed rapidly in the beginning, but when it came to actual fighting, they lacked a killer instinct, and their techniques, though perfect in form, lacked power. He made a decision to test her. "You can start now."

Rising from the bed, he fell into a stance, spreading his legs wide, his buttocks only inches from the floor. "This is a *kiba dachi*. Do it!"

She rose also, assuming the stance alongside of him. His back was straight, she held hers rigid. Although she felt a pull on her thigh and buttock muscles, she knew her form was perfect and thought to herself, this is easy.

"My white belts hold this stance for forty-five minutes while participating in blocking and punching drills. Originally, this horse stance was developed for fighting on boats or horseback, depending on which ancient Chinese tale you believe. It teaches solidarity, earth contact, center of real balance; you are stimulating your power center and the pain involved in strengthening the kiba dachi aids in developing a strong fighting spirit."

As he spoke, the stance which had initially seemed simple now tried her muscles. She felt tremors beginning in her bent legs.

"As it begins to hurt, don't fight it," he said, sitting back on the bed. "Give in, bend your knees more—sink deeper into the stance."

She did and the pain eased a bit. He watched silently and she realized he meant to see how long she could hold the kiba dachi. I'll show him, I'll put my mind elsewhere. I wonder what Darkchild is doing right now and if he knows he's jumping at the Garden this week? I wonder if we'll take a ribbon?

But her thoughts turned to her legs all too soon. Sweat formed on her brow as she mustered all her athletic control to maintain the suddenly excruciating posture. Her whole body began shaking. He sat, observing her struggle, then walked behind her and swept at one ankle with his foot, the same test any white belt would be subjected to in the dojo. She crashed to the carpet. "Get off your ass," he said coldly, just as she would be told in the dojo, "get back into the kiba dachi."

She did, feeling even more pain in resuming the torturous posture.

"I shouldn't be able to sweep you like that. Sink lower.

In the dojo black belts will always sweep at your stances, and the floors are not covered with fancy carpet."

She held out for five minutes, much to his surprise. He had seen strong men succumb after one minute. He was pleased with her display of strong will and toned muscle, but knew she still could not deal with his dojo's brutal training. "Tell you what, I'm going to give you private lessons for a while, until you're ready for class downtown. Okay with you?"

"Super!" she exclaimed, thinking how much she'd see him that way.

"Good," he said, still in his stern sensei's voice. "Six *every* morning. You have to make your instructor's breakfast first, then have your class. You certainly have the room for it."

She suddenly was exhausted—it seemed the longest day of her life. "When do I start?" she said, thinking what fun it would be to have breakfast with Khan every morning.

"Tomorrow morning. I am leaving now."

Her spirits plummeted. She assumed he would stay, that she would sleep in his arms. But she was fast learning not to assume anything where he was concerned. Well, she thought as her eyelids closed, I'll see him in a few hours for my first class. She was asleep before he left the apartment.

When Anton's phone rang, the Nightwalker was jarred to the present. Amazing, she thought, listening as he finally spoke to Ritchie, he could hold a rational conversation. Up until now, he had only talked to the television, ranting while he waited for this call and the opportunity to hit the back streets of Honolulu to continue his debaucheries.

Establishing that everything was still go—Maui's Haleakala Crater was still a marijuana exchange point—and setting up a meeting early tomorrow morning with Ritchie, Anton dropped the phone and exited, slamming the door.

The Nightwalker activated. Leaping from her condo's lanai to Anton's, she pulled at his sliding glass hurricane door. It was locked! Her mind raced, evaluating the door, the type of lock. There were no windows facing the lanai and the entire wall was glass with only the sliding door capable of opening. It was but a slight piece of metal across the door, not a drop lock. She focused. I feel you, Mother. I feel you, Y Shin Sha. Her chi rose, vibrated. She threw it from her, directing intrinsic energy at the small piece of metal, concentrating, concentrating . . . The metal moved.

In the condo she removed the infinity transmitter from the phone and slipped it in a pocket of her camouflage fatigues. A quick look around. A holy mess! His bed.

Picking up the pillow where his head had lain, she stared at it and was suddenly overcome with hatred and grief. In a gesture passionately denying a scream, she thrust her face into the pillow. His scent filled her nostrils.

Anton returned within the hour, having replenished his supply of cocaine, and began yet another session of unsuccessful phone calls to escort services. Finally angered, out of numbers to call, he took more drugs, then stripped, and looked at himself. "A fucking Marine. I'm a fucking Marine. Ran a whole fucking army," he yelled, remembering a time when *real* virgins were available to him.

1981, Taiwan

Inspection and breakfast over, Mikel Anton returned to his tent. "Let's go! Keep going. There *is* nothing else!" he chanted, savoring the fullness of his rock-hard belly. Good food! Man food! At first the troops had puked when they ate raw meat. Now, three years later, they showed bulk! They didn't deserve him or the top condition he had whipped them into. But then, it wasn't their choice to have him as their commander, he knew that. Any one of them would find joy in his death. Anton laughed aloud, wishing a fucking dirty gook would have the balls to try an assassination. Nothing pleased him more than a fight to the death. That's why he walked among them, ate with them—a dare none, not even his enforcers, had the courage to accept. Cowards, staring into their bowls of food, crack troops because they were more afraid of him than any enemy.

Making his hands into tight fists, Anton dropped on his knuckles to the wooden plank floor. Knocking off one hundred push-ups, he felt a welcome burning visit his triceps. Opening his huge hands, palms on the floor, he effortlessly swung into a perfect handstand and executed another hundred push-ups. Anton had used these handstand push-ups to win money in bars around the world. He swore, as he performed the phenomenal feat, he would never become a leadbelly!

Calisthenics completed on schedule, he sat at his desk, left hand automatically caressing his green and brown fatigue pants, pulled tight by his granite-hard rectus femoris. His right hand took a pen. He was working on next year's training schedules.

He didn't know if he would be on this job next year, but that made no difference. Maintain discipline! Discipline was his religion and why he was such a valuable employee.

He glanced at a folding table holding a chess set. The fucking government gook who came once a month was coming tonight. It gave Mikel great pleasure to trounce him at chess. The envoy had a case of Chinese superiority, a haughty Mandarin attitude, making it obvious he felt demeaned dealing with a black! The government people hated and feared the commander even more than the soldiers. Mikel was proud of that. "They hate me because they need me." He was unequaled. When officials came to judge and report to the dictator, they saw immediately the troops' perfection—exactly what Anton was hired for—and hated him even more.

Anton looked forward to the monthly chess game. He surmised his opponent took lessons, for each time the envoy returned, his game had improved. But Mikel always won. Laughing aloud, he recalled particularly embarassing defeats he had socked to the high-class Mandarin chink bastard. His left hand massaged his thigh harder now; his big, square-tipped fingers dug deep, moving with the rhythm of his thoughts.

Across the tent, in a space between the cot and the canvas wall, Yu listened to the low murmurs Anton made at his desk, the sudden outbursts of laughter. Yu polished the high black boots the commander would wear when he mounted and rode with the men. The devil changed uniforms many times a day, and each time his boots required diligent cleaning. The boy's left hand was now minus a pinky tip, cut off by Anton's favorite Marine Raider stiletto, punishment for dust in the cot springs.

Head down, crouched low behind the cot, the boy polished and polished, doing his best to remain innocuous.

Mikel foraged through papers. By the time dawn broke, the tent already steamed and his sweat dropped onto the papers. He paid the heat no attention, his back never touching the chair. Even seated, his spine was rigid. Outside, jungle birds saw the sun and their shrieks heralded its rise. The thump, thump, thump of soldiers running drills with forty-pound backpacks sounded through the tent's canvas walls.

Anton frowned at a notation made months earlier, *hating* loose ends. The woman thing . . . Pushing the director's chair from the desk, he paced, lacing his fingers together, methodically cracking them as he thought it out, wondering if he should employ his female stoolie. He suddenly spat at full volume, causing Yu to start. Anton hated his informers most of all.

Anton personally monitored all Taiwan villages, and he had come across a mountain community with a difference. He was always sensitive to, and disturbed by, difference. It could herald danger, an uprising. But this particular difference was in the women. He shook his head. How the hell could that disturb him?

In his opinion nothing yellow men did was right, with one exception—the way Chinese treated women, keeping them inferior, using them only to breed and serve. Females had no say in this society, could not own property, and were themselves property of one man or another.

He had a dogma when it came to women. "When they put them on the front lines, then I'll respect them." He glanced to the framed, smiling picture of pretty blond Ziba Ganiyeva, taken in 1934. One of the USSR's premier snipers, the fresh-cheeked young girl held her M189/30 scoped rifle proudly. She had had three hundred Nazi kills to her credit. "Now that's a woman. They don't make them like that anymore," Mikel said. The photo, cut from a magazine years before, was the tent's only picture. Chortling, he thought that those few ever inside his tent probably thought the sniper was his woman—a laugh.

He used women only for sex, no tenderness involved. As soon as he was serviced, she was booted from his bed. And he would have none of the fancy whores populating

Patou, the Taiwanese town that was a brothel for hundreds of Japanese men coming by the plane load each day to fuck their brains out, then go home. Nor did he frequent the now popular discos like 2001, right in Taipei, where a handsome man like himself could easily pick up a girl at no expense.

The fact was, Mikel Anton did fear something. *Women with sexual knowledge*, who could laugh at him, a prisoner of premature ejaculation. Long ago he had given up trying to control his juices' uncontrollable flow. He could give no woman pleasure and he hated all women for his shortcoming.

On his village tours, he noted innocent girls. Learning their names, he sent for them when his balls ached for sex. He picked virgins as young as ten, knowing full well that after being with him, she would be treated like a leper by others. No man would take her into his household, not even her father would give her food or shelter, no matter how she begged. She would be cursed and starve. Mikel could care less. He did a few of them favors by slitting their throats.

Disturbing Mikel now was the memory of two girls he first raped and terrorized then killed. They had *not* displayed animal cringing like the others selected for his one thrust of pleasure. Those two girls from the same village, pretended to be afraid. *He did not smell their fear*, and Mikel could always smell fear.

Heeding his instincts, he had obtained an informer among the women of that village. He had come across her by accident. She was a grotesque, fat, badly pimpled bitch, with the fucking nerve to smile at him! Instead of kicking her in the stomach, his first impulse, he had her brought to him.

Her name was Wi, fourteen, and she kept her eyes down sidling into his tent. The blue cotton pajamas they all wore could not conceal the pounds of loose, jiggling flesh. "You may look at me now. I brought you here to talk to me," he said, concealing his profound distaste. "I can see you are not stupid like the rest. Tell me about the women in your village and their customs." He smiled at her.

She babbled stupidly, of women's work.

He stopped her. "Tell me something different about the women in your village."

"Nothing," she said, squirming, then paused and reconsidered. "Except maybe the 'Time of the New Ones' . . ."

"What is that?"

Delighted that she had interested him, the ugly girl anxious to please, spilled words quickly. "Each year, girls who are to marry go to the woods. They purify themselves with herbs to accept man's seed, learn medicine for childbirth and healing, and go through rituals only for women."

Fucking amazing, he thought, a few miles from Taipei and they lived as they had hundreds of years ago, witchcraft medicine, hocus-pocus . . . "And what happens during these rituals, who teaches them?" he asked, still smiling.

"No man ever chose me, so I have never been to the Time of the New ones." Coyly she batted her stubs of eyelashes. "I think older women teach the younger."

"I shall make it so next year. You shall be my eyes and my ears."

By the horrible creature's reaction, he realized she thought he wanted her for a wife! Jesus! He laughed incredulously recalling her simpering attitude. Of course, this whole thing was unnecessary—probably nothing going on with the women, miserable, weak bitches they were. But one hundred percent security was the only way. The Marine way, and a gathering of desirable young virgins titillated him as did having a spy among them. He closed his notebook.

Glancing at his motto on the wall, he chanted it. "Let's go! Keep going! There *is* nothing else!" Yes, *excellent* these mottos he dreamed up. Even better were the fighting moves coming to him in the night. He thought of one. Shit! How he missed his company, the hand-to-hand combat sessions.

He went to a cupboard and rolled up some excellent marijuana, part of his pay. He laughed as he smoked, thinking how it was death for any Taiwanese to be caught with pot. When the right feeling came, he stripped. In a loincloth he stood again before the mirror and reenacted his dream fights, following patterns seen in his sleep. They came clearly, strength flowed through him, and a strange power seemed to hold him. Dripping with sweat, moving with terrifying beauty, he repeated and repeated his dream kata, whirling, leaping, punching, and kicking in planned fury for hours. Finally he fell to the wooden plank floor.

Yu cowered in terror during the display. Because he had to always be within earshot of the monster, the boy had no choice but to hear the sounds, see the frenzy. He cursed the fates placing him close to this crazed demon. He was praying Buddha for the commander's death while the devil lay passed out on the floor, when he thought he saw a flash of light in the tent over the commander's prone body. The boy negated it, assuming his troubled mind could imagine anything. He turned his back so not to even look in the devil's direction.

Mikel came to on the floor, having experienced a strange and chilling dreamlike vision. An occurrence happening a few times before in these Taiwan mountains. There was a something . . . a, a . . . ? He tried recalling the dream, a weird being snapping its hands. The mercenary could not even describe it to himself. The word "shining" came. "I must be fucking crazy," he murmured. "This land of gooks is sending me off the deep end."

He called for Yu to bring fresh clothes. He would eat, then wait for the envoy and his chess game. While he dressed, he thought of infiltrating the Time of the New Ones, the sacred marriage training. It would be a relief from the boredom of this job. He made a mental note to interview the ugly one again soon.

As Anton's brain danced with cocaine in the next condo, the Nightwalker crouched at the tile wall. Forebrain fastened on Anton's murmurings, her subconscious returned to Khan and the morning after the karate tournament.

Manhattan, 1977

Six A.M. on the dot. Fluffing her hair, wearing her best smile, Grey threw open the door, expecting Khan and her first karate class.

"Make my breakfast!" demanded a female specter with one purple eye swollen shut. "And give me courtesy. I'm a black belt, you're a white belt." Her sneer left no doubt as to her opinion of the lowly rank.

More out of shock than martial arts propriety, Grey bowed. "Osss, Sensei."

The sneer became, if possible, more derisive. "Don't call me sensei," the specter spat. "Sensei is only applied to black belts over the rank of third dan. I'm a first dan. Address me as 'Ms. Backer.' " And, attired in jeans, leather jacket, and sneakers, a red, well-worn canvas bag slung over her shoulder, Carol Backer entered Grey Coltrane's life like a tornado visiting Kansas.

"What shall I wear?" Grey asked Carol, serving the delicious breakfast she had risen at five to prepare for Khan, thinking this was certainly not as she had envisioned things. She poured freshly squeezed orange juice into Carol's glass. Where was her champion of the day before, her lover of last night?

"Any workout clothes. Have a gi tomorrow. Make me more toast. Show me where to change my clothes. Hurry up! He says for me to be finished by eight thirty!"

Later, Carol in a gi and Grey in a sweat-soaked Danskin unitard, faced each other in the ballet room. Grey's forehead ran with rivers of sweat and her chest heaved. She attempted quieting her rapid breathing, the result of Carol's unrelenting half-hour warm-up: two hundred fast jumping jacks, an arduous stretching session, one hundred sit-ups, and another two hundred rapid jumping jacks.

Carol lectured, pacing in front of Grey, who was rigidly locked into *kilska* (attention position). "Knuckle push-ups are the test of the man. First you make a fist. Like this." Discontinuing pacing and rolling her fingers into two solid fists, Carol thrust them under Grey's nose. "Then you drop to your knuckles and execute push-ups." Doing just that, the brown-haired black belt pumped push-ups with ease, her bare knuckles pressing the shiny wood floor. Then, hopping to feet, she said, "Your turn. Make a fist."

Grey made a fist.

"Not like that, stupid! Look. Roll your fingers tight like . . . Hey. You can't make a fist. Not with those nails." Carol's one open eye burned with contempt for Grey's long, beautifully manicured nails.

"I'll have them short tomorrow," Grey managed saying as control of her breathing returned.

"Now! Bite them off! That's what they made me do in the dojo," Carol said, as though the incident was a fond memory.

"Bite them off?" Grey said, not sure she heard correctly.

"Fucking *now*, white belt."

Grey did, including one patti nail.

Carol interrogated Grey during a break she allowed her to take in a zen meditation position. "You work here? Who owns this place?"

"This is my apartment," Grey answered, her knees kissing the wooden floor, her mind focusing on the pain in her legs after a particularly torturous half hour of practicing one stance. She's trying to kill me, Grey thought, wondering how she would get through the rest of this class.

She had listened incredulously to Carol's long list of things to do and not to do. Under other circumstances, Grey would have laughed. Khan's karate system sounded like a combination of Marine boot camp, college hell week, St. Anne's, and Hare Krishna ritual. Carol made it clear that physical punishment would result from infractions or refusal to comply with the axioms, no matter how bizarre. "Like if you don't bow to a black belt in the street. When he sees you in the dojo, he'll punch you out. Or if you don't do what a black belt says fast enough, you have to do knuckle push-ups," Carol promised.

With Carol's fighting prowess from yesterday's karate tournament in mind, Grey was not about to test her authority and was cooperative as possible. I actually begged for these classes, she reminded herself. God! Wood and shins don't go together, she thought, concentrating again on the pain she suffered in the meditation position.

"No shit! This place is yours?" Carol looked closely at the kneeling Grey. "How old are you?"

"Twenty."

"Where did you get the money?"

Grey's green eyes were frank. "My husband died and left it to me."

*   *   *

"Carol!"

She spun around, facing him, naked from the waist up; clad only in gi pants and black obi. "Osss, Sensei." She bowed, then waited.

They were in the black belt locker room, in front of Carol's locker, where she was changing. Other black belts in various states of undress were changing into street clothes after class. Making sure not to pry into Sensei's business, they kept their backs toward Carol and Khan.

"How was it this morning?"

"She's half-ass weak. Can't do push-ups. Bleeds easy from the knuckles, too," Carol said satisfactorily.

"Did she cry?"

"No."

The sounds of students cleaning the main workout area drifted through the dressing room walls.

"I want her ready to enter this class in three months. You understand? History, ceremony, meditation, terminology. All basics—stances, kicks, open and closed hands, blocks, breathing. Three katas"—his wide, slanted eyes narrowed—"or your ass is grass."

"Osss, Sensei," she said, bowing in acquiescence to the monumental task.

"Black belts, what is your last virtue?" he yelled.

"Nothing is impossible!" was immediately yelled back at him by everyone in the locker room, including Carol.

"You still have the prettiest chest in the locker room," he said softly, then walked out.

Carol turned back to her locker, her nipples hard.

"Hey, Mama, how 'bout some of that fire? Some for me, huh, pretty mama?" a handsome six-foot black belt crooned at Carol, cocky now that Khan had left.

"In your dreams, faggot! Unless you're good enough to knock me out and bull some off," Carol said without even looking at him.

The six-footer went back to dressing. Other men began laughing and throwing raspberries at him. "Faggot. She called you a faggot, bro. Are you going to stand for that?" There were loud catcalls.

Carol, stepping from sweat-soaked gi pants, paid absolutely no mind to her crazy dojo brothers. She had been an inhabitant of this locker room, this inner sanctum (where as an underbelt, she heard rumors of weird goings-on) since the day two years ago he had made her a black belt and told her to act like one, too.

She could handle herself in the black belt dressing room. A lot of the rumors were true. It could get rough, certainly raunchy. Nobody bothered her, though. She'd take anyone's eyes out who tried. But female underbelts were open game. One way or another, their stints in the dojo proved short. Only Carol had ever remained to climb the ranks through the grueling four years to black belt.

I'd like to punch the rich bitch out, popped into her head. Rolling the gi jacket and pants and tying the roll with the obi, she pushed the concise bundle into her red canvas bag. Then, lacing her Nike running shoes, Carol reflected on the interrogation she had conducted of Grey.

Yeah, Carol thought, yanking her leather jacket from her locker. I'll train her ass. Real good. So I can have a piece of it in the dojo. Still thinking of Grey, she exited the black belt locker room, bowing to those of higher rank, not even noticing the nakedness of some. After Khan it was hard to pay attention to another man.

Soaking in epsom salts for the third time that day, Grey read from the *Book of Bushido*, explaining the samuri's complicated honor code. It was but one of the books on a list Carol had tossed her upon leaving. "Read all of these."

Grey called Herbert, but he called her back to say none of the books were available at Brentano's. "Too specialized. I'm going to try the Village, Chinatown, and martial arts supply stores."

"Would you pick up a white gi and a white belt, too?"

Putting the *Code of Bushido* aside on the edge of the bathtub, turning down the corner of the page, marking the section explaining how it was preferable to commit honorable suicide rather than lose face, she sank, sighing, deeper into the hot water; then moaned at the pain movement caused.

Darkchild had seemed to laugh at her that afternoon. She was not able to ride, was absolutely hamstrung. Never, she thought, not even in the practice of gymnastics had she suffered such muscle aches. She put Darkchild through his paces on a lunge line, then walked him in the park, trying to ease her aches. "Darkchild, you wouldn't believe this woman. And my God, I have to face her in the morning."

She suddenly realized as she lay in the epsom salts that Carol had so overpowered her, she hardly contemplated Khan. She looked at her hands, where the pain of raw knuckles nagged. The phone next to the bathtub rang.

"How's your body?" Khan's deep voice asked.

"Great. It was a wonderful class."

He laughed. "Well, in that case, I'll tell your instructor to work you harder. You're supposed to be in pain."

"Oh no. I lied. I'm a basket case."

"Never lie to your Sensei. Your instructor will make your next class more difficult, so you will value the telling of truth." And with that as good-bye, he hung up.

I must remember not to joke about martial arts with him, she thought, picking up a typewritten list of Japanese terminology lying on the bathroom floor. Well, at least I have enough studying to occupy me in the bathtub. Looking at her breasts half covered with water, she thought about Khan. I'm going to be the best student he's ever had, she promised herself.

I'm the best student he's ever had, Carol said to herself the next morning as she walked through the still dark streets toward the subway. She would test for nidan (second-degree black belt) soon. Then she would be on her way to *sandan*. That was her goal, to be a sensei. Then he would consider her more seriously. "Fuck off," she told a man who stuck his tongue obscenely out at her, cradling his balls with one hand. "Subway freak." She boarded the trian, and as it headed uptown, she thought to her first meeting with Khan.

She had been twenty-three and was already at the dojo as a purple belt. The chief instructor, a sandan named Ralph, was adequate. He turned her on to the kick and punch aspects of karate,— nothing like Khan's whole spectrum of the martial arts. Her training originated with a bet between Ralph and an instructor from another school. It was Ralph's contention that a woman could be made to fight as well as a man. Carol was living in the neighborhood, hanging around the school. She became the guinea pig, and a good one. She took right to it.

When the College of the Streets received a Rockefeller grant, it hired Khan. He kicked Ralph's ass, raised Ralph's rank, and gained his respect along with everyone else's. The dojo changed.

Suddenly there was esprit de corps. Khan taught them bushido. He made them a family. "If your dojo brother is in trouble, you help him. It's your duty as a karateka." They kicked each other's ass in the dojo, but he united them against all outsiders. Their numbers grew until they went to tournaments two hundred strong, Khan always leading them to victory. Their school was unbeatable. They had something special. They had Khan.

All the students were in love with Sensei, each in their own way. Hero worship for the kids, the men experienced comaraderie along with awesome respect. For Carol, the only woman, it was all those things—plus much more.

He had dominated her from the beginning. "I don't allow underbelts to smoke cigarettes," he said, coming up behind her outside the dojo after her first class with him. She had been cocky on the mat, checking him out with her knowing cat's eyes.

Quickly extinguishing the Winston, she thought, Who the fuck does he think he is?

"That means all the time. Not just around the dojo, you understand? You owe me one hundred for the butt you just dropped," he said, doling out knuckle punch-ups, "and another one hundred every time you smoke. I want healthy belts, not cancer cases."

At the time Carol was working at the Electric Circus, a wild East Village disco. She sold tickets, smoking a half pack of cigarettes each night in the glass cage. Some of the security men were black belts, and they must have reported her continued smoking. She found out the next week.

It was after a brutal four-hour class in which she had been hurt sparring by a chest punch. They didn't give her any slack for being female. Rubbing where it ached, she approached the student dressing room. Two black belts blocked her way. "You're not going home now, purple belt," one of them said.

"Why not?" she said defiantly.

"Because," the other said. "You owe Sensei one thousand good ones, and he told us to stay until you give them up. That's your cigarette count," he said, grinning, enjoying his assignment. They all thought she was a smartass.

They kept her there, making her pump the thousand push-ups. She screamed when she couldn't go on anymore and collapsed. But they hit her with the bamboo *shinai* and that hurt worse than the push-ups. When it was over, she could see white bones where the skin on her knuckles was long gone. There was blood all over the floor, which the bastards made her clean before leaving.

He was waiting for her outside. "Learn your lesson?"

"Osss, Sensei."

He took her upstairs to his living quarters, bandaged her horrible hands, and got down with her. Carol never smoked another cigarette or made love with another man after that.

There had been a boyfriend before Khan came. The chief instructor had given her boyfriend rank over her because she was a woman, too sure of herself. "So what?" she said to anyone ragging her about it, "I can still punch him in his goddamned nose anytime I want. Brown belt or not." And she could.

Now, at twenty-seven, the black belt with the black eye on the uptown train looked at her hands with callused knuckles. Not pretty hands, like the twenty-year-old rich bitch's. It had been a month after those thousand push-ups before Carol could even close her hands.

Khan had been fair—he had given her the brown belt and made the guys respect her. She shared his bed for a while, but he didn't make her his woman, move her into his quarters the way she hoped. Even when he made her scream with passion, he seemed somehow removed from her.

In the winter, looking out his bedroom window, watching him clad only in a loincloth as he meditated on the roof in the snow, like it wasn't freezing out there, she began fathoming how deep his removal from her was, how very different he was. He had drifted away, making love to her less and less often. It had been a year since the last time he had invited her to his bed.

Carol still considered herself his. She could wait, too.

She was with him everyday. She even worked in the College of the Streets' administrative office, where he had gotten her a job. She was at his side at tournaments, demonstrations, parties on weekends, and in his classes every weekday. *She* braided his war lock.

Other women came and went. Some came to classes to flirt with Khan, always a mistake. The dojo's hard realities were a rude awakening. Usually the brutal calisthenics would eat them up. The warm-up alone went on for hours. Once on that floor, you didn't come off until Sensei ended the class, or the ambulance took you away, which had happened a few times. Women, especially those who came to look cute in a gi, were sorry they ever considered it and would remember the class for the rest of their lives. When a woman came on the mat, sparks would fly. If she lasted any time, sooner or later, there would be a confrontation between Carol and the new one. There had been no contest so far.

No, Carol mused, the women in the dojo didn't last and the ones outside it didn't last, either. She watched him become bored with them. He needed a woman who could stand by his side. Sometimes, especially when he talked about the "Way of the Sword," he referred to sons he would have and how he would school them. He wasn't going to get sons without a mother for them. Carol figured sooner or later, he'd realize she was right under his nose.

By the fourth day of Carol's terrorization, Grey's body ached worse than ever. Contrary to her expectations, she was not loosening up, much the opposite. Each class was another test of endurance, a reaching of yet another pain threshold.

Carol ingeniously extended Grey's workout a half hour, ordering breakfast ready by six and Grey in gi, too. The black belt then bypassed the kitchen, going straight to the ballet room. She sat on the floor, eating in front of the mirrors, barking commands between mouthfuls. She demanded seconds and was not unabashed at requesting thirds.

The brazen black belt was also diabolical. Once after ordering Grey to assume a horse stance, she appeared to drop off to sleep. Grey, straining thigh muscles in the merciless kiba dachi, looked at the sleeping woman whose black eye was now purple, yellow, and slightly off-green. She must be exhausted, too. I wonder why she does this? Is she paid? When Grey could hold the stance no longer, the pain too much too bear, she shifted slightly ever so slightly.

Carol's good eye darted open. "Gimme twenty for moving."

And where was Khan? Where, Grey thought, ending a series of one hundred reverse punches, feeling fire in her biceps spreading, consuming her entire upper body. Carol gave her a minute break. Grey collapsed, flat on her back. Where was Khan? Exhausted at the end of every days, sleep took her before she could even contemplate his silence since that one call. God, I'm tired. She tried separating her vertebrae against the wood floor, an unsuccessful attempt at unlocking her poor upper body.

Intensive karate under this relentless witch was happening at an already busy time. Grey could not neglect Darkchild's training, nor stop the flow of his workouts, although she changed their time. His first competition was Sunday. After Carol's initial class, she gave herself no further respite for aches and pains and hurried to the stable daily, after a hot soak.

Khan finally made an appearance on Thursday morning as she completed her two-and-one-half-hour torture session. Why now, when I look like this? She waited by the door after the doorman announced his arrival in her new, sweat-soaked gi, looking like a potato sack with a rope around the middle. No matter how many times Carol had showed her, she couldn't get the gist of the intricate obi knot.

Opening the door and seeing him filling up the space, she gave him courtesy and, looking into his eyes, the pain in her body stopped for a moment.

But Khan was distant in his attitude. Back in the ballet room, he watched silently as Carol put Grey through her paces. Oh, Darkchild, I know how you feel. Actually, she thought she did quite well until it came to the push-ups. Then she felt like an ass, struggling to do one real push-up on her raw knuckles. Feeling even more of a fool, her arms giving out, she flopped like a dead fish onto the perspiration-covered floor.

Instead of chastising her, Khan turned to Carol. "She

looks like garbage. Her obi isn't tied correctly. Give me one hundred now!''

As Grey left to shower, after saying virtues, Carol was glaring hatefully at her and pumping out push-ups.

When Grey returned, Carol was gone and Khan was no longer the stern instructor. He led her to the bedroom, where, pulling a sheet from the bed and laying it on the pink carpet, he said, "Take off your clothes." He displayed a small brown glass bottle. *"Ti Da Jow,* every white belt's best friend.

"On your stomach," he said when she was naked, and massaged her with the Chinese brewed herbs for an hour, during which he never spoke. Her groans were the only sounds. With magic hands he found all the painful spots, almost as though the pain were in his body, she thought.

First his administrations were deep, working out the anguish. Then the massage became gentle, soothing. Her body felt warm, in accord with itself. Drifting off to a peaceful sleep, she awoke only when he slipped inside of her.

From the condominium next door, Mikel Anton broke into the Nightwalker's thoughts by leaving a six-thirty wake-up call. She surmised he took a sleeping pill.

When satisfied Anton was sleeping, the Nightwalker also rested. Easing onto the double bed, she slept immediately and had a familiar dream, a dream she once hurtled within for years, involving those who made the Nightwalker what she was:

She was in excruciating pain. A woman with a shining aura named Mother, who might have been Chinese but for overlarge, radiant eyes, touched her and made the pain go away. Flash of a lovely young Chinese girl named Lo Ling, always smiling. Smell of jasmine. An Oriental man named Y Shin Sha, compellingly virile, wearing a red beret, doing strange, snapping hand things, suddenly not human, taking off his beret, turning into a frightening alien with antennae. *Khan dead.* She screamed, "Mother help me." Awful pain. Mother touched her, took the pain. Smell of gardenia. A pipe, a syringe. Women climbing trees. Y Shin Sha striking trees with lightning hands and feet, disappearing, reappearing, leaping effortlessly into tall trees. Pain. A bloody fetus. Soldiers. Pain only

Mother could take. Mother was hacked to pieces. Blood everywhere.

"No, no, don't hurt Mother," the Nightwalker screamed aloud. Nothing must happen to Mother! Fighting and kicking, the Nightwalker flailed at the air with such ferocity that she threw herself from the bed, severely cracking the nightstand's sharp corner, and awakened on the floor to blood and pain.

Lying there, splayed on the carpet, sweating and shivering in the aftermath of the nightmare, head throbbing with pain, she remembered another agonizing awakening from that same dream world into the Time of the New Ones, when virgins gathered, preparing for marriage. The horror of horrors had happened, her husband was dead, she had drifted in coma for almost three years. It was Taiwan, she was under a healer's care . . .

11

"Mother, please, I'm in pain!" Grey's words rang in her ears as she came awake to concerned eyes. Eyes with the unmistakable ovals—epicanthic folds included—of a Chinese.

The whole face came into blurry view—a young girl's, not the face Grey sought. "Mother, please, I have pain," Grey heard herself whisper. Then the face she did seek, Mother's face, framed in shimmering light, came into focus. Mother's eyes, radiant and wide, also held concern.

Mother raised a palm to Grey's forehead. Familiar emanating tingles pushed Grey's pain into the background. And then, not in a voice Grey could hear, but rather within her mental pathways, Mother answered, "Yes, I know, my child. And you may have medicine, but less, and soon it must stop. You are better. I am needed by others. This is the Time of the New Ones, and you must learn to overcome the pain yourself." Mother took her palm away.

The pain returned. Grey quickly thrust her arm toward the Chinese girl, Lo Ling. *How do I know her name?* Lo Ling plunged a syringe into the offered vein.

Grey felt the prick, instant relief, drifting . . . Through the lovely enveloping haze she gazed at the dark eyes and luxurious black hair belonging to the fifteen-year-old girl who so deftly administered the needle. Velvety beauty. The girl was Chinese, but reminded Grey of Llana. *Llana.* "Khan," Grey screamed, "Khan!"

Lo Ling immediately held a small, smoking clay burner under Grey's nose. Grey sniffed hungrily at the pure opium. *How do I know to do this?* Euphoria and colors returned along with sharp smells. She felt Mother pick her gently up, and she reverted to dreaming far, far from reality. But just before she did, she glimpsed Y Shin Sha, dressed like a commando in camouflage uniform, a red ascot at his neck, a red beret concealing his antennae of her dreams. He was close, peering at her.

Lo Ling watched Mother pick up the poor, wasted foreigner like she was a feather and carry her to the camp clearing, where, by Mother's side, shaded by climbing trees, the foreigner would lie still, deathly pale, until someone moved her.

It had been so for almost three years, since Y Shin Sha (Nightwalker) had brought the foreigner, an inch from death, bloody in his arms, to the camp. But now Lo Ling was hopefully excited because the foreigner's extraordinary green eyes had again opened in comprehension. Her patient had first awakened six months ago.

Lo Ling had often held the comatose foreigner, always when feeding life-sustaining juices and herbs, but much of the time, Lo Ling cradled the beautiful Westerner just to love her. Did not Mother teach *love as the most powerful component of healing?*

That day, six months ago, the foreigner had suddenly pulled from Lo Ling's arms, screaming "Khan" over and over, just as she had a few moments ago, then lapsed into a coma again. Lo Ling had been very frightened.

Lo Ling sighed, a breathless little sound she often made, and looked at Y Shin Sha, who also watched Mother carry the foreigner away. Even from this distance, she could feel his chi. This Nightwalker was like a summer storm filled with crackling energy which heightened into lightning bolts when he became agitated. And he often became agitated. He did not return her gaze.

From behind a tree in the heavily wooded area, an obese girl named Wi squeezed a pustule on her chin and observed Mother leave with the sick foreigner in her arms.

The always complaining, indulged shopkeeper's daughter was even more miserable than usual. Sore feet. Hands scraped bloody. Worst, her ponderous belly was empty. Despite her discomforts, Wi concentrated on spying for the commander. But would her intended believe? Did she believe, even though seeing with her own eyes?

Picking at her face, the fat girl watched Lo Ling, who

she had despised from first sight, roll the sick foreigner's pallet. Lo Ling's slim beauty made Wi feel even more like a cow. Lo Ling looked with love at Mother's incredibly agile son. When Wi asked about him, Lo Ling said he was Y Shin Sha, whatever that was!

The Nightwalker, Wi observed, gave his attention only to Mother and the sick foreigner—when he was present. Wi had been in this accursed camp for only two days, but already established the Nightwalker was not a permanent fixture. He flitted in and out of the camp, seeming to pop from nowhere.

For almost three years the commander, a handsome black American ruthlessly hunting rebellious Taiwanese for the government, had contacted Wi intermittently, asking about the women in her village, promising to send her to this marriage training. The pimply faced girl, believing the commander loved her, waited to hear from him, hard put to keep her secret. I have a man, Wi ached to proclaim to her mother and the village girls who never included her. I am wanted, trusted, *by one you all fear*. Now she too feared, beholding bizarre things she would have to report. Would he believe? What had she gotten into?

Only twenty miles away the object of Wi's concern, Taiwan's secret weapon against T.I.M., sat naked on a towel-covered chair at his desk. The commander's solid black form ran with sweat as he worked in the hottest part of an intensely hot summer day. The cloying heat lay heavy, even stilling the never silent birds and insects. Anton looked down at his balls pressing the white terrycloth towel, there to catch his copious perspiration. One was darker, swollen more than the other. Reaching his right hand, he cradled and felt at the lump in that ball, probing with his first finger until finding the remaining seat of pain deep inside the testicle.

He still didn't know what had happened that day almost three years ago when he had experienced the most excruciating pain of his violent life. Mikel Anton was having an interesting afternoon until then . . .

He was in a gorge encampment. A scout came, telling of an insurrectionist nest, a martial arts sanctuary; men, monks, master, a foreign man—a giant, the scout said, all cut down by the commander's troops.

Leaping to his horse, Mikel raced to a scene of slaughter and rape. There was a naked white woman in the courtyard, sprawled on her back, a soldier atop her, his ass pumping hard. Other soldiers, who waited their turn at the woman, looked at the commander with fear; Anton waved a hand in approval. Their spoils.

Among the dead, Anton then saw the magnificent giant crawling through the dirt. Blood ran from his mouth and bullet wounds in his wonderful chest. Anton laughed, exhilarated by smelling blood, excited by the killing, *recognizing the woman and the giant.* A high-ranking commissioner had sought them for years, had ordered them found and returned alive. Each month the government envoy mentioned fighting champion Khan Sun and his woman, who had embarrassingly managed to elude the commander.

Amid the carnage, Mikel sprang into action. Grabbing a soldier's bayonet, he plunged it into the champion's stomach, at the same time locking eyes with his beautiful victim, seeking his reaction, the special enjoyment of seeing into a man's eyes as he killed him. He was disappointed. His victim's lids merely dropped. Too bad, this would have been a worthy adversary, a great sparring partner. Anton wished he had been here earlier to savor the fighter's death to the fullest.

Once more admiring the champion's splendid musculature, he withdrew the bayonet from Khan Sun's stomach, jerked Sun's body over by the wrist, and was administering the coup de grace when he experienced a horrendous pain in his balls. He could have sworn he was kicked! Thought he saw a flash of something . . . But there was no one near him. The pain certainly took the joy from his bayonet thrust. It also took all his years of military discipline squeezed into that excruciating second not to scream aloud.

Somehow he got to the base pool of a nearby waterfall without the men, busy raping and plundering, realizing he was hurt. As he passed, still more soldiers waited their turn at the woman. Blood from her temple mixed with the earth, making a dark mud pillow for her head. She was unconscious or already dead.

Anton sat in the cool water until dark. Riding his horse at a gallop still brought painful reminders of that day. He had never returned to that place. Let the bodies rot! Anton recalled an inexplicable energy surrounding him as he had sat in the water nursing his screaming testicles, as though the very air rejoiced in his pain. After that experience his sleep patterns had become worse than usual, his fleeting slumbers almost always terrifying nightmares featuring the strange being who had snapped his hands.

When able, Anton had begun his mad marijuana workouts again. A few times the frenzied athletics ended in seizures. Bothered by his fewer hours of sleep, he took to eating candy bars for quick energy and instead pushed himself into hypoglycemia, so a low-level headache was his constant companion. He paid attention to none of these things and drove himself as usual. Now, taking his hand from his groin, he let go those thoughts and returned to his paperwork.

Anton had been away from the mountains for almost a year, first in Taipei, then about the island, securing waterfronts against communists. Now returned, he suddenly lusted for a young girl.

The mercenary thought about Wi, the ugly one he had made his spy years ago and finally sent to "marriage training." She had gone with a group of eight. Eight virgins, nine if you included the ugly one. Shuddering, he laughed aloud. It still amused him. The fat-pimpled-gook-pig had actually thought he would choose her! He needed some fun—a diversion. "Ready my horse," he commanded, knowing Yu would fly from the steaming tent with the order. Anton decided to catch up with the ugly one, and planned to think also, on his ride, how to best present the Americans' bodies to the envoy. The couple would be bones by now, picked clean by nature's scavengers. Perhaps this was the time to have them "found."

Eleven-year-old Yu did fly from the tent. The boy's screams still rang in the night from Anton's brutal sodomitic attacks. Ashamed to be alive, Yu only looked at the ground as he ran through the camp and told a soldier to prepare the commander's mount.

Mother entered the clearing on the second day in the Time of the New Ones. As always, her shining presence awed those Taiwanese women present. Sinking to their knees, the women touched their foreheads to the ground. "We greet you, Mother," they said and waited for her tapping staff, signaling their day's start.

Mother took the platform seat where she would remain for most of the day. The sick foreigner lay sleeping by her side.

The training began. Mother watched as she always did. The three ranks—disciples, big sisters, and new ones— ran in the form of the snake. Running women weaved in and out of the giant trees, their blue pajamas flashing against the brown trunks. It was easy to tell which were new ones. They often tripped and their chests heaved with desperate reaching for breath. Big sisters kept up. Disciples ran with the grace of forest deer, their black-slippered feet barely skimming the ground.

The blue snake slithered for an hour. Some new ones fainted. This was expected. They would rise in their time. The fasting contributed to light-headedness, and this first week weaknesses were overlooked.

The climbing began. Effortlessly disciples silently ascended the giant trees, pulling with true grips from branch to branch. Wasting no motions, sure-footed disciples quickly disappeared into the treetops, where, hidden from view, they sang. Their cacophony radiated dimensions of freedom and exaltation.

Big sisters followed the song into the trees. They had already attended at least one Time of the New Ones, and were returned desiring someday to be disciples. Some big sisters were only teens, married but a year. Their ascent was slower than the disciples, nor was it perfectly quiet. Big sisters slipped, started again. Fresh blood decorated branches where hands poorly selected grips, closing on sharpness. Finally they, too, were hidden in the treetops.

The new ones attempted the climb. Not one could even pull her body to the first branches, even though vine clusters dangled enticingly to help. And Mother saw who tried and who gave up.

After the allotted time for struggling new ones, they were commanded away from the trees. Then the disciples, together with big sisters, scurried thrice more up and down the trees. The new ones watched, amazed. And though it appeared the foreigner slept, impressions formed in her sick mind.

*   *   *

The pain receded from the cracking blow at the night-stand, enough for the Nightwalker to pull herself off the floor and go to the bathroom. She washed away the blood, then returned, exhausted, still shaken, to the bed. *I must sleep*. The revenge of Anton must be correctly done. Rest is important. Cushioning her head on a soft pillow, she willed herself into another slumber.

Manhattan, 1977

As the end of May approached, Grey's life was too full. Soon her three-month stint with Carol would be over, and she would start evening classes at the dojo. Surviving Carol's classes, learning uncountable new things—many in Japanese— and showing Darkchild was in combination a herculean feat. Every second was taken. Llana came to the stable on a Saturday so they could keep up with each other's lives.

Dressed in a plaid shirt, jeans, and sneakers, Llana sat with one leg thrown over the arm of the tack room's old, cracked leather chair. She watched Grey, in sweatshirt and jeans, hair tied back with a bandanna, assiduously scrub a saddle mounted on a wooden two-by-four. Grey had spread *The New York Times* under her work area. The tack room smelled great—leather and wax.

Happiness further enhanced Llana's velvety beauty. She smiled all the time now. Her June wedding with Grey as maid of honor was but five weeks away.

The two best friends had just finished laughing, at Grey's expense. Grey had described Friday's karate class, during which she and Ms. Backer front kicked each other in the stomach. It was only funny in retrospect. The actual experience had been no laughing matter.

Initially, Carol had drilled Grey for an excruciating hour of nonstop front kicking, slowly at first, for perfect form and control, then furiously—as in combat.

"If you put the kick out at fifty miles an hour, you should pull it back at one hundred. That's so you don't hang the kick and give your opponent something to grab you by," Carol lectured, then demonstrated repeated front kicks. Her leg was a blur. Her gi made sharp, snapping sounds.

Grey threw fast kicks until her legs felt like lead and she thought her racing heart would burst through her chest. Carol finally halted her.

Standing, facing Grey as she panted and perspired, Carol said, "Kick me, plant it right below my obi, low stomach," and offered her middle.

Grey threw a tentative, slow kick. The ball of her foot just grazed Carol's gi.

"Not like that, stupid! Like this," Carol yelled, kicking Grey in her stomach.

"Oufff." Grey doubled over in pain.

"Get yourself together, white belt. Soft gut, that's your problem. Kick me!"

Grey did, mustering all the power she could. Carol's stomach was hard underfoot.

Carol never moved. "Nothing, you've got nothing!" she yelled, snapping another solid *migeri* into Grey's midsection.

So had gone the seemingly interminable class. Carol and Grey traded unequal kicks, Grey attempting to tighten her abdominal muscles to lessen the pain while silently swearing to toughen her stomach.

"What does your personal drill sergeant look like?" Llana asked. She had been to the dojo to meet Dan after classes, but had not been able to catch a glimpse of Carol.

"Why can't somebody invent something better than saddle soap? It's so much work," Grey said, stopping scrubbing for a minute, wiping the perspiration on her forehead with a gauze bandage wound around her hand. "Ms. Backer has kind of a gamin look, freckles over her nose, about five four, actually delicate features. Elizabeth Ashley type. I guess if I didn't know what a monster she is, I'd be more complimentary and say she was pretty. She has beautiful yellowish eyes—like the cat's eye marbles we used to play with. At this point it's difficult to be objective," Grey said, rubbing her sore stomach.

"Is Khan really worth going through all this? I know I introduced you guys, but I never meant to put you on a path to getting killed."

Grey laughed. "It's bad. But in a couple more weeks the worst will be over. I'll be in shape then, same as the rest of the students, and I won't hold back the class. Once I'm in the dojo it will be clear sailing," she said confidently. "As far as, is Khan worth it? Emphatically yes! He's made me glad to be alive. And you know what? I love martial arts! Even with Ms. Backer on my case," she continued with the enthusiasm of a new convert. "I just read the *Tao of Jeet Kune Do* by Bruce Lee. A profound book. You should read it. And Llana, the martial arts is a way of life. A powerful challenge, and character-building."

God! Llana thought, she sounds like Dan. What have I done? "I'm already a karate widow before I'm even married. Is my best friend going to succumb also?" she teased.

But Grey was serious. "You really ought to try karate Llana. You're a good athlete. You'd love kata."

"No thank you. See these?" Llana held up two hands, the left adorned with a sparkling engagement ring, her long tapered nails perfectly manicured and a bright poppy red. "They're showing Dan's paintings next week at the Pierre Matisse Gallery and they have to look good. Besides," she grinned, "I'm a lover, not a fighter."

Grey wanted to talk about Khan. It used to be just the opposite, she thought, returning to saddle scrubbing. Llana had always rambled on about Dan, and I had never been able to get a word in edgewise. But the tack room was getting busy, and it was difficult to talk intimately. The door opened and Charlie walked in, came to Grey, and said, "They're here."

"Come on with me," Grey said to Llana. "I have to walk Darkchild in and out of a van he's traveling in tomorrow, so he won't spook in the morning." Darkchild was competing in New Jersey this time.

Darkchild's first big show, open jumping at Madison Square Garden, had been a disaster. Grey, karate-sore muscles aching so badly that she felt her seating precarious, had not been a great asset. Darkchild was nervous. The audience of thousands, bright lights, loudspeakers. The big stallion had knocked down one gate and refused another.

The next show, though, had been a success. Darkchild placed fourth. Now trainer Jack Brian held great hopes for tomorrow.

When Grey and Llana were back in the tack room, this time alone, Llana said, "Lemme see your knuckles."

Grey ceased polishing a stirrup and unwound gauze from her right hand.

"Jesus!" Llana said, feeling like a kid staring at her friend's wonderful boo-boo. "Doesn't that kill you?" she said with awe.

Grey contemplated her gory knuckles, the product of the daily torture session on the bare floor, with the same deference as Llana. "Especially since every time I make a fist, the scabs break open again." Grey wound the gauze around her knuckles and, picking up the stirrup, returned to polishing it. "Wanna know how she finally got me to do push-ups?"

"I'm fascinated. How?"

"She ran into my kitchen like a crazy woman, got a knife, and held it point up, where my chest would drop if I let go of my body weight. She held that knife there, right under me. I knew she'd let me stab myself." Placing the gleaming stirrup on a table, Grey picked up a pair of reins and reached again for the saddle soap. "She really scared me into doing my first real push-ups. Then she said"—Grey imitated Carol's abrupt voice and manner—"See, you faggot white belt? You coulda done it all along."

"I don't believe you're really doing this," Llana said.

"The worst of it is," Grey said, "she's perfect. That's what's killing. She makes me feel like a bumbling idiot. But that won't last. I'll learn."

Llana leaned closer. "Khan must be all I said, huh?"

"More," Grey said, and just then made a mental note to buy a black garter belt. Reaching to the floor, she ripped off the front page of *The New York Times*. "Ford Renews Criticism of Carter and Defends the Pardon of Nixon," the headline read. Crumpling the page, she used it to apply solvent to a stubborn black spot on a rein. Letting out a breath that was more of a sigh, she said, "I wish I saw more of him."

Khan remained elusive. When with him, she was in heaven, a deliriously happy place of Khan and martial arts. He never mentioned her classes or commented on her wounded knuckles or her forearms, blackened from Carol's merciless blocking drills. But he was always ready to talk martial arts theory. They had long discussions about things like contempt of death and pain, and why it was a sin to allow oneself to be harmed. They mulled over karma, explored the strange martial arts marriage of destructiveness and healing attained by great masters. Sometimes he told her stories. Like the one about Wing Chun she had requested after the tournament. Now he was willing:

Four or five hundred years ago, in a province of Canton in China, there was a Buddhist temple inhabited by monks and nuns who trained in martial arts and taught the local people.

The government of that time frowned upon such practices, not wanting the people to know the fighting ways, which made them rebellious and hard to control. And so they burned the monastery to the ground, thus quickly solving the problem. But four monks and one nun escaped the purge by fire. Each took a separate way, reasoning they would be less likely to all be captured and could spread the teaching by going in many different directions.

The lone woman found a place to settle high in the mountains. By herself, after much meditation, she came to realize her martial arts were not really good enough to compete with men. She spent the next ten years in isolation, building a fighting system: simple, direct, and economical, it would turn a man's energy against himself.

During this period of developing the superior fighting system, the nun would go every now and then to a village, to a bean cake maker, for her supplies. One day the baker begged the nun to take his daughter, Yim Wing Chun, away from the village for her own safety. The local bully, who controlled by fear, had seen Yim Wing Chun's great beauty and requested her hand in marriage. Horrified by the prospect, the baker beseeched the nun to save his lovely child, who was distraught and threatened suicide before she would make such a match.

The nun took the girl, keeping her for three years, and during that time she trained her in the new system of martial arts.

Yim Wing Chun returned to the village and her father's home, but the time away had made no difference. The ugly, brutal man had not forgotten her, but wanted her even more. Angered at having lost the beauty in the first place, he went to the bean cake baker and beat him savagely. Then he called for Yim Wing Chun. The girl, furious over her father's suffering, confronted the bully in front of the whole town. "I would fight you, and if you can beat me, then I will marry you," she challenged.

Infuriated at being publicly confronted by a woman, the bully ran at her with flying fists.

But Yim Wing Chun was not there to receive the beating. Simultaneously she avoided his onslaught and dealt him such a blow that he fell to the ground and had to be carted away, for he could no longer walk.

In the crowd witnessing the victory by the local beauty was a famous opera star who was also trained in martial arts. The handsome actor fell in love with the fighting maiden and they were married.

Yim Wing Chun taught her husband the simple fighting system. He named it "Wing Chun" after her, and schooled his kinsmen in it. The system was kept within this particular family and local village people for many centuries until a young man by the name of Yip Man moved to Hong Kong and brought the system out of the bamboo curtain.

It was the famous Chinese movie star and martial arts master, Bruce Lee, trained in the Wing Chun fighting style, who brought the system to the Western world.

"I thought his system was Jeet Kune Do?" Grey said accusingly.

Khan laughed. "Been doing your homework, haven't you?" He was obviously pleased at her knowledge. "Jeet Kune Do is the system Bruce Lee created. But his own background was Wing Chun, pure and classical."

"Tell me about Bruce Lee. Do you know how he really died?"

"That's another story, another time."

At times like these, when they had made love and he shared ancient stories, she loved him with heart-bursting intensity. She would lie, arm bent under her head, curled up facing him, watching his beautiful face as he talked and trailing her fingers over his wonderful body. It was an opening up, she thought, when he told the tales: a humanization of the stone-cold, hard man he was most other times.

She loved just looking at him.

He never talked about Vietnam. She didn't ask, being afraid to know. She would rather lose herself in the fascinating, mystical new world he was unfurling.

He taught her to chant a mantra. Facing each other

cross-legged, intoning an ancient Sanskrit prayer, they drew deep breaths filling their bellies with air. "*Om namo guru dev namo.*" Their voices joined and the chant's resonance rode on their escaping breaths. Grey found herself alive with a tingling energy never before experienced. "Your first chi awareness," he told her later when she asked about the strange sensation.

Trying to bring him into her world, she invited him to Darkchild's shows and called him about events her crammed mailbox announced—ones she thought he might enjoy. Studio 54 opened. Mick gave a party for Bianca. *The Greatest*, a screen biography of Muhammad Ali, premiered. Stevie Wonder, whose album, "Songs in the Key of Life" was top on the charts, had a concert . . .

Khan accepted none of her invitations. He was constantly busy. Once I'm in the dojo, she thought, I'll see more of him.

Meanwhile, it had been a week since they had been together. Khan had become the center of her thoughts, the catalyst of her days. Her karate-sore body ached for his lovemaking. Somewhere buried deep inside her, thoughts of a permanent future with him were formulating. She thought of his lips—so soft. His tongue—so demanding.

"Hey, Cochisa." Llana's voice crashed into her thoughts. "Stop mooning over Khan. I'm here."

"Got me that time," Grey acknowledged, grinning, then finally finished cleaning tack, put up her soaps and polishes. She and Llana went off, arms about each other's waists, to discuss Llana's wedding and whether she should go to Jamaica or Mexico on her honeymoon.

The Nightwalker was jarred awake, her short slumber broken by sharp pain—my head! She staggered outside onto the lanai and, holding one hand on her skull, breathed in the Honolulu night. Held by headache, probing a sore lump, the Nightwalker's thoughts returned naturally to Mother, who had healed her when she would rather have been left to die.

Taiwan, 1984

Mother looked lovingly at the women before her. Big sisters served the disciples fruit, then retreated themselves to eat fruit. The new ones watched, bellies crying, knowing it would be a full week before they ate. In the cool shade, Lo Ling bowed as she approached Mother, her hands proffering a clay vessel of pure rainwater—collected only for Mother. Lo Ling's eyes shone with devotion.

Mother drank the water given by her favorite, her shining constant, giving no indication of her special feeling for Lo Ling, this most precious daughter so full of love, laughter, and strength. Mother returned the empty vessel to Lo Ling.

Lo Ling spoke, "Two new ones are sick, Mother."

"Bring them to me."

"This is Kua," Lo Ling said, pushing forward a slight, frightened girl.

Beaming love on the scared new one, Mother projected a "knowing." Probing the girl's belly, finding a tumor, she began a shrinking process. "This one shall fast on the juice of green grass instead of water—many bowls of grass juice, three times each day. Morning and night she must also run the grass juice through her lower portion," she instructed Lo Ling. Mother gave thanks for the opportunity to help and turned her mind to the second girl Lo Ling pushed forward.

"This is Wi," Lo Ling said.

Mother reeled as negative vibrations reverberated from this obese new one. Her sickness—eating of the insides by the mind—was difficult to heal. Self-destruction was far more devastating than the simple tumor she had just dealt with.

Looking with sorrow at Wi's festering acne, Mother knew this most serious illness must be treated carefully. "This one shall stay with you also," she imparted to Lo Ling. Lo Ling would have the patience. Mother knew this new one would probably not remain among them. But she would try as she always did. Mother opened her channels to Wi, something she did not normally do at this point with new ones. *Your body must first be physically tempered and spiritually synthesized before it can understand its work now.* But the communication only scared Wi, and she gave no response.

The sick foreigner who had been allowed one pipe of opium lay by Mother's left side.

The business of the camp went on. The new ones went to their tasks. During their fasting week they would be part only of the running snake and attempts at climbing. The rest of the time, the new ones labored, even weaving the blue cloth clothing them all.

Big sisters carried six-foot wooden staffs to a clearing, where disciples taught them fighting moves for hours. Sounds of wood against wood rang in the air.

Mother watched, Lo Ling always at her side, now and then dispatching the girl with a message to the training women that changed confusion to clarity.

The foreigner lay still within dreams in which she was like Alice down the rabbit hole, chasing after Mother for relief, hurtling from beautiful visions to pain and horror. "Mother, I have pain," she said aloud. Mother's left hand dropped and settled on her head. The pain went away.

Late in the day all but the disciples were sent from the clearing. Mother rose and went to them. Circling her, the disciples waited for precious moments to come. Only once each year, in the Time of the New Ones, would she teach. For the remaining months, practicing secretly in their villages, they would try to perfect themselves. Rapt with attention, the disciples listened and watched.

Of all the disciples, Lo Ling, an unwanted child, had been longest with Mother. One too many for a poor peasant family, left to die in a field, Lo Ling had been found by Y Shin Sha and brought to Mother like the sick foreigner. It made no difference, Lo Ling thought. No matter how many times over the years she had watched Mother in motion, she would never become used to the beauty and perfection. Lo Ling's very soul sang joyfully. It was finally time for the learning. Fastening her mind as Mother taught her, Lo Ling swore to absorb every precious move. *This time I will miss nothing of the new knowledge.*

The morning of the sixth day of the new ones, Mother felt a strange slowness.

Lo Ling awoke the same morning, glancing at her charges. The foreigner, now waking intermittently each day, lay peacefully sleeping. Lo Ling gave thanks for that. It was a great trouble when the foreigner was awake, silently weeping, refusing food by clamping her lips. Lo

Ling had to force herbs and juices down her throat. Even then the weeping continued. During the day Lo Ling propped the foreigner against supports, lifted her to her feet . . . But it was Lo Ling who made the movements; her patient was like a crying cotton doll.

Sighing, Lo Ling glanced at the next pallet. Kua's ovarian tumor had stopped bleeding. Pleasurably, Lo Ling saw Kua's grayish pallor receding and a healthy glow beginning.

Wi was the least changed. Even in sleep the deep frown remained between the pulled-together eyebrows. Lo Ling had to goad Wi to her tasks. Thinner after six days of fasting, Wi's skin, reacting as toxins left her body, was worse than ever. Although Lo Ling carefully explained this fast would purge the sores and clear her skin, it was as though she were speaking to the air. Personally wondering what the man who would marry Wi looked like, Lo Ling thought Wi very lucky to have found him.

Lo Ling's time with these charges took from her precious learning. Still, she harbored no resentment, only a will to do better, to heal, so Mother would be pleased.

A whoosh sounded outside her bamboo hut. Lo Ling hoped it signaled morning showers to replenish rainwater, the only sustenance she ever saw Mother take. Lately Mother's tingling, shining force seemed less strong. That is foolish, Lo Ling chided herself, let me put thoughts of Mother losing strength away. Mother is constant and always will be.

Across the quiet hut, Wi was pretending sleep, knowing she had to work if Lo Ling realized she was awake. Not relishing another day in this weird hell, she lay immersed in the familiar waters of hatred. From childhood Wi had hated being fat, ugly, different. Now she hated hunger, running, climbing. But most of all, she despised beautiful Lo Ling, the favored disciple, offering only love, who would not be baited or pulled into Wi's darkness.

As hunger cramps assailed her, Wi let go of hate and examined fear. Wi feared Mother unto death, having felt the sorcerous probing, a tingling violation, and having seen the incredible faint light about Mother's head that sometimes brightened. She had heard Mother's words *within* her head! What manner of creature was this? Had Wi not promised her intended to discover the secrets, she would have surely fled this accursed camp. She contracted the place between her legs that would belong to "him." There was much to find out in this Time of the New Ones. Laboring to her feet, Wi rolled her pallet, hating how Lo Ling smiled sweetly at her.

Mother took careful stock of the new ones this morning of the sixth day. Here and there especially gleaming eyes bespoke commitment to the Way. "Bring the sick ones."

Lo Ling led Wi and Kua forward. Mother sent a knowing. Kua's killing growth was shrinking. Probing electromagnetically, causing the tumor to further shrink, Mother turned her mind to Wi. The same sickness festered. Looking at Lo Ling, Mother saw concern in her most beautiful child. She feels she has failed me because of this new one, or perhaps she senses my time grows short. When the trials are over, I will send her from me—spare her what I can.

Mother concentrated again on Wi. Strange. This new one should not be here. Yet there is purpose inside her. Strange. I have never felt one like this. Beaming unconditional love, she sent them to their tasks and took some water from Lo Ling.

As Mother watched the climbing, Grey became fully awake and wept the entire morning. Lo Ling went to her many times, but nothing could affect the eternal sadness that had taken hold. Mother realized her depth of pain, also knowing it was only abject weakness keeping this different one from killing herself as the awful combination of drug withdrawal and painful memories overtook her. So different, this one, Mother thought, from the Asians she was surrounded by. Mother felt close to this one who suffered so. At first, when she had been almost dead, she had always remained with Mother, had slept in Mother's hut, and lain under her healing hands for hours at a time.

Mother observed climbing with special care this morning, the day before the trials began. Some of the new ones made it to the low branches of the trees. Others in their hunger had completely given up. Tonight new ones would break their fast, and with the fruit would have the "words," wisdom of Mother. After the trials there would be selections. Those chosen could return once a year for the rest of their lives. But, Mother thought, what would they find next year? Sadness settled over her. Would she be here? Her precious children . . . She put away sadness—it would be as decided.

Through the agonies of drug withdrawal, Grey realized that mercilessly macabre, twisting fate had placed her with Khan's legendary Wing Chun nun. A real psychic—capable of telepathic communication, magnetic healing, and God only knew what else. God? There is no God!

Grey did not care which of her dreams was real and which was fantasy. Memories she knew were real assaulted her, punctuated always be the *face of the man she watched kill Khan*, a face etched in fire in her mind. She had no conception of time, not an inkling that years had swept by as she lay in a coma. Khan was dead and her belly was empty.

Grey attempted escaping tormenting reality by retreating into dreams, but was denied even that by her cramped gut screaming for opiate and by Lo Ling's never ending, gently demanding administrations.

Neither did the camouflage-uniformed man give her peace. Standing over her, he often did what she recognized as Wing Chun Gung Fu hand forms, and his heavy chi bathed her in energy—an energy absolutely electric. She thought she remembered actually being moved by it. Sometimes he was wrapped from head to foot in black and green with only his eyes exposed. She did not even have the curiosity to wonder. The fact that Khan had been right, that *she* was now where he had dreamed of being, was the devil's own joke. Denied retreat to colored, scent-filled opium dreams, she existed behind a veil of tears lifting only when she slept.

With the weeping foreigner by her side, Mother watched disciples teach big sisters the Way of the Sword, knowledge strictly forbidden to them by their men. Strange, man's fear to develop strength in females. Humans were strange beings, making war on females of their species, ignoring Earth's freely growing food, killing other living creatures, sickening by eating them. Even then, Mother reflected, curative herbs for the diseases inflicted on themselves were readily available. Her great dark eyes glanced to a tamarind tree with feathery foliage. Rich in calcium and phosphorus, its fruit was laxative in quantity. Trees heal. Even people were programmed for self-healing and had capacity to heal each other. Yet man mostly ignored nature's healing bounties to make medicines causing yet more sickness.

A big sister displayed a flair with her blade, cutting the air with graceful arcs. That one will soon join the disciples, Mother thought.

It was the disciple's time, and Mother went to them. Now again, the singing inside of Lo Ling. Oh joy of joys. To move with Mother through forms. Life was too good. She was the luckiest, the most joyful of females.

And Mother saw that of the disciples, only Lo Ling was truly one with her form. Mother's shining grew a bit stronger. Lo Ling saw the glow, and her own happiness heightened.

Later, Mother watched the new ones break their fast with mangoes. How they appreciate the sweet fruit. Will their minds absorb as easily as their bellies? As always, sweet Lo Ling was by her side. For the first time new ones heard Mother within their mental pathways.

"The ways you learn now are foreign to your upbringing and learned religion. *These are the right ways.* You have not been taught thinking, yet you are capable of thought and decision. Fasting, food of meditation, the disciples' example, and practicing the martial arts Way, opens your minds and educate your souls."

Mother became emphatic and her shining grew. "Beware religious and political leaders with presumptuous powers of authority, for there is only one sin—to impose your will on another! There is only the law of the Creator who loves you. *You* are sacred, beloved, destined to save the human race!"

The new ones, virgins about to marry, taught from childhood that as women they were nothing—certainly not sacred—were horrified. The words eerily reverberating in their heads were anarchy. In Taiwan, anarchy brought death.

"Your bodies are sacred vessels housing your souls. It is your duty to protect those vessels. You are not meant to be men's slaves. Men have wrought destruction, polluting Earth and the atmosphere, allowing evil to take hold and procreate. You can teach, you can rule.

"This training strengthens you and brings peace of mind. You will be able to teach your daughters their own worth and teach them the Way. Eventually man and woman will stand together to raise humanity's consciousness. You must not dwell in faintheartedness, but manifest physically and spiritually becoming part of the universal living light. Learn to heal, use nature and love's power. You must be strong to counter evil. There will be times that you must fight, even kill. And that also will be your duty, and you will know when."

Mother understood the disbelief on the young faces before her. Simple folk. She probed each, seeing if there was any comprehension. "Morning brings the week of trials. Trials that show how strong you are, how worthy." She left then, exhausted by the telepathic communication, the ability for which was growing weaker inside her.

Mother advocated nature's cures above all others, the Nightwalker mused in the Waikiki condo, filling a shower cap with ice cubes. She wrapped it in a dishtowel and returned to bed. Y Shin Sha had sometimes appeared in camp with precious ice. Her head atop the icepack, she returned finally to sleep, determined to rest her body fully for the grand finale it must soon face.

Manhattan, 1977

Carol seethed with hatred during the three months of training Grey. *She would never forget having to do push-ups in front of a white belt.* One *he* was fucking. In Carol's world of Khan and karate, there could be no greater insult.

To compound her suffering, the damn white belt rich bitch was well-coordinated and picked up things fast, and Carol was locked into teaching to the best of her ability. Further martial arts advancement had much to do with her teaching expertise. "Judge an instructor by his students' prowess," Khan said.

And, Carol thought, her manners! "Miss Fucking Prissy Missy," Carol said aloud, peering into the cloudy, cracked bathroom mirror she shared with another roomer in a lower East Side tenement building. Her eye was back to normal, and she was glad of that. It had taken almost six weeks for all bruising to disappear. She pretended she didn't care what she looked like, but that was not the truth.

Carol patted her silky, shoulder-length hair, brown with reddish highlights. Pulling it tightly back and up, she made her yellowish eyes elongate and slant like the rich bitch's. Yeah, her fucking manners. Pink napkins. Fancy ones. Made of real linen. All folded fancy on the fancy breakfast tray with the fancy breakfast on it.

And her bathroom! Fucking fancy everything in there. Goddamned bathroom, Carol thought, bigger than the room I live in. Fucking gold and crystal faucets on the sink and bathtub.

And her kitchen. Carol had not been able to bear returning to that exquisitely beautiful room of flowered tiles with the bird and the plants—that kitchen out of a magazine.

And her hair. Carol let her own hair fall around her face. Nice hair, a little wavy. She thought about Coltrane's masses of gleaming, fancily cut, blazing auburn tresses, halfway down her ass. Carol imagined her scissors hacking away Coltrane's hair, followed by a razor shaving her head. Fucking rich bitch white belt—probably be beautiful bald.

I almost had her crying, Carol thought, remembering with satisfaction that the day before she had swept Grey's feet, crashing her to the wooden floor at least ten times. But fucking Miss Prissy Missy had figured out the kiba dachi and finally sunk low. After that, Carol wasn't able to sweep her. Then Carol had sensed triumphant feelings emanating from Grey. Thinks she knows something. Wait until the dojo!

Carol walked down the paint-chipped hall to her austere room, where a sword and a pair of steel *sais* hung on the grayish wall. The weapons and her black belt diploma were the only decorations. One small, washed-to-no-color polyester rug covered the bare wood floor. Picking up her red canvas bag from the white chenille bedspread, she slung it over her shoulder and, locking her three locks, headed into the morning darkness.

Maybe if I make him jealous, she thought, walking on

Avenue A. Some junkies dealing in a doorway of an abandoned, burned-out building checked her out. Recognizing her as from the neighborhood, the junkies went back to business.

She thought specifically of Gary, who had made a pass at her the day before. Gary was a tall, redheaded actor. He was handsome, a second-degree black belt, a funny guy—joked a lot. Used to have a Puerto Rican girlfriend, hot stuff. Carol didn't know what had happened to the girlfriend. Gary was a friend of Dan's. Now, Dan was a sexy guy. But everybody knew he was getting married. The guys gave him hell about it in the locker room. No, it would take too much work to get Dan horny. But Gary—now there's an idea, I never thought of making Sensei jealous.

In Greenwhich Village, Khan contemplated Washington Square Park. It was a beautiful, warm May day. The park could use more trees, he thought. Gazing at the neoclassic town houses bordering on the north, which had survived the demolitions craze at the end of the nineteenth century, his eyes settled for a moment on the statue of Garibaldi, hero of the Italian struggle for independence, who had visited New York in 1850. He thought of the N.Y.U. student story that the statue turned his head when a virtuous girl passed by, although no one has ever claimed to have seen it do so, the excuse being perhaps the statue looks in the wrong direction.

Khan knew everything about this park. Researching Greenhich Village was a hobby he pursued to take his mind from the present. Here Henry James had lived and wrote the novel *Washington Square* and long, long before that, it had been a potter's field. I wonder how many New Yorkers know this park sits on top of a cemetery, he mused.

He sat on the back of a park bench, his feet on the seat, near some chess players. These old men were here all day, every day. Khan watched hippie college kids from nearby N.Y.U. play their guitars, and roller skaters as they skated backward and executed fancy moves. Drug dealers meandered here and there, taking advantage of the good weather, offering loose joints and assorted hard drugs. The park was small enough that from his vantage point, Khan could take it all in.

Welcoming sunshine settled warmly on him, calming, softening, making things bearable. He thought of the dojo, with a screaming, pleading junkie tied to a pole. Khan had been with the junkie three days and nights, detoxifying him. How many times had he done this? Didn't even know anymore, lost count. Twelve, fifteen? Most of them went back to dope. A few stayed clean. This one was a vet.

He thought about Grey. Peace. The quiet bedroom with the blue satin sheets. He supposed she put them on the bed for him. When she was asleep, he wandered her house, looked into the linen closet. All the other sheets were flower-covered.

Her library! The ridiculous books and magazines she read. He laughed out loud, causing one of the chess-playing old men to stare accusingly for breaking his concentration. The old man stared pointedly at the big Eurasian, but decided to say nothing, returning to his chess board. Khan returned to amusing thoughts of Grey, how she had actually told him with that serious look on her face, meaning every word, that she intended to "educate herself to life through literature."

He tried to think of something wrong about her, but couldn't. He tried to think of anything about her he didn't like, but couldn't. He probed further. Well, maybe her naivete. But then, that made her different.

Khan saw one of the dojo kids, Peter. Peter didn't see Khan. A retarded kid barely pedaled by on a blue Schwinn. Peter blocked the kid's way. "Gimme your bike," Peter threatened. The retarded kid got off his bicycle and stood crying as Khan's student pedaled off on it.

I'll handle it in the dojo next week, Khan thought. They all took so much taking care of. He'd been taking care of them for years. Enough? Would there ever be enough time to pay the karma he had earned under the Agent Orange sky? Karma he charged himself with for his "wet work" in Vietnam?

He thought again of the waiting junkie and how he had gotten him: Khan was at a buddy's karate school in Newark, New Jersey. A pit of a city. He brought a pair of husky-shepherds for his friend, whose downtown dojo was constantly broken into. The two men were spending the night in the street-floor school, working out and getting the guard dogs used to new surroundings.

At 3 A.M., the dogs positioned themselves by the back door, leading to an alley, barking furiously. The karate instructors opened the door, finding two men both puking their guts from bad dope. The guys were vets who explained they began their habits in Nam. Khan let them in to sleep for a few hours. One of the vets told Kahn how much he wanted to kick heroin. Khan gave him his card. "If you're serious, come see me." The vet showed up two months later, flying like a kite—all shot up, swearing he wanted to kick.

"You're high now, man. It's not gonna be like this when the shit wears off," Khan said. "It's gonna be cold turkey."

The junkie begged. He got what he begged for. Khan tied him to a pole upstairs in the heavy bag room. The walls were padded with acrobatic mats, as was the floor. The guy could scream all night in there. Khan made him work out until he passed out. When he woke up, Khan made him work out again. He wouldn't give him candy bars, either, like the junkie begged for, just steaming mugs of Chinese herbs. The junkie sweated stink.

He couldn't get away from Nam, Khan thought. No matter how hard he tried, it followed, reaching inside to meet the silent scream he carried deep in his gut.

"Hey, Khan, wanna sit in?" The big Eurasian was a known figure in the Village, East or West. Friends of his in a conga band were getting ready to jam. Khan enjoyed the drums. Sitting in, he lost himself in the pok-ta-pok-a he beat out. A crowd gathered around.

He thought about Grey again as he played, standing at the tall conga drum in the spring sun. How she lit all up when she saw him. Grey naked, sleeping. How her pubic hairs curled. He felt himself grow hard.

He thought about how incredibly rich she was. He thought of being hung from a tree in Nam, naked in a cage so small he could only crouch on bamboo poles with wide separations between them—the Cong poking at his bare balls from underneath with sharpened sticks. His hard-on went away.

He thought about the hundred thousand he had in the bank. All the money over the years from Uncle Sam. *Mucho* hazardous-duty pay. He had never spent anything all those years. They gave him clothes. They fed him. He was imprisoned. He was hospitalized. They gave him mustering out pay. After eleven years he was "too specialized." Twenty-five thousand, cash. Bye, it was nice knowing you, soldier. Captain. Thanks a lot. Uncle Sam really enjoyed having you.

He needed to let off steam, he thought, leaving the conga band. Steam. Something for his black belts that night. He headed east, back to the junkie.

Black belt class. Anything was liable to happen. That's why it was exciting, Carol thought as she dressed. Everyone in the locker room felt the same way. It was quiet. The bullshitting came after. Now they wondered what Sensei had in store.

As Carol bowed onto the floor, she took in the sake bottle heating on top of the steam pipe. The last time Sensei had had sake for black belt class, they had all gotten drunk, then had a "breaking party," which in dojo language meant smashing pine boards until 3 A.M. This class ended when Sensei felt like calling it quits.

Khan's voice rang out, "*Zen mukso, sazi.*"

Twenty-five black belts dropped to a kneeling meditation position, their eyes closed. Khan spoke the virtues, and the black belts repeated each line after him.

"The Martial Arts are my secret; I bear no arms.
May God help me if I ever have to use my art.
Love is our law
Truth is our manifestation
Conscience is our guide
Peace is our shelter
Nature is our companion
Beauty and perfection is our life."

Now Khan's voice boomed and the black belts raised their volume in answer, filling the dojo with their thunderous unison.

"I shall find my strength as a karateka

I shall always be aware
I shall be quick to seize opportunity
Nothing is impossible!"

From their kneeling posture, the black belts bowed to Khan, touching their foreheads to the floor. "Kilska", Khan ordered. As one they leapt to their feet and stood at rigid attention: every hand in a fist, every toe on the same line.

After an hour-and-a-half warm-up they ran freely with sweat and their gis were soaked. He formed them into a line again. "You guys have to function stoned. What if you're out partying and get attacked, have a hassle?" With that justification, he fed them hot sake.

Filing by Khan, Carol tossed the small cup of hot rice wine down, then returned to the back of the line. She passed Khan four times and was totally wasted by the time he turned the pipes on. The black belts watched with amazement as the dojo filled with white-gray steam. Only the area near Khan's desk, where they lined up, stayed relatively clear.

"Start the sparring," Khan yelled, and pushed them, one by one, into the fog. After a few black belts were swallowed by billows of steam, sounds of fighting were heard. "Build your awareness," Khan yelled. He sent Carol in.

Someone hit her the minute she entered the surrealistic atmosphere. "Fuck!" She took the blow on her shoulder. Quickly, instinctively, she began whirling her arms non-stop, creating blocking circles fending off kicks and punches coming at her. Feeling a body underfoot, she dropped to the floor, flat on her stomach, finding herself in an absolutely clear space about six inches high, where there was no steam. Marcos lay there, watching everyone's bare feet, staying out of the way, thinking he was so clever.

"You better not let Sensei catch you," Carol whispered and jumped back to her feet to face the thrilling unknown.

After two hours in and out of the steam, Carol was too exhausted to make much of Gary in the locker room, where it was proudly agreed by all the black belts their Sensei was crazier than ever, and the class they just survived would become legend. Carol did make sure, though, to walk from the locker room next to Gary, hooking her arm through his and looking into his eyes as they passed Sensei's desk and exited the dojo.

Marcos was still in gi, pumping out hundreds of push-ups Sensei had ordered as punishment. Khan knew about the clear space under the steam—that's where *he* had evaluated the action from. You couldn't fool Sensei, he didn't miss a trick.

Khan was jealous. He silently put a name to the emotion as he caressed the hard steel of his favorite gun. This was the first time he had ever recognized feeling the sentiment and it bothered him. He prepared to shoot.

It had begun the day before when Grey had called him:

"Khan, please come to New Jersey, please, to the horse show tomorrow. You've never seen Darkchild. It'll be a lovely day, we can take a picnic lunch."

"I have too much to do."

She gave him the address. "In case you change your mind," she said, disappointment in her voice.

After hanging up, he thought about how she squeezed fresh orange juice for him in the morning when he stayed there. The silly tray with a flower bud in a tiny silver vase. Croissants and exotic preserves, guava and mango, the newspaper. Breakfast in bed, like he was a stockbroker or something. He reflected on how he had made her dress up the last time they had been together.

He had dumped her lingerie drawer onto the carpet and pawed through gossamer things until he found a white lacy garter belt. "Don't you have any black?" He had her put it on with white stockings and white satin four-inch heels—and nothing else. There were candles burning. In their flickering light he made her pose for him, raising her arms over her head so that her full breasts were pulled high, enjoying her embarrassment as she postured. Even in the candlelight he could see her blush. He guided her to the foot of the bed. "Lean over." He thought about how her ass looked when he took her from behind over the edge of the bed with the lace garter belt on. He made arrangements to go to the horse show without telling her.

It was another warm, sunny day, the New Jersey countryside greenly lush from the sky. The helicopter, owned by a friend, a former Green Beret captain who ran a charter company, dropped Khan at the edge of the parking lot. Waving good-bye to his buddy as the chopper lifted off, he headed toward the main gate. You could tell it was a society affair by the cars. Rolls and Bentleys, Porches, Mercedes, a profusion of horse vans. A tweedy-looking family unloading a big wicker picnic basket from the back of a brand-new station wagon looked with curiosity at the exotic man who came by helicopter.

Paying his way in, Khan found a seat high on a bleacher, losing himself in the Sunday afternoon audience. The show ring was large, set up now for open jumping competition. Khan assessed the crowd—rich. The competitors —fancy riding clothes, beautiful horses. Then he saw her in a warm-up ring on a giant black stallion. So that was Darkchild. Khan was impressed. The horse reared—highstrung—but Grey controlled him. Khan watched her lean over the saddle and talk to the horse, reaching her hand forward and touching him just below his ear. The big animal quieted down. Khan felt the beginning of pride for her.

He checked his program. She was the fifth competitor. He found himself tense, waiting for her to have her try. The jumps were very high. Number three took a spill. The crowd went "ahhh."

When it was Grey's turn, it didn't look good. Darkchild was obviously nervous. But she kept whispering in his ear, leaning over the saddle, sticking her magnificent ass up in the air, making Khan think about the white garter belt.

She prodded the big horse forward and sailed cleanly over every jump. Beautiful! Khan was thrilled, experiencing as much exaltation as when he had earned his first trophy. It surprised him.

He felt eyes on him and turned to his side. A cool, elegant blond in a blue silk dress, one rope of pearls. "Would you like a drink?" She offered him a flask. He swigged the expensive brandy, enjoying the warmth as it went down, glanced at the wedding ring on the blond's finger as he handed back the beaten silver flask. "Thank you."

"Chinese and British, from Hong Kong," the blond said in cultured tones to the fascinating man dressed in soft, burnished leather sitting next to her.

"Close," Khan said, turning back to admire Grey, who was the hit of the show even though Darkchild placed second.

The first-place winner, a magnificent strawberry roan who had jumped his heart out, took a definite backseat to the famous, beautiful heiress. Cameras were everywhere. The photographers surrounded Grey and Darkchild, wearing the second-place ribbon on his bridle. The strawberry roan, wearing a multicolored winner's garland of flowers about his neck, was almost ignored. T and A gets it every time, Khan thought.

As he watched, he was amazed at how Grey handled the press and the crush of people pushing to meet her. He saw Llana and Dan in matching cable-knit sweaters, touching each other, the way they always did when they were together. An older couple he surmised to be Grey's parents. The woman was fiftyish, pretty, a little plump. A brown-haired Grace Kelly type. The man, slim, white-haired, tall, proud. Khan saw Grey's cheekbones on the face and knew it was her father.

Just then a tall, dark, unusually handsome man in a light khaki suit approached Grey. She froze. So did her parents. Even from the bleacher, Khan could see the tension in Grey's body, confusion on her face. The man took her hand and, avoiding the bandage, kissed it.

Khan felt the hairs on the back of his neck rise. He saw Dan and Llana move closer to Grey as though defending her. The well-dressed man continued talking to Grey. Smooth-talking, Khan knew by the body language. The man leaned close to her. Photographers surrounded them. Khan had seen enough. Leaving the bleachers, he made his way back to the edge of the parking lot. He was only there a few minutes before the helicopter returned over the horizon to take him back to New York.

Now, later that night, Khan emptied the Walther PPK into the target. Perfect grouping. He stared down the tunnel-like basement shooting range at the target—the silhouette of a man. He reloaded the gun. *I wonder if they're fucking right now?* He chastised himself for the thought.

He had important things to do in his life. A master to find. A way to follow. No broad was going to interfere with his life. Especially some jet-set, horsey-set . . . No. She wasn't like that. She was special. He wondered if she *was* with the man at the show. They looked like they belonged together.

"Sensei, can I try your gun?" Carol said.

They were underneath an almost impossible-to-find Bowery dojo of a karate master. The shooting range was secret. It was doubtful if any gun ever fired there was registered.

"Sure." He handed over the Walther to Carol and watched as she followed his example. "Good group," he said, noticing how pleased she was at his rare compliment.

"Son of Sam is using a .44-caliber Charter Arms Bulldog," she said to draw him into conversation, for everyone was talking about the murderer on the loose.

He glanced at his watch. It was ten. Grey should be home by now, enough time to put the horse away. She had a 6 A.M. class. She should be home.

"Keep shooting," he said to the six black belts he had brought with him and went upstairs.

On the first floor, the dojo looked like a school gym except for the circle of heavy bags. He asked the Master's permission to use the phone. Khan had a lot of respect for this master who had brought karate to America from Japan. The only Caucasian to have received rank from Yamaguchi himself, he was a hard man. The heavy bags were filled with rocks. It was a school legendary for its brutality and classic adherence to Japanese GoJu style. Khan had aligned himself with the Master when he had come to New York. He had had to do that. Otherwise he would have been a *ronin*, an outlaw, a black belt with no allegiance.

He dialed Grey. The phone rang ten times. He put the receiver down, bowed to the master, and went downstairs, back to the underground shooting range and his students.

What the hell was he doing even wondering if she was with another man? What did he care? He took Carol home with him to prove it.

For Grey, Darkchild's wonderful showing was overshadowed by Andre Bugueot's appearance and left hollow by Khan's absence.

"You were *magnifique*," Andre said, his magnetism no less than she remembered. She was caught off guard, confused and shocked by his materialization. Family and friends hustled her off, but not before he begged to be allowed to call. She refused. What a day!

Between silk-flowered sheets at ten thirty, bone weary, full of anticlimatic feelings, last thoughts hit Grey. Khan, why don't you call? Oh God! Carol in the morning. She practiced counting in Japanese. *Ich, ni, san, chi, go, ryuku . . .*

12

A sixth sense woke the Nightwalker. In two moves she reached her listening device. Anton's phone was ringing! Her computerized watch said 3 A.M.

"Don't send me an ugly one," Anton's sleepy voice rasped. "And make it quick."

The Nightwalker surmised an escort service had located flesh to Anton's order and was sending it over. *He doesn't want an ugly one.* She wondered if he even remembered the unsightly spy he had planted among innocent girls preparing to become women in the Time of the New Ones . . .

Taiwan, 1984

"I do not want to be a disciple," Kua broke the silence after Mother's speech. Guilty because her ovarian tumor was healed, yet unable to contain her trepidation, Kua's scared young eyes sought Lo Ling's. "What will happen to me? I know the secret of Mother!"

"You will learn medicine, Mother will wipe secret memories away. You will marry traditionally and no harm will come to you," Lo Ling gently said. Then looking at the twenty new ones, the youngest disciple spoke: "It is your choice to accept the trials." A challenging gleam lit Lo Ling's soft eyes. *Llana, like Llana,* Grey flashed in a millisecond of cognizance.

Lo Ling voiced the challenge: "Those wishing to pursue the Way, come forward." Ten did, most from Wi's village with its tradition of stalwart females. Wi was among them.

Later, Wi lay on her pallet watching Lo Ling braid the foreigner's bright hair and coo to her in singsong. The foreigner paid no attention and never stopped crying.

Wi had attempted speaking to the wasted Westerner, but received only blank, tear-filled stares. Wi drifted to sleep, thankful morning would bring the trials, heralding an end to this madness!

Next morning, new ones realized the awful seriousness of the trials. The instant they tried mounting trees, making the same attempts they had for the last week, disciples, who had before encouraged new ones, now ran at them screaming and swinging bamboo sticks. With no anger on their parts, disciples methodically beat the new ones, leaving only one possible escape for the terrified new ones—into the trees.

As the violent scene unfolded, Mother watched. Y Shin Sha, the Nightwalker, stood near Mother and weeping Grey. He looked often at Grey, as though wondering if the trial penetrated her tears.

Some new ones were bleeding. All of them, including fat Wi, finally gained the giant trees, demonstrating the power provided by that incredible human resource, adrenaline, even to the weakest. But for new ones thinking they were safe, there was another lesson. Within the trees were more disciples with sticks. It was terrible. Before it was over, new ones lay unconscious and hurt at the foot of the trees.

"Please, I'm in pain, please," Grey said, begging for medicine. Lo Ling packed herbs on two places where Grey's skull was cracked like an eggshell. Lo Ling was pleased with how it had healed and the herbs she used also had prevented thick scars from forming. She knew her patient's head was painful still, as did Mother, who gave permission for a pipe.

Lo Ling brought opium. The Nightwalker watched. The youngest disciple administered the pipe, then held Grey as the trials continued.

Grey felt wonderful! In a blazing garden, flowers bloomed a million shades of red. Her olfactory cells exploded with the attar of roses . . . Mother was a winged angel. A penis army chased Grey, one eyes' spitting white death. *Khan is dead.* Grey attempted clearing her aching head. "Help me, Mother." She opened her eyes for a second, saw a shadow that said, "Of course, my child, let me take your pain." Then Mother's tingling, loving warmth, relief. "God bless you, Mother," she said within her dreams. She sniffed the pipe: ambrosial fragrance of new mown grass. Y Shin Sha turned alien. "I'm dying now," a tiny fetus said. Grey began screaming and screamed until Mother laid her hands on her.

At dusk, new ones, beaten bloody, blue pajamas torn and covered with dirt, knelt before Mother and thanked her for their trial. Disciples stood sternly behind, armed with bamboo sticks.

"Enjoy the trial, my children. *It is yours for the week.*" Mother communed.

None of the new ones was more horrified than Wi.

The next morning, deep in the woods, Lo Ling schooled girls who had not chosen the trials. Scurrying up a thirty-foot mangosteen tree, she picked its ripe purple fruit and twigs, then leapt deftly to the ground. "This dried rind decoction alleviates diarrhea," the exquisite youngest disciple lectured. She showed twigs. "One end should be chewed until frayed, then used to clean the teeth."

Grey sat against a tree. The Nightwalker crouched motionlessly by her side, blending perfectly in camouflage garb with the surrounding foliage.

Lo Ling tried including Grey and spoke directly to her. "These women will go among the people, curing, caring for others." Thinking Grey did not understand, she tried to mime her words.

Grey's tears had finally ceased, but she showed no interest, staring as though Lo Ling was not there. Lo Ling stroked Grey's cheek, looking with sorrow at the Nightwalker, who had suddenly disappeared and just as suddenly returned with an adorable infant monkey which he held toward Grey and smiled. Lo Ling felt a pang. Y Shin Sha had never smiled at her.

Grey turned her head away. The Nightwalker held the monkey, rocking back and forth on booted heels, a mime in despair. Lo Ling would not accept Grey's behavior and forced her to stand.

The third morning of the trial, Mother gazed at Lo Ling, who was compelling Grey to walk in the shade of a forty-foot capulin tree with drooping branches and peculiarly odored soft leaves, used for teas. The youngest disciple spoke continually, attempting to spark her patient. "And see"—Lo Ling waved a hand at the great trees where new ones suffered trials—"some new ones already escape the sticks, learning to survive like jungle animals in precarious situations." She walked faster, forcing Grey to keep pace. "New ones learn there is always hope, inevitably a way to overcome adversity. As you will."

Confirming that she understood the spoken dialect, Grey spoke for the first time in a dead voice. "There is no hope."

Joyfully surprised, Lo Ling kissed Grey. The Nightwalker's eyes lit. Mother, who missed no interplay, was so delighted her shining brightened.

The next morning, before any stirred and night still ruled the sky, Grey rose shakily from her pallet and moved, zombie-like, from the hut and into the woods. Walking until exhausted, she sank to the ground, her back against a tree, and stared into the fading night.

Wi also was awake, for this the morning she was to meet Anton! Exhausted and badly bruised, she had not slept a wink, dreading what she must report. She looked at Lo Ling's pallet, where her keeper slept. Wi had seen the foreigner depart and knew she should stop her or awaken Lo Ling. She almost did, but then she realized the foreigner's wandering off was a stroke of luck, providing the excuse Wi needed for leaving herself. When questioned later about her absence, she would say she left seeking the foreigner. Wi quietly left the hut.

Lo Ling opened one eye as Wi exited. Realizing Grey was also gone, she ran to the door, and in the fading moonlight she saw Wi run across the clearing. Lo Ling followed.

Mother lay on the floor of her hut, body racked in spasms, her shining on and off. The fit abated. Her shining steadied, but was very faint. She could not rise. The Nightwalker came to her aid, helping her to stand. For a moment the two touched foreheads. Mother attempted to regain her composure as the Nightwalker, distraught with grief, held her.

Wi made her way clumsily through the woods. On the one hand, she burned for the commander, picturing his chiseled face, magnificent physique, thinking of his absolute power. On the other hand, she was terrified of his reaction to her information. In her agitation, although she passed by her, Wi failed to notice Grey.

Lo Ling saw Grey against the tree, but continued after Wi, sensing the fat girl was up to no good. A short distance farther, Lo Ling was horrified to witness Wi meet Anton, accompanied by a cadre of brown-uniformed soldiers. Although she had never seen the infamous commander before, there was no doubt as to whom she now beheld. Her blue cotton clothing blending with the not-yet dawn, the youngest disciple crept so close, she heard the dreaded commander speaking.

"A thing man, a thing woman, with what?" the huge black said with scornful disbelief to Wi.

Wi made circular gestures about her head, vainly attempting to recreate a shining aura. Wi babbled about magic, teaching of rebellion, a sick foreign woman, the thing Chinese man wore a uniform, could leap into trees, be gone in the blink of an eye . . .

"Shut up! Stupid crazy ugly bitch," the Commander barked. Wi shrank. "Return before you are found missing. Say nothing of my presence."

Anton watched Wi scurry away, believing nothing of the ugly one's hocus-pocus fantasies, but aroused by her recount of a sick foreigner and a uniformed Chinese man. A guerrilla fighter? T.I.M.? He would wait a bit, then follow his informant's trail to this camp. Mikel's anticipation heightened. He tapped his boot steadily with his black leather riding crop, impatient to get to the fun.

Lo Ling was in a panic. I must warn Mother! She prayed.

As though her prayers were heard, a loud rustling and snapping of brush announced the arrival of a messenger on horseback who handed an envelope to the Commander.

"Motherfucking bad timing," Anton mouthed, reading its contents. He mounted his horse. Lo Ling slipped away.

Wi, quaking with terror, no longer deluding herself she was loved or wanted, made her way to face another day of trials. She was startled by Lo Ling in her path.

"You have betrayed us!" Lo Ling accused, tossing her head so her sheet of hair swung to her back.

Wi's fear and venom converged and exploded. Picking up a rock, she ran at the beautiful teenager blocking her path.

Easily avoiding Wi's wildly swinging arm with a singularly deft movement, Lo Ling twisted Wi by the wrist into a painful lock. Wi dropped the rock. If she moved now, she would break her own arm. Wi screamed.

Grey heard the screaming and stood. From her vantage point on a rise, she saw all that took place as the sky lightened.

Anton, departing the area for his encampment, also heard the screams and galloped toward them.

Lo Ling's forearm snaked across screaming Wi's throat, clasping one hand over one wrist. The bone in Lo Ling's forearm became a clamping, solid bar. Wi's windpipe was crushed. It was over in two seconds.

Mikel Anton burst on Lo Ling, Wi's body at her feet. Jumping from his horse, he raced for the teenager. Lo Ling spat full in his face, kicked his knee, and, hands outstretched, jumped for his throat. She was grabbed by soldiers.

As Lo Ling's spittle ran down his face, Anton drew a stiletto. He raised the knife high. Grey's eyes widened. The glint of deadly steel, Anton's face. Khan's death came rushing back to her. Anton plunged the knife repeatedly into Lo Ling's chest. Then sweet Lo Ling lay, her blue jacket saturated with blood, next to Wi. Without a second glance at the two bodies, Anton mounted and galloped off, followed by his men.

There was a knock at the door in Anton's condo. He answered it. Evidently the prostitute was not too ugly. The Nightwalker heard him invite her in. It was almost 4 A.M., and she prepared to wait out yet another of his sick encounters.

Manhattan, 1977

Carol was ecstatic. Her strategy had worked, she reasoned. Jealous of her attentions to Gary, Khan proved it by taking her back to his bed. And to further secure her regained status as paramour, Carol also attacked from the flank—with a newspaper.

On Monday morning in the subway station, she picked up a discarded New York *Post*. There, on page six, was a photo of the rich bitch staring into the incredibly handsome face of Viscount Andre Bugueot. "Is it on again?"

the caption asked. Underneath the half-page picture, two columns of gossip rehashed the couple's disastrous engagement along with detailed backgrounds on both of them.

Carol consumed the words with hopeful hunger. *She's got a boyfriend*: rich, a real hunk, with a fucking title! She won't want Khan. Maybe now she won't even come to the dojo. Suddenly the dingy subway was a wonderful place. Carol ripped the page from the newspaper. Later that evening, just before class, she placed it on Khan's desk.

"Grey," Llana's voice rang with excitement, "I'm at the Pierre Matisse Gallery. Jacqueline Onassis just purchased one of Dan's paintings. She saw the canvas yesterday and came back to get it today. God, Grey, Dan's going to her apartment to supervise the hanging—and she's actually coming to the loft to see more of his work."

"Oh, Llana, you must be in heaven. What was she wearing?"

"First day, all white—jeans, cotton shirt, and tennis sneakers. Today, a red Chanel suit."

Grey, herself clad only in a gossamer Dior bra and bikini panties, held the phone with one hand. With the other she pushed her gi and white obi into a Fendi carryall. In an hour-and-a-half she was to begin her first dojo class. "Llana, I want to hear all about it, but I have to run now—"

Llana began sobbing.

"Llana, what's the matter?"

"Grey, I have to talk to you. Right now! Can I come over? I'm just on 57th street."

"Of course. Hurry."

Grey anxiously awaited Llana's arrival. What could possibly be wrong? Crying was out of character. Pre-wedding jitters?

Picking up a gilt envelope containing Llana's wedding present, Grey tied it with a gold ribbon and made a floppy bow. I'll give this to her now, she thought, to cheer her up.

Grey had wracked her brain conceiving Dan and Llana's present. Since Grey only had to order a luxury to have it, deciding on what was her only problem. The young heiress had considered everything from matching mink coats to a silver service once owned by King Ferdinand of Spain. She inspected an ancient Japanese block print, a Fabergé rock-crystal vase holding flowers made of cabachon rubies. Nothing was right. She had to thrill Llana; the offering must be perfection itself.

The wedding gift remained frustrating until a board meeting at Fowler Enterprises requiring Grey. Wearing a pinstripe Adolfo suit, heading the long table in the boardroom, Grey listened to boring financial reports. Then an extensive list of new acquisitions was read, and among them was a travel agency. That's when she got the idea.

Dan and Llana had remained indecisive about where to honeymoon. They had narrowed their choice to two places neither of them had been, Jamaica and Mexico, but couldn't decide which, and the wedding was only three weeks off.

Grey arranged a fairy-tale honeymoon—Jamaica *and* Mexico. First-class flights, chauffeured limos, yachts with crews, and light planes, at the newlyweds' beck and call. Dan and Llana were booked into royally appointed bridal suites stocked daily with champagne, fruit, cheeses, caviar, and flowers. They were to be serenaded by marimba bands in Mexico and reggae in Jamaica.

Designing the spectacular honeymoon helped take her mind from Khan's unexplainable behavior. She pretended it was her own honeymoon she was planning. I can go on a trip like that anytime, she mused, fussing with the packet's bow. But by myself? What fun would that be?

Her thoughts turned to Darkchild's trainer and their conversation of the week before. "Darkchild needs a rest, Ms. Coltrane, and so do you. Overtraining is no good," Jack Brian said, pulling thoughtfully at his chin. "This is a city. Some Kentucky bluegrass would do that horse just fine. Give me the word and I'll arrange it. Darkchild should graze for the summer. That is," Brian continued, "if you really want to enter Olympic trials with him next year."

What about me? Would Kentucky bluegrass fix me? Why was Khan being such a mystery? He was so taciturn now, as though she had done something to offend him. She could not imagine what.

She had not seen him, except in her dreams, for almost two weeks, during which she suffered for want of him. Then he called suddenly out of the blue. "Want to see *Star Wars*?"

He sounded—how? Remote? Impersonal? It's *you* I want to see. "Yes, I do. I'd love to," she said.

The movie was fabulous, but far overshadowed by his physical presence, and she only anticipated his hands on her body.

The concept of the "Force" in *Star Wars* greatly appealed to him. It made for a long dialogue between them after the movie, over delicious, tangy curries and wine in a dimly lit Indian restaurant with colorful wall hangings. A turbanned man sat cross-legged on a platform in front of a golden Buddha, strumming a sitar.

You are the "Force," Grey reflected, tasting fiery mango chutney. Searching his eyes, she attempted to see into his mind, looking for the part of him relating to her.

He came back to her apartment and ravished her. With his infinite sexual skills, he brought her to orgasms so stabbing she became frightened she would die. She woke during the night, reached for him, and found herself alone.

The next morning after Carol's class, Grey went searching for a wonderful present for him. He often wore leather, suiting his confident stance. She found an exotic leather parka fashioned by Alaskan Kute Eskimos. The salesman in Bergdorf said it was likely "chewed soft," as though to justify its five-thousand-dollar price tag. The white, hooded parka was embroidered with buff leather, beaded with hand-carved horn, and lined and trimmed in wolf fur. That's Khan, she thought, examining the wildly beautiful thing, visualizing him with his dogs in the snow. Instinctively she knew his size.

That had been eight days ago. The parka was in her closet now. She didn't know how to give it to him—or when. How not to offend him. A thank you for classes with Carol? Revenge was more fitting. Blessedly, those tortuous sessions had reached their finale last Friday. No "well done" from Carol—not even a civil good-bye, just an exit.

I'll show the parka to Llana, ask her how to give it to him. *Where is she?* Maybe she and Dan had quarreled.

Maybe she's pregnant. God, I wish she'd hurry. I can't be late. Llana *never* cries. I'm going to see Khan!

A sense of urgency overtook her. She glanced at the mess on the pastel-flowered silk eiderdown quilt on her bed. Three books lay open at her place in each. *The Karate Dojo* by Peter Urban was almost finished. Picking up the small red book, she quickly scanned "Ceremonies Upon Entering a Dojo" one last time. I *am* prepared for tonight. She gathered up travel folders, bright with tropical colors, that would give away her surprise and hurriedly pushed them into the drawer of an ormolu nighttable. In the process she shook a Chinese rose-filled vase on its surface. Pink petals fell from swollen blossoms, scattering onto the rug.

She picked up a note from the quilt and read it again: "Grey, my nomadic life no longer has meaning. I cannot forget you. I am obsessed. I must see you. I beg, I beseech. The American Ballet Theatre festival celebrating Michel Fokine is presenting *Les Sylphides* and *Le Spectre de la Rose*. Please, please accompany me. Andre."

She ran her finger over his engraved gold and red crest on thick cream notepaper, then tossed his plea into a Baccarat crystal wastebacket. An earlier note, a few days before, giving his address as the Carlyle, had invited her to Liv Ullmann's Broadway performance "Anna Christie" and to meet the actress after the show.

She thought about Andre as she continued picking up clutter, then fallen rose petals. Each time she moved, her muscles, which had undergone a radical change during three months of training, flashed in definition. Andre certainly knows how to tempt. And he does know my tastes. But I've met a real man. One more exciting than any hero of all the fairy tales and novels I've ever read. Exotic, fearless, handsome beyond belief, intelligent, skilled at war and love. With thoughts of Khan, her nipples, suddenly hard, pushed at her wisp-of-silk bra. The doorbell rang.

Llana wore a white, ruffle-necked Yves St. Laurent blouse, an easy linen skirt in a cream and white weave, and Chanel shoes, cream slingbacks with black toes. Her shiny black hair was starkly pulled into a chignon, secured by an ivory pin. Chunky, curved gold earrings lined with small emeralds, a present from Dan, flashed at her ears.

Grey whistled. "Llana, you look luscious—if it weren't for your poor eyes." Llana's red-streaked eyes clearly declared her state of agitation. "Come on, sweetheart, tell me what's wrong," she said, taking Llana by the hand to the bedroom. They sat on the bed. Llana kicked off her shoes and sighed. Grey put her arm around her shoulders. "Tell me."

Llana began crying again. "Dan wants an open marriage," she sobbed, feeling better as soon as the words were out. Speaking quickly as if catharsis would change the situation, she continued. "We were having this talk after we sold the abstract to Mrs. Onassis about sophisticated marriages, like she has. It's all been written in the columns. She and her husband signed an agreement before they wed as to when they would spend time together and stuff like that. We got onto the subject of how, if people really love each other, they accept whatever the other wants. Somehow the conversation got around to fidelity and extramarital affairs. Dan said he thought an occasional affair could keep a marriage alive!

"For example, he told me about this married couple he knows who have two children and love each other madly, but have affairs with others. They're writers. Very enlightened, he said. They tell each other about the affairs. Details!" Llana's voice went from plaintive to derisive. "I guess they get off on each other's sexual high jinks."

Grey, still clad only in underwear, worried about the fleeting time, yet was more worried about Llana. She handed her a tissue from the crystal box on the nighttable. Wiping her eyes, Llana began talking again while abstractly focusing on Grey's clearly defined abdominal muscles above her tiny panties.

"Then I asked him, more to be a smart-ass than really considering what I was saying. You know, Grey, just to tease. We were drinking champagne, celebrating . . . I asked Dan, 'Would you like to have an open marriage?' expecting him to tell me I was the only woman he ever wanted." Llana's voice became an absolute wail. "Grey, he said yes! His eyes lit up when he said it, too. He doesn't really love me, not really."

"Wait a minute," Grey said, "you're madly in love with each other. How can you say that?" She picked up Llana's hand, touching the fiery four-karat marquis diamond there. "Your lives are twined together so beautifully before you're even married. Dan's career has become yours. And you're going to be successful at all of it, including your marriage. I think you're taking a conversation too seriously. How much champagne did you have? Is Dan seeing other women?"

"One bottle. None I know of."

"If he were, what would you do?"

Llana's whole demeanor changed. The tears stopped. She sat straight on the bed, dark eyes snapping fire. "I'd kill him. I'd kill her."

Grey, reminded of who Llana's father was, had a vision of little Llana blasting away with a giant shotgun at Dan and some faceless woman. Grey lost the picture as Llana's tears began again. "I'd die. I don't know what I'd do."

"Well, it's gonna be all right. Dan was just kidding, I'm sure," Grey said, standing, forced by the time factor to cross the room and open one of many mirrored closets. An interior light illuminated rows of jeans, spaced well apart, draped over flower-printed chintz hangers. The same whimsical print lined the closet walls.

Llana broke in. "I know. I know it sounds like a tease. But I'm scared. Really, Grey. We talk about things like that when we make love. About being with other people, what we'd do. Well, mostly Dan talks. It's been stimulating —freaky. But nothing ever happened. But, my God, this afternoon when we were talking, he said, 'Wouldn't you like it if I brought home a handsome man as a surprise and the two of us fucked you?'" Llana's crying escalated. "What kind of marriage would that be?"

"An exciting one, by the sounds of it," Grey quipped, trying to cheer Llana up.

Llana's dark eyes were accusing. "Grey, Dan's the only one I've ever had sex with. He's man enough for me for the rest of my life."

Pulling washed-out Levis from their flowered hanger, Grey said, "I know, sweetheart. I really do. Khan's man enough for me, too. I feel like sitting down and crying with you. I don't understand Khan. I have everything" —she waved her hand at her surroundings—"and I can't share it with someone I love. I don't even know how he feels about me and it's driving me crazy. Know what?

You're lucky. Dan loves you, wants to marry you, and that's forever. You'll work this out. Who knows, maybe open marriage is better than having a cheating husband. Honey, maybe he's joking to see how you'll react.''

Llana began sobbing again. Grey could not help but think, why now? I'm going to Khan. I'm going to the dojo class for the first time. Oh, Llana, why now? She went to Llana, hugging her.

Weeping in Grey's arms, Llana suffered a double dilemma. The truth was, she had only told part of what caused her anguish. The other thing that had driven Llana to tears concerned Grey, but Llana was afraid to tell! She had never withheld anything from Grey, and this was momentous. Guilt had propelled Llana to Grey's apartment as much as Dan's promiscuous statement—actually, more so.

Llana knew about Carol. She had listened, eyes wide with astonishment as Dan recounted Khan's renewed interest in Carol, which Carol proudly flaunted, he said, at every opportunity. Dan also told of Carol's flirtation with his friend Gary, the actor, and Gary's subsequent growing infatuation with Carol. "It's Peyton Place, dojo style," Dan laughed, not realizing how absolutely horrified Llana was at the gossipy tidbits. So, over the phone the past weeks, Llana had listened to Grey's laments of unrequited love, knowing the real reason for Khan's indifference. What a bastard he is, Llana thought as she sobbed. Not bad enough that Khan was fooling around with a woman he had continued sending to Grey's house every morning; Llana had found out Grey faced *real* danger in the dojo.

Miserably perplexed, Llana had finally told Dan of Grey's secret private classes with Carol and her upcoming joining of the dojo.

Dan was flabbergasted. "That's insane," he said, then told Llana scary and violent Carol stories. "Carol is violently jealous. She'll really hurt Grey. I've seen her beat up girls who just flirted with Khan.

"She's really mysterious, too, hard to read. Always got that red bag with her, acts like she's got the Hope diamond in there. But one thing is clear: Khan is the rising and setting of her sun. Lately she's upstairs in his apartment a lot of the time, cleaning like a German house-wife. The place sparkles."

Now, Llana watched Grey as she pulled on jeans, readying for what could be destruction. If I tell her about Khan and Carol, it will break her heart. But I have to stop her!

With no idea of Llana's inner turmoil, Grey offered more soothing words. "Dan's surely teasing. It's gonna be okay."

"Grey, don't go to the dojo tonight!"

Grey was shocked. Not see Khan? "Llana, honey, it'll be all right. We'll talk later, I promise." But, she thought, what if Khan wants me to stay with him after class? I haven't seen him in almost two weeks. He'll probably take me to dinner. Oh, Llana, why now?

"No, Grey, you don't understand. It's really rough down there. Dan's been telling me. I'm afraid for you."

"Hey, take it easy. I'm ready for whatever. Remember, I've been training with the dragon lady for three months. Look at me, I'm muscles all over," she said, flexing her arms, making her biceps flash. "I can do fifty push-ups on my knuckles, even if they do bleed." She slipped off the washed-out Levis and reached for another pair. "My old jeans are too tight around the thighs, from horse stances." Grey lifted her leg and pointed her toes, displaying the curving quadricep muscle of her upper thigh. "I'm a strong athlete, Llana. Don't worry. This is a challenge I'm looking forward to. Nothing could stop me," she said, tossing the gift-wrapped packet at Llana. "Here, darling, Happy Wedding. This will cheer you up—it will have to, 'cause I'm leaving now!"

Pulling a turquoise T-shirt on, she grabbed the Fendi bag and shook her auburn hair to order. "Just lock the door behind you when you leave. I love you. Talk to you later—promise," Grey said, and ran from the room.

It was fifteen minutes until class time when Grey entered the dojo. Dan, already on the mat stretching, saw her immediately. She bowed properly, then stood, obviously wondering where to go. Oh boy, Dan thought, watching the ravishing Ms. Coltrane as she looked toward Khan's desk, where a terrific commotion was taking place. Dan saw Grey's features arrange themselves in disbelief as she took in the scene unfolding there.

The noises were loud cries coming from a young boy in a gi, kneeling on the floor. On his stooped shoulders were two large cinder blocks, one atop the other, which he held in place with his hands. "Please, Sensei," the boy pleaded, "I didn't do it. I didn't take his bike."

Nearby, dressed in street clothes, watching in a mildly interested daze, was a retarded boy.

"When you're ready to confess, just let me know," Khan said matter-of-factly. "Until then, those blocks are part of your body."

"How cruel," Grey thought just as Khan saw her standing there. With a lurching heart she noted how light and shadow caught his extraordinary cheekbones. She smiled, saw by the caste of his eye she shouldn't have. Immediately she bowed. "Osss, Sensei."

"The underbelt dressing room is that way." He pointed and went back to some papers atop his desk.

Accompanied by background pleas of "Please, Sensei," from the boy holding cinder blocks, she followed the direction of Khan's finger. Canvas bag over her shoulder, she walked the wooden space bordering the tatami mats. Others passed her in gis, coming from the dressing room. There were already sixty students on the mat in various stages of warming up. Grey saw Carol, wearing a headband, doing a split. She saw Dan. Coming to a sign, "UNDERBELT DRESSING ROOM," she moved aside a curtain and entered.

To her consternation, the room offered no privacy. Instead it was completely open and filled with men and boys in various states of undress. With a sinking heart, she thought of her wispy underwear. She smiled, a weak attempt at friendliness. No one returned the gesture.

Crossing the room, she placed her bag against the wall with others, knelt next to it, and took out her gi. Still on her knees, back to the students, she pulled off her sweatshirt. The catcalls and whistles were instantaneous, even from the little boys. Whipping on her gi jacket, mortified, she rose to a standing position still facing the wall, hoping the canvas jacket covered her bikini-clad bottom. Slipping off her jeans, Grey jumped into her gi pants with all the speed she could muster. "Class ass," a fifteen-year-old said reverently as she walked from the dressing room, adjusting her obi.

Bowing, Grey stepped onto the tatami, surprised at how right the smoothly woven matting felt under her bare feet. *As though I belong.* Glancing at Carol to see if her instructor had any directions to give, she saw only a glassy hardness in Carol's eyes. Grey stretched, picking a white-belted man with glasses who looked like he'd been around awhile, and imitated him.

"Sensei, I did it," yelled the boy under the cinder blocks. No one on the mat appeared to pay any attention to the strange scene, yet no one missed the interplay.

"Come here," Khan said to the retarded boy, who still stood patiently by his desk. The boy obeyed. "What's your name?" Khan said, smiling at him.

"Frank," the boy said slowly but distinctly.

Standing, Khan draped his arm around Frank's shoulders. "Well, Frank, this is Peter. He's sorry he took your bike. He's going to return your bike." Khan faced Peter, now minus the cinder blocks, but still crying. "And he's going to teach you karate and be your best friend. Right, Peter?"

"Osss, Sensei," Peter said.

"After class you go home with Frank and tell his parents you're his new big brother, understand?"

Clarity dawned for Grey. Khan wasn't cruel, he was just and loving. *Khan, I love you so, please be proud of me.*

"Start the run," Khan commanded.

The mat came to life. One hundred and thirty students, all except the black belts, began to run in a huge circle around the edges of the mat while throwing vertical punches. Black belts holding bamboo shinais stood in the center of the underbelts, who ran faster and faster. "Close the spaces," black belts called whenever any distance occurred between students, meaning someone had slowed.

Grey ran the first five minutes easily. After all, jogging was her pleasure, stamina no problem, and she had thrown uncountable punches in the last three months. But as the running and punching continued, the pace escalated and the back in front of her moved away. "Keep the pace, close the space," she heard Carol yell. It was directed at her.

Grey ran faster, wondering how long this lasted even as the pace picked up again. Her arms became lead that punched. The only sounds were bare feet on the mat and snapping gi jackets as punches were thrown. She heard loud breathing and realized it was her own labored breath ringing in her ears. Her respiratory system was taxed to maximum, and her chest now burned with exertion. "I said, close the space," a black belt yelled at her. Precipitously, her stamina went. She didn't know how long the class ran and punched, only that her legs tried to pump with a life of their own, her heart beat faster and faster, and the opening between her and the man in front grew ever wider.

"Last warning," Marcos called to her from the center of the circle, waving his shinai at her. Mouth open, gasping for air, she tried to close the space, couldn't. Her gi was soaked with sweat, making it a heavy weight. The man behind ran into her. Suddenly a pain, like a burning fire, shot across her back as Marcos cracked her with his shinai. She screamed and could not stop screaming. Suddenly she was hysterical with pain, exhaustion, Khan's rejection . . . And it all culminated in a keening cry seeming to come from someone else.

"Get her off the mat," she heard Khan say. And she was grabbed, pulled into the dressing room, thrown against the wall, where she continued sobbing uncontrollably.

"Karateka, don't cry. You understand?" the boy Marcos with the crazy eyes yelled. "You can't cry in the dojo." But she couldn't stop. She was shaking with sobs, and the horrible pain across her back intensified.

"Damn white belt. Fucking girl," Marcos said. "Stop crying."

She heard Khan's voice over her sobbing. "Marcos, get back to the mat. Start meditation." Then he was in front of her. "Stop it. Stop crying."

"I can't, it hurts. He hit me," she said, gulping sobs.

"He was supposed to. You broke ranks on a forced run. That's standard procedure here. I said you couldn't take it. Now get out. Go home."

She knew if she did, she would never see him again. She had embarrassed him, proven herself a piece of fluff.

"No," she said, "please. I'll stop crying." She gasped for control.

"Then get yourself together," he said and was gone.

Grey was left alone in the dressing room with her pain

and tears. She could not stop the burning where the shinai struck, but forced a stop to her tears. She had to, and after a long minute of struggle, she did.

She went into the dojo and bowed onto the mat again. Everyone except the black belts with their shinais was in meditation position. She heard the shinai's crack as it descended on the back of a green belt who had shifted from strict *zazen* posture. The green belt made no sound, straightened his back.

She joined the white belts, dropped into zazen, making *sure* her back was straight. Nothing would ever make her risk the shinai's bite again, she swore.

Khan watched from his desk with mixed emotions as Grey reentered, taking her proper place. Okay, so she's got guts and determination. He already knew that. Hadn't he watched her on that giant of a horse? But what she had just done—returning to the class—that took more. That took real spirit.

Well did he know the exquisite pain of the delicate artificial sword used in kendo practice. The shinai's forerunner, thirty-two pieces of heavy-linen-covered reed, had been invented by the great Japanese sword master, Ono Tadaaki in the 1600s, and remodeled into the more flexible, present-day version of four bamboo strips in 1750. Kendo was created because *kenjutsu,* the art of the sword, was too dangerous to practice, resulting in loss of limb and life. The shinai's advantage was the student could confidently strike without cutting, could concentrate on force and rapidity of blows. Kendo is swordsmanship minus the sword, although it is said, the shinai is clothed in the sword's spirit. Since its invention, the bamboo sword had been used by martial arts masters and zen priests to instill contempt of pain.

Khan remembered well his many hours of zen meditation. His father had left him as a youngster for three years in the Byodo-In Temple, in Ahuimanu Valley on the Hawaiian island of Oahu. Those first three months Khan had undergone sixty hours of meditation before he could begin kendo and calligraphy; the priests struck him with the shinai as he meditated. Finally, blessedly, he was able to go so hypnotically deep, he felt no pain. For a moment he pictured the classic temple, its many roofs covered in green tiles, its spectacular setting against a background of fluted cliffs. It was a place where time brought no change, an exact replica of the Byodo-In Temple in Kyoto.

And while the boy Khan had learned ancient ways, his father had been at Hickham and Pearl Harbor, teaching those same ways, creating a new breed of special forces men to go off and die.

He had thanked his father for that training when he was a prisoner in a cage. And that time in the trap in the tree, he had been able to accept oncoming death stoically because of the zen training. How would his students apply the training? How would Grey Coltrane? Why the hell did she need it?

He looked at her beautiful face in meditation, lids closed, concealing her startling eyes. He knew her back burned like fire and would for days. Why? Why had she come here? Could she have fallen in love with martial arts truly? It wasn't him she was after. She had her prince. That's how Khan thought of Andre after reading the *Post* article and determining never to see her again. She would only confuse his life, deter him from his Way. Then again, that portion of his mind he did not control, that connected to his groin, took over. He wanted her— once more.

He had invited her to *Star Wars* and dinner, surprised she went. Evidently a prince wasn't enough. Perhaps she wanted a prince and a priest. Maybe she was some kind of freak he hadn't encountered. The *Post* article said she'd been married to one of America's wealthiest men. How then was it possible for Khan to take her virginity?

He had been genuinely surprised when Grey entered the dojo. He had almost forgotten that Carol had been training her every morning. With no comments or complaints his yellow-eyed cat had followed his orders to the letter and completed the herculean task.

Khan glanced at Carol, standing with her shinai. He knew what type of claim she wanted on him. But he had lately begun to formulate plans of his own and they did not include marriage. He saw Carol's streetwise eyes flicker toward him, knew she had caught vibrations he was thinking of her.

Well, whatever Grey wanted she would be treated no differently than anyone else here, and no matter how strong her spirit; this was no place for her. But now she'd have to back off herself. He wouldn't kick her out.

"Begin the virtues," he commanded, taking his place at the head of the class as all the voices blended.

"The martial arts are my secret, I bear no arms . . ."

"Rubbers!" You must be fucking crazy!" Anton screamed at the young hooker cowering against the wall.

"Please, Mama-san says for against AIDS," the young Korean girl pleaded, holding forth a package of condoms.

Crouched at the tile wall in the condo next door, forced by her unrelenting surveillance to listen, the Nightwalker's subconscious returned to Anton's murderous past and her own past, and fate's diabolical weaving of them into one cloth.

Taiwan, 1984

Grey emerged from the woods at sunrise, moving zombie-like still, but it was a deceptive slowness, for within her boiled a caldron of hysteria as her mind replayed pictures of Anton stabbing Lo Ling to death.

Hearing a small crying sound, she spotted the source of the mewing. The baby monkey Y Shin Sha had offered and she refused was in a cage, shivering, lonely. Lifting the door of the cage, she took the animal out, looking into its wide, scared eyes. "Poor thing," she whispered, holding it close. The little monkey, feeling her warmth, gripped her pinky tightly with its tiny fist. That creature's touch pulled her from the brink of insanity.

Then Anton's face filled her mind.

Y Shin Sha, the Nightwalker, came from Mother's hut and saw Grey holding the monkey. Their eyes locked. In that instant she dedicated her life to Mikel Anton's annihilation.

Grey led Mother and the Nightwalker to where Lo Ling and Wi lay dead. Mother's shining pulsed, her arms raised wide to heaven, heart-wrenching grief plainly written on her face.

And then beautiful Lo Ling, the unwanted child raised by Mother, was buried by her. The Nightwalker took Wi's body away.

It was the Time of the New Ones and the trials continued. Besides Lo Ling's awful absence, there was another difference. Grey was no longer adrift but watched, keenly focused on everything taking place. And she ate.

One day when she thought no one could see, she stood before a great tree. Reaching up her painfully thin arms, she grasped a dangling vine and attempted pulling herself up. She proved much too weak for the task, but tried several times before sinking in exhaustion to the ground.

The Nightwalker, who never let her out of his sight, leaped, kicking high in the air, his eyes glimmers of merriment.

At the end of that day, Grey approached Mother. "May I be a new one?"

Mother considered this different daughter, whose startling beauty surfaced as her face and body filled out. "When these trials are done, the Time of the New Ones is complete. Then you shall learn the Way. Now is time for sustenance. Grow strong, my daughter." And Mother was overjoyed even though a part of her grieved for Lo Ling, who would have been ecstatic at this moment. She enthusiastically embraced Grey.

The Nightwalker leapt into a tree, then to the ground. On the last day of the trials, the new ones stood before Mother, every one of them able to elude the disciple's striking sticks and knowledgeable in healing ways. The young women glowed with strength and confidence. How beautiful my daughters are. Mother shone. Grey, who was stronger, also stood, next to the Nightwalker.

Mother looked at the stately climbing trees and, nearer, at spiny-trunked tree ferns with young coil-tipped leaves that could be peeled and eaten. She gave thanks for her surroundings that helped in all things. "I am proud of you, beloved daughters. Next year in the Time of the New Ones, you may return. The final trial you now face will mark you forever as—" Breaking communion, Mother looked at Y Shin Sha and the Nightwalker led Grey, not to be privy, away.

The next day, the women were gone. Mother, Grey, and the Nightwalker remained, along with Lo Ling's spirit, which would never be gone. And Grey's training began.

Drinking great amounts of grass juice several times each day, she quickly gained strength. The green juice alone brought power rushes. Not many days passed before she was climbing great trees. Each day Mother covered Grey in tingling energy and shining light, and the Nightwalker threw heavy chi on her. Swiftly accumulating a vast store of herbal knowledge, Grey came to know trees as life givers.

Mother schooled her in Wing Chun, that method of simultaneously blocking and striking, the foundation of which is economy of motion. Mother stressed proper position, the key to success in Wing Chun's technique. Grey practiced long hours with Mother at Wing Chun's unique sensitivity training called "sticking hands." She and Mother hooked their arms, rolling them back and forth, and the Nightwalker watched with approval. Grey thought of Khan's tales of the Wing Chun nun. Oh, Khan, you were right, you *knew*. She trained harder, the better to grow strong for revenge.

Soon she was able to imitate the beauty of movement Mother possessed and follow through ancient forms as old as martial arts themselves. Grey felt a strange familiarity, a core consciousness, as though she knew these movements from a previous time. Within those times, some of the anguish inside her receded and she almost felt joy.

And Mother saw that this beloved daughter's aura momentarily sparked and that this daughter moved in perfect sync with her, even more perfectly than had Lo Ling, and Mother knew peace that the knowledge was safe within this one.

There were times when Anton's face left the forefront of Grey's mind, and natural curiosity did take over. Had the dreams in her coma been real? Were Mother and Y Shin Sha other than human? Or would she simply soon awake? Was this just another dream and when she woke, Khan would be there and her baby would still be inside her?

No. Her belly was as empty as life without Khan. Curiosity abated. Anton's face consumed her and there was nothing left but that.

But the Nightwalker spurred her speculations awake again. He seemed such an odd coupling of emotionless savagery and comedic mimicry. Grey wondered where he went when he disappeared.

Close up, the Nightwalker did not appear like other

Chinese. His eyes, exaggeratedly angled, were overly big, the pupils seeming oblong, solid black. If I pull off his red beret, will antennae spring up like in the opium dreams? That thought scared her. Y Shin Sha was like a praying mantis, she decided. Grey approached Mother. "I do not want to be a new one. I want to be Y Shin Sha."

Mother was taken aback. This was not as she had expected, but this one was different. Mother probed Grey, confirming again her left and right brain hemispheres were fused. She could receive, perhaps this was meant. She gave permission.

Anton's loud voice pulled the Nightwalker back to the present in Waikiki.

Infuriated by the Korean whore's refusal to have sex without a condom, Anton literally kicked her out of his condo. Opening the door, he grabbed the frightened girl by her hair. "Fucking whore, gook, pig," he yelled, planting his foot on her ass, sending her flying into the hall. Slamming the door as she slammed into the wall across from it, he returned to bed.

Next door the Nightwalker, breathing a sigh, rose from her crouching position and let her earphones drop to the floor. Naked, she stretched her lithe body, glimpsing it in the bathroom mirror as she did. She switched on the light and, swinging her hair away from her neck, stared at the deep brand there. Her fingers played across it. "Soon Mikel Anton, soon," she vowed in a singsong. Her fingers searched her hair, finding those places no hair grew, where her skull had been crushed. She dropped her hair. What did it matter? Who would ever run his fingers through her hair again? "Soon Mikel Anton, soon."

Clicking off the light, she left the bedroom and lay on the bed. The picture window showed the sparkling lights of St. Louis Heights and Manoa Valley. Khan. Khan.

Forcing her eyes closed, she lulled herself to sleep with remembrances of a disastrous first karate class and Khan.

13

The voices of one hundred and sixty students reached a crescendo: "May God help me if I ever have to use my art."

Grey's voice blended, fervently shouting the virtues. Despite her pain, she was thrilled at being part of such resounding energy. "Nothing is impossible," she yelled, and began pumping knuckle push-ups with the class.

Soon the tatami, so smooth underfoot, was another torture to endure; the mat's close weave became tiny knives cutting her knuckles. She withstood the new pain by concentrating on her burning back struck by Marcos's shinai. When the push-ups were over, she gazed abstrusely at the blood on the mat. It might have belonged to someone else.

In the same trance-like state, she kept pace with the white belts' half hour of grueling abdominal exercises, *beginning* with one hundred knee-to-chest "crunches," and valiantly fought back tears threatening to recur. My back, my back. The pain was steady anguish.

Generally, she was in shape for the workout, rigorous as it was. Making this different than other calisthenics was constant black belt pressure.

Obviously, no black belt wanted assignment to white belts—dojo nothings, nonbeings. Those black belts pulling the undesirable duty paraded among the white belts with shinais and brutal feet sweeps, searching for mistakes: dawdling, weak stances, poor form. Physical punishment was immediate. It was nothing like St. Anne's gymnastic classes or even three months of classes with Carol. They had prepared Grey physically, but not dispositionally for what she now faced. That realization came as she dealt mentally with her wounded back, reminded of Khan's warning karate was not for her *in his dojo*.

I climbed the ivy at St. Anne's! With that thought Grey drew from a deep well of reserve and continued.

"Line up for blocking drill."

She found herself paired with a tall purple belt. They bowed to each other and commenced. Grey was thoroughly familiar with this drill and approached it confidently.

She soon found out, though, that as black and blue as Grey's forearms had become from countering Carol's blows, there was no comparison. Carol was smaller than Grey. Her present purple belt partner was six foot and strong. Even though she blocked, angling her arms correctly, she could feel them being bruised again and again. Again she made no complaint, but focused on her back. The punches she threw were of no consequence to her stone-faced partner, and his solid blocks hurt her even more. Necessity forcing her to invention, she shifted off center line, diverting the blows instead of taking them full force.

From across the mat, Khan, who missed nothing, saw Grey instinctively using *taisavaki* (the art of avoidance), a skill he taught students at green belt rank. Even her footwork, by accident probably, was correct.

Carol saw Grey use taisavaki also. She had been stunned when Grey first entered, knowing with womanly instincts that Grey was here for Khan. No matter what the newspapers said, the rich bitch was here for Khan!

With knowing pleasure, Carol had watched Coltrane weaken during the forced run and bring the shinai's sting upon herself. Foreseeing exactly that inevitable moment, Carol had taught Grey punches, built her stamina with jumping jacks, but never prepared the neophyte for running *and* punching that taxed one's respiratory system to the extreme. "Well, Sensei," she would say if Khan blamed her for Coltrane's failing, "there wasn't enough space in that dance room to run her." She would get away with it. He might make her do push-ups, but it wouldn't seem engineered. Neither would the other nuances Carol had contrived, guaranteeing Coltrane would have it doubly tough. Ever so subtly, Carol had made sure Coltrane would be a dojo fuck up.

Carol had made sure not to be the one hitting Coltrane when she fell behind in the run. She would give Khan no reason to suspect jealousy on her part. Carol fingered the leather *tusba* on her shinai as she watched Coltrane's blocking from across the mat. She would stay away from Coltrane unless Khan assigned her the white belts. You taught me to play chess, she thought, glancing at Khan, so handsome it hurt to look at him, so tall he towered over everyone. I'm playing to win now.

What joy Coltrane's hysterical screams and uncontrollable crying had given Carol, well aware of what Coltrane suffered. Pampered bitch. See how much you can take, she had thought. Now, she was shocked seeing Coltrane naturally use taisavaki, a skill Khan had had to *teach* Carol—and it had taken her awhile to catch onto the tricky premise.

Carol felt a foreboding but shook it off, reasoning she was close to her goal. Her personal belongings all were packed, ready to be transferred to Khan's quarters. Once I move in, it will be game over, checkmate.

In the rear of the dojo, under the red and white battle flag, fronting a mirrored wall, second-degree black belt and Stanislavski-trained actor, Gary Reddington, led brown belts through *sanchin kata* while using the mirrors to keep his eye on Carol. My little dominatrix. Cat, yellow-eyed bitch, flower.

Gary, by nature of his profession a keen observer and by his own nature a roaring romantic, easily read Carol's jealousy and unsuccessful try at paying no attention to the overly beautiful white belt so disconcerting the dojo. The play continues, Gary thought, watching his best friend Dan drilling purple belts to break choke holds. He winked. Dan rolled his eyes in answer. Gary glanced to second-degree black belt Pierre, his other best friend.

Pierre, a handsome, light-complected black man with close-cropped hair except for a thin, braided war lock in imitation of Khan, was gentle and soft-spoken until he drank; then it took Dan and Gary's combined strength to control the raging bull Pierre became. With a conspiratorial wink Pierre also acknowledged awareness of the transpiring dojo drama.

Gary checked Carol again in the mirror while moving in kata. Jewish Princess. He had investigated her in the same manner that his revered acting master, Sanford Meisner, advocated researching a role. He even knew what besides a gi was in her red canvas bag. He had seen its strange contents today, for after Carol had left the locker room, he had slipped into her bag one perfect rose and a sonnet.

Teaching his charges testicle kicking and eye gouging in retaliation for attempted stranglings, Dan considered the unfolding saga. He was sorry for Grey's experience and at the same time madly stimulated. It was all so sexual. The sweet S&M of the dojo: Carol's jealousy permeating the air like spicy food smells before dinner; suffering by the new white belt beauty, suddenly "Little Nell" of the dojo, and another woman where Carol reigned supreme. The students emanated curiosity, you could almost *hear* their speculation. When Grey had gone hysterical, Dan had thought, Well, that's the end of that. Then she reappeared on the mat! Now, you could tell by her manner, though shocked, hurt, pressured, that she thought she was through the worst. Little did she know!

Well, Dan thought, it would be the conversation, over beers, later with Gary and Pierre. It was going to be hard to joke about it, though, knowing Grey so well. He wouldn't tell Llana what had happened, Dan decided. It was embarrassingly private—something only the dojo could understand.

"On your knuckles." Khan's voice sliced the air, stopping thoughts and actions. He left them on their knuckles, arms fully extended holding body weight, for five minutes. "What is pain?" he yelled at the end.

"Karatekas feel no pain," the whole dojo yelled.

The class returned to various assignments. Khan observed from his desk, mostly contemplating the teaching quality of his black belts. It was important to him to leave that legacy. He was proud of his belts, loving those he had spent years training and knowing personally. He would take them to the "All American," he decided, at Madison Square Garden. One last time. It wouldn't be like the old days, when he returned from Nam and that competition was the hottest in the country, attracting thousands of participants. Then the greats like Owen Watson, Ron Van Clief, Ulio La Salle, Albert Cheeks, Malachi Lee, Louis Delgado, Toganashi, Chuck Norris, and many more, had attended. Most of them were under "The Butcher" Frank Ruiz. It was Ruiz, trained by Peter Urban, grandmaster of USA GoJu, who had combed the country, collecting ronins, (black belts without allegiance) to form the mighty Nesei GoJu nation. Ah yes, Khan remembered with pleasure, you could get a good match at the Garden then.

Now it was different. They covered your hands and feet with protective polyester. The judges eliminated fighters for excessive contact. And the former champions, those wonderful gladiators Khan had enjoyed sparring with, were now scattered over the world. Van Clief, known as the "Black Dragon," made movies. The most charismatic of them all, Owen Wat-son, also had made a couple of martial arts movies, then disappeared, ending what could have been a brilliant film career. Some were instructors now sending their students into the much gentler tournaments. Or they were dead—like Malachi Lee— mysteriously. A few became lazy, stopped training, developed lead bellies. Never me, Khan thought, touching his lean, hard waist. Ruiz, that rock of a man, former Marine and CIA agent, never beaten by a human opponent, was devastated by a car going eighty as he changed a tire by the roadside. Ruiz, great champion and sensei, saw the car bearing down on him, and at the last moment he stood and threw a side kick. That's what saved his life. Otherwise he would have been hit broadside and killed for sure. As it was, Ruiz was hurled hundreds of feet by the impact and most of his bones broken. Many operations later, he was still a regular at tournaments. For a couple of years, he had been on crutches; then, steel pins inside his leg bones, he finally walked unaided and even returned to the mat—a living example of the karateka's indomitable spirit.

No, the tournament wouldn't be the same, but he would enter his dojo, Khan thought, and his students would take the major trophies, for his was one of the last schools practicing "the old religion."

Dan, Gary and Pierre, his crazy gang of three, would do him proud. He looked at them now, knew they were reading each other's minds. They were good guys, always joking. Each so different, yet so alike with their intensity. Gary's acting, Dan's painting, Pierre's martial arts—

and his women. Of the three, Pierre put in the most dojo time. Often Khan would come downstairs and Pierre would be there by himself. Khan finally gave him his own key. Dan and Gary kidded Pierre relentlessly, said he spent excessive time practicing karate to escape the amorous relationships he so enthusiastically formed, then felt trapped within.

Khan looked to black belt boys he called his "Twin Dragons," blond Romulus and black Rebulus, both sixteen. They were nicknamed after the legendary Roman twins Romulus and Remus, abandoned as babies, suckled by a wolf and raised by a shepherd. Khan had seen fit to alter the one name a bit, but he made sure to tell the boys the story. It was one they could relate to, having been abandoned themselves. Khan was their shepherd, the streets of New York their wolf. The Twin Dragons were of equal height. My kata champions, Khan thought. They always performed the same kata together; like Olympic water ballet pairs, synchronization was their specialty.

By Buddha, Khan thought, time flew. They were going on seventeen. They had been twelve when Khan forced them from a rat-infested, condemned building where they were barely living, skin-popping dopers. Not yet formal addicts, but on their way. Now they slept on futons in the heavy-bag room. Khan clothed them, fed them, sent them to school. He loved all his "sons," but these two boys and their progress over the years had brought him special reward. He would have to make plans for them . . . He forced the thought from his mind. It would be very difficult. He would face it then.

And Carol—once more he contemplated the only woman he'd ever given a black belt. He knew her so well he could read her mind. Well, he would let her move in. It wouldn't mean what she thought, though. He would also face that when he had to. His "dojo daughter." Sometimes he felt almost incestuous making love to her.

Enough thinking. Time to teach. He would give them what he could while he could. As far as making plans, he decided to talk to someone whose wisdom he respected. Khan had been raised to heed the advice of older men. He would take his decision-making to the grandmaster.

Rising from his desk and opening the swinging gate in the cordon railing, Khan walked onto the mat. At his signal, brown belts and black belts closed a circle around him. Only they received his instruction. Underbelts were always envious. They would have to wait until they achieved those ranks before Khan would teach them personally.

Inside the circle, Khan took Carol's shinai and demonstrated with incredible rapidity the *men* (forehead), *kote* (forearm), and *do* (side) blows. "Remember, good strikes are delivered in well-defined places using the upper third of the shinai.

"Remember, kendo practice is meant to train the body *and* mind, to build a strong soul, to strive relentlessly for improvement, to respect human courtesy and honor," he lectured his adoring audience.

During Khan's time with his upper belts, the white belts were taught hold-breaking by the purple belts. Grey dutifully extended both wrists as commanded, and a green belt—even more of a hulk than her purple belt blocking partner—grabbed both her wrists with his hams of hands.

"In order to break this hold," her purple belt teacher said, "turn both your wrists quickly outward. Thumbs have no gripping power and you will break the hold."

Although her main focus of attention was her painful back, she by rote followed directions. They were correct. Despite her partner's power, Grey easily broke his tight grip. After this drill was repeated for a half hour, her wrists were as bruised as her forearms. Mercifully, at the point she could bear no more pain, she heard the call for virtues, knew it was the class's end. Thank you, God.

Virtues over, she left the mat with the underbelts, walking past Khan's desk. He was being interviewed by a reporter armed with tape recorder and camera. He did not look at her. The black belts remained on the mat as she hurried to the dressing room, hoping when she changed, the interview would be over and she could talk to Khan, that he would ask her to stay with him. She would not be accusing, she promised herself, still using her gi jacket to change under. This time there were no jeers when she took the jacket off, her back to the others. Instead there were whistles of wonder. My back must look awful, like it feels, she thought. Dressed, she rushed out.

Khan was not at his desk, nor did she see him anywhere in the dojo. Carol stared triumphantly at her from the mat. Crushed, Grey exited quickly, before Dan could talk to her. She was too mortified by what had transpired to speak to him.

Once downstairs, her hair lank with perspiration, she reached for the car keys in her jacket pocket. Her arm refused to move. She stood on the street next to the Mercedes, realizing her arms and wrists ached to the point where they just wouldn't work.

A gentle voice spoke. "Ms. Coltrane, could I drive you home?" It was the white belt with glasses she had first imitated in the dojo.

"How do you know my name?"

"I'm a photographer for the *Daily News*. I've taken quite a few pictures of you in the last couple of years." He rushed on, "Look, I've had a first class here too. I know what you feel like. Please, let me drive you."

Beaten and defeated, Grey accepted the offer and they drove uptown. Once at her apartment building, with the car in the garage, she offered the kind photographer cab fare to his home. "No, I don't live far away. I'd like the walk. Good night, Ms. Coltrane." She realized once she was upstairs that she hadn't even asked his name.

Carol gasped when she unzipped her red bag in the dressing room and saw Gary's rose lying atop the Shakespearean sonnet. "That son of a bitch," she said. *Gary saw inside her bag.* How dare he? Doesn't he knew I'm Khan's woman? He's weird, his crazy poetry. Sexy, though . . . And I started it. *But he saw.* "Fuck!" She read Gary's note. "I would have you for mine, Isis, sweet bitch, my small Aphrodite, my Sabra." She read the sonnet: "Shall I compare thee to a summer's day, thou art more lovely, more fair . . ." and was not quite so disturbed. So he saw. Big deal. He'll just think I'm a little more nuts than he already knows I am. Nothing matters. I've got Khan. Everything will be all right soon.

For Grey, the night brought little sleep to offer succor. There existed no comfortable position for her bruised body. The couple of times she did drift off, nightmares began. In one, Ed, Khan, Llana, and her mother terrifyingly blended into one many-headed monster chortling, "I told you so." Another dream brought a vision of Carol hitting Darkchild with her shinai. Darkchild was hobbled and couldn't fight back. She was liberated from nightmares when pain awoke her.

The next morning, she thought of how wretched she was. Even more so than when she had been married to Ed Fowler. Her back's flaming pain was a reality she could not disavow. The view of the bruise in the mirror was astounding. A diagonal stripe from shoulder to midback was already a rainbow of colors ranging purple to yellow. Khan, why do you hate me? What did I do? Pain and embarrassment suffered the night before by no means dimmed her passion for him.

Five hours later, Grey bent over her kitchen sink, trying to effect a miracle healing before class. She had ingeniously devised an ice bag to cover the fiery stripe on her back by filling a pillowcase with ice cubes, rolling it into a long tube, and laying it across her diagonal wound. At first the ice had made it hurt more, but now the wound was numb and relieved. A thick terry towel folded over the edge of the sink cushioned her breasts. Both her arms were immersed in the sink, filled with hot epsom salts. The cold on her back contrasted with the heat on her arms. *What a picture I must make.* She had a laugh at her own expense.

Suddenly she felt differently about the dojo and Khan. *He's not rejecting me, he's testing me. This is how he gets, cold and removed, that's all. He'll see I mean to train seriously and everything's gonna be okay.* "Right, Jose?"

The cockatoo hissed at her.

"You look like an ice-cream cone that needs licking," Dan said to Llana. Since the weather had gotten warmer, she had taken to wearing only beige and white.

Standing in her white linen suit, a glass of wine in hand, she merely stared accusingly at him.

He couldn't stand it. He hated sulking. Fixing his penetrating gaze on her, he said, "All right, that's it! Time to talk this out, once and for all. Take off your clothes. I want to be able to touch you everywhere."

Llana felt herself begin to melt. Taking off her suit, she stood in a white silk strapless teddy. He pulled the tortoise pins from her hair, watching black tumbles of hair spill onto her naked shoulders. "Your eyes are dark purple pansies," he said, picking her up and carrying her upstairs to their bed.

Once they lay side by side, naked, her petite body seemed even smaller by comparison to Dan's six-foot muscular frame. "I hate sulking," he said.

She just lay there. He touched her nipple and watched the brownish-pink rosette pucker in response. His hand trailed to her rosy stomach and he made circles tracing her belly's soft roundness. She just lay there. He put his finger on her clitoris and pressed. Her breathing changed. He thrust his finger inside her. She moaned and reached for his hard penis.

"No," he said, his finger still inside her. "Now we talk."

She tried to maintain her moody demeanor, but couldn't and moaned again.

"So you don't want an open marriage. Okay, I understand, and that's fair. We won't have one. But we will have truth between us." Taking his finger from its warm place within her, he put his hand again on her belly. "I love you. I want you forever, Llana. I want to put babies here. I don't ever want to lie to you, I want absolute truth between us. So I offered you an opportunity. If you don't want that, okay. I would never want to be a married man cheating on his wife and lying about it."

"Are you now?" Her voice was a tiny whisper.

"No. It's just I want us to have real understanding." He lifted her body easily, settling her on his erect penis. With his hands around her tiny waist, he moved her up and down and spoke over the soft moans of pleasure she could not stifle. "If you don't want to marry me, be my mistress."

"No. Wife," she said, riding sensations of ecstasy, barely able to say the words.

"Wife?" He thrust up, holding her still.

"Wife," she gasped.

"There will never be another woman for me. It'll be the best life you ever had," he said and brought her to screaming orgasm.

Later, lying on the bed after they both were satiated, Llana looked down through the railing at Dan rummaging through the icebox. He was always hungry after they made love. "Look in the blue bowl, there's leftover meat-balls in sauce."

"Mmmmm," he said, uncovering the blue bowl and saw it contained papers instead of meatballs. He took the papers out and read them. "All right!" he exclaimed, reading Grey's note and her incredible itinerary for their honeymoon.

"The meatballs are in the yellow bowl," Llana called, watching his sandy head again bend to the refrigerator. It will be a good life, she thought, believing his vow of fidelity, thinking how much fun she'd just had getting the matter clarified.

Then he was sitting cross-legged on the bed beside her, eating cold meatballs with chopsticks. Together they pored over the wedding present from Grey.

Then she became sober again. "What's going to happen to Grey?"

"I don't know, baby. Grey Coltrane is on a rough trip. But it's her life. You have to let her live it. Make her own mistakes."

"But can't you help her at the dojo?"

"No, honey, it's everyone for themselves. Forget it! We're getting married in three weeks."

The warm evening was made even hotter for Grey by the leotards and tights she wore under her jeans and a cotton shirt. She had the cab drop her at St. Mark's and Third, thinking a stroll would loosen her up a bit. Walking across St. Mark's Place, dreading the encounters bound to come, she was at the same time filled with the anxiety of seeing Khan.

Young lovers were everywhere, strolling arm in arm, hand in hand, making her miserable with thoughts of Khan. There was a line at the Gem Spa on the corner of Second and St. Mark's for ice cream and chocolate-covered graham crackers. Grey turned south on Second Avenue, acknowledging none of the passes and drug offers men made to her. Lifting an aching arm, she adjusted her strap on her shoulder and began mentally running and punching, preparing for the tortuous warm-up. I will do it. I will. She steeled herself by reminding herself of the childhood story, "The Little Train That Could."

Khan was not in the dojo. Carol was.

This time there was laughter in the dressing room when her leotards and tights were seen as she changed. She was suddenly mad. I don't care. Laugh. I'll show you. I'll show you all.

It wasn't the running and punching or even black belts with their dreaded shinais that made the warm-up awful. She held her breathing under control, kept pace with the class, threw steady punches with her aching arms. It was her back! Her leotard strap and sweat-soaked gi rubbed the wound as she punched. The pain was intense.

The class was ten minutes through running and punching when he entered. Her whole being centered on him. See, Khan, I'm keeping up. I love you. He did not even glance her way.

Finally, her heart racing, she completed the run without incident and stood at attention. Her back burned more fiercely and her arms were two vestiges of pain hanging at her sides, but she was proud. Then, in sudden panic she realized push-ups were next. She knew her arms wouldn't hold her. Oh, no. God help me!

The door of the dojo burst open and a young giant entered. He was black, easily six-foot-six, perhaps nineteen. His loud voice boomed across the room as he addressed Khan, who sat at his desk. "Where's the master? I want to pay a mat fee."

His hackles rising but his face expressionless, Khan stood. It was a "dojo bust." I'm tired of all this, he thought. "Are you a black belt?" he said.

"That's right, and so are my boys," the young giant said, stepping aside to reveal two nasty-looking but smaller young men behind him, one white, one black.

"The mat fee is five dollars apiece. The dressing room is that way," Khan said quietly, his wide, slanted eyes revealing no emotion. "Marcos, show these gentlemen where to change."

Carol's attention was jerked from the rich bitch by the entrance of these fools. Nobody got away with that shit in Khan's school. They were real asses, she thought, sitting with the class at Khan's command. Carol knew Sensei was really upset because he broke routine, stopped the warm-up, didn't call for push-ups.

Walking onto the tatami, Khan began demonstrating uraken uchi technique to the class. The visitors bowed onto the mat. The giant, now in a black gi and frayed black belt, led the way.

"Kilska," Khan called.

The class jumped to their feet.

The three newcomers joined the black belt lines.

Khan continued teaching, calling a student forward to demonstrate practical application of the back fist. "The uraken uchi uses speed instead of power," he said, slowly arcing the back of his fist into the student's face. "This is a whipping technique," he said as his knuckles brushed the student's nose. "You can strike center-face from the front, or"—pausing, he stepped to the side and placed the back of his huge knuckles against the student's cheekbones—"from the side."

Watching closely, Grey remembered the winning points Khan had scored at the tournament with just that blow.

"I don't think that would really work," the visiting giant bellowed.

It was very still in the dojo as Khan's voice, now softer than ever, answered. "We'll see when it comes to the sparring." He continued demonstrating for another minute. Then, his voice almost a whisper, Khan announced, "kumite."

Electric charges shot about the room. Dan, Andy, and Pierre transmitted excitement to each other. Marcos was almost jumping out of his skin. Romulus and Rebulus were itching for action. Carol began breathing faster, felt her nipples harden against the rough canvas of her gi.

Khan signaled Pierre forward and the rest of the class to zazen. Pierre and Khan bowed to each other and began sparring. Khan barely touched Pierre with his kicks and punches as the two men moved in slow motion. Khan was setting the pace in an exercise of control.

Marcos was next. Again Khan was gentle, slow, patient.

Grey, watching, not understanding what saved her from the calisthenics she could not have performed, was mesmerized by Khan's movements as he sparred without contact. Even though she did not comprehend the situation at hand, his next words were spoken in so low a tone, she realized something unusual was happening.

"Would one of your friends like to spar?" Khan said to the young giant.

"Yeah, man, that would be real," the giant boomed,

his loud voice contrasting Khan's, and nodded at one of his companions. The seventeen-year-old black boy eagerly sprang to his feet and came forward.

"Carol," Khan commanded. Jumping forward with a grin on her face, she bowed to him, then squared off with the confused boy, who had never expected to face a woman, especially one half his size.

"Begin," Khan said.

Carol's lightning-quick round kick instantly lashed out at her opponent's face. Splat. Her instep contacted his cheek, immediately followed by a snapping front kick into his groin. The visitor hit the mat, screaming and pulling his legs to his chest. Carol bowed to Khan and waited. His nod told her to rejoin the other black belts. He paid no attention to the writhing form beside him.

"Perhaps now you'd like to join me?" Khan's voice was honey-sweet and he smiled as the young giant jumped to his feet.

When they squared off, the giant was taller than Khan by two inches and outweighed him by fifty pounds. Suddenly the black man screamed "Aiee" insultingly into Khan's face.

Khan snapped. Like lightning he was on the giant, striking him twice in the face with the uraken uchi, the one that "wouldn't work." At the same time Khan's right leg moved between his opponent's legs and, snapping against the inside of his knees, swept out the man's feet so he crashed to his knees like a tree brought to ground.

Then Khan began slapping. Back and forth—the Japanese interrogation slap, it was called. The whole dojo rang with the slapping sounds as the back of Khan's hand, then his palm, hit either side of the kneeling giant's face, which snapped in the direction of each blow.

"You stupid ass!" Khan yelled, now out of control as he continued the slaps. "Don't you know I could have killed you?"

"Please Sensei, please stop," the giant, who seemed smaller now, pleaded as Khan's powerful blows drove him backward on his knees. But each of Khan's words was punctuated with another slap. Blood came from the corner of the giant's mouth.

"Get in that corner and give me a thousand push-ups, you understand, you asshole?"

"Yes, Sensei, please, sensei."

"And your friends, too."

The three visitors were soon pumping knuckle push-ups for dear life.

Khan again took his place at the head of the class, but his racing adrenaline prevented him continuing his teaching. He paced back and forth, looking at the three doing push-ups. He walked to them, stood seething over the giant's broad back. Without warning Khan swept out the man's tree trunk arms with his foot. As the giant crashed face-first onto the mat, Khan stomped down with his heel, planting his foot solidly in the middle of the prone man's back. "Give me your instructor's name," he yelled.

Carol enjoyed a feeling of absolute intoxication. As she held her back ramrod straight in meditation position, adrenaline rushed like a wild river through her body. She drank the excitement, loving it, needing it. He choose *me* to fight for the dojo's honor. I wish he had let me kick the other one's ass, too. She listened as Khan spoke to the offender's instructor on the phone and knew the three would face holy hell when they returned to their own school. She looked into the mirrors, back to the five lines of white belts, checking Grey's reaction to what had happened.

Grey wasn't hard to find. Positioned directly under a light, the highlights of her hair blasted like a beacon. Carol saw no expression on her perfect face. Grey's eyes were very wide and fresh sweat poured continuously from her forehead even though she was still. Fuck her, Carol thought. I'm it. Then she felt Gary's eyes on her and experienced yet another rush of adrenaline.

A vertigo close to drunkenness gripped Grey. The pain of the scourge on her back was a hundred times worse, permeating her like water reaching to every corner of a cloth. Having to remain still during the violence she just witnessed, burning pain always there, became almost a holy experience, an adoration of her own pain. Thoughts of the nuns at St. Anne's whipping themselves abruptly flashed into her mind as she fought tears.

Through it all, she had felt pride as Carol demolished her opponent, though she was sure Carol could care less about *her* admiration. She had watched Khan turn the cocky giant into a sniveling midget with clashing sentiments bordered by physical agony: fear, horror, disgust, pride, then unexpected titillation. Now only pure desire for Khan remained. Somehow her pain seemed to purify her of yesterday's disgrace. *I belong here. I'm doing what you want. Want me!* Hard as she tried, she could not transmit her thoughts to him.

Talking to the idiot's instructor calmed Khan. They even had a laugh over the incident before the conversation ended, and Khan was satisfied more punishment would be handed out to the offenders.

Not paying any attention to the hundred or so students who remained on their knees, Khan replaced the phone receiver and took a moment to think.

Dojo busting—an old martial arts tradition, could be traced to ancient schools in China, which had aggressively "visited" rival schools. He had dojo busted himself, especially when he first came back from Nam. When he took over this school, he continued the practice. He would take eight, maybe ten of his students and "visit." It was courtesy for the host school to invite him and his students to work out.

As Khan's reputation had grown along with that of his students, it was many an unhappy instructor who had invited the group onto the mat. He remembered one man, a phony black belt with a school in Connecticut who cried. "Please, don't ask me to spar in front of my students. This is a business, I have kids," the cowardly faker begged Khan. The bogus black belt's students, who were banished to another room, overheard the conversation and deserted the school.

Then there was the dojo bust of all dojo busts. The Count Dante affair in Chicago, which ended with many deaths. The story is told that students grabbed martial arts weapons off the walls to defend themselves, but those dojo busters had guns. Count Dante, the infamous black belt they had come for, was absent at the time.

Oh, what the hell does it all mean? He got kicks that way then. It was fun taking Carol along, making her fight first, psyching everyone by putting a girl up, the way he had today. He thought about her techniques. She was on. Especially the way she had taken advantage of her opponent's millisecond of hesitation.

He stood and went onto the mat, walking the lines of

students, thinking. Suddenly he didn't want them looking at him. "*Zen mukso*," he said, giving the command to close their eyes, and continued pacing the ranks. He was naggingly restless—suddenly horny. He passed Carol, thought about later, upstairs. He paced more lines and came to the white belts. Grey's ashen face was pouring sweat. He saw her whole body was shaking, noted her trying to control the shaking. When he walked behind her, he saw the back of her gi soaked with blood. What does she want from me? Goddamn it!

"Class dismissed," he commanded. "Say your virtues." Without any explanation he left the dojo.

After virtues, saved by the grace of God from a full class, Grey painfully pulled herself to her feet. She was heading toward the dressing room when Carol blocked her way, holding a tin bucket and a toilet brush. "Newest white belt in the dojo pulls latrine duty," she said with a grin.

14

The Bleecker Street pub was "established in 1808," according to its brass plaque. The dimly lit interior boasted dark wood, a low-beamed ceiling, and a sawdust-scattered floor. Within arm's reach of every table, metal-banded, age-darkened wood barrels filled with peanuts stood like sentries. Patrons threw empty shells to the floor, where fresh sawdust and crushed peanut shells blended into a unique aroma. Dan, Pierre, and Gary, who lingered over beers at a corner table, were used to the smell, for the three often gathered here after class.

"Did you hear that gargantuan asshole talking to the underbelts outside the dojo?" Pierre asked.

"I don't guess he was bragging about his kumite," Dan said. "Jesus, Sensei slapped the shit out of him. I'm surprised he could talk."

"Well, he could," Pierre said. "I heard him say Khan's the *fifth* great Sensei who's kicked his ass. He was proud as punch, called himself a 'Sensei buster.'"

Their laughter at the absurdity of it all was interrupted by the waitress, dressed as an Elizabethan tavern wench in a blouse cut so low that the beginning of dark around her nipples showed. "More beers?"

"Only if you'll be mine forever," Pierre said, smiling lazily at the buxom blond.

"We'll keep him tied," Gary said. "Bring the beers."

The waitress walked away, looking back several times over her shoulder to smile at Pierre before she disappeared.

"Man, don't you have enough women?" Dan said.

"I'm trying to repopulate New York, you know that," Pierre said in jest, at the same time seriously referring to his present problem. One of his girlfriends was pregnant and refusing to have an abortion. His steady girlfriend, a pleasingly plump designer he had been with for years, would have a fit if she found out. Pierre smiled at the tavern wench's overly pronounced frontage as she returned, leaning near him, placing brown Budweiser bottles on the table. He resisted a strong urge to plant a kiss on her nearest breast.

"You should have," Gary said when she left. He looked more like a burly mountain man everyday in the beard and moustache he was cultivating for an off-Broadway role.

Pierre's laugh acknowledged Gary's telepathic powers. Then he spoke. Pierre's low, raspy voice, little more than a whisper, made people pay close attention. "Five bucks WBB does not come back," he said, changing the subject. "WBB" was their acronym for the dojo's newest student and stood for "White Belt Beauty."

"Done," Dan said, knowing Grey would return. If she had come back for today's second class, she'd be back for more. Until she faced Carol!

"Change that wager," Pierre said. The light-complected black man immediately sensed his mistake. "Five bucks Carol wastes WBB before the week is out."

There were no takers.

"Well, she has a break. The dojo's being painted," Pierre said. "Only black belts work out for the next two days, upstairs in the heavy bag room."

Blue-eyed Gary, who had been daydreaming as he gazed at an old tintype of Pancho Villa hanging on the wall, spoke, "Did you see Carol duke that guy off. He never knew what hit him!" Unabashed admiration rang in his voice.

"You must have got your cookies on that one," Dan said. "What is it with you, man? Randy for a dominatrix to whip your ass? You a masochist, man? What turns you on, anyway? Carol is too tough!"

"Yeah, man," Pierre agreed. "Lost your Irish macho?"

"No, guys, you got it all wrong," Gary said, grinning. "I seek to conquer! Bring her to her knees, turn her into my adoring slave." His blue eyes focused on Pierre. "Make fighting babies," he said, flashing a devilish grin.

"You're crazy," Pierre said, activated by the word "babies" to straighten in his chair. "Carol is older than you. She's varsity nuts. But most of all—in case you haven't noticed—she belongs to Khan. Sensei will kill you!"

"No, he won't," Gary confidently replied, reaching into a nearby barrel for another handful of peanuts. "He doesn't really want her. She pushed in. It won't last."

There was a moment's silence as the other two men contemplated Gary's truthful insight.

"Yeah, okay. But what makes you think she'll want you?" Pierre rasped.

"Once I get her alone, it's game over. You're not the only freak in town," Gary said, throwing a peanut at Pierre. Pierre deftly caught the peanut and fired it back at Gary, who ducked it, then turned his gaze on Dan. "I want to ask you a real favor, Dan."

"Name it," Dan said.

"Ask Carol to your wedding."

It was Dan's turn to sit up straight. "You must be kidding," he said. "She's antisocial." He racked his brain for excuses. Grey was the maid of honor. Khan was best man. Carol at the wedding would be disaster! "She'll start a fight. She probably doesn't own a dress," he said.

Gary looked really disappointed. Dan sipped beer and considered the dilemma. Deciding he couldn't refuse Gary, he put the beer bottle decisively down, making a noise on the table. "Okay, she's got her invite," Dan said, watching Gary's grin materialize. "You look like Paul Bunyan, you big cheese," he said affectionately. "But you have to watch Carol like a hawk. *If* she does come, and I don't think she will—"

"Five bucks she does," Pierre interjected.

"Done," Dan said, and continued warning Gary. "You have to promise. If she starts to act up—"

"I won't take my eyes off her," Gary promised.

The three friends ordered a last round. Gary and Dan had decided to grow war locks, like Pierre, in time for the All American. The task was simple for Gary, whose hair was already long for his upcoming Norseman's role. He could just braid a piece. Dan had short hair. Would it grow in time? They made bets.

At eight the three parted. Dan walked to Soho, contemplating Llana's reaction when asked to send Carol an invitation. He decided to just give one to Carol. Hopefully she wouldn't come. If she did, he'd explain to Llana on their honeymoon. He felt suddenly cornered by the thought of Grey's incredible honeymoon present. Three-

way loyalties pulled at him. Llana, Gary, Grey. He shook
his head. Considering his position, the artist reasoned, it
was best to let things happen as they would. One thing
was for sure—it was going to be an interesting wedding
day!

Pierre stayed behind, talking to the tavern wench.

Gary went shopping for a dress.

Once home from the dojo, Grey, acknowledging she
needed help desperately, called Debbie the makeup artist
at her home. Luckily, Debbie was there and, hearing of
the problem, rushed over, curious as hell. She walked in
bearing a large aloe plant in an earthenware pot. "Bloody
God!" she said, viewing the oozing mess on Grey's back.
"Lie on the bed and let me fix you."

Grey meekly obeyed, just thankful someone was taking care of her.

Debbie expertly split a white-spotted green aloe leaf,
exposing its clear healing gel. She laid the leaf, gel side
down on the open wound, where it formed a natural
bandage, sticking to Grey's back. It took four such leaf
applications to cover the whole bloody stripe. The cockney makeup artist talked as she ministered to her famous
client.

"The Egyptians immortalized the aloe plant in hiero-
glyphics inside their pharaohs' tombs, and their doctors
recorded its wonders on parchments.

"Aloe is a godly gift, according to them. Egyptian
queens claimed it the secret to their great beauty and
Nefertiti is reputed to have used aloe, mixed with the
semen of Nubian slaves, as a face lotion."

Grey laughed, noting a new butterfly tattoo on Debbie's
hand as the redhead split another aloe leaf. "Debbie, you
lend spice to any situation." Then she became silent,
reminded of the time Khan had rubbed her with *Ti Da Jow*
to soothe her aching muscles.

Using surgical tape, Debbie completed a well-secured
bandage. "That should hold all night, luv, if you can
sleep on your stomach. It'll be pretty much healed by
morning, closed for sure. I'll just let myself out," the
chubby makeup artist said, leaving the aloe plant by the
bedside, wheeling a golden rheostat on the wall until the
bedroom's many lamps went dim. How unbelievable this
was! she thought. Grey Coltrane mutilated in a karate

class! Wouldn't *Rolling Stone* love that as a banner head-lining an article?

As Debbie closed Grey's front door, she made a mental note to bring her Nikon to Llana's wedding, where she would be doing makeups for the bridal party as well as being a guest. Then she rushed off to dinner with guitarist Robert Fripp, who had just inaugurated a collaboration with David Bowie: they were cutting an album called "Heroes" and Debbie was *mad* for gossip when it came to her celebrity clients. English rock musicians were all the vogue, and she had recently done album cover makeup for Queen and Alice Cooper. The Sex Pistols wouldn't go on camera or to a party unless Debbie prepared them.

But now no celebrity interested her as much as Grey Coltrane. She had queried the *Enquirer*. They would pay plenty for an exclusive on the heiress. Grey's press was spotty lately, they said. Bugueot was about town with other beauties. Grey had not surfaced with a new beau, and the *Enquirer* was absolutely frothing for news of her.

Comforted by soothing aloe, Grey thought of what a friend Debbie had become. Then, of course, her thoughts turned to Khan and their last time alone. Funny, she thought, how many different ways two bodies can fit when they're cuddling. She recalled the feel of him next to her. How she threw her leg over his, her breasts against his ribs. Her arm, so delicate across his heavily muscled chest. Falling asleep that way, holding on. Waking and changing position. Her slight movement waking him so he took her again, slipping easily inside her in the night. Finding herself alone near morning . . . Tears of wanting him wet her pillow before she finally slept.

Khan walked the Village restlessly that same night, upset with himself for losing composure with the giant ignoramus—I almost went off, really off!—and at Grey for coming to his school to bleed. He paced the streets until he reached Chinatown, Little Italy. Finally he ended up on the Bowery, at the Master's.

Only one light illuminated the chess board as the two men played for hours and talked. The giant dojo lay darkly silent in the background. The legendary heavy bags, filled with rocks, hung in shadowed lines like mute sentries behind them.

"Women can turn perfectly good dojos into whorehouses," the Master said. In his late fifties, he was square-faced and dark-haired. He made a move, his knight threatened Khan's bishop. "That's why I have my Women's Lodge 0007.

"*My* female students have class on Friday night and Sunday afternoon. Every two weeks, they come to Thursday men's class. *Only to spar.* It is serious that way. The women learn to face men's power, but have no time to disrupt the dojo, like trying to look sexy when they do kata."

Khan laughed appreciatively.

The Master continued. "After the women's Friday night class, a Catholic priest from the corner church teaches them chess. I require it. They learn logical thinking and to stop all that girl stuff."

Martial arts men were known as extremely sexist, and this master fit the mold well, referring to himself as a male chauvinist prince.

Laughing again, Khan moved his bishop, attacking the Master's main defense line, then contemplated the older man as he studied the board. Martial artist of martial artists! This grandmaster had brought karate to America and personally proved it worked. He was as well a published author, humorist, libertine, philosopher . . . He drank with great gusto from life's well, and his teachings had produced the greatest of modern-day karate men. His karate system had spread throughout the world, with schools in Italy, France, Brazil . . . Khan was proud of his allegiance to this man, but he needed more—to go further into the mysteries, where this teacher could not take him.

But he felt his tension receding as the Master, during the course of their chess playing, astutely commented on the personal problems Khan put before him.

The Master moved—devastating to Khan's attack—then he scrutinized the younger man as he bent his head studying the chess pieces. The Master, an insomniac, had enjoyed many nocturnal hours with this "son," who consulted him now at this pivotal point in his life. Khan's war lock, pinned up to a small circle, showed in the light.

Magic, the Master thought, he believes in magic. He

recalled Khan's words tonight, his plan to seek a legendary psychic woman master. "Bruce Leeism," the master had said, which was what he titled these now popular beliefs in Chinese fairy tales bolstered by kung fu films crediting Chinese martial artists with powers beyond human. He abstained from flights of fancy and was a practical man, trained in Japanese logic by Master Yamaguchi and Master Kim themselves. A punch for a punch. You could count on that, the Master who was also a zen master, thought. But young men must go and seek their dreams. Especially this one, this formidably skilled warrior so disturbed by war—so different from any other the Master had trained. This Eurasian, a martial arts priest in an era when there were none, and who planned to raise sons to be the same. "You are locked into another time warp," he told Khan.

The Master had been active in the bloody, freezing, loathsome Korean War. He had dealt out death, been nearly dead and survived it. A handsome man, he also was besieged by women, made to feel obligated by some, enchanted by the beauty of others. Ultimately he married an uncomplaining Oriental woman who raised his two children, kept his house, and never came to the dojo. His life was the dojo. As much as any man could understand this younger man now searching the corridors of his soul—the Master did. He also understood when it was time to stop searching and get on with life's business.

"I have a new *koan*," he said to Khan.

Khan looked up expectantly from the chess board. Koans are insoluble zen riddles, words or phrases meaningless to the intellect, but at the same time having the power to illuminate. Koans do not make sense, nor are they meant to. There are thousands of koans:

The Master says, "What is moving, the wind or the flag?" An answer might well be, "Neither, the mind is moving."

Koans are statements of spiritual fact to be intuited and not understood. An answer may be a leap to a new level of truth:

A student is busy studying, hoping to find enlightenment. The Master picks up a brick, begins rubbing it.

"What are you doing?" asks the pupil.

"Trying to polish it until it becomes a mirror," the

Master replies. Then addressing the pupil, he says, "What are you doing?"

Zen masters use unorthodox methods of awakening students to the truth. In zen, laughter is significant, jokes frequent. The master may shout, shake students, box their ears, or hit them with sticks. Khan prepared himself for anything.

"What is the sound of one hand clapping?" the Master asked him with a most pleased expression on his face.

Khan contemplated, knowing better than to offer the obvious "Silence" as an answer. "The sound of one hand clapping . . ."

The Master could not contain himself: "A slap across the face of a stupid student!" he yelled, causing Khan to break into loud laughter.

Leaving the Master, Khan again wandered the streets, his spirit eased. It was good to have another viewpoint, he thought.

The sidewalks still held the heat of the day. His six-foot-four, muscular frame strained at his open chamois vest and blue jeans as he walked until there was no more land, to Battery Park, where Staten Island Ferries were berthed. It was a 4 A.M., too late for any boats to be moving.

He stood at the water's edge, silvery with moonlight, for over an hour. Just still, thinking . . . Carol, the Way, the cage, Grey's eyes—golden sparkles around her irises, like little suns dancing inside emeralds—the blood on her back, the blood of so many others, the cage . . . Near dawn he headed uptown, decisions formulated.

Grey arose the next morning, grateful to find Debbie's miracle cactus had sealed her wound and removed its pain. Immediately dire expectations of that night's karate class filled her mind. But knowing Khan would be there negated any thoughts of not going, no matter the consequences. She went to Darkchild.

She walked the black stallion on the bridle path. She hadn't ridden him since her first karate class, but felt no guilt. Jack Brian had said Darkchild needed rest. The Olympic trials across the country next fall would be grueling. She had agreed to Kentucky grazing and was traveling with the stallion this weekend in a plane she had chartered after investigating commercial airlines. None would permit her to be with her horse in flight. Leaving Darkchild, she steeled herself to face God only knew what and went to the dojo.

"NO CLASSES UNTIL FRIDAY. DOJO BEING PAINTED" was posted on the door. Relief washed over her immediately, followed by despair. *I won't see Khan.*

She roamed the Village in the warm June evening, ending up on St. Mark's Place. She sat on the steps of a brownstone with a gang of punk rockers in cutout leather. Their amazing hairdos—mohawks and shaved patches and cherry-blue-yellow streaks—attracted her. She felt comfortable on this street where people were so bizarre; her famous face brought no recognition. She considered moving to the Village, closer to Khan. *Friday, I'll see him Friday.*

She filled the next two days with Darkchild, healing her body and thinking constantly of Khan. She continued ignoring Andre Bugueot's constant stream of flowers and invitations. Aches eased, bruises receded.

That evening, she approached the dojo along with a tall black man who looked vaguely familiar. Then she remembered him from the tournament: the purple belt schoolteacher who had so patiently explained the action. She remembered his name—Ed. She smiled at him, then flushed with embarrassment, thinking he had probably been in class during her mortification and in the dressing room for her Dior underwear.

"Hello," Ed said in his lilting Jamaican accent. Speaking quickly as they neared the door, he said, "You're having a hard time, but you're coming along." He smiled encouragingly. "Just remember, hit hard!" Then he entered the dojo ahead of her. Nobody wanted to walk in with a white belt.

Wondering who she was supposed to hit hard, she saw Khan at his desk and drank in the sight. A white gung fu jacket accented his bronze skin and when he looked up, her heart skipped a beat. She fixed her gaze directly on his as she bowed, willing him to acknowledge her. He did not, his gaze seeming to pass through her. *I'm going to wait outside after class.* You have to come out sooner or later, she thought.

Two days of rest had served her well and she moved through the forty-minute warm-up in the freshly painted hall with no mishaps. Heart pounding, biceps and triceps pumped with blood from punching, she felt strong. She even managed to keep up with the push-ups, although her last twenty were by no means perfect, and avoided the shinai's sting.

Kata was called, and white belts were banished to a corner, where Pierre led them through a solid hour of basic forms. Thank you, Carol, Grey thought, moving assuredly through three white belt katas holding her own. She began feeling confident. Even her gi seemed to fit now, to feel right. In the mirror her correctly tied obi hung at a jaunty angle on her hips. *I look like I belong.*

Either from the corner of her eye or in mirrors, she kept constant track of Khan. The dojo was crowded after being closed for two days, and many times she could see only his head as he moved from group to group.

"Kumite," he ordered.

She dropped into zazen in the white belt circle, wondering who was sparring, then realizing she was. Alarm gripped her. *What a stupid ass I've been.* Watching fighting all the time. The tournament, the dojo bust. Listening to all Khan's stories . . . Never equating contact with herself, oblivious to the obvious.

Marcos, crazy, wild-eyed Marcos, their black belt custodian of the moment, was already sparring with a second white belt. Grey watched with horror as he mercilessly pummeled the white belt much bigger than himself. The student, a cop from Long Island, blocked frantically to little avail.

Khan walked to the white belts and observed. Grey felt his presence along with mounting terror. Marcos dismissed the cop, nodded at Grey. "Next."

Someone handed her a mouthpiece. Inserting the rubber protective device, she jumped to her feet, entered the circle, and bowed to Marcos. Khan also entered the circle, assuming the position of sinban. "Ajami," he said.

Immediately Marcos punched her in the stomach. As a black belt sparring a first-timer, he used control, regulating his power to "light contact." He knew what Sensei wanted.

Grey felt as though a horse had kicked her. "Oufff." She doubled over. Instantly Marcos swept her. She landed hard on her ass, then sprawled to her back, bumping her head. The mouthpiece flew across the floor.

"On your feet," Khan said, handing her the mouthpiece.

She scrambled up and, facing Marcos, reinserted her mouthpiece. Marcos smiled at her.

"Ajami."

She stared, wide-eyed and stricken with fear as Marcos advanced kicking. She attempted a weak block to no avail. Marcos front-snap kicked her stomach, vertical punched her chest, then swept her again. Bip, bip, bip. She struck the tatami full force on one hip, then flopped onto her back.

"On your feet." Khan's voice was flat, impersonal.

Trying not to cry, she again struggled to her legs and faced Marcos.

"Kick, punch, bite, sweep, do anything," Khan said. This time his voice was derisive. "Ajami."

But she was rooted to the mat, frozen with terror, exactly as she had been when surrounded by the gang in Central Park. Now she had no Darkchild to defend her.

Marcos swept her. She crashed to the floor yet again, spread-eagled on her back. Marcos heel-stomped her stomach. Waves of nausea overtook her.

Khan watched with distaste as she bounced off the floor like a rag doll in gi. He thought of the Master's words of last night and disagreed. If women were going to train, they should learn along with men. Well, he thought, she wanted karate, she's got karate. "On your feet," he said. He could smell her fear as she painfully hauled herself up once again.

As Marcos and Grey squared off, her eyes were wide with fright. Hurt, desperately panting, she felt spittle collecting around the unfamiliar mouthpiece and running from the corners of her mouth. It was obvious she was a split-second away from crying and was not going to fight back.

Carol watched from the purple belt ring, where she supervised sparring. Rich bitch was a coward! Carol gloried in Grey's refusal to fight and the pitiful sight she made, flopping like a turtle on its back, drool running from her lips, with Sensei right there! Carol couldn't have planned it better herself.

Friday evening always meant sparring. Sensei maintained that it set students up for the weekend, just like the fighting film the students would attend en masse afterward.

Carol had been delighted when Marcos had been assigned the white belts. Nasty little bastard. Only Sensei controlled him. Carol remembered when Marcos had been a thirteen-year-old junkie. Now, still painfully skinny at seventeen, he was Khan's shadow, lived for Sensei's approval, moving like a robot to his commands. Marcos would kill in a second if Khan ordered. Carol thought Marcos looked like an insane speed freak, with his eyes so constantly wide. Khan once told her Marcos even slept with his eyes open. And now that crazy Puerto Rican was kicking the shit out of Grey Coltrane. It was difficult for Carol not to smile.

From amid his green belts, Dan suffered for Grey. He needed all his years of karate discipline to refrain from running across the dojo and rescuing Grey from Marcos. WBB was taking a serious whipping.

Black belts hated white belt sparring assignment. That's where they were likely to get hurt out of stupidity. New white belts had no control and became overexcited, turning into windmills of uncoordinated techniques. If the white belt was big and heavy, a black belt had it extra tough. You weren't supposed to knock them out or break bones. As a black belt you taught respect via hard knocks, hard sweeps. In a street fight, if someone was swinging at you with no control, you'd put an immediate stop to it, but in the dojo, with the white belts, you had to keep going. Dan saw Marcos was in a bad mood.

In the white belt ring, Marcos rolled his eyes at Grey, Sensei moved close to Marcos. "Grab some," Khan said, his dark eyes cold. He knew how to make a person fight. "Ajami."

Marcos jumped forward and thrust his hand inside the opening *V* of her gi jacket. His fingers closed on her breast and squeezed.

She screamed. Her cry cut the air as Marcos's hand violated her. "Remember, hit hard!" The schoolteacher's words catapulted into her frenzied mind. And she did.

She assaulted Marcos, who dared to insult her so. But in her mind it was Khan she now attacked. A culmination of shame, rejection, and pain suffered at his hands blended into explosive anger, transforming her into a punching, kicking, wild-eyed screaming hellcat.

Blocking furiously, Marcos hated not being able to knock her out.

"Yami."

With difficulty she ceased her fighting frenzy, not daring to disobey Khan's command. But in an uncontrollable continuation of raging emotion, she leapt suddenly backward and into the air, executed a perfect back handspring, and came, like an auburn-haired bolt of lightning, to her feet on exactly the spot she had begun. *Then* she bowed to Khan.

Her green eyes lit with fiery defiance, chest heaving with never before expressed anger, she looked directly into the eyes of the man to whom she had given her virginity, whom she loved, and who had just taught her life's most profound lesson—to protect herself! "Osss, Sensei," she said.

"That's not in the program here," Khan said, indifferent to her gymnastic skill. "Gimme one hundred." Maintaining an air of city imperturbability, he turned and walked away.

The Nightwalker leapt from her bed and, taking up her listening apparatus, monitored Anton as he, grumbling, received his wake-up call. After showering, he dialed Ritchie's number. "I'll meet you in half an hour," he said, then hung up the phone, and left the condo.

The Nightwalker hurriedly pulled on shorts and a T-shirt. Sneakers in hand, she entered the hallway just as the elevator door closed. Not wanting to wait for another and miss trailing him, she ran down the stairs and outside onto the street. He was just rounding the corner onto Kuhio Avenue. With no time to put on her shoes, she followed him barefoot.

He walked the length of Waikiki, unaware he was shadowed. He had caught an hour of sleep at most and was in an awful mood. What the fuck did Ritchie want, anyway?

Watching him from across the street, the Nightwalker was also aware of the beautiful sunrise over the mountains to her right. Pale brown zebra doves, barred with black and blue, abundant in residential areas, cooed wel-

comes to the morning. Odd, she thought, in the midst of
this loveliness, I watch whom I will kill.

Then he turned onto Ena Road and made his way to
an already busy restaurant, Eggs and Things. Through
the picture window, he saw Ritchie at a table with two
other men and a waiting place for him.

It was not necessary for her to enter the small, crowded
restaurant. She would be satisfied just keeping an eye on
him and the picture window made that easy. Standing
directly across from Eggs and Things, she noticed a small
wooded area behind her. Into it she went.

A waitress in a blue-checkered apron poured coffee for
Anton and left him with a menu. The men at the table
waited while he read it. The Nightwalker saw everything
clearly from her vantage point.

Once again in a wood she was truly at home. Like old,
familiar friends, the trees comforted her. While watching
Anton eat breakfast and confer with his employers, she
thought of how she had asked to become a Nightwalker
and how Mother had agreed and given her to Y Shin
Sha.

Taiwan, 1984

The Nightwalker took Grey into the woods, where he
crouched motionlessly for hours, expecting her to imitate
him until her limbs screamed, and he put things in her
head. Not the way Mother did, not a communing. Grey
would just *know* things when she was with him, like how
to slow her heartbeat and become one with nature so that
even animals did not sense her presence. She knew also,
when she was with him, he was only Y Shin Sha, and that
was the sum total of his being. Like a ninja, but beyond.
Oh, Khan, you would have loved the Nightwalker. Then
came tears and hate of Anton.

The Nightwalker seemed to disappear. She never knew
if he really did, or could leap so quickly it only appeared
that way. And he could throw his chi as a weapon,
striking where he chose. He put into her doubting mind
these were easy things to do, that matter and mass were
only magnetically trapped light. He was simply joining
that light, disassembling and reassembling. He trained
her in illusion and disguise.

When she had difficulty, Mother would augment the Nightwalker's lessons. Grey could not cope with waiting in ambush, and Y Shin Sha only let her suffer through. Mother gave her the key, teaching her to separate her conscious forebrain, which would stay aware, from her subconscious, which could drift. Using this technique, Grey became two at once, and with this double brain activity also came a release from her horrible memories. She relived happy times before Khan's death and was soon able to remain motionless for hours, free of physical pain. She eagerly began awaiting stalking time with the Nightwalker and those periods of introspections.

Sometimes the Nightwalker settled his gaze on her and she felt strange. And sometimes when he did his violent, snapping hand form, he emanated yet another kind of power. Sexual? She rested such momentary flashes and concentrated on violently snapping her own hands.

She thought of her denial of God. How could there be a God letting Khan and her baby die and Mikel Anton live? But when she was encompassed by Mother's loving force, she doubted her own doubts. Confusion reigned inside her.

Y Shin Sha taught her to make poisons from toad's goiters, globe fish, boxfish, and from plants. She came to know bedeviling trees, like the stinging tree: its oblong leaves bore poisonous hair on their upper surfaces and stinging spines on the veins below. Contact caused itching, prickling, then small red spots, followed by stabbing, radiating pain lasting three hours, then duller pain, swelling, and enlarged lymph nodes which would persist three days. Water and rubbing did not relieve but intensified the pain.

Dipping tiny arrows and spearheads in lethal fluids, Y Shin Sha hunted and killed. In the same manner, he taught her to make sedatives so strong that someone would appear as dead after taking them, to use yam bean, whose mature seeds inside the brown pods could be crushed along with its leaves and put in streams to stupify fish. She learned to use a spear and blowgun.

The Nightwalker, with no need to climb, laughed soundlessly at her from above as she ascended. Her acrobatic prowess reawakened. The day came when she leapt and landed nimbly next to Y Shin Sha on a tree branch.

Granted, the branch was quite low, but it was a start, she thought with satisfaction.

The Nightwalker made powder from stone that stopped bleeding. He trained her to walk soundlessly, even over leaves.

He fought in his mind. She remembered Khan telling her of Chinese mind boxers. At midnight, mind boxers entered a standing trance, practicing martial arts only in their minds. Yet when called upon to defend themselves, they were fully prepared and deadly accurate. The Nightwalker shared this knowledge with Grey. She would just know he was mind fighting and wanted her to do the same. And she mind fought. Always her opponent was Anton. Then the Nightwalker let her know that thirsting for revenge could weaken her, for emotions interfered with efficiency. She chanted an ancient Tibetan mantra to clear her mind and imagined a faceless opponent.

One night, Mother stood over Grey's pallet and saw with pleasure that the gauntness was gone and beauty restored. She probed. Yes, still able to bear children. Mother threw her shining, giving healing knowledge as Grey slumbered, knowing this beloved daughter would be able to call on it when needed.

Covered in shimmering light, Grey shifted on her pallet and a fleeting smile played across her face, something Mother saw only when she slept. At that moment, the slowness overcame Mother and she could no longer continue.

The next day, Mother placed a sword in Grey's hand. Overcome with thoughts of Khan, Grey learned her first sword form, thinking thoughts so painful she cried, but never ceased her movements. She visualized Anton before her, imagining each swing of the curved Mantis blade hacking his body parts. This arc a hand, that slice an ear. She cut him to death every day.

One morning, shaded by Nicobar breadfruit trees, Grey followed Mother through a sword form. Mother suddenly dropped to the ground and, shining only faintly, lay at Grey's feet.

"Oh God, please," Grey prayed, scooping Mother into her arms. "I love you, Mother, please be all right," she chanted, that moment acknowledging Mother as the center of her world.

"It is the slowness," Mother faintly communed.

"What herbs, Mother?"

The communing was even fainter now, a distant thing in Grey's mind. "There are no herbs. My time is ending."

"I will die with you then, Mother."

"No, my daughter." Mother found the strength to touch her forehead to Grey's.

Then Grey knew what Mother wanted from her. She must promise to be the keeper of the knowledge, a guardian of what Mother had taught. "Yes, Mother. I am the One," Grey said, willing to be anything in order to help Mother.

Mother's shining brightened again and Grey's panic receded. Now I have pledged, she will be better. Let Mother be all right.

From then on, Grey's concentration was two-edged, shifting between her obsession with Anton and Mother's well-being. As days passed, Mother seemed well, her shining was constant, and Grey's training progressed with no further interruptions.

Living to train, to be near Mother, she fell into this mode of life as though it were a normal one and her companions usual. Always an aching space in her heart held Khan.

She had no idea of how much time passed in her life. What day was it? What month? What birthdays had come and gone. Am I twenty-seven, twenty-eight?

Nor did she know how she appeared. With no mirrors to contemplate, grooming consisted only of cleaning herself and plaiting her hair reaching her knees. Nothing mattered, except Mother was well and Y Shin Sha continued to make her in his image.

Grey discovered why she had been sent from the new ones' final ceremony when Mother communed it was time to promise adherence to the Way and to teach it always. "A trial of pain will be yours, my daughter."

"I will take the oath, Mother."

From the always burning fire, Grey was branded as she knelt. Screaming, she was marked for life by a red-hot iron searing an eternal circle into her neck. Mother communed at the same time. "You must return to life among your own people."

In the days it took for the burning brand to heal, Grey

was haunted by Mother's words. A return to America loomed like a future jail sentence. But as her training continued and no more mention was made of her leaving, Mother's words faded into the background.

Y Shin Sha cornered a rabbit in a highland rattan forest. Remaining in a crouch, he scurried and blocked the rabbit's way each time it attempted a break. It was a game the Nightwalker was enjoying much more than the rabbit.

Suddenly several swiftlets flew from the rattan, startled by men and horses interrupting the jungle's normal noise pattern.

Y Shin Sha was gone. The rabbit scampered to safety.

Anton and his troops appeared.

"Go ahead," Anton ordered an officer. "If you locate the camp, take prisoners. I want them *all* alive." He dismounted, standing at a precipice overlooking a deep gorge, and waited until the men were out of sight, then produced a marijuana packet. Dropping the reins of his mount, he moved to the cliff's very edge and sat gazing across a spectacular view. Lighting the marijuana and drawing deeply, he settled back against a guava tree. "Too bad I don't have any warm, intimate moments to relive," he said aloud, negating his acknowledgment of the beauty before him.

It had been months since Anton, busy with emergency after emergency, had been in these mountains. Otherwise, he certainly would have hunted human prey at the women's camp long ago. In his time away, he had been madly titillated by memories of Lo Ling's fighting him before he killed her. Would there be other beautiful little girls who would resist him?

His mind drifted under the marijuana's influence. A problem had surfaced. The dictator had personally confronted Anton about the missing American couple and his failure to locate them. Seemed the woman's enormous fortune made her internationally important. That, plus the fact Taiwanese curried American favor more than ever, made explaining the couple's mysterious disappearance imperative. Except it was no mystery to Anton.

Now pressed, he knew he must return to their death site. Should he get rid of the bodies? Or should he "find" them and claim the murders as T.I.M.'s work? That would cover him, blame it on T.I.M. But then again, he reasoned within his marijuana haze, there had been many witnesses as he bayoneted the man—his troops. Even though they were participants in the killing and raping, torture could loosen any tongue. And they did hate him.

He did not relish returning to that monastery death scene. The unexplainable injury suffered there haunted him almost as much as his recurring nightmare of a specter doing martial arts, contributing further to his nearly sleepless nights.

Further irritating the commander was the actual matter of T.I.M. The motherfucking guerillas *were* somewhere in these mountains with superior organization, judging by two recent successful operations: a government weapons depot robbed of its entire cache, and the mining of a bridge open only to government use, plus the fact they remained hidden among the people. Well did Anton remember fat Wi's tale of the camouflage-uniformed man. The key? An adviser from another country's military? Was the women's camp the uniformed man's headquarters? Perhaps his harem? That amused Anton and he laughed aloud while thinking he better ride quickly and get to the camp when his troops did.

His chortling was immediately silenced by the appearance, out of nowhere, of the very man he contemplated. Anton acknowledged Wi was not crazy. What stood before him seemed other than human.

Y Shin Sha snatched the joint from the startled man who sat against a guava tree. Assuming a one-legged posture, grinning diabolically, Y Shin Sha dangled the joint teasingly.

"You're the fucking dream!" Anton said disbelievingly.

The Nightwalker answered with a snapping hand dance and Anton saw his nightmare come to life. The huge black man rose and, towering over the apparition, reached for its neck.

The Nightwalker was suddenly not there, but just out of reach. Striking another posture, he made foolish faces, holding the marijuana joint high. Anton, enraged, advanced.

Y Shin Sha leapt over Anton, landing behind him, and from the rear, taking advantage of Anton's open-legged stance, Y Shin Sha kicked him precisely in the testicles. The toe of his combat boot struck home.

Anton experienced the *same awful pain he had felt at
the monastery*, then the air reverberated with the *same*
weird, silent laughter as at the waterfall. Now, from
pain's center, Anton knew the source. The reverbera-
tions grew, causing his skull to feel as though it would
burst. Feeling fire in his groin, chaotic pressure in his
brain, Anton turned. Facing the Nightwalker, screaming
at the top of his lungs, Anton charged.

Y Shin Sha danced lightly left, and Mikel Anton plunged
screaming over the precipice. The Nightwalker watched
Anton fall, land in a tree, fall from that, and then,
obviously hurt, drag himself into the jungle foliage. Then
Y Shin Sha was gone.

Mother and Grey were in the camp clearing. A basket
of newly picked papaya lay nearby as Mother covered
Grey with shining and communed.

Experiencing the "feel of Mother," extraordinary
tranquillity in midst of immensely high radiations, Grey
thought, I am addicted to this feeling. Suddenly it became important to solve this incredible woman's mystery.
"Mother, where are you from? Are you—"

Grey's question was interrupted by Y Shin Sha's sudden
appearance. He touched his forehead to Mother's. The
wonderful feeling of Mother retreated as he did.

"Come, my daughter," Mother communed and, following the Nightwalker, ran from the camp. Just as
Mother, Y Shin Sha, and Grey gained the cover of the
jungle, brown-uniformed troops burst into the clearing.

"The fire still burns," one soldier shouted. "They must
be near." Fanning in a circle, the soldiers entered the
woods, seeking their prey.

The running three were moving swiftly when Mother
stumbled. "I go no farther. It is time," she said, touching
her forehead to Grey's, throwing all her remaining energy.

The very essence of Mother radiated into Grey.
"Mother, don't leave me. I want to die with you, Mother!"

"Remember your oath, my child. Go to your people."

"You are my people. Mother, don't leave me!"

"I *am* always with you, my daughter."

And with their foreheads still touching, Grey experienced all-encompassing dizziness and phenomena of such
bizarre nature, she never knew if it really happened. It

was as though a pillar of light filled her head. A pillar of light seeming to come for Mother and within it, a vision.

Mother rose from her elderly, pajama-clad body like a butterfly emerging from a cocoon—young, radiantly beautiful, with magnificent wings. Wearing the angelic majesty of Grey's dreams, Mother hovered in the shimmering light. "I love you, my child," and her shining was again a wonderful warm envelope.

"I love you, Mother."

And then dizziness, and vision were gone. Mother's body lay on the ground, looking like any elderly corpse.

The sounds of the soldiers drew close.

Looking to Y Shin Sha through tears, Grey was abruptly struck with what she saw. He looked terribly alien. His strange black eyes were half hidden in concentration as he looked at Mother's body. At that moment his eyes opened fully. She realized then that they were slit like a cat's.

The Nightwalker returned to the present. In the restaurant across the street, through the picture window, she saw Anton in heated conversation. Ritchie had a newspaper in hand and slapped it several times emphatically as he spoke. I have to find out what's going on. Deciding to go in, she put on sunglasses.

Everyone in Eggs and Things checked out the lady coming in the door. Coffee cream tan, thick auburn braided coronet, elegant and remote, even in shorts and T-shirt. Anton was too busy arguing with Ritchie and his partners to do more than glance through her, and Ritchie, also wound up in the fracas, never recognized her as his black-haired, kohl-eyed Sufi dancer.

A waitress led her past their table to be seated, and the Nightwalker spied the headline on the *Honolulu Advertiser* at Ritchie's hand. "BIG ISLAND MARIJUANA BUSTS."

"Can I get the paper?" The waitress poured freshly brewed Kona coffee into a mug, left a menu, and went to accommodate the request. I'm famished, she realized, sipping the rich coffee.

Anton's table was two away and she couldn't hear well, but it was clear he was disagreeing with the others. The waitress brought the newspaper, and after requesting a double order of macadamia nut waffles, scrambled eggs, home fries, and freshly squeezed orange juice, she contemplated the paper.

The president's newest push against drugs meant thirty-three helicopters just for marijuana hunts in the Hawaiian Islands. And those copters were seriously busting growers on the Big Island, where most of Ritchie's product grew. *No wonder they're excited! Are they changing plans?*

The old Hawaiian tintypes decorating the restaurant were for sale. Leaving her table, she went to the wall backing Anton's table and seemed to be studying one, then another. She drifted closer, paused at a tintype of Queen Kapoliani and her court. She moved again until at King Kamehameha's portrait as a child, she was in hearing distance.

"*Better on Maui,*" Anton's voice was insistent.

Ritchie's answer was more an anguished plea—she could tell by his manner he didn't want to rile Anton. "But I have to—"

She interrupted. "Do you know how much this is? Amazing, isn't it, how American clergy got Hawaiian queens into European gowns. Lovely, yes?"

The four men looked blankly at her. She used a New Zealand accent, since summertime in Hawaii meant many New Zealand tourists. She continued looking at them, her mirrored sunglasses reflecting their faces.

Ritchie finally said, "I think you should ask your waitress."

"Oh yes, good idea." A last admiring look at the tintype and she went back to her table, tingling with the excitement of having been so close to Anton, having looked into his eyes.

The waitress brought her food. Stalking now, one part of her played a role, eating, aware and focused on her prey, another part went back to 1977, a summer Friday night in New York City, just after her first sparring session.

Grey pumped knuckle push-ups happily. *Veni, Vidi, Vici,* she congratulated herself, *I proved myself.* At the front of the dojo Khan announced the Friday night movie was *Drunken Monkey* and told its legend:

"Drunken monkey is a bizarre fighting style originated

centuries ago by a prisoner in a bamboo cage in a bamboo forest where monkeys were the alarm system. If a human or large animal approached, or if a prisoner attempted escape, monkeys set up a hue and cry, alerting the guards.

"One prisoner, a martial artist convicted of subversion against the corrupt government, witnessed an amazing phenomenon: A guard left a wineskin behind. A monkey grabbed it and ripped a hole, drank the wine, and quickly was drunk. Other monkeys gathered, then attacked the drunken one. But drunken monkey's bobbing, weaving, almost-falling over and high-pitched yammering proved disconcerting to the others. The curious monkeys came close to observe. The drunken monkey devastated them with a ferocious hitting, biting attack, then fled in mirth.

"During his years in the bamboo cage the martial artist developed a fighting system based on that drunken monkey's example. Upon his release, the martial artist traveled through China, teaching the inebriated monkey's style."

His story finished, Khan said, "We'll discuss the techniques in tonight's movie, so pay attention," and dismissed them.

Grey was jubilant. It's movie night! Recalling her last time with Khan, when he had taken her to *Star Wars*, she thought how wonderful it would be sitting next to him, vindicated, a fighting dojo member, knowing Khan would drop his instructor's demeanor and be again her longed-for lover.

15

Outside after class, Carol told herself she shouldn't feel jeopardized. She had just came onto the street alongside Khan and watched Grey Coltrane almost keel over in shock. Carol kept her face an open sneer aimed at Grey, sitting on a blue Chevy talking to two underbelts. What's the matter, bitch, just recognizing who's with the man? Carol moved closer to Khan. Black belts milled, gathering in preparation for Friday night movie. Underbelts could come, but had to follow behind and keep out of the way.

But Carol's sense of peril persisted, due, of course, to Grey's metamorphosis from sniveling coward to glorious gladiator. Grey had "come out," shown a karateka's fighting spirit, and in her attack on Marcos, she had extemporaneously delivered, form perfect, reflexively flowing kicks and punches and properly terrifying kyiis—results of Carol's training. Grey's stunning gymnastic display had shown grace, beauty, power! Topping it all, her display had sparked the sense of impending doom Carol tried unsuccessfully to deny. Khan said gymnastics were part and parcel of martial arts.

With her thumb Carol hitched the strap of her canvas bag higher on her shoulder, continuing to eye Grey coldly. Dan, Pierre, and Gary spilled onto the street, laughing, pummeling each other. Dan walked to Grey sitting on the Chevy and kissed her. Carol was incredulous. *They know each other?* She watched Dan introduce Pierre and *Gary* to Coltrane.

Suddenly the fucking white belt was holding court. In attendance were the three best-looking, sexiest, most popular black belts in the school, including her Gary! Carol watched Grey smile into Pierre's dark eyes, laugh at something Gary said.

322

Like a queen watching a new consort enter the throne room, Carol saw her domain crumbling before her. She pressed against Khan, making it obvious she was where she belonged. She felt something from him. What? Jealous his black belts flirted with Grey? Did he want his reject back? She speculated, reevaluating Grey, these events, what they meant to her future plans. The shaken black belt noted with further dismay that the rich bitch, wearing faded jeans, running shoes, and a turquoise cotton blouse knotted at the waist, was a *vision* perched on the old blue Chevy. Her hair was enchantingly disarrayed: the shaggy waves curled softly in summer humidity —a moving, glowing frame for her gorgeous face smiling enticingly at the gathered men. Carol was getting sick.

I've got to get pregnant! It hit like lightning, and she congratulated herself on the simple, brilliant thought. Why didn't I see all along? *Pregnant*. He'll marry me then. The diabolically reassuring thought became a satisfied smile playing Carol's gamin face. She felt Gary's eyes on her and looked at him. He stuck his tongue out. Crazy nut! But she was pleased. Even if she didn't want him, he was hers.

Sixty students walked the East Village streets. As Khan led, Carol alongside, black belts laughed and joked with Sensei in the summer night. It was a familiar sight, and local shopkeepers and residents called greetings as the school passed. A woman in a babushka and apron in front of her Ukranian restaurant presented Khan with a big bag of warm-from-the-oven cookies. "For the movie," the old woman said, patting the adored karate instructor's broad shoulder. Years ago, Khan had ousted this neighborhood's predatory junkies and muggers, instigated student patrols, and remedied the mostly elderly Eastern European residents' sad plight.

Grey found herself, like a leaf caught in a river current, drawn along with the class toward Chinatown. "Come to the movie," the photographer, Robert, who had driven her home, invited. "Yeah, come to the movie," said Ed, the schoolteacher walking on her other side.

She had been talking to them when Khan and Carol had come from the school together. She had been planted on the car directly across from the school door waiting for Khan, her aching, bruised body wanting only him, when Khan and Carol came through the door. Carol's victorious sneer spoke volumes. Overwhelmed by the sight, Grey stared back. Then Dan came, kissed her, brought his handsome dojo brothers. Grey somehow found the composure to socialize, all the while feeling Carol's eyes, consumed with awareness of Khan across the sidewalk. Dan's whispered "Well done" was not able to gladden her as it would have a few moments before.

Being part of the school journey was a short interruption in her ambivalent thoughts of Khan. Are you really with Carol? Is it she's a black belt and gets to be close? Was I only the body of the moment? Maybe I'm paranoid and Carol's creating an illusion.

Inside the Sun Sing Theatre, Grey sat between Robert and Ed, four rows behind Khan and Carol. Armed with dried anchovies, cuttlefish, and sticky plum candy, Grey could not find a comfortable position for her bruised hips.

The Hong Kong-made film was spoken in Cantonese, captioned ungrammatically in barely legible English. The latter made no difference. It was the fighting scenes everyone came for. Students laughed and talked as did the mostly Chinese audience in the old, beat-up theater. Small children ran freely in aisles. The audience was never quiet and when the fighting scenes ensued, the audience yelled appreciation or criticism.

Khan watched between Carol and Dan. He had seen the drunken monkey legend many times and found this particular version interesting. The choreographer was talented, and the young master playing the prisoner made for a good drunken monkey. He poised on one foot, the other held in the air angled askew, making drunken giggles, acting the fool. It appeared he had no balance, was completely stoned. This behavior always duped the bad guys into complacency, whereupon the drunken monkey master kicked ass. Once the actual fighting started, he became a veritable windmill of spinning, wheeling, flying devastation.

Khan chuckled aloud, recalling a tournament during which he had gone drunken monkey. When "Ajami" was called, he hopped on one leg, making bizarre faces and high-pitched giggles. He wobbled his head and like an idiot, let his tongue hang from his mouth, scaring his opponent to death. It was bad enough to draw Khan Sun as an opponent, but to witness his insane carryings-on and not know what was coming next was awful. Khan scored on his startled opponent at will.

Hearing Khan chuckle, Dan said, "Good drunken monkey, isn't it, Sensei? Is that how you're going to look in a tux?" Dan's upcoming nuptials were foremost in his thoughts. The invited black belts were excited also, expecting the party of the year.

Khan smiled at Dan, proud his dojo son was building the life he wanted. He would test Dan soon for shodan. He looked to his right and saw Carol's profile in the flickering screen light. He would test her for nidan. Time for her to climb rank. Carol turned, smiling. "Good drunken monkey," she said, and Khan thought, the plans I've made will give her a solid future. And now, it seemed, he had another dojo daughter.

Grey had proved she had fighting chi. It wasn't controlled or yet understood by her, but it was there. Khan had been secretly thrilled when Grey had popped that gorgeous back handspring like it was nothing. He had always wanted a gymnast to train, but never considered the possibility of that gymnast being a woman. Buddha! He could train her beyond any student he had ever worked with. But, he reminded himself, I won't be here, and even if I were, she probably wouldn't keep training. Today's session only *began* the year of trial required to rank as green belt and thereby attain recognition as one who took martial arts seriously. Then again, he considered, after three months with Carol, Grey was already a quarter there. Time had passed, he realized. She had stuck that out—must have been a bitch, he thought, glancing at Carol and chuckling again. Carol had done a superb job. She was a hell of a teacher. He was drawn back to the film as the star went into action.

Yeah, you could learn a lot in a cage, he thought as the young master on-screen concluded fighting, leaving six prone bodies. *His cage*, where he could only crouch, had swung from a tree. No monkeys to entertain him, only the stinking gooks below. Fucking Cong with sharpened sticks. *He* was their entertainment, their monkey. They laughed when he shat or pissed, which wasn't often because they fed him only twice a week, watching him almost starve, keeping him barely alive in case he might be used in negotiations. Khan appreciated the drunken monkey legend because he knew he had learned a lot in a cage.

Like how to get out! He had duped his captors by urinating on the same spot, weakening the bamboo, then began on another spot. Bamboo is tough, and it had taken months to prepare the cage for escape. During that time he had had to adjust his crouch, for he could no longer keep his feet on those two urine-soaked poles. He had to broaden his crouching stance, moving his feet wider apart, adding more pain to the already excruciating pain in his legs. They were atrophied from no movement and never being able to straighten. Then, finally, the time was right to escape.

An unsuspecting woman with a small child and a gathering basket stumbled upon the Cong camp near dusk. Khan watched a guard's swinging machete simultaneously lop off the little boy's head and the mother's hand raised to protect her child. Laughing and jabbering, the Cong staked the woman down while she screamed, tying her so she was spread-eagled next to her child's head and her own severed hand. As the woman's life's blood seeped from her arm's stump, the Cong lined up for intercourse.

With new entertainment his captors forgot the special forces captain in the overhead cage. Khan pushed the bamboo and fell like a lump to the ground below. Pulling the body he could not straighten through the jungle by arms kept strong with isometrics, like a crippled gorilla, Khan dragged his bent and wasted legs. Yeah, you could learn a lot in a cage.

He thought again about Grey's moment of truth, how well she had done. He pictured the disbelief in her crushed emerald eyes as he exited the dojo with Carol. Actually, she has balls, he thought, coming after me. He wondered if the prince awaited Grey at home and if they laughed together over her karate adventures. I wonder what the prince thinks of her bloody back?

Without wanting to, he thought about how breathtakingly beautiful Grey had appeared, sitting on the car with the whole dojo panting to get next to her. "Women can turn a perfectly good dojo into a whorehouse," the Master had said. She probably collected men like others collected stamps. There had been a moment when he wanted to snatch her off that car and hurt her—hurt her for almost making him care, then turning out to be just like everybody else, except worse, because she wanted to add him to her collection. Well, Khan wasn't collectible!

The movie was fast approaching the culminating fight scene. Khan noted the Ghost Shadows, a powerful Chinese youth gang, was in the theater in force. He became more aware of Carol as she pressed her shoulder against his, wanting so much . . .

After the film, as the school gathered outside the theater, many of the students were wobbling in drunken monkey stances. About forty Ghost Shadows emerged. Martial arts buffs from all over New York spilled onto the street. There was always a moment after a good fighting film when violence could erupt. Chi was in the air. But the Ghost Shadows respected Khan, who had once acted as the mayor's liaison when an escalating gang problem in Chinatown exploded in death, violence, and front-page headlines. Khan negotiated a peace. Some Ghost Shadows dipped in martial arts courtesy as they passed him, and their leader stopped to talk with him, as did a couple of other senseis.

Carol, standing to the side, opened an envelope Dan had just given her and read his wedding invitation with genuine surprise. She ran her finger over its raised engraving. Classy, really classy. She looked at Dan, talking with another black belt, George, a blue-eyed, blond bounty hunter who drove to Khan's Manhattan classes from Long Island three nights a week. A real Clint Eastwood type, he went after escaped prisoners, bail jumpers, and wanted criminals with a sawed-off shotgun and a lot of balls. Dan and George began to drunken monkey at each other. Carol smiled. Crazy dojo brothers. Looking again at the invitation, she thought, I've never been to a wedding. The black belts had been talking about this one for a long time in the locker room, giving Dan hell about the "yoke and collar." Carol heard his fiancée was gorgeous and hot. Well, she'd have to be, fine as Dan was.

I have nothing to wear. Now that the invitation was in hand, Carol realized how much she wanted to go. Her work clothes would never do. Fuck! She thought then about Grey's wardrobe and the fucking nerve of her coming downtown in jeans like ordinary people. Running her finger again over the raised engraving, Carol savored the cream-colored wedding invitation. Checking Khan, she saw him socializing. Her eye wandered to a hole-in-the-wall candy store with an advertisement for " BUBBLE GUM BY THE BOX" in the window. She darted across the street.

Gary, watching her run to the candy store, said to Dan, "Did you see her with that invitation?"

"Like Fagan relishing stolen coins," Dan said, and drunken monkeyed on one leg. Gary drunken monkeyed back, then headed to the candy store, where he watched Carol through the dirty plate glass window, talking to the old Chinese proprietor. Seeing she was buying bubble gum, Gary opened the door, causing bells to jingle, and walked in. Carol looked up. "Osss." She made a quick bow, returning to her conversation with the Chinaman.

Gary walked to the glass counter filled with little toy soldiers and, standing close to Carol, stared at her. She didn't like that. She had given him courtesy because he outranked her, being a nidan, but that was as far as it went. "What do you want?" she said.

"To buy some bubble gum, short stuff," he said and grinned down at her. "How much for the whole box?" he queried the Chinaman. Quick bargaining ensued. Gary acquired the Bazooka for half the asking price. Paying for the bubble gum and taking a piece himself, he read the comic wrapper, then moved even closer to Carol. His six-foot frame towered over her five-foot-four. Reaching behind her, he pulled open the zipper of her red bag and dropped in the bubble gum box. He closed the zipper.

"Why did you do that?" she asked, moving away.

"A present from me to you," he said, smiling, moving closer again.

"Get away from me. What do you want anyway?"

"To find out if you're going to Dan's wedding."

"I don't know. Haven't made up my mind. Why?"

" 'Cause I want to dance with you at a wedding."

"You're crazy!" she said, and ran out the door.

After the drunken monkey movie, Grey was invited to join her classmates for Chinese food but declined, being emotionally and physically exhausted. She needed epsom salts desperately, and she was due at the stable to tranquilize Darkchild at 5 A.M. for his trip to Kentucky. But most of all, she wanted to go home because she was terrified Khan and Carol would be together at the restaurant. By that time she decided she didn't want to know the truth—it was just too much for her.

In the Honolulu restaurant, by a combination of behavioral study and lip reading, the Nightwalker determined that Anton made his point stronger than Ritchie and partners and would have his way, doing the deal on Maui as planned. With her spoon she captured the last tiny bits of macadamia nuts drenched in butter and blueberry syrup on the otherwise empty plate. The waitress freshened her coffee and Anton prepared to leave. Paying her check, she waited until he departed and once again followed him onto the street, where he headed back toward Diamond Head. Probably going to get some sleep, she thought, knowing he had had next to none. Better to watch over him while he slept than while he debauched. She did hope he'd get back to talking on his phone and provide her with positive information. As the Nightwalker trailed the black man along Kalakahua Avenue, a group of soldiers walked on the other side of the street. Their brown army uniforms reminded her of those of Anton's Taiwanese troops and she remembered being hunted by them.

Taiwan, 1985

Y Shin Sha picked up Mother's body and was gone.

Grey was alone and the soldiers were almost on her. She cut into the foliage and in her blue pajamas and black rope-soled slippers traveled swiftly, first through familiar surroundings, then far from the area where she had spent the last three years of her life.

In unfamiliar terrain with sounds of her pursuers clearly audible, she came to the edge of a huge gorge and looked into its depths, where steaming springs announced themselves by pillars of smoke. Deciding she could be trapped there, she looked up. Climbing was better, she determined.

Two hours later, in a highland forest, she entered a dense clump of rattan, reasoning that their leaf tips with sharp, curved thorns was a deterrent to any searching for her and knowing that good drinking water could be obtained in the rattan's hollow stems. She was well hidden: some of the spiny stems grew twenty feet, others twined and climbed one hundred and twenty.

She stayed in the rattan for a day and a night, eating the gelatinous pulp of its small fruit, at the same time sweet and acid, and feeling a difference in herself, as if an essence of Mother and Y Shin Sha remained inside her.

That day and night, she wandered in and out of a trance, planning Anton's death, waiting . . . Once a bird's cry caught her attention. A blue parakeet was impaled by its wing on a thorn. Hands tingling, she pulled the bird off the long thorn. Its punctured wing bled. Holding the parakeet, she loved it. The bleeding stopped. She opened her hands and the little bird hopped, chirping, from her, branch to branch, then flew off. She realized she possessed healing talents. "I feel you, Mother."

Time passed, and as she crouched, her mind working below Alpha, she twice heard soldiers. Were they some of the same soldiers who had raped her and killed her baby? Strangely, she felt no fear, giving her an inkling that some of Y Shin Sha's talents were also hers. That inkling was positively reinforced by what happened after sundown.

Sensing something nearby, even though it was night, she saw a deadly pit viper at least five feet long about to crawl over her slippered foot. Grabbing the snake behind its jaw and by its body, she flung the pit viper high into the rattan, impaling it. Then she knew. Her senses *were* keener than normal, her reflexive actions beyond ordinary, her strength and mind powers more than products of training.

Then she knew nothing could stop her. Touching the unending circle on her neck, she chanted. "I am Y Shin Sha, I am Y Shin Sha." She left the rattan with Mikel Anton's face imprinted on her mind's eye.

The Nightwalker was waiting for her, holding the five-foot pit viper she had killed.

Y Shin Sha wore no expression, but as usual she simply knew what he wanted her to know. He was aware of her self-revelations within the rattan, was pleased with her behavior, and wished her to follow him.

She trailed his lithe figure through deep foliage with no sad thoughts of Mother or tears for her demise. Part of the something that had happened to her dictated she would never cry again.

For days they traveled through gorges. Many times she hid while Y Shin Sha made contact with young men. It was obvious he was training them and that they were members of the Taiwan Independence Movement. With the intense young men gathered around him, the Nightwalker taught them to handle weapons and explosives from caches he uncovered. How did he produce these modern-day weapons? She never saw him talk. Did the boys understand him as she did? Whatever their form of communication, it worked. She often saw the men doing the snapping hand form Y Shin Sha had taught her.

Once, when she thought she was alone, bathing naked in a hot spring, the Nightwalker suddenly appeared at its edge. In his camouflage uniform and red beret, looking for all intents and purposes like a handsome, patrician Chinese, he peered at her.

Feeling no modesty for her nudity, she knew because he wanted her to that he had seen her nude many times before. Then she experienced a feeling she used to have when she and Khan thought they were alone, in a secret place where they used to meet. And then she realized Y Shin Sha had been watching her ever since she had come to these mountains—even when she made love.

The Nightwalker gave no indication of leaving, so she came from the spring and felt his eyes on her as she dressed. *I will never have sex again in my life*, Grey thought at that moment. She looked defiantly at the Nightwalker to see if he also thought of sex. Can he read my mind or just put things into it? But the strangely slanted eyes were impenetrable. He only wheeled and headed north. She followed, head whirling with remembrances of Khan's touches, ones she would never feel again.

One day they came to a freshwater stream where purple water hyacinth was massed: their growth was dense and buoyant like a light raft. Y Shin Sha rolled quickly over the floating weeds in crossing the stream. Grey did the same. Once on the other side, the Nightwalker pulled scores of hyacinth, hanging them to dry on nearby trees.

Reaching under the weeds, he caught fish, laying them on the bank also to dry, and left her, returning hours later with sweet potatoes.

As she watched, he used the now-dried purple water hyacinth flowers, which because of their high phosphorus content burned readily, to make a fire. No longer wondering how she knew these things, she accepted the knowledge as part of her. He buried the potatoes beneath the fire and while they cooked, she joined him in the snapping hand form, feeling their two chis blend.

Then she shot arrows with deadly accuracy while he watched. She thought, What a lovely way to kill Anton, and pictured Anton's head, an arrow piercing his temples.

Later, she ate the fish and sweet potato as the Nightwalker watched. Suddenly he made her know what had happened to Anton. She pictured the black man's fall into a gorge, saw in her mind's eye Anton still alive, dragging his hurt body into the jungle. Y Shin Sha left him alive for me to kill. Good, she thought, he understands. And then she peered directly into Y Shin Sha's eyes, trying also to understand this mysterious being, a part of whom she seemed to have inside her. What she got back shocked her.

He meant to enforce Mother's will. She would have to leave Taiwan!

"No!" she said aloud, throwing the remains of her food into the fire. "I will hunt him and kill him. I will not leave here until he is dead!"

Then Y Shin Sha was the alien again; his eyes opened wide and the slits showed. Picking up a stick, he hit her foot hard. She was astounded, realizing this was no joke. He meant to beat her! She ran.

He chased her for two days, and never could she hide from him or outdistance him. Sometimes he would be in a tree overhead, laughing at her, making the air vibrate with his mirth, causing her head to hurt, then would suddenly descend, and hit her with the stick. In her mind's eye she saw the new ones' trial as they were chased by stick-wielding disciples and realized that was exactly what Y Shin Sha was doing. He was providing a trial both to further her education and impose Mother's will.

And so it went, and as the new ones had been, she was

beaten and bloody when she finally made her escape from Y Shin Sha into an American Air Force base fifty miles from Taipei.

Now she trailed Anton through the streets of Honolulu, three years after Y Shin Sha had herded her with a stick. Anton continued toward Diamond Head, most likely headed to his condo to sleep as she had surmised.

At that moment, the man calling himself Charles Halehana unscrewed the mouthpiece of the phone inside Anton's rented condominium.

He and the boy were now situated in an apartment down the hall on the same floor. Setting up the monitoring equipment, discovering his infinity transmitter in Anton's phone not working, he just entered the black man's condo after making sure it was empty.

The transmitter was gone! Halehana's mind raced as he replaced the mouthpiece. Had Anton discovered and removed the device? He remembered that the boy had heard someone come in the apartment after his own departure. That someone had searched the room and unscrewed the mouthpiece. Did that person come back and remove it? Most likely, the big man conjectured, his foot pushing one of many bent beer cans on the floor as he looked at the disgusting mess about, a filthy temple to excess and sexual deviation.

Pornographic magazines, a whip, handcuffs. The rejected packet of condoms on the carpet where they had fallen that morning from a terrified whore's hand. Empty candy wrappers and tinfoil packets once holding cocaine. A half-eaten hamburger in a white cardboard container. Dried pizza remains . . .

I could just wait here and kill him—get it over with. He thought again of his adopted son, Yu, how much the boy needed to see Anton die. *Let things stand,* he decided. *No, I don't think Anton removed the infinity transmitter. If he had discovered it, he would have left it and put misinformation over the phone. Better yet, he would have tried to set up whoever put it there. That was more his style. Whoever hunts him can't have the kill—it's mine!*

As the big man exited Anton's condo, he looked at the door of the next condo, where the desk man had told him a gorgeous widow holed up. His mind flashed to his former intuitive feeling that a female also trailed Anton. She had preceded his tracking of the mercenary at the Alabama gun school and the Georgia anti-terrorist training camp. He thought of the listening devices he had found on Anton's phone in New Orleans.

He knocked on the door, prepared to excuse himself for being at the wrong door if she answered. He waited. Nothing. Using the same pick that had gained him entry to Anton's condo, the big man entered the "gorgeous widow's" living room.

On Kuhio Avenue, Mikel Anton hailed a pedicab operated by a good-looking blond boy. Youngsters came to Honolulu from all over the world to pedal tourists in carts fronted by bicycles called pedicabs. They made a few bucks, some sold pakalolo, but mostly they had a good time and developed terrific leg muscles.

The Nightwalker sped up to keep pace with Anton's pedicab. Her green eyes on his broad back, her mind wandered elsewhere.

Manhattan, 1977

In her apartment Sunday night, having returned from Bluegrass Farm and settling Darkchild in, she felt as if her weekend in Kentucky had been a dream, except for the freedom of knowing she would not have to be at the stable every day.

Grey Coltrane's visit to the Bluegrass Farm was an event eagerly awaited by its owners. Unbeknownst to her, the local newspaper's society columnist was informed of the dinner party and hunt to be given in her honor. The columnist, mad to score points with other publications, called the New York *Post*, the *Enquirer*, the *Star*, the *Daily News*, and *The Los Angeles Times*. The woman thought awhile and then called *People* magazine, *Vogue*, *Harper's Bazaar, Town and Country, Time,* and *Newsweek*.

Darkchild's flight had been uneventful. A mild tranquilizer had kept the stallion docile. They were met by a shining silver horse van and a limousine, and whisked into early morning Kentucky sunshine.

The farm was acres upon acres of rolling hills, sweeping meadows, patches of forest, lakes and streams, decorated by race horses on sabbatical, mares in foal, yearlings kicking up their heels, and fillies in heat. Darkchild needed no prodding to join them when he was turned loose. Since the tranquilizer had worn off, he took a moment to lift his head and smell fresh grass. His nostrils quivering with excitement, Darkchild picked up an even more enticing scent. A last prancing circle around Grey, one last whinny, and he was gone, tail and mane flying, in hot pursuit of a delicate palomino mare named Lady May. "Have fun, Darkchild, I know how it is."

The twenty-year-old heiress spent that sunny Saturday enjoying the grass herself, walking barefoot for miles. Every now and then Darkchild came galloping past, sometimes with his new friend. They were a wonderful contrast: Darkchild so gleaming blue-black, the mare burnished tawny gold with sparkling white mane and tail.

In her solitary wanderings she came on a secluded lake. Prompted by the heat of the afternoon, she removed her jeans and checkered cotton shirt, lay them at the base of a stately weeping willow, and swam nude in the cool water for an hour. Afterward, lying by the edge of the lake, allowing the Kentucky sun to ease her aching, bruised body, she thought of the night before and her dojo traumas, how she had faced physical fear and conquered it. As the sun warmed her breasts and belly, she realized that experience had been a profound revelation of her own courage and capabilities. *Khan, you showed me part of myself I never knew I possessed. It makes me love you more. How many times have you made love to me?* Tracing circles on her flat stomach, she began counting. *Not enough.* She was revisited by sensations that his touches brought: tingling groin, swelling nipples.

Darkchild broke her reverie by running circles around her and splashing through the water's edge, getting her wet again. The horse was laughing, she was sure of it. Darkchild's lady friend joined him. Grey stood, patting the two horses, talking softly to them while the sun dried her. Then, dressing, she worked out.

Stretching first, she did kata, and the moving meditation brought an inner peace. She ended the kata session by drunken monkeying around a bit and then burst into laughter at the quizzical faces of the two horses watching her strange gyrations.

At the hunt Sunday morning she was disconcerted by the unexpected appearance of the press and mounted ahead of everyone to escape photographers and questioning journalists.

It was a thrilling chase. Astride a beautiful roan mare, auburn hair flying from her cap, she remained in the forefront of the pack riding after the hounds. The exhilarating two-hour hunt was followed by an opulent brunch attended by two hundred. She spent a few more hours with Darkchild and Lady May, then waved a teary goodbye to Darkchild. The black stallion, a picture of contentment, seemed to question his mistress's emotional distress. *I'm all right, what's the matter with you?*

Now, back in Manhattan all her thoughts centered on Khan. Before falling asleep, she even considered calling him. *And what?* she asked herself. *Ask him if he's sleeping with Carol?*

At Monday night's class, Grey encountered a round-robin sparring session with all the white belts and a disgustingly filthy bathroom. She came out of the round-robin the worse for wear, having caught an assortment of kicks, punches, and sweeps. But she dished out some, too, and the awful fear was a tiny bit less. She needed no special treatment to find her fighting spirit and was again impressed by how serious a lesson sparring was. This "facing the tiger" was indeed stressful. Khan paid her no attention.

On Tuesday, she began learning a more intricate blocking system requiring simultaneous blocking and punching. She spent two exhausting hours drilling it, then faced an hour of round-robin sparring. She swept someone for the first time.

Whenever the opportunity presented itself, she watched Khan, trying to fathom his inscrutability and his feelings toward Carol. To no avail. He remained distant, never demonstrating anything but a sensei's demeanor to Carol. Grey was frustrated, miserable, forced to face the possibility she had lost all communication with Khan. The only plus was that she was caught up by the awesome challenge of karate training.

On Wednesday night, after a grueling four-hour class, a half hour of latrine duty, and still no acknowledgment from Khan, she made up her mind to send him the parka. Also, it was time for her to consider what to wear to Llana's wedding.

Llana, following the latest fashion, did not pick her attendants' dresses but instead assigned colors and let each choose her own. Grey was to wear violet pastel, but the frothy chiffon creation in her closet wouldn't do now. It plainly showed her bruises! Even though her back felt much better, she still bore a wide purple stripe visible in the low-backed gown. And her arms . . .

Ralph Daniels called, needing her at a fund-raiser to save St. Anthony's Children's Hostel, a project she had been part of since her days as Ed Fowler's wife. Dealing with the city of New York and the Franciscan Order of Friars was a mire of red tape and archaic holy laws, but the lawyer was optimistic that Grey's appearance would make success more likely. She agreed.

By Thursday, her dojo brothers saw yet more of her sculptured body than the skimpy underwear of her first day. *Her body was now public domain.* She was featured in several scandal sheets, including a six-page photo spread in the New York *Post*'s centerfold. "NUDE BATHING IN KENTUCKY FOR RECLUSIVE TWENTY-YEAR-OLD HEIRESS" was the caption of one photograph showing her lying naked at edge of the lake, nipples and pubis blacked out by a censor's pen.

The press refused to drop the Fowler name from hers. "GREY COLTRANE FOWLER AT JET-SET KENTUCKY NUDIST HORSE FARM" read another paper's caption. The picture depicted Grey standing naked between Darkchild and Lady May, a hand on each horse. Again her nipples and pubic area wore little black blocks. But the picture Grey's dojo brothers loved best was one captioned: "ECCENTRIC MILLIONAIRESS GREY COLTRANE FOWLER—DOES SHE NEED PSYCHIATRIC CARE?" showing Grey in jeans and shirt doing drunken monkey.

There she stood, barefoot, on one leg, the other askew in the air. Arms raised, hands hung near her face, fingers open, her face was contorted, eyes rolling, head lolling to one side, and her tongue hung from her mouth.

Carol saw two of the papers before finishing work. Grey's nude photos were more than she could bear. The perfectly sculptured body, her beautiful breasts, the picture between two gorgeous horses with Grey looking like a wood nymph come to life, and the drunken monkey pose! That picture spoke of expertise. What fucking right did a white belt have to make like a martial arts expert? Carol's hand shook with anger, holding the newspaper. Maybe if Khan saw it, he would be mad a white belt didn't know her place and kick her out of the dojo. Then again, he might like it. Thinking of Khan looking at Grey's naked perfection, Carol was sick. Then again, if Sensei wanted the rich bitch, he'd have her. Oh fuck! She threw the papers away, not able to handle yet another worry. She was loaded with them.

Hurriedly she picked up her red bag lying next to her desk. There were sounds of things knocking together inside it. The worker next to her looked curiously. "Got a problem, sister?" Carol snapped. The woman looked quickly away. Carol Backer was not the most popular person in the office.

Hitching the bag over her shoulder and throwing a last dirty look at the woman, Carol rushed out. It was five and her schedule was more than usually cramped. She planned stopping at a fancy second-hand clothing store, on the upper East Side. Having scraped together thirty-five dollars, she intended to somehow outfit herself for Dan's wedding. Because classes began at seven-thirty on Thursday, she'd have to hurry.

As she rode the crowded uptown subway, she reviewed events so far thwarting her becoming pregnant. Khan had not made love to her in almost two weeks. Was it coincidental Grey Coltrane had been in the dojo for that same amount of time?

Over the weekend, when she had intended putting her propagative plan into action, Khan had fasted. Carol hung out with the other black belts upstairs in his apartment. They had free rein of the place, except for the bedroom and his library. Only she was allowed in those rooms. The black belts partied, listening to Khan's incredible record collection, talking martial arts, going downstairs to the dojo, working out, coming back upstairs, hanging out.

But it wasn't the same without Khan. He was on the roof, where he'd been for two solid days, drinking only water and brewed herbs, sitting in lotus position for hour upon hour, with only the dogs out there with him. At midnight Master Pedray, Khan's weapons instructor, would come by.

Pedray was Filipino, soft-eyed, soft-spoken. A small man with big martial arts expertise, he practiced and taught forty different weapons. Pedray was secretive. No one knew where he lived. Khan addressed him as "Master," but Pedray was proud of the fact he had never formally been ranked beyond third-degree black belt. An Air Force communications expert, who had been stationed in Okinawa for eight years, Pedray had spent his off-duty time training in Okinawan martial arts, specializing in weaponry, achieving a third dan. That had been years ago and Pedray had never returned to his senseis in Okinawa to be ranked, although he continued advancement.

So for the past few days, the only communication Khan had had was with Pedray, sometimes referred to as "The Shadow."

At night, Carol lay in Khan's bed, peering through the window at the two men. Since Master Pedray said steel took energy from the moon, he and Khan worked *sais* and swords from midnight until dawn, first practicing technique, then fighting. The ringing of steel on steel went on for hours.

Khan broke his fast on Tuesday, after four days. He was gaunt and peaceful—and not horny. Carol hated when he got like that—inside a spiritual fortress with no place for her. The last time it had happened, Khan had ended their sexual relationship for over a year. But he was different this time and it confused her. His attitude toward her lately was unusually benevolent, almost gentle. He even let her onto the roof for one session with Master Pedray—and that was unheard of! Carol brought her sais, a pair of heavy steel three-pronged swords, and Master Pedray schooled her.

Carol was very proud of that. No woman worked sais. The master showed her beautiful moves. She would blow minds in weapons competitions at tournaments.

But how to get pregnant? She focused on Dan's wedding. Carol knew Khan was Dan's best man. With Gary chasing her, hot to "dance at the wedding," she intended rekindling the jealousy that had gotten her back to Khan in the first place. It would be a party—a wedding was romantic. She had to get a dress!

Grey spent Thursday afternoon with Halston, explaining her problem. Without blinking an eye, he called for a measuring tape, carefully recording the length and breadth of the bruise on her back. After that he examined her arms. Together they selected the silk chiffon which was to be tinted barely violet and silk-screened in strategic places.

While she was at home preparing for class, Ralph Daniels called asking if she had seen the day's papers.

"No, I haven't," she said. "Why?"

"Well, I suggest you do, Mrs. Fowler, then get back to me. We'll have to issue some sort of statement. Several board members called. They mostly say the public display is . . . Well, actually, they're questioning your sanity, and your position on the board. I think you should sue for invasion of privacy."

She had returned to her apartment and was reading her press when the phone rang again. It was Debbie, the makeup artist. "Healed up, luv?"

"Yes, thank you, Debbie, you're a real friend in need."

"Quite a splash, ain't you?"

"Oh, the papers," Grey said nonchalantly, like she wasn't aghast at the pictures spread on the kitchen counter.

"Yes, luv. What's it you're up to in the photo with your clothes *on*?"

"Drunken monkey," Grey stated flatly, wondering if her mother and father had seen the papers, if Khan . . . Oh God! "What are you wearing to Llana's wedding?" she said, changing the subject.

It took all her courage not to go into hiding. At the dojo she was not in disgrace, much the opposite. She might have thought she was Joan of Arc returning victorious from the wars, so exuberant was her greeting. Her dojo brothers clapped and yelled when she entered the dressing room. Pictures of her naked hung on the walls. Several of the students had cut pictures from the paper and asked her to sign them. Everybody was all smiles in the locker room.

The mat was another story. It was a hard class. She had her first session with spinning kicks and badly stubbed her toe when a white belt bruiser blocked a kick she threw. Khan was, if possible, more remote. She immediately noticed his weight loss. The high-planed cheekbones were more pronounced, causing his strong face to take on a delicacy that was at first surprising, then made her ache for him more than ever.

Terribly dejected after class by his denial of her existence, wanting to escape from all the people who had seen her naked in the pictures, she limped on her stubbed toe to her car and was just about to pull away when Dan appeared at the window. "Good drunken monkey," he said, leaning into the Mercedes with a big grin on his handsome face.

Relief broke over her, taking the form of uproarious laughter shared with Dan. She didn't care then if she was naked all over the papers. It felt so good to laugh! Feeling a lot better, she drove home, pondering the quandary of what to say to people like her family, who were going to need explanations. She couldn't come up with a solution. She could only think about Khan.

Khan received the parka Friday morning. "Thank you for putting me in touch with my own courage. You're the best sensei in the world. Your student, Grey Coltrane," read her note.

Putting the Kute Eskimo parka on, experiencing the wolf fur lining's softness, he walked to the mirror. I look like Genghis Khan, he thought, taken with his image. Putting the hood up, he turned from side to side. Then taking the parka off, he laid it on the bed and touched the bone beading, the fur, the butter-soft leather. A majestic offering from a magnificent woman with great martial arts potential.

Students often gave him gifts, usually when they made green belt, always when making black belt. This jacket, though, fit for a pasha, was more than a grateful student's offering. An attempt perhaps to buy him for her collection? Whatever her reasoning, he *loved* the parka.

Llana sat on a kitchen stool, feeding dough into a steel noodle-making machine bolted into the blue tile counter, turning its handle slowly. As raw noodles came out the other end, she chopped them to size, then hung them on a thin wooden rack running the length of the counter. "Mama, this machine must be a hundred years old. Why don't you get an electric one? It does all the work for you."

"It would be hard to get used to a new way," her mother said, standing at the stove, wooden spoon in hand, cooking and testing. "The sauce is good today," she said.

"The sauce is always good, Mama," Llana said pensively.

"What's the matter, baby?" Her mother's soft, dark eyes looked at her. It was like looking into her own eyes.

"How did you do it, Mama? All these years, seven children, being married to a handsome man like Papa—always doing what he says? When he goes away, don't you wonder, Mama? Don't you wonder if there's other wom—"

"Shhhh!" Mama interrupted. "Don't talk that way. That's your father—have respect! Shhhhh."

"But, Mama, we're adults now, we can talk."

"Not about your papa. A woman respects her husband."

"Why, because he's a man?"

"Yes. Men are different. It's different."

"How?"

"Men have to go off some. You have to not look at what they do, as long as the husband comes home, goes to church, is a good father, provides. A woman's place is—"

"Mama, don't say it. Why do you have to be so, so . . . stereotyped!"

"What is this 'stereotyped'?"

"Oh, never mind, Mama. Mama, why don't you learn to speak more English?"

"Why? My family understands Italian. Come," Mama said, "let's go upstairs."

Llana followed meekly, like a child again. God, I miss Dan! Her parents had insisted she move home for the week before the wedding. "The daughter of the house will be married out of the house," Papa said. Llana felt virginal again. She hadn't seen Dan for three days and wouldn't until tomorrow night at church rehearsal. They spoke for hours on the phone. Dan understood, knowing how Papa was and how important it was to Mama for Llana to be there at home. Tons of relatives were already in town for the wedding. There would be twenty-five for dinner tonight and at least that number every night until the wedding. It was just so hard, after sleeping with Dan every night . . .

Llana was so proud of him. There was a family dinner at the house, and afterward Dan went into Papa's office with Papa and her brothers to smoke cigars and drink brandy. Dan winked at her when they returned to the living room and rejoined the women. Llana breathed a sigh of relief. Obviously her brothers liked Dan. It was Papa she had worried about, what with she and Dan having lived together. But it was all right now. She had gone to Mass with Mama and confessed. Jesus. She did penance forever for living in sin. Now she was washed clean—the daughter of the house, at the house.

Upstairs in Mama's bedroom, the gown was on the bed, looking like a pile of clouds. A fitter and her assistant were resewing seed pearls covering the hem, bodice, and train. "God, Mama," Llana said as she stood with the gown on, after they so carefully slipped it over her head. "I can't believe you were this size."

"And your Nonna Rosario, God rest her soul. You are the third generation to marry in this dress."

It was the most beautiful gown ever, Llana thought, looking into the mirror at its paper-thin silk and handmade lace, delicately ecru with age. She tried on her veil and Mama started crying. "Oh, Mama, stop it," Llana said, laughing and teary herself. She knew the wedding was going to be Italian grand opera. It was the only way her family knew how to conduct themselves at weddings.

"Someday your daughter will wear it," Mama said. Tears ran down her cheeks as she pointed out a loose seed pearl to one of the seamstresses. The two women had been working on the gown for weeks, and thousands of little pearls had been resewn, tiny tears in lace painstakingly repaired.

After the fitting, Llana resignedly returned to the kitchen with Mama and daydreamed about making love to Dan between phone calls to Grey. Due mostly to Llana's environment, she and Grey had regressed to secrets and giggles.

Llana was determined to use her wedding day to reconcile Grey and Khan. That's what Grey wanted and, right or wrong, if that's what her best friend wanted, that's what was going to happen! That Carol creature wouldn't be around. Llana had arranged dinner seating so Grey and Khan would be next to each other. They would walk the aisle together, her hand through his arm. Grey once again looking like Scarlett O'Hara in a soft picture hat. Champagne would flow, romance would be in the air.

Before Friday's class, Khan wandered the empty dojo, pausing at hundreds of photographs backing his desk, reading inscriptions, recalling moments pictured, students gone, tournaments won . . . He laughed softly to himself when one picture reminded him of how he had liberated it from another dojo. Picture stealing was a traditional dojo game. It was not uncommon to walk into another school for the first time and find a picture missing from yours.

He wandered into the black belt dressing room, looked around, walked out, went into the hall, opened the door to the student bathroom, preparing himself for its usual awful odor and was disconcerted by freshness instead. Several daisy-shaped, flower-smelling deodorizers were stuck to now sparkling tile. A small sign on lined note-paper written in red ink and a clear script, was Scotch-taped over the sink. "THIS IS YOUR BATHROOM. PLEASE KEEP IT CLEAN." There was a roll of toilet paper in the holder, something else he had never seen there.

Face reflecting his bemusement, Khan reentered the dojo and looked into the underbelt dressing room. Seeing newspaper pictures stuck on the back wall, he went closer, then did a double take as he saw Grey naked. Moving from picture to picture, he studied each, read captions. Khan paused longest by the photograph showing Grey with Darkchild and Lady May. Any man in his right mind would want her, he thought. Then, lastly, he came to the drunken monkey picture. His rich laughter filled the dressing room and wafted into the dojo.

That night, he pulled Grey from the white belts and took her to the rear of the dojo. "Do a back hand-spring," he said. She obliged. "Give me a front, one and a half," he said next.

Across the mat, Carol, who was tired and out of sorts, put a group of brown belts through kata and watched with horror as Khan probed Grey's gymnastic abilities. Fucking rich bitch was all lit up like a Christmas tree!

Carol thought about blasting a nine-millimeter at Grey and blowing her head off.

When one of the brown belts relaxed his stance, Carol swept at his calf. He hit the mat on his ass and looked at her with fleeting hatred. "Gimme one hundred," she said to him, consumed with hatred of Grey and anxiety over Khan.

Nothing was going right for Carol. She hadn't found a dress that afternoon and had made things worse for herself by abandoning the thrift shops and wandering Bonwit Teller, hating the well-dressed women and salesladies peering askance at her jeans and Nikes. She had put out the word to local boosters, wanting to buy a stolen dress. They laughed at her. Thirty-five dollars wouldn't even get her a hot dress!

Class ended with a fierce sparring session during which Khan matched Carol against Gary. He swept her a few times, which made her really mad, and managed to block her techniques no matter how she tried to get to the big redhead. He outweighed, outreached, and outranked her. His blue eyes laughed as he bounced her around. It was a bad day all around.

In the black belt dressing room, in the back near her locker, Carol pulled off her soaking gi jacket and threw it to the floor. She knelt to her bag, opened its zipper. Her gasp was heard across the room as she pulled a turquoise chiffon dress spangled with silver bugle beads from the bag. Underneath lay dyed-to-match shoes and a silver evening bag. She held the dress against her body, looking at it in disbelief. Then, raising her eyes, she looked into Gary's. "For dancing at weddings," he said.

16

On the morning of Llana Dellagio's wedding, she clipped the headline of *The New York Times*, "ISRAELI WITHDRAWAL LINKED BY MONDALE TO 'REAL PEACE' PACT," and pasted it on the first page of her wedding album. By the afternoon, peace in Israel was the last thing on her mind as she sat in the wood and mirrored dressing room of the church, surrounded by bridesmaids, sisters-in-law, and flower girls.

The door opened, admitting Grey and Debbie. The plump, redheaded makeup artist had been working for hours on bridesmaids and wedding party members in the next room and had just finished with Dan's mother and Grey. It was the bride's turn.

Debbie looked at Llana, wearing a white slip, sitting in a straight-backed chair, looking lost in the midst of the confusion and commanded, "Everybody out, except for Grey and workers." Two seamstresses knelt on the rose carpet, still plying needles on the gown, hanging on a dress form. Supervising them was Mrs. Dellagio, resplendent in floor-length coral chiffon.

"Thank God you're here, Grey," Llana said, brown eyes wide, face scrubbed clean. Her profusion of black hair, washed, conditioned, and brushed until it shone like a raven's wing, hung like a loose sheet to her waist. She looked sixteen—and scared.

Debbie, experienced with nervous brides, went right to work. " 'Air first," she said in heavy cockney, pulling a hairbrush from her pink smock.

Mrs. Dellagio, her own gleaming black hair twisted in a heavy chignon, left the seamstresses and relieved Debbie of the brush, looking suspiciously at the purple streaks in the makeup artist's hair. "I'll make the braids," she said with finality and began vigorously brushing and plaiting

Llana's hair. Debbie could tell she had done it a million times before.

"No one will notice me," Llana said, back to herself a bit as her mother's hands flew in her hair. "My maid of honor is too beautiful. Grey, let me see the back."

In violet silk shoes, Grey turned slowly around. Her ankle-length violet chiffon dress bore butterflies of iridescent bugle beads and paillettes. Tiny butterflies danced along her arms. One big butterfly on her back sparkled so, it seemed to fly. A matching chiffon picture hat framed her face and hair. Debbie had employed violets and browns to enhance her tilted green eyes and a muted pink on her full lips. Violet velvet streamers encircled her tiny waist and fell tantalizingly from the picture hat.

"Absolute Scarlett," Llana proclaimed in full approval.

Mrs. Dellagio finished winding a perfect coronet of Llana's thick braids, and Debbie deftly threaded seed pearls through it, creating a crown from which Llana's veil would fall.

While Debbie assiduously plied her craft, choosing a shadow of ground pearls to highlight Llana's dark eyes and pink pearly blusher on her rosy olive skin, Mrs. Dellagio fussed at the fitters and Grey stood guard at the door, admitting no one.

Finally, Debbie, Mrs. Dellagio, Grey, and the two seamstresses inspected Llana, fully gowned and veiled, as she stared into the full-length mirror.

"You're the most beautiful bride in the world," Grey whispered.

Mrs. Dellagio was talking softly in Italian, touching her fingers to her lips and crying, which made Debbie glad the bride's mother had refused makeup. "Uh, uh," the makeup artist admonished Grey, who looked teary herself. "No sopping my work, luv."

Then the bridesmaids and little flower girls were back in the dressing room. The flower girls grabbed the end of Aunt Llana's train. Eight bridesmaids formed a line.

"Grey, you go now," Debbie said, thrusting Grey's rose and violet bouquet into her hands. Opening the door to the church, she let in organ music. Grey walked as though in a dream toward the church's center aisle, where Khan, who had not attended last night's rehearsal, waited. The dream continued, becoming reality as Khan, resplendent in a tuxedo, offered his arm. They walked, he towering over her, to the dais, where they separated, standing on either side of the priest, and stared at each other as the wedding party made their way up the aisle. Dan came forward, so handsome in his cutaway, his dark eyes fixed expectantly on the satin-ribboned aisle, waiting for his bride.

Gasps and tears gave proper homage to Llana's radiant beauty as she appeared, a shining jewel, on her father's arm, eyes huge under her gossamer veil, looking at Dan.

Dan's mother, a handsome blond woman in teal silk, and Mrs. Dellagio cried openly. Mr. Dellagio's eyes were brimming and Grey was hard put to keep tears away. It was Khan's presence, so overpowering she felt faint, that kept her from weeping at the moment's beauty. He was too magnificent in his tuxedo. Grey stared blatantly at him during the ceremony, wanting him so much she could die.

Suddenly, with Llana and Dan right there being married, as the priest's hand was raised in blessing, unbidden thoughts of Khan's full lips touching hers came to mind, followed by memories of when last they had made love. The way he rode her with commanding exquisite certainty . . . Shivers ran down her spine, and her eyes flickered in passion. She thought his nostrils quivered. Do you smell me? She thought of Darkchild and Lady May. Maybe I should turn, show you my rump, and run. With that thought her smoldering gaze was replaced by an impish grin. She smiled at Khan.

Llana and Dan were man and wife. Grey's heart skipped a beat at the poignant moment Dan lifted Llana's veil and kissed his bride. She traveled the aisle again with her arm through Khan's, then entered a waiting limousine, and sat next to him. They shared the limo with Gary and his bridesmaid, Mary Beth Katrine, whom Grey had not seen since Mary Beth had been a bridesmaid at her own wedding to Ed.

Blond, blue-eyed Mary Beth, possessor of the longest hair at St. Anne's, looked scrumptious in pink-watered silk. The famous tresses still hung from a pink picture hat in a luxuriant sheet to her hips. Mary Beth stared at Khan. He smiled at her. "My name is Khan," he said.

The two young women talked as the limousine sped

toward the country club reception. Khan and Gary remained still. Grey was terribly aware of Khan's muscular leg next to hers. One part of her made small talk with Mary Beth while her other self, the one that really mattered, talked silently to Khan.

The wedding party piled from the limos into the sprawling, slate-roofed clubhouse, forming a reception line. Before the first guests arrived, Grey and Llana caught a moment alone. They hugged, not having to speak, then pulled apart.

"I've got champagne hidden in a bush," Llana said, and they laughed, remembering Grey's wedding shower, forever ago. Radiant with happiness, Llana looked to where Dan, Khan, Pierre, and Gary talked with Roberto and Donato, two of her brothers, also ushers. Mary Beth joined the men's group, then Dan's mother. "Go get him, Grey," Llana said, "before Mary Beth does."

"And every other woman in the world," Grey said, noticing how Dan's mother looked into Khan's eyes as Dan stood proudly by.

Then they took their places in the long reception line, Llana at its head, Grey next to Khan. The next forty minutes they kept busy greeting guests. Grey noted how easily Khan assumed a diplomatic composure. He was taking the same attitude toward her also, a polite manner adopted just for this day.

A flashbulb popped in her face. Then the Nikon's wielder, Debbie, daring in low-cut black beaded dress, trimmed in ostrich feathers, was kissing her. "What a smasher you look, luv. And who's this?" She stared at Khan and moved toward him. "Debbie, how do you do?" She extended her butterfly-tattooed hand, which Khan politely shook before passing her up the line toward the bride and groom. The back of Debbie's dress was cut to a *V* below her waist. Light violet streaks in her short, dark red hair stood up with little black feathers attached to the ends.

Roberto, Llana's twenty-seven-year-old unmarried brother, standing on Grey's other side, stared after Debbie. "Quite an outfit," he said, displaying perfect Dellagio teeth in a lazy smile. He was tall and broad-shouldered with rich black hair and big brown eyes like Llana's. Unbelievably, this was the first time Grey had ever met

Llana's famous brothers. Their reputations proved true, for each was more darkly handsome than the next.

"Ready for some champagne?" Roberto asked Grey, taking her mind off Khan. "I've had about all I can take of this"—he waved his hand, indicating the reception line. "Besides, after all these years I think it's time I get to know Llana's best friend."

"I can't leave, not yet," she said, looking at some fifty more people making their way toward them, but really not willing to leave Khan's side.

"I'll give you another ten minutes, then I'm coming back to insist," Roberto said, and headed for the sumptuously catered cocktail party in full swing. Mrs. Dellagio stopped and began berating him for leaving the reception line, then melted as her handsome son planted a placating kiss on her cheek and said something in Italian.

Llana looked down the line at Grey. She raised an eyebrow toward Khan and peered with narrowed eyes at Grey. Go ahead, her look said, go for it.

Okay, Grey said to herself, this is it. She drew a breath for courage. "It *would* be great to have some champagne," she said brightly to Khan, who must have heard Roberto's offer.

"Yes, that would be nice," he said, patiently shaking the hand of an eighty-year-old great aunt of Llana's.

"I thought—I thought maybe we could talk," she said softly.

"About what?"

You and me. I want to talk about you and me, she wanted to say. "Oh, just talk," she said instead, like an idiot.

"Sounds fascinating," he said. Then the expression on his face changed suddenly, causing her to look in the direction of his gaze.

Carol Backer was working her way through the reception line, accompanied by George, the bounty-hunting black belt from Long Island.

Grey almost fell over. Carol was delicately lovely in a turquoise chiffon toga banded with a silver belt, and most of her hair was caught in a thin silver wire headband, the rest in enticing wisps about her face.

As Carol stopped in front of Grey, they shook hands

like two programmed robots, then Carol moved to Khan, stood on her tiptoes, and kissed him on the lips.

"You look beautiful," he said. Carol beamed, demurely dropping her eyelashes while George shook Grey's hand.

"Time," Roberto said, returning with a crystal goblet of champagne.

Taking the proffered wine and looking into Roberto's liquid eyes, Grey said, "Yes, I need a break." Hooking her arm of sparkling butterflies through his, she abruptly left the reception line, no longer caring for propriety.

As they walked past Llana, Grey saw the shocked expression on Llana's face as Carol offered her congratulations and Dan introduced them. Llana's eyes met Grey's and disavowed any knowledge of what was happening. Then her countenance changed, showing loving approval as she saw Grey's arm hooked through Roberto's. Llana's dark eyes spoke to Grey. Why can't you love someone else? Isn't my brother gorgeous?

Grey decided to make a real effort to get drunk!

By the time the three hundred guests had left the clubhouse after the reception and spilled onto the lawn, where an enormous, medieval-looking tent with heraldic flags waving, for dinner and dancing, Grey had consumed four glasses of champagne. She was cornered by Debbie and her Nikon.

"Who's that?" Debbie asked, indicating Khan.

"My karate instructor."

"Now I understand," Debbie said. She looked appraisingly at Grey. "And who's that?"

"Pierre."

"Introduce me, luv, will you? He looks just my type."

Khan was already seated at the head table atop a podium when Roberto escorted Grey to her seat next to Khan's at the end of the table. Llana had made sure there would be no gentlemen on Grey's right to distract her from Khan, who sat next to Mrs. Dellagio. Roberto solicitously pulled the chair out for Grey. "Dance later?"

"Yes, of course," she said, smiling warmly, thinking how nice he was as he left. Then, terribly aware of Khan overpowering the space next to her, she looked from the podium to the colorful array of guests seated at large, round tables. Six tables in one section held only young people: black belts from the dojo, St. Anne's alumnae, and unmarried friends and family, a particularly attractive group. Grey could see the excitement as they met each other. Roberto smiled from one of the tables and she returned the smile, feeling Khan's electricity at her side and champagne coursing through her head.

At the center of the head table, the bride and groom were besieged by well-wishers. Llana's veil, now attached to the back of her braid-and-pearl coronet, was a frothy white cloud framing her dark beauty. Mr. Dellagio stood, and silence reigned in the huge tent as the handsome, silver side-burned father of the bride proposed a toast.

Guests clinked silverware against glasses, an Italian wedding custom demanding that the bride and groom kiss. Dan and Llana responded in kind. Every few minutes the clinking began again and the couple kissed.

"Cute custom," Grey said to Khan, who had just finished speaking with Mrs. Dellagio, and reached for her champagne glass, which the waiter kept filled. Directly before her was the table where Carol sat between Pierre and Gary.

She's an enigma, Grey thought, sipping Dom Perignon. You'd never know by looking at her now that she's a lethal weapon with a drill sergeant's mouth. Carol's silver-banded waist was enticingly small, and her low-draped chiffon bodice revealed cleavage enticingly large. She was openly flirting with Gary. Debbie, at that table, too, drowned in Pierre's eyes whenever she put aside her camera, which wasn't often.

From the corner of her eye Grey observed Khan, wondering if he was bothered that Carol batted eyelashes at Gary. Seeing no particular reaction, she thought, He doesn't care about anything. Well, the hell with it, then, neither do I. And turning her green eyes' full power on Khan who had not responded to her small talk, she said, "Do you like the parka?"

"It fits well," he said, turning again to Mrs. Dellagio, who had adopted Khan and now urged him to eat his hot appetizer before it cooled.

The nerve! Not even a thank you. Grey picked at her escargot, watching as Khan expertly manipulated the snail holder and tiny fork with his huge hands. She thought again of his ease in the reception line, remembered Dan so proudly reiterating Khan's background as a special forces officer, captain of SEALs. Of course he would have social skills at his command.

Her need for him became heart-searing fire that leapt into her eyes. "If you don't make love to me anymore, I'm going to die," she blurted, then was aghast at the words that had involuntarily left her lips. Clapping a hand over her errant mouth, she made a physical effort to stop more words threatening to tumble out.

"I think you've had too much champagne," he said, fixing her with his wide, slanted eyes.

Mortified, she turned away to watch the guests, mostly men, who came to the podium one by one, shook Mr. Dellagio's hand, then presented an envelope to Llana, who stuffed it into a bulging white satin drawstring pouch.

Grey didn't speak to Khan again. Drinking more, barely picking at the delicious food, she managed to isolate herself and was unaware of exactly when dinner ended and a band began playing. Then she joined with everyone else, forming a big circle so that the bride and groom could dance at its center. Llana and her father danced, followed by Dan and his mother. Of course the best man and the maid of honor were called into the circle. Khan whirled Grey in a waltz. The iridescent butterflies on her dress sparkled under the lights, and the assemblage applauded and commented on what a beautiful couple they made.

Finding herself tipsy, Grey would have stumbled had Khan not held her firmly. As streamers from her hat and waist flew in the circles of the waltz, she felt like a rag doll in his strong grip. Too soon the dance was over. "Please don't leave me," she said, hating herself for subjugating herself, close to tears.

"There will always be someone to take care of you," he said. "You don't need me." He walked her pointedly toward Roberto.

"I hate you. I hate you. you rotten bastard son of a bitch motherfucker," she spat, and ran past Roberto toward the ladies room.

Khan saw Llana follow hurriedly after Grey, thinking how really drunk she was, highly amused by her tantrum and gutter language. Where was her prince? Roberto also looked after Grey as she exited, and Khan realized he was jealous. Disliking the feeling, he turned toward the dance floor.

The lights were now dimmed, and in place of the staid waltz band, a young deejay spun "Slowhand" by Laura Nero and Eric Clapton. Carol danced with Gary. A realization dawned suddenly in Khan's head. *Gary is in love with Carol.*

Relief washed over him. He read real caring in the way Gary hovered protectively over Carol. She in turn looked into his eyes and smiled. She looked lovely, really lovely, Khan thought. He could have been knocked over with a feather when she had come through the reception line, looking like a real lady instead of his foul-mouthed guttersnipe. He waited to see if jealous feelings surfaced as Gary said something that made Carol laugh. No jealousy, relief—loss of guilt.

Suddenly stifled by the press of people, Khan headed through the guests, outside to a beautiful, balmy Long Island night. A half-moon was softly bright and legions of stars twinkled in a black velvet sky. Locating the constellation Orion, then the Big Dipper, he strolled around the perimeter of the huge tent. Strains of the Eagles' record of the year, "Hotel California," played pleasantly in the background. Spying a wrought iron bench beneath a tree, he stopped to sit, stretching his long legs. As he gazed at the sky, his big frame blended into night's shadows.

In the ladies room, Llana wiped Grey's tears. "Baby, stop it, stop it. Give him up. Oh God, why did I ever introduce you to him?"

"Oh, Llana, I'm ruining your wedding!"

"No, you're not, you turkey! Come on, let's go outside and talk."

Ashamed for burdening Llana on her day of days, Grey forced herself to stop crying. Dabbing her eyes with a tissue and peering into the mirror, she said, "God, I've ruined Debbie's work."

Llana determinedly led Grey from the ladies room. "Don't ask how I arranged what you are about to see," she said as they came to a canvas tent wall. Hooking the train of her gown over one arm, she lifted a canvas edge with the other. The two scurried under, entering the starlit June night.

Llana strode to a nearby bush. "My stash," she said,

pulling out a blanket and a champagne bucket with a chilled bottle of Dom Perignon and glasses.

They spread the blanket on the lawn, and like two lovely birds come to rest, they settled in their finery onto it.

"You're really married," Grey said, taking Llana's hand, where a simple band now accompanied her diamond engagement ring.

"Yes," Llana said, the seed pearls in her hair drawing moonlight, sparkling like tiny, captured stars. Smiling her most devilish grin, she said, "Dan says he's putting me in bondage for my wedding night to prove I'm forever tied." She wiggled in her wedding gown. "I can't wait."

Grey laughed, then began crying again.

Llana's face became serious. "Dan invited Carol," she said. "He had to. You see, Gary is in love with Carol and he's Dan's best friend."

Grey stopped crying. "Does Carol love Gary?" she asked hopefully.

"No," Llana said, realizing Grey had to face reality. "Carol loves Khan."

As Grey gulped her entire glass of champagne, she threw her head back and in the process caused her picture hat to fall off. Refilling her glass, she looked at the stars. "It's an impossible situation. He treats me like—"

Llana interrupted. "Forget about Khan—he's only gorgeous. You can find someone who will really love you, Grey. You need to start dating—stay away from the dojo."

Grey jumped to Khan's defense. "He's not only gorgeous! He's wonderful and talented and brilliant, and the only man I've ever made love with. I can't get him out of my system."

"Yes, you can," Llana said adamantly. As she sipped champagne carefully from a fluted glass, she leaned forward, taking care not to spill any on her gown. "We can solve that dilemma tonight. You have to make mad, passionate love to another man. That'll make you forget about Khan. Roberto is crazy about you. All my brothers are tens. I introduced you to Khan and started this whole thing. Let me show you there's other men in the world."

"Oh God, I think I'm going to be sick," Grey said.

Suddenly the moon and stars were blocked by Khan's

massive form, throwing a shadow over the two women on the blanket. "Get back to your husband, woman!" he commanded in his deep voice, scaring Llana half to death. Scooping Grey in his powerful arms as though she were weightless, he said, "Make her good-byes. She's leaving now." He turned away, Grey in his arms, and was swallowed by the night.

Llana hastily returned to her wedding party, bursting to tell Dan what had occurred.

Commandeering a limousine, Khan gave Grey's address and deposited her in the backseat, sliding in beside her. Through her alcohol haze, fighting nausea, she tried to fathom what was happening, then decided just to accept the fact he was next to her, was taking care of her, and deal with not throwing up in his lap. She burped.

He laughed and pulled her into the circle of his arm, where she fell asleep. The limousine sped along the Long Island Expressway toward Manhattan until it was snarled in heavy traffic caused by the end of a Frank Sinatra concert at the Forest Hills Stadium. Khan contemplated Grey's beautiful face in repose, musing over her conversation with Llana.

He had been sitting on the bench under the tree when he had heard soft feminine voices, clear in the still night. Watching with amusement, hidden from view in the tree's shadow, he watched Grey and Llana spread their blanket and break out the hidden champagne. His amusement drained away when they began discussing him.

When Grey declared she had never had another man, Khan recognized the truth in her champagne-slurred words. And when Llana suggested Grey make love to her brother—a distinct possibility, considering the Italian's steady pursuit and Grey's state of inebriation—anger overtook him. He stepped in and took what was his.

It was, all in all, a very interesting bit of eavesdropping, and Llana's remarks also confirmed his own realization of Gary's feelings for Carol.

Like a wire stretched to its limit, Carol Backer was ready to snap at the merest increase in tension. Hadn't she been forced to watch the interplay between Khan and Grey all evening? From the moment she saw them walking up the aisle of the church, Carol had known it was game over, no matter how she played out the farce of her and Gary. Gary had arranged her ride with George. Gary had been waiting, handsome and burly in his tuxedo, outside the church with the silver headband in his hand. He had put it on Carol's head and tucked her brown hair into it. "Hey, I'm an actor, remember? Into makeup and hair. Trust me. Don't you want to look beautiful? You are, you know," he admonished over her protests.

And I do look beautiful, Carol thought, until seeing Grey and Llana. After that she had no delusions. The opulent surroundings, music and laughter, became nothing to her. The champagne and caviar might as well have been beer and pretzels. Now, as she danced with Gary, the two empty seats at the head table spoke volumes. Khan was stolen, and in the circumference of Gary Reddington's arms, Carol plotted her revenge.

Gary Reddington held the bundle of smoldering dynamite who tonight, in her silver headband, was Diana, goddess of the hunt. Carol's caught-up hair showed her big cat's eyes and delicate cheekbones to great advantage. The only problem was that her yellow eyes flashed with jealous anger instead of passion for him.

Gary did his best to relieve Carol's misery, even arranging for her to catch Llana's bouquet. He didn't know if that made things better, but he did think it momentarily took Carol's mind off Khan and Grey and what she probably considered her public rejection. Carol caught the fragrant bouquet Llana lobbed suspiciously directly at her. The guests applauded Carol's catch as Gary said, "That means you're going to get married soon."

"Yeah," Carol said, smelling the flowers, then pinned him with her eyes. "To who?"

"How about me? Don't I look great in a tuxedo?" He stroked his satin lapel, smiling.

"What is it with you? What exactly do you want from me?"

"Right now," Gary said, stepping closer so that his six-foot frame closed her off from the milling guests, "to have another glass of champagne and dance again." His blue eyes held her. "Later"—he pulled her by the waist, close, so she felt his power—"to make love to you," he said, his voice husky.

Despite herself, she experienced a shiver of anticipation. "Never happen, and you can have your dress back, too," she said. "Fucking creep. I belong to Khan!" And whirling turquoise chiffon, she strode off to find George and see when she was going home.

"She is not facing reality," Pierre said softly behind Gary, "and you are getting nowhere. *And* you owe me ten dollars. The Red Sox just clouted the Yankees 9-4. Catfish Hunter is my man!"

"That's not true about Carol," Gary said. clasping his arm about Pierre's shoulder and aiming the black man toward the closest bar. "She's falling in love with me. It's just going to take her a bit of time to realize it." He smiled. "And how's your romance going?" He gazed pointedly at Debbie, deep in conversation with Dan at the wedding cake.

Pierre laughed as he leaned an elbow on the leather bar they came to. He accepted a long-stemmed glass of champagne from the barman.

"Did she ask you a million questions?" Gary said. He fished in his pocket and put a ten-dollar bill on the bar in front of Pierre.

"Yes," Pierre said, pocketing the money, "mostly about Khan. She makes me nervous. Now, Mary Beth—she's my type." Then he laughed. "Did you catch the scenario when Llana tried explaining to her mother and two aunts, in Italian, what a war lock is?"

It was Gary's turn to laugh. "No, but you can fill me in on that one later. I have to get back to my dojo darling. I promised Dan not to take my eyes off her."

Grey awoke the next morning still in the circle of Khan's arm. Sketchy memories cut through a pounding headache. The return to her apartment. Did she really throw up? Had Khan solicitously held her head, then put ice packs on the back of her neck and forehead? Had she then answered questions he put to her for what seemed hours? Questions about marriage to Ed, her engagement to Andre, the horse show where Andre had surprised her by appearing out of nowhere? Yes, it had all happened.

She examined Khan as he slept, her eyes squinting against the cruel champagne hangover. He was so big that his massive frame sprawling across her king-sized bed made it seem small. The half-covering sheet exposed his sculptured chest and arms, outlined his curving thighs, and the fullness of his big genitals. So, she recalled, was the memory of his lovemaking real. She moved closer, touching him. Thank you, God, for answering my prayers.

The Nightwalker turned her mind to hating Anton, sitting like a pasha in the pedicab ahead of her. The mercenary had evidently hired the handsome boy pedaling for a Waikiki tour. It was nine in the morning, and keeping a half-block distance between her and Anton, she trotted along Kalakaua Avenue and its beach-front high-rise hotels. Thousands of tourists already baked on Waikiki Beach. Sweat poured from her and she welcomed the workout, passing many other joggers along the beach.

She could tell by the way the blond boy kept turning and talking to his passenger that Anton was being gregarious, which from him could only mean bad news.

Grey looked at the sea: a turquoise mirror reigned near shore, but the surf was up a half mile out, and hundreds of surfers rode the waves. She jogged past a walled area forming a giant pool; beyond the wall the whole Pacific came rolling toward her, white-topped wave after white-topped wave.

Anton's pedicab turned onto a shaded side street and parked under a tree. She sat on the curb, watching. The blond boy and Anton were deep in conversation. Then Anton got out of the pedicab's backseat, and the blond boy lifted the leather seat and took something from under it. Anton handed the boy money. She assumed it was in exchange for marijuana, for pedicabbers were known to be a source on Waikiki Beach. Amazing, she thought, he's moving tons and hasn't got any for himself.

She followed the pedicab to an ABC store where the boy stopped, left Anton in the cab, ran in, ran back, and pedaled around the corner again, where he handed Anton rolling paper and waited while Anton rolled a joint. They smoked together, Anton's handsome face all smiles.

He looked then like a smiling picture she had stolen in Georgia, at an anti-terrorist training camp where she, posing as a New York-based journalist, talked the old colonel who ran the camp into letting her take the training course and into the files. She remembered finding Anton's picture, holding it as though it were sacred, running her finger over the shiny surface of the black-and-white snapshot. Smiling. He smiled when he killed, too.

The colonel had come in then, smelling of scotch, trying to talk her into staying on the grounds instead of the hotel she drove from every day. She knew better, the first woman ever there, because the general wanted publicity, the only female in a para-military camp of sixty hardened men.

The instructors were surprised by her prowess on the shooting range. The Nightwalker had taken advantage of the ten-day course, enjoying the hand-to-hand combat every morning, the electronic surveillance classes bringing her to date on the latest equipment, the better to hunt Anton with. She thought often of Y Shin Sha there, especially during an unconventional weapons class including blowgun and spear. It was six months after he forced her from Taiwan. Was he still there? Would he be there forever? Was he ever there? Yes! Grey knew it was all not a dream by the fact she was trained as no other.

The same sixth sense that had alerted her to the poisonous viper on Taiwan continued to protect her in the camp. Grey knew a towering Sioux Indian named Twin Eagles lay in wait as she mounted a spiral staircase toward a second-floor bathroom set aside for her use.

The firearms instructor, he had cast his slicing eyes on her when she first appeared. His violent chi warned her that day as she climbed the stairs toward where he hid, meaning to accost her. She did a turnabout, avoiding the situation, for she needed to stay longer and get information on Anton. The Indian eventually came down the stairs, pegging her with his eyes at the desk where she studied bomb diffusion stats, not understanding how she eluded his trap. She relieved herself in the woods after that.

At the Waikiki Banyan, Halehana searched the widow's condo. Strange, nothing to show anyone lived in the place. No food in the icebox or cupboards. Camouflage fatigue pants in a drawer, not normal apparel for a woman unless she was military. He switched on the bathroom light. Makeup. Wait a minute! He picked up a small black box, opened it, recognized its contents: cork black facial camouflage. A sixth sense overtook him. Despite his oversized frame, he sprang lightly onto the bathroom countertop and searched the housing of the florescent light. His big hand came up with a suction cup and earphones. Dropping it back in the hiding place, he left the condo and headed back to his own.

Yu was waiting for him, tape recorder set.

"I dropped a device," the big man said.

"I know," Yu said, "I heard you close the door."

"Someone else is watching Anton—a woman. She just might be stupid enough to follow him to Maui and get in the way. I'll have to think of a way to throw her off the track."

Anton's pedicab was on the move again. The Nightwalker jogged after it along the beach, feeling the sun and trade winds, wondering what she'd do the rest of her life, starting in under two days' time when the past was reviewed and her prey was dead.

Manhattan, 1977

"DASHING MEN WITH PAGAN WAR LOCKS DECORATE WEDDING ATTENDED BY MILLIONAIRESS GREY COLTRANE FOWLER," the *National Enquirer* captioned the little photos on its front page. There, pictured in profile to show their small braids, were Dan, Pierre, Gary, and George the bounty hunter. The big picture on the page showed Grey and Khan formally dressed, sitting next to each other, taken at just the angle to show Khan's pinned-up war lock. A small, sketched-in black arrow pointed to his war lock. "Are the Kinky heiress and the Mysterious Eurasian Karate Cult Leader Headed for the Altar?" asked that caption. Inside were more pictures and an article.

Grey added the pages to her growing pile of recent press clippings. Additional nude pictures, clandestinely obtained in Kentucky, continued to be published. Rumors connected them to a ruthless paparazzo who had abandoned Jackie and taken up Grey. As each exposure of her body hit the stands, Ralph Daniels initiated another lawsuit. The lawyer also appeared before the press, reading a statement condemning the publication of the pictures. His statement was carried nationally on television news, which gave the scandal sheets yet more to write.

The story and pictures taken at Llana's wedding were not the grist of lawsuits, but did herald an end to the heiress's relationship with Debbie, who had obviously taken the pictures and written the detailed accompanying story. To Khan, that story showed how the sensational press displayed life out of context, making him realize Grey's vulnerability and understand how the Andre Bugueot stories happened.

Two weeks after the wedding, Grey and Khan still were together day and night. She attended every class at his school, but there was no way to discern from his behavior there that he spent every night making love to her. If anything, he was more stern and demanding, harder on her than any other white belt. Life was sweet for her. By evening, karate. Nights in Khan's arms—except for her parents.

Besides saying that she had disgraced the family forever with her nude pictures, Grey's parents were critical of her relationship with Khan—and during one heated conversation her father prejudicially referred to him as "other than white." So, with Llana away, there was only Khan to talk to, and that was fine with Grey. She began once again to fantasize permanent life with him.

She had dealt with Carol's hate by ignoring it these last two weeks, and had not yet come into physical contact with her, but it was a distinct possibility. Each class, as black belts were assigned to underbelts, Grey held her breath. One of these days, Carol would have a chance to hurt her and probably succeed. Fear of Carol was a price she paid to be near Khan.

As for Carol, she trained with more fervor than ever. The black belt was soon to test for nidan, and Sensei applied ever more pressure in the dojo, which was fine with Carol, for it meant he focused attention on her. But that was only in class. Her personal life was a shambles of confusion and bitterness.

The day after the wedding, Carol purchased a snub-nosed .38 special from a junkie, then painted Grey's name on the barrel with red nail polish, and waited for

Monday in her sparsely furnished room, staying the week-end in solitary confinement: not eating, pacing, handling the .38 or twirling sais.

Carol carried murder in her heart and the .38 in her red canvas bag on Monday morning. What a shock it was when Khan came into the office and told her to move her belongings into his quarters.

It didn't take long. She accomplished the move after work, before class, and shelved the idea of shooting Coltrane. *She was living with Khan.* But was she? He was never there, except to change clothes or hang out a bit with the black belts. She slept by herself. She surmised he was with Grey, but had no positive proof. He treated Grey like any other dirt garbage white belt in the dojo. Worse. Carol didn't dare question him concerning his whereabouts, fearing he might tell her to leave. So she waited—as in the past. He would come round. After all, he had moved her in.

She sought the opportunity to let Grey know, but the moment never presented itself. They were certainly not on speaking terms and she was never assigned the white belts; another opportunity she also patiently awaited, fantasizing Grey with missing teeth and a broken nose. Meanwhile, Carol let Gary Reddington know she was living upstairs to cool him down. Amazingly, it made no difference and the big, sexy redhead continued his hot pursuit.

It was a steamy Thursday evening. Grey and Ralph Daniels were being shown around St. Anthony's Hostel by Brother Ignatius, a saintly Franciscan friar who main-tained the temporary home for abused children and had been discovered harboring a few of them permanently, against church regulations. Grey had been fighting finan-cially to make it a legal home for those children, but this was the first time she was actually at the Hell's Kitchen facility. "If it weren't for our number one volunteer, we never could have protected these kids this long," the gentle, brown-robed friar said, throwing open a door to reveal a playroom filled with children and Carol Backer passing out cheap toys from her red canvas bag.

"She's here every evening after work, before her night school and on weekends. Sent to us from the Lord," the priest said, eyes skyward, while Grey was trying to back from the doorway so Carol didn't see her. I knew no one could be that completely awful, Grey thought, as the priest continued talking and Grey watched Carol tenderly pick up a little girl and wipe away her tears. "But," he said, sharing a secret with the heiress who could save his beloved kids from an unfeeling state orphanage, "I think she has a boyfriend who beats her, for she's always black and blue."

Class that evening in the oven of a dojo was particularly trying. Khan was training Grey in gymnastic kata routines created especially for her. Pushing her beyond her limit, then harder, he ended every session with a hundred push-ups, even if she made no mistakes. Tonight's routine was a killer: spinning dragon-tail sweep from the floor, into a rollout, into a back handspring, into a double-flying split kick in the air. He made her repeat that series for an hour *after* the usual killer warm-up, and then, when she was almost dead, called kumite, ordering her coldly back to the white belts.

She was just pulling the Mercedes away from the curb when he came onto the street with Kyoshi, his favorite dog. He smiled at her and the dichotomy was complete. Now he was her Khan, no longer stern Sensei. Her resentment at the merciless workout faded with his smile.

"Want to meet the zen master?" he said, changing his mind about walking Kyoshi downtown when he saw her.

"Sure," she said, opening her door, leaning forward for Kyoshi, who hopped immediately in the back, where he began panting and drooling on the leather seat. She switched on the air conditioner, following Khan's directions, the big dog's hot breath on the back of her neck.

It seemed a deserted warehouse on a deserted street. Khan made a horrendous racket banging on fortress-like double steel doors until the Master opened them. He was not the white-haired, bearded, elderly Oriental she expected, but dark-haired, dark-eyed, square-faced, six-feet tall, and bulky, in his late fifties. The Master was dressed in a black gi with no obi, the jacket hanging free. Draped about his thickly muscled neck was a white towel, and his feet were in leather thong sandals.

Khan bowed, introduced Grey. As she bowed to him, the Master absorbed her astounding beauty, the parked Mercedes with Kyoshi on guard in the back, and understood why Khan was hard put to get the girl out of mind. Making a broad gesture with his arm, he boomed, "Welcome, my dear," and led the way through a labyrinth of hallways disguising the entrance to his school.

Once inside, after giving proper courtesies, she studied the famous school with fascination. The giant gym was in semi-darkness, but she could still plainly see hundreds of slogans posted high on the walls, the biggest of them proclaiming: "ZEN EQUALS: ZEAL, ENERGY, NOW!" Whole walls were covered with memorabilia, trophies, plaques, group pictures of students. Many pictures of the Master, always with the towel about his neck. They walked by rows of heavy bags, by an official-sized boxing ring complete with ropes—and still the school went on. They came to the Master's desk, where the only bright light shone. The Master sat at the large, cluttered desk, indicating chairs for Khan and Grey.

She was nervous in the presence of this man whose books she had read and whom Khan so respected. It was a shock to see Khan kowtow. She was very concerned about acting properly herself.

Reaching a hammer hand into a drawer, the Master produced a gin bottle and, pulling three water glasses to him, poured the same goodly amount of gin into each and handed them around. He raised his glass in toast.

She tossed her drink down in imitation of the men. She dealt quietly with the burning sensation, but could not prevent her eyes from watering.

"So, my dear," the Master said to her, "you are a student of karate. Do you enjoy the martial arts?"

Sitting very straight in the chair, she smiled at him. "Oh, very much. I love karate. It's really fun," she said in her brightest manner.

The Master's voice changed. "Fun? I didn't know karate was 'fun.' " His patronizing tone made her realize she had said the wrong thing. The Master tilted his head toward her. "And what rank are you, my dear? How much time have you put in at this 'fun'?"

"White belt," Grey said, her face burning. "I've been training five months."

"Ahhhh, a student embarking on a long journey. I have something that will help you along the way. Would you like that?" He spoke in even more condescending tones.

She knew she was trapped, looked at Khan. His face was blank. He was Sensei again. "Yes, thank you, Master, I would," she answered, extremely apprehensive. Dojo legends abounded concerning this master's exploits— how he choked students into unconsciousness teaching his famed *aiki-jitsu*. She was suddenly terrified he would want to give her an aiki lesson, or any kind of lesson. Stories Khan had told her about his diabolical zen humor flashed through her mind.

The Master continued speaking condescendingly to her. "Do you know what meditation is, my dear?"

"Yes, Master," she said, thinking of her time in Khan's classes in zazen position.

"Well, that's good! Then you should enjoy some zen meditation," he said, standing suddenly and gesturing for her to follow him.

They came to a door which the Master opened, revealing a perfectly dark room. Trepidation growing, she followed into the room.

"Now, do you know the meditation position?" he said to her as if she was a small child.

"Yes, Master," she said, dropping to the wooden floor in a zazen, back straight, hands properly clasped in her lap. She closed her eyes, anxious to display proper form.

"Good, good, that's quite good," he said. "I'm going to leave you for a little while and let you listen to the words of one of my very own teachers, the great Master Kim. Do you think you can stay still, my dear?"

"Yes, Master," she said in a small voice.

"Good, good, you do that," he said, switching on a tape recorder, closing the door, leaving her on her knees in the black room with her eyes shut.

A droning voice began. The "Itness of It" was the subject. For thirty minutes the one-tone voice spoke on the itness of it, during which time she suffered excruciating pain in her legs, but was terrified to move. For all she knew, the Master and Khan could be watching through a peephole. Now and then, as the tape voice hummed on, faint laughter came from the other side of the door.

Finally, blessedly, the tape stopped. The door opened. "How are you doing, my dear?" the Master asked.

"Fine, Master," she said, still with her eyes closed, anticipating standing, knowing her cramped legs would kill her as the blood returned.

His voice boomed at her. "Good, good, very good. You're ready for the other side." The Master turned the tape over and closed the door again.

The next half hour Master Kim's voice expounded on the "Thatness of That." None of her attempted mental ploys—thoughts of Llana's honeymoon, picturing Carol as an off-hour ministering angel, reliving Khan's love-making—took her mind from the pain. Awful cramps gripped her and through it all, the voice droned. Finally it stopped.

"Very good," the Master said, returning that exact instant. "Why don't you join us, my dear?" he said, leaving her to the agonizing task of getting to her feet.

It took about five minutes for her legs to come painfully back to life. Stepping tentatively, she walked from the dark room toward a two-armed lamp with a green glass shade on the Master's desk.

Approaching, she saw the men were playing chess. She was abruptly angry. *They laugh and play while I suffer!* Khan looked at her expectantly. Keeping her face blank, she sat where the Master indicated.

"And was that fun also, my dear?"

"No, Master," Grey said.

"And how would you describe it?"

"Educational," she said, praying the answer would not earn her further meditation.

"Good, good! First zen lessons are often educational. Remember, to experience pain is to break the shell that encloses your understanding. You are quite bright, my dear. You will make a fine martial artist someday if you work very hard." The Master looked at Khan. "Perhaps your Sensei will send you to my women's lodge to train when he leaves."

Leaves. When he leaves? Her anger was replaced by fear.

The Master said to Khan. "When are you leaving, my son?"

He's taken the ball out of my hands, Khan thought, seeing her incredulous expression. He had not wanted her to find out like this. "In two weeks," he said flatly, watching her face.

"And how long are you intending to stay?" the Master asked.

"Perhaps forever," Khan answered.

Outside the Master's school, Khan and Grey sat silently in the Mercedes. She reached to turn on the radio, then changed her mind, hooking her hands on the steering wheel. Kyoshi's breathing was the only sound. "Are you really going away?" she said, staring ahead at the deserted street.

His voice was gentle. "Yes."

Oh no, God. Please, God. "Where are you going?" Her grip tightened on the steering wheel.

"To Taiwan."

It all rushed to her: dedicating his life to the Way of the Sword, finding the perfect sword master, the legend of the psychic woman master who was a Wing Chun nun, his fantasy of finding her. She had thought he was merely dreaming. Sweet Mary, mother of God! "I can't live without you," she said and began crying.

He usually hated tears, but now he accepted hers. He thought as he looked in the dim streetlight at the svelte beauty with cheekbones that could cut glass how changed she was from when he first met her. It was difficult now remembering her inclination toward insecurity, the quiet moods. Lately she absolutely glowed. Her personality had taken a new dimension, confident, even forceful. He knew the changes were due to his influence. And he knew everything about her now. She could be trusted.

He had never trusted a woman.

"They will make you soft, take your manhood if you let them," his father had warned little Khan, who cried as he was taken from his mother to a zen temple in Hawaii to learn to be a man. And when even his mother broke the faith, it seemed to him his father was right. For did she not desert him by dying while he was away, leaving only dim memories of soft, touching hands, blond hair, cerulean eyes, and a lilting voice singing Russian lullabyes?

In special forces, the nineteen-year-old Khan was actually schooled to mistrust women. "Remember," the SEAL counter-terrorism instructor cautioned, "a woman is more deadly than a man. In that split second when a man looks into the eyes of a gun-holding woman to see if she really means it, that's when she blows him away. Shoot a woman before a man!"

They were right. Buddha! How many times had he witnessed women making bombs out of themselves in Nam? And the stories—Cong women with razor blades hidden in their vaginas so American soldiers fucked themselves to death. He didn't know if that was possible, but when he was in Saigon, horny as hell, he made sure by sticking a banana inside the woman before he entered her. Then he prophylactically sheathed himself against the penicillin-resistant strains of veneral disease the armed forces constantly warned about. If he slept after such sex, it was with his razor-sharp knife at the woman's throat. If she moved, she died.

Now he looked at Grey silently crying, staring out the windshield of the Mercedes, and saw the whiteness of her knuckles caused by her death grip on the steering wheel.

With a gentle touch of his hand, he turned her face toward his, looking searchingly into her tear-filled eyes. The pain he saw there became the horrible pain in his mother's eyes when he was torn from her. He suddenly cared to the very fiber of his being that she was in pain. His words were simple, yet the most important he ever uttered in his life. "Marry me," he said, feeling the shock of his question pass through her, seeing her eyes widen in wonder. She pulled her face from his hand.

"You see"—his voice only hinted at the depth of emotion he felt—"I can't live without you, either."

And as though a magical shining cloud settled on them, they were enveloped in the miracle of each other.

"Be my wife, come with me," he said, watching her tears stop. He traced her jaw with his finger. "If you can live without the luxuries you're used to."

"Oh God yes, I'll marry you, Khan." Her heart was singing. "Luxuries never brought me happiness. *You* are my happiness!"

Khan, hardly believing he had proposed, hardly believing she had accepted, silently admitted his love. I am content to be with her.

She laughed, aglow with realized love. Swiping the

tears on her cheek with the back of her hand, she said, "I want to hear all about where we're going to live and what language I'm going to speak. Where shall we get married? When? By whom? What about Darkchild? Oh, Khan, I don't have to give up Darkchild?" she said, suddenly terrified he would say yes. "And, and"—her black lashes dropped—"do you love me?"

"Whoa," he laughed. "Yes, I love you." He put his arms around her. "Of course you don't have to give up Darkchild. I love you," he said again, savoring the strange words, tasting them. His face was only inches from hers. He kissed her cheek, the tip of her nose, the softness of her closed eyelids. "I love you." Then his mouth descended to hers, relishing it: the kiss was like a shared glass of ritualistic wine, a pledge to their future together.

The Nightwalker jogged a half block behind Anton's pedicab until it turned into Ala Moana Park and came to a stop along a sea wall. Across the water hundreds of sailboats were docked at Waikiki Yacht Harbor. Anton was talking fast and the blond pedicab driver was looking a bit uneasy—his expression said he might have bitten off more than he could chew by befriending this passenger. Anton was getting excited, cracking his fingers in that special way that announced to her trained eye he was an aiki expert. From her vantage point the Nightwalker cracked her own fingers. *I know exactly how I will kill you.* Had it not taken her almost as long to plan that as the years to locate him?

Again the "then what?" thoughts were at her.

Lying on a park bench near her was a paper someone had left behind, a big island publication, *Save Hawaii*. She picked it up, glancing at articles warning of the dangers of food irradiation, voted down so far in Hawaii but looming as a threat. Big papaya growers wanted it. Lists of pesticide-contaminated wells on each of the islands took up pages. On Oahu, a community called Mililani seemed particularly hard hit. The lists of its polluted wells went on and on. Articles told of the thirty-seven different chemicals found there, thanks to pineapple and sugar cane growers.

Mother would be horrified, the Nightwalker thought, keeping an eye on Anton and the blond boy as she did. I can fight polluters. She touched the unending circle on her neck, her oath in mind. I will teach the Way.

Would you have me stay here in Hawaii, Khan?

The sun beat hotly down. At the edge of the water, two outrigger canoe teams slid their six-man outriggers into the ocean. The men were in wonderful shape, muscles straining at their paddles as they chanted and headed toward the open sea. None of their bodies were as beautiful as Khan's. He was her Adonis.

Manhattan, 1977

Driving north on the West Side Highway, both Khan and Grey were silently enthralled by the enormity of what they had just decided, thinking on a multiplicity of levels, sorting the million things each would have to do. Even the big dog in the backseat caught the new mood and nuzzled his black nose at Khan over the seat.

Cruising Amsterdam Avenue in the Seventies, they looked for a restaurant. The neighborhood was rapidly changing, trading up—beginning to look like the Village with artisans taking over small shops, sprinklings of gourmet food stores, handmade clothing boutiques opening one by one. The pedestrians were young, casually dressed, restaurants all over the place . . .

Parking at a meter, they walked hand in hand up Amsterdam, looking at eating establishments, joining throngs of Friday night strollers and shoppers. Kyoshi, without a leash, stuck to Khan's left heel as if glued.

"Let's go in the one that smells best," she said, tossing her head, swinging her long hair off her shoulders in the heat. Then she caught a whiff of curry in passing an Indian restaurant.

"Bet," Khan said, pulling at her silky hair, agreeably noting how everyone passing stared. The men ogled her, whose skimpy tank top and tight, washed-out jeans accented her full breasts, tiny waist, curvy hips, and long legs. The women gaped at him, whose huge size and exotic handsomeness made him so different from other men on the street.

We are a hell of a couple, he proudly thought, beginning to think a whole new way. He draped an arm protectively around her and felt her nestle close as they walked, become a moving part of him.

They stopped simultaneously at 79th and Amsterdam, assaulted by tantalizing aromas, and followed their noses through the glass portals of Crab Heaven, laughing at its name. Kyoshi settled onto the cement by the door as Khan directed.

Inside, bottles of sherry, assorted spices in round metal racks, and bowls of peppers rested on the wooden tables, draped with bright checks. Neither had eaten since morning and they were famished.

Lobster bisque liberally laced with sherry took the edge off their appetites, followed by soft-shelled crabs sautéed in garlic accompanied by sliced raw tomatoes, zucchini, and onions with a tangy dip. Eating ravenously, sipping crisp Rhine wine, they resumed talk of their future.

"Now ask me questions," he said, noting how pink her lips were without lipstick, scrutinizing her face, gazing at his fiancée as if for the first time. Lips—soft and full, made him think of her pussy lips, pink and soft and full. He felt himself stirring. She radiated sexuality, he thought.

"When shall we get married?"

"Right away, as soon as possible," he said, watching her beautiful smile light her beautiful face. *She's mine.* Her next question surprised him. He thought she would ask about Darkchild.

"How are my martial arts?"

"You are a smart ass. You know you've got me at a soft moment. But, my pretty,"—he smiled, and the "look," the one meaning he was going to make love to her, passed over his face—"you'll pay later for your bold question."

She shivered. Sex with Khan was never knowing what was next, except it would be thrilling.

"I'm proud of you, and I'm going to make you the best woman martial artist in the world," he said matter-of-factly, cutting a crisp soft-shell in half. "And, to answer your next question, after we're settled, Darkchild can be shipped or flown over along with Kyoshi and a bitch," he said, greatly relieving her anxieties.

"Tell me about Taiwan."

"You'll see soon enough. We leave in thirteen days.

It's a dictatorship. One million Mainlanders ruling thirteen million Taiwanese. Lots of unfair oppression. The island itself is very beautiful."

"Is the woman master you're going to study with the psychic Wing Chun nun Chiang Kai-Shek is said to have kidnapped from Mainland China?"

She doesn't forget a thing I tell her, Khan thought, pleased. He sprinkled red pepper from a can in the rack marked "X-TRA HOT!" onto his crab half. He ate it and tears broke in his eyes. Taking a moment to recover, he laughed. "I wish it were that easy. You don't exactly put an ad in the local paper for her. The story goes she's hidden in the mountains. If she's teaching martial arts against the law, her head would bring a price. I intend to find a sword master, apprentice myself, then begin a search for her."

Like looking for the leprechaun and pot of gold at the end of the rainbow, her practical side thought. Her romantic side loved him more for dreaming his dreams.

"To be married without Llana—and Dan," she said, shaking her head.

"When are they coming back to New York."

"Not for another two weeks."

"Will you make marriage arrangements? City Hall is fine with me, I have no religious preference."

She was suddenly taken with an idea to rendezvous with Dan and Llana in Mexico for a wedding, but remained silent. A surprise for Khan, she thought. Her husband. She drank him in, this exotic superman, thinking of the monumental task ahead. Change her entire life in thirteen days. Telling her parents would be an experience.

"Let's get some champagne," he said. "I'm going to spank you for your boldness, make love to you for hours, then teach you to braid my war lock."

There was no dissent from her.

Hours later, in a moment when she was a vessel of burning pleasure, he spoke. "Tell me you'll never have another man."

"I'll never have another man," she said, feeling him thrust faster inside her and the white-hot fountain of sensation they were in erupted. A ragged cry ripped from deep within him. She gripped his shoulders as she convulsed, as he shuddered, then quivered with aftershocks until his head dropped against hers and he was still.

He lifted himself on his elbow and gazed with a look that suddenly terrified her. What could be wrong?

"It will be difficult. There are no liberated women in the Orient," he said, shattering the silence.

She laughed in relief. "This is a white belt you're speaking to, remember, Sensei? The one with latrine duty. I eat humble pie now."

His deep voice was serious still. "You'll always be subordinate to me. Not just in the dojo. Do you really understand? It's not a game I play, but a life I live and you'll live it, too. Think carefully, Grey. Be sure. You're beautiful, rich, famous. You can have any man you want." He put two fingers on her lips, stifling her attempted protest. "You weren't raised to be wife to a man like me. It'll be hard for you. It won't be fair and I'll always be the boss. I'll go away and leave you, maybe for long periods of time. I want children, at least three sons, maybe four. Where we'll be living, it's like regressing in time a thousand years. No one speaks English. Theirs are alien customs, a sexist society." He took his fingers from her lips.

The expression on her face was as serious as his as she also raised herself on an elbow. He thought perhaps she was reconsidering. "Am I really beautiful?" she said, then stuck out her tongue.

He laughed. "All right. But you have to get some rank. Sensei's wife cannot be a white belt, even if she is the world's most beautiful woman. And—I told you about being a smart ass!" He was suddenly all motion. She felt herself snatched in his huge hands, she was across his lap, and he was spanking her. "Say I will be respectful to my husband, lord, and master," he said, smacking her bare buttocks.

"Never," she said, trying to wiggle away, feeling his growing erection against her belly.

This time the smack was harder. "Say it," he said, administering yet another resounding smack, watching her gorgeous ass quivering.

"No!"

"Stubborn, huh?" He whopped her harder. This time he could see his hand print.

"I will be respectful to my husband, lord, and master."

Then his lips were kissing the stinging hand print. He turned her over. For a moment that seemed to last forever, he held himself poised above her. Then, with an indrawn breath, he lowered his hot flesh to hers.

Later, as she slept in the curve of his arm, he gazed at her perfect face. *I trust her.* Inhaling her hair's fresh scent, he thought of his extremes in obtaining that trust. Perhaps someday he might even tell her she had been placed under surveillance worthy of a master spy, followed, watched with binoculars—until he had been satisfied as to her activities. Finally his paranoia had been squelched. He felt no guilt. It had all been necessary. Otherwise, he could never have come to this peace he now felt. He looked at her head cradled in his arm and swore nothing would ever harm her.

17

Anton did a slow burn sitting in the blond kid's pedicab. He had already sprung for a thirty-dollar tour and twenty-five dollars for a solitary bud wrapped in plastic he and the boy polished off. The kid wasn't going for the idea of a session in Anton's room. "Take me to the Waikiki Banyan—the long way!" Fuck it, let the little bastard pedal his ass off, Mikel thought, settling his weight back into the seat, hoping to make it harder to pedal the cab. The kid headed for Kuhio Avenue, then to the Ala Wai Canal, pedaling along its banks. Marshmallow clouds were piled onto peaks of the lush Koolau mountain range in the distance. Anton stewed. No sleep, no good drugs, sex suddenly seeming unobtainable. "Turn here!" The blond moved back onto Kuhio, where Anton had him go into another ABC store and buy five packs of chocolate-covered macadamia nuts, which he ate as the ride continued.

The pedicab driver had thought to tell his passenger to fuck off a few times, but something had stopped him. Maybe self-preservation, he told himself as he moved past the International Marketplace. There was only a few more blocks to go, and he had the pain-in-the-ass's money in his pocket. He'd be rid of the granite-faced black in a few minutes.

Anton continued his angry reverie. Ritchie and his fool partners were scared shit! A few busts and they were peeing in their pants, wanting to wait even months before making a next move. No way! He wanted the motherfucker who had ripped off the last three loads. He had had to kiss ass to get his way. Fuck, what had he come to? Since he couldn't at that moment shoot the prick who was trying to ruin him, he focused his evil thoughts on the boy who pedaled his cab, and rejected his sexual overture.

In a condo down the street, a boy who never had the luxury of being able to refuse Anton's overtures, who had instead been his slave, looked at his adopted father, who spoke and pointed to myriad surfers, plainly seen from their ocean view.

"You'd be a good surfer. You're nice and lean. What say? A lesson? Now?"

But Yu had other things on his mind, and playing in Hawaiian waters was not one of them.

Downstairs, in the courtyard, Anton's pedicab came to a halt. The Nightwalker was not far behind. She was certainly close enough to see Anton grab the blond boy by his bunched-up T-shirt, jerk him off his feet, then bang him against the side of the pedicab. Several other people saw also, but no one, including a blue-shirted security guard walking by, wanted to get involved. Near to tears, the blond boy reached into his pocket and returned Anton's money to him. Anton stalked to the elevators with never a backward glance. The pedicabber pedaled off, and the Nightwalker waited until the elevator doors closed on Anton, then headed upstairs herself.

18

Manhattan, 1977

Driving to karate class, Grey passed a black Ford near her garage entrance. She had seen it a few times before, she remembered. Easing into Fifth Avenue traffic, she switched on the radio. "Hello, New York, this is Frankie Crocker, your chief rocker."

Accompanied by the dulcet-toned WBLS dee-jay, she rehashed her last, hectic days. Blood tests, calls intercepting Llana on honeymoon, the wonder of Khan, fear of Carol . . . Real concern for the children Carol cared for at St. Anthony's Hostel. Now Carol and Grey had the same aims inside the dojo and out, although Carol was not aware of Grey's involvement in the abused children's plight—and Grey was not about to enlighten her. She'll think I'm invading all her territories. Grey wondered if Khan knew of Carol's loving volunteering, then put her mind to some of the million other things to do in the coming days, including the test for green belt.

Frankie Crocker spun "Best of My Love" by the Emotions, number one on the charts for five weeks. She glanced at her gold and steel Hublot watch, drove faster. There had been an awful phone call with her parents, not too different from the one when she had intended to marry Andre. She told them of her impending marriage to Khan and listened to her father shout over the den phone while her mother cried through the bedroom extension; neither would give Grey a moment to speak her feelings. She ended it by hanging up. That was two days ago and her parents' attitude continued to disturb her, especially Daddy's accusation she was no longer capable of making decisions.

In a hurry, she ran a caution light at 63rd and Fifth.

Hearing a screech, she looked in the rearview mirror and saw the black Ford run the red light behind her. Recognizing it as the same car she had noticed when leaving the garage, it dawned on her that she was being followed. To make sure she wasn't misjudging the situation, she swung a sudden left onto 62nd Street and watched in the mirror. The Ford did the same. She drove around the blocks back to Fifth. So did the Ford.

Sure she was followed, she slowed, seeing in her mirror the black car's occupants, two burly men in suits and ties. Frightened, determined to lose them, she cut in and out of traffic and through side streets. The now ominous Ford kept up with her. After a harrowing, careening, high-speed chase through Chelsea, she finally lost her pursuers in the Twenties. Adrenaline racing, she continued toward the dojo.

About to pull into Avenue B, she again spotted the black Ford—parked near the school entrance! Swerving, avoiding Avenue B, she drove to the nearest pay phone, dialed the dojo, held her breath as the phone rang. Khan answered. Relieved to hear his voice, she hurriedly told him of two men so blatantly tailing her. "They're parked near your entrance," she gasped, "but I don't think they saw me."

"Keep cool," he said, "I'm not going to let anyone hurt you, understand?"

"Yes, Khan," she said, her breathing evening as his voice calmed her.

"Drive onto Avenue B like nothing's wrong. Drive past them. Just before you get to the corner, angle your car like you're going to make a U-turn. I want you to block them without them realizing what you're doing. Can you handle that?"

"Yes."

She turned the Mercedes onto Avenue B and drove slowly by the Ford as though she hadn't a care in the world. God! The men were big.

She advanced past the black car, then angled the Mercedes just past the Ford, closely blocking it. She made sure not to look at the two men staring at her, and peered about the street as though deciding where to park, imagining the men talking about what a dumb broad she was. Sitting in her car, playing a dangerous part, she felt the same excitement she experienced before sparring. That excitement escalated as *screaming* brown and black belts poured onto the street.

Led by wild-eyed Marcos, the students used metal garbage cans to barricade the black Ford. Marcos jumped onto the Ford, ran from the hood of the car to its trunk, leapt off, grabbed a garbage can, and banged it against the Ford's front fender. Others joined him, screaming, crashing the car with garbage cans. The noise was horrendous!

The two men inside the Ford were flabbergasted. Blocked by Grey's Mercedes on one side, hemmed by garbage cans and gi-clad crazies on the other, they locked the doors and made sure their windows were rolled up. One of the men reached into the glove compartment as if to go for a gun. But it was a bluff. Seeing that, the students began violently rocking the Ford while Marcos jumped up and down on the rocking car's hood, grimacing grotesquely through the windshield at the wide-eyed men.

Khan came from the school and approached the Ford. At his signal the students moved away. "Had enough?" he asked in a booming voice he knew penetrated the closed windows. One of the men, built like a dumpster, nodded and rolled down his window.

"Okay, what's the story?" Khan said. "Why are you following her? You guys have a choice. Tell me what's going on and you can split. Otherwise, I go back inside and leave you with my friends here." He waved a hand and Marcos came close, grinning.

The two men talked.

"Why were they following me?" Grey asked in the dojo.

"On the mat, white belt" was Khan's only reply.

As she changed in the locker room, her adrenaline racing from the incredible street scene, Khan was on the phone.

The next afternoon, George Coltrane and John Parish, Grey's former brother-in-law, were in Coltrane's office. Parish was standing near the window as a helicopter hovered dangerously close to the building. "It's not police, maybe building maintenance," he said to Grey's father, watching a thick rope drop from the helicopter. Suddenly a huge man dangled from the rope, and before Parish could say anything, the man crashed feet first through the window.

Shaking particles of broken glass from his jumpsuit and combat boots, Khan grabbed Coltrane by his Brooks Brothers shirt and Parish by his Christian Dior. Jerking both men off their feet, he spoke while they dangled, nearly choking, like puppets from his huge hands. "Hi, I'm Khan Sun," he said to George Coltrane. "Shall I call you Dad?" He threw the two men across the office onto a leather couch. "Now listen to me, you weasels. I don't know why you're having Grey tailed, but I surmise it's something to do with trying to get her money. Call your goons off, you understand? Otherwise I'm going to hurt you." And with the two men cowering on the couch, Khan reached out the window, grabbed the hovering copter's dangling rope, and was gone.

The phone rang. Ashen-faced, Coltrane answered. Listening for a moment, he hung up, turned to Parish. "That was the detectives. They are *not* on their way here and don't want anything more to do with this."

Parish, equally ashen-faced, rubbed his throat where Khan had gripped him. "Jesus, did you see the size of him? I guess this wasn't such a good idea." Then calculation replaced fear in Parish's eyes. "Jennifer can take her into court. Fowler and Fowler should be in Jennifer's hands, not someone whose own father will testify she's not sane," Parish said, looking pointedly at Coltrane.

Carol sat in "her house"—that's what Khan called the apartment—when he confirmed her worst fears. "Love her! He wants me to love her," she said aloud.

It was four days since Khan had dropped his bomb, charting her future, too. She was to give her martial arts allegiance to the zen Master and attend his classes along with the other black belts. She recalled Khan's words for the millionth time. "I'm going to make you a sandan before I go. I know you just passed your test for nidan, but you can carry the rank, and I'm making you chief sensei. In other words, it's going to be your school, income included. And this"—he waved at the living room as he stood near a window—"is your house now. Don't you see? You'll have your job in the office, money from the school, a home. You can pull your life together the way you always wanted."

"Not without you," she said as his other words—"I'm marrying Grey and leaving for Taiwan,"—burned in her brain.

As he spoke, he saw the beginnings of the rising hysteria that later smothered her. He pulled her to him. "I know you love me. But if you really love me and want what's best for me, love Grey. Give her the same allegiance you'd give me."

The entire dojo was in shock. Sensei was leaving! Marcos was the most upset. He had already moved into the Master's school, as had Romulis and Rebulis, but he was handling Khan's coming departure worse than any of the others—except Carol, who was one step from catatonic stupor. She went to classes, but other than that, she did nothing. She had not shown up for work in days, but just sat in "her house." She was so despondent that she even neglected her children at St. Anthony's Hostel, something she'd never done since the first day she walked in there years ago.

It was 9 P.M. when she took the emergency keys to the building from Khan's pegboard and went downstairs to the office. Once at her desk in the empty office, she wept, and stayed there crying until three in the morning. When there were no more tears left, she went into the dojo. It was empty, yet filled with Khan, and she stood there, feeling as though she was sinking into quicksand—smothering. The feeling became so oppressive she could hardly breathe. She went back upstairs into the bedroom where she had waited alone so many nights. *I knew it, deep inside I knew it.*

She walked into his library and scanned the bookshelves, the martial arts literature he held so dear, the record collection he so prized. She heard sounds of the dogs patrolling the roof and saw their shadows pass by the window.

The all-night gas station on the Bowery gave her the two gallon cans of gasoline. She was very careful to wet each book, each record jacket. When she finished soaking down "her house," she proceeded to the dojo, pouring gasoline on everything he held precious. Dan's huge painting that Grey had purchased and then donated to the school hung high. Carol had to swing the gasoline can to splash Khan fighting the dragon. She began crying again. "Love her. He wants me to love her."

Grey's phone rang at 5 A.M. It was Ralph Daniels. One of the children from St. Anthony's needed an emergency operation. There was no health insurance and St. Vincent's Hospital wanted guarantee of payment to treat the deathly sick child.

Khan stirred awake next to her and she told him the news, then she and Khan raced to St. Vincent's Hospital in the Village. Grey explained her connection to the children as she did.

The apartment and dojo were burning. Flames licked the walls and tatami mats in the ground floor dojo and could be seen through the plate glass window as Carol left the College of the Streets. The loaded .38 was in her canvas bag. She headed for Grey's Fifth Avenue apartment.

Just before she reached the corner, a squad car screeched to a halt next to her. She thought about running, getting rid of the gun. But a police officer had her by the arm before she could sprint away. Resigned to being arrested, she climbed into the backseat of the squad car by the door a policeman held open. That's when she saw the Franciscan priest sitting there. He told her Kelly, a little girl Carol dearly loved, had ruptured an organ, had been taken to St. Vincent's Hospital, and was calling for Carol. "You have to come," Brother Ignatius said, looking into Carol's eyes and watching them fill with panic. He did not even bother to ask why she had been ignoring the kids these past days.

As the police car sped toward St. Vincent's Hospital, fire engine sirens cut the predawn silence in the East Village.

It was Marcos who called the fire department. He was asleep on a bunch of towels in the black belt dressing room, having disobeyed Sensei's orders to lock the school that evening and go to the Master's. Marcos loved the Master; after all, he was the grandmaster, his sensei's sensei. But losing Khan was losing his father. Like a dog needing to sleep on his master's sweater when he was away, Marcos spent a defiant night curled up behind the lockers.

Crackling sounds from the dojo awakened him and he smelled fire. Skinny as a wire, graceful as a fencer, the seventeen-year-old went into action, calling the fire department, then racing seven flights of stairs to alert Carol. Upstairs, he found more flames, Carol absent, and an empty gasoline can. He beat the fire with wet towels and kept the dogs from harm.

Carol sat on a lone chair just outside the operating room, where she was left to wait with the sick five-year-old girl while Brother Ignatius went to the business office to meet the hostel's benefactor, whom Carol knew existed but never met, and who was paying for the surgery.

Carol held Kelly's hand. Already sedated, barely awake, the little girl was comforted by her presence and even though drugged, she maintained a grip on Carol's hand. Finally a medical team, given the go-ahead by the admitting office, wheeled the child, who did not want to let go of Carol's hand, into the operating room. Unfamiliar with prayer, Carol now immersed herself in it. God, she silently asked, save her. I'll be good for the rest of my life. She jumped suddenly to her feet and strode the hospital corridor to the nearest ladies' room. In a locked booth she took the .38 from her red bag, dismantled and cleaned it of fingerprints, and wrapped the gun in toilet paper. Leaving the booth, seeing no one else in the ladies' room, she stuffed the revolver to the bottom of the waste bin. See, God? I'm being good. I won't hurt anyone, she continued her inner dialogue as she raced back to the operating room hall. And whoever this benefactor is, God, I'll be her slave for life.

At that moment Khan and Grey came into view, accompanied by Brother Ignatius. The brown-robed priest thrust Grey toward Carol. "This is our savior," he said, "and her fiancé." The priest could not understand why the three people he introduced all went rigid.

Carol, Khan, and Grey stared at each other. Carol wanted both to strangle Grey and kiss her feet. The two conflicting urges became so strong that Carol actually looked from Grey's throat to her shoes.

Then, considering her promise to God and all Grey had done for the abused children Carol loved so much,

Carol felt she had no other choice, and during the hours the little girl was under the knife, she was truly civil to Grey. There was even a moment, as Carol cried for Kelly, when she allowed Grey to put a comforting arm around her shoulders. For his part, Khan was completely out of his element in this drama. He merely watched and tried to absorb the unbelievable fact that Carol had hidden her child-caring self from him for years. When he incredulously asked her, "Why?" she sincerely told him she had thought he would think her a wimp not worthy of the dojo. He could only shake his head at her logic.

Then the drama underwent a drastic change as Khan found out about the fire, which Carol, in her agony over Kelly, had forgotten. The dogs were safe, but there was extensive damage to the dojo and the apartment. Khan wanted to kill Carol. He came down the hall from the phone with murder in his eyes, and Carol thought he probably knew of her intent to shoot Grey, too.

The giant Eurasian grabbed Carol and threw her against a wall. "She tried to burn down the school, kill the dogs," he said to Grey as she grabbed his arm, thinking he had gone crazy. A white-coated hospital attendant paused in the hall, wondering if she should call the police.

It was Grey who defused the situation by pleading for Carol. Khan allowed her to pull him around the corner, away from the pitiful figure of Carol wringing her hands and crying.

"I love you so much," Grey said. "I understand her because of it. If the situation were reversed, knowing the facts, I think I'd do the same. Don't hurt her, Khan. Who's going to love those kids?" Even as she begged mercy for Carol, Grey still reeled from the discovery that Carol of all people in the world was a hostel mother. That the black belt's mysterious red bag was filled with toys and gifts for the children of St. Anthony's was mind-boggling.

Eventually Khan accepted Grey's pleas. "I'd set fires if you left me," she said, her eyes filled with compassion.

His anger abated, Khan watched Carol waiting to know the little girl's fate, even feeling sorry for her. The martial artist thought back over all the years he had known Carol, how loyal and loving she had been to him, how she had waited . . . He experienced great guilt at not having been more sympathetic, taking a greater interest in Carol's life outside the dojo. Grey is changing me, he thought. I'm getting soft. Carol in mind, he went to make another phone call

Ultimately, after an unbearable wait, there was good news. The surgery was successful, and Kelly would live. The little girl's first word when she awoke in the intensive-care unit was "Carol." Khan, Grey, Carol, and Brother Ignatius were all there to hear it. A look passed between Carol and Grey, and though there were no words to describe it, a bond was established between the two women.

Then everyone was gone, leaving Carol with Kelly. Seeing her was Kelly's best medicine. The child's eyes never left Carol's face until she drifted back into sleep.

It was night when Carol emerged from the Seventh Avenue door of St. Vincent's and realized she had nowhere to go. The apartment was still hers, but was filled with char and smoke fumes. Exhausted, broken, and defeated, unable to think clearly, she walked, looking down at the stone steps. Raising her head, she saw a car at the curb. Its door was wide open and the interior light seemed to beckon her. She drew closer and saw Gary Reddington in the driver's seat, smiling at her, just before she got in.

The whole school attended the ranking ceremonies in the Master's Chinatown dojo. The ceremonies began with the Master sharing anecdotes of his great, revered sensei, Gogen Yamaguchi. "My sensei," the Master said proudly, looking hard at Khan's students sitting in zazen, "had signs in his school prohibiting bleeding on his mats, forecasting dire punishment for those who did!"

From her prone position amid white belts, Grey wondered what punishment for bleeding could possibly be, but of course refrained from asking. I only hope I don't bleed today!

"White belts testing for green," Marcos called.

Grey joined a group of ten testing, and with two hundred karateka looking on, she performed the katas called for. Moving through her favorite, the Golden Swan, she felt Khan's eyes on her and knew he was proud.

Next was sparring, and although woefully outmatched

by the black belts she faced, she managed to maintain footing with her now well-developed taisavaki. Getting out of the way had become her speciality, and during four matches she did not score any points, but neither was she swept to the floor.

As her chest heaved after the sparring, she stood with the other white belts before the Master. Marcos held boards for breaking, and one by one the white belts broke a single board with a *shuto* (knife hand). When her turn came, she said a prayer, then sliced through the wood as if it were butter, and let a breath of relief. She had passed her test!

Just then the Master stepped forward and congratulated the white belts on their performance so far. "But lest you take your elevation to this new rank of learning lightly," he said, "I think it best you break two boards now." He took his seat again.

She tried to quiet doubts, knowing they would detract from her try at two boards. She had never broken more than one and that only recently. Remembering Khan's words, "If you take a fast-action picture of a karateka breaking boards, you will see the wood started to break before he ever touched it. It's his chi preceding the actual technique."

Gods of the martial arts, help me, she silently pleaded. She felt Carol's eyes on her and looked up. Since Kelly's operation, Carol had resumed her role as Grey's teacher and was fully as relentless as Khan in the dojo. She was already filling the chief sensei's shoes, and there was much stir over her elevation among martial artists in New York City, where it was unheard of for a woman to hold such a position, especially in the city's hardest-fighting school. I'll kick your ass if you fuck up, Carol's look plainly said.

Marcos held two boards in front of Grey. One student had just failed to break them and retreated in defeat, having failed his test. She visualized the wood breaking, then concentrated on the little pad of fat protecting bones in the side of her hand that turns to callus and becomes a lethal weapon. If she didn't hit the boards with exactly that part of the hand's under edge, she would break her bones instead of wood.

The Master nodded. "Ayiiii," she cried, swinging her shuto. The boards broke!

An hour later, standing with the underbelts who had passed their tests, Grey received a new green obi. Tying the stiff new belt correctly, filled with a fine sense of accomplishment, she joined the other green belts. The black belts had tested privately before Khan and the Master at an earlier date, and wore their new ranks proudly.

Ceremonies over, the Master invited all for hot sake in celebration and good-byes to Khan. Grey was feeling no pain from the rice wine when the Master approached her. "Come and let's talk, my dear," he said, leading her away from the crowd. The new green belt was very frightened of being alone with the Master. With his zen meditation lesson still painfully fresh in her memory, she dearly hoped he would not decide to teach her anything. God, I hope he doesn't give me an aiki lesson, she thought.

"You are very beautiful, my dear," the Master said in a quiet spot where there were two chairs, indicating she sit next to him. "And that can lead to 'shunting.' Do you know what that means, my dear?"

"No, Master," she said. God, he makes me feel like a little baby when he talks to me.

"Shunting means getting things the easy way," he said. "A person as good-looking as you can shunt through life. Or," he paused and looked meaningfully at her new green obi, "you can ignore the fact you are overly beautiful and work extra hard to avoid shunting and thereby live up to your full potential. Which will it be?"

"I will avoid shunting at all costs," she said immediately.

"Good, good," the Master boomed in approval, then peered searchingly at her. "You are marrying one of the best martial artists in the world. Are you aware of that?"

"Yes, Master."

"He is also a disturbed personality warped by war. Do you understand that also?"

"Yes, Master," she answered seriously, looking full into his eyes and waiting for advice she hoped would be forthcoming. Khan's moods could be mercurial and she was sometimes at a loss to know how to deal with his sudden changes.

"You'll do just fine. I think you have good instincts. Just remember, your husband is different, and he is a real warrior. One that will forget about you at times and find battles to fight. Now, enough of that talk. What is it you will be careful of in your career as a karateka?" He looked at her expectantly.

"I will be wary of my own beauty," she dutifully said.

"Good, good, very good," the Master shouted, pulling her to her feet and back to the party. "It is important you name your first son after me. Do you agree?"

"Yes, Master," she said on the verge of laughter, relieved the session had only involved a talk.

Later that night, lying next to Khan, anticipating his lovemaking, she told him of her conversation with the Master. Khan laughed. "Isn't he wonderful?"

"Absolutely," she answered. "Will we name our first son after him?"

"Yes," he said, then closed his eyes. "In anticipation of our forthcoming marriage," he said in a formal voice, one she had not heard before, "we should prepare ourselves for this union by not making love until we take vows. Do you agree?"

"Do I have a choice?"

"Not really," he said.

"Well, then, I agree," she said, looking at him, marveling at the fact he was really hers. She considered what the Master had said about how different Khan was.

Then he opened his eyes and gazed at her lying naked next to him. "Cover yourself, woman. You're enticing me. Our wedding night will hold a thousand delights." He went to sleep.

It was Grey's last meeting with Ralph Daniels at Fowler and Fowler. All pertinent business was finished. Daniels congratulated her on her upcoming marriage, expressing his best wishes for her future. She was just about to leave when the gray-haired attorney handed her an article cut from *Time* magazine.

It was titled "Spies Among Us." A college professor and his wife, originally from Taiwan, both "certified residents" who owned a home in Pittsburgh, were the subjects of the article. In May, when the school year had ended at Carnegie-Mellon University, where Wen Chen taught statistics, he and his family had flown home to Taiwan for the first time since leaving in 1974. During their sentimental return home, the professor was picked up by Taiwanese security police and questioned for thirteen hours about his "anti-Taiwan" activities in the U.S. He was found dead the next day with all his internal organs ruptured, thirteen broken ribs, and a fractured pelvis.

The *Time* article went on to say that Chen's death had sparked congressional concern that the dictatorial government of President Chiang Ching-kuo maintained a network of agents, especially on campuses, to keep an eye on the half-million Taiwanese in the United States.

"How awful!" she exclaimed, handing the story back to the lawyer.

"Mrs. Fowler, in your best interests, I think it advisable you choose another country to absorb Oriental culture. Mainland China would welcome you. I seriously wonder about your safety in Taiwan," he said, looking across his desk at her; always stunned by her beauty, genuinely caring for her. My God, he thought, what is she doing to her life? The lawyer forced himself to remain silent and keep a neutral expression on his face, knowing he had said as much as he could.

She smiled. "I really appreciate your concern. I know your motives are sincere. But my future husband has specific reasons for going to Taiwan. He would never lead me into danger. We are not going to Taiwan to involve ourselves in politics, but to study, so put your fears to rest."

Ralph Daniels knew when a conversation was over. He could not press the point any further. But privately he would worry. In these days of terrorists and kidnappers, she was so well-known. He almost gasped, assaulted by a clear vision of horrors to befall her. The moment passed. The elderly lawyer bid his good-byes, but after Grey left, he offered up a silent prayer that his chilling vision of her future had been a thing imagined. But somehow the prayer seemed empty—as though Daniels knew he saw her tomorrows.

There was nothing left to do in New York. The seemingly impossible tasks were accomplished. It was a bittersweet time. Good-bye tears, last conversations, last looks at beloved faces, a last tournament.

There was a quick morning flight to see Darkchild in Kentucky. Khan was fascinated by the big stallion and insisted on riding Darkchild bareback. He whipped off his shirt, let down his war lock, and in jeans and sneakers grabbed Darkchild's mane, vaulting to his back. After first rearing, Darkchild accepted Khan's mastery and galloped off in the open Kentucky field, with Khan playing Genghis Khan on his unsaddled back. Grey, astonished and visited by a tiny ping of jealousy, knew she would never forget the picture.

It seemed impossible to keep the surprise wedding plans a secret from Khan, but she pulled it off, mainly because he was busy every second himself.

Finally they were at Kennedy Airport. As far as Khan knew, they were to marry in the airport chapel in San Francisco during a layover before flying to Honolulu on the first leg of their journey across the world. A nononsense ceremony, he thought.

"But this plane is going to Mexico," he said in the waiting area by the gate.

"With a San Francisco stop, where we get off," she lied.

Content with her explanation, still distracted by poignant good-byes, he boarded the 747.

To her relief, he fell immediately asleep, the same way he had on the flight to Kentucky. She had counted on that to carry off her surprise.

"Wake up, we're in San Francisco," she said, keeping up the charade until they were pummeled and hugged by honey-tanned Dan and Llana at the Cozumel, Mexico, airport.

Khan was flabbergasted Grey could have kept such a surprise from him, and seeing Dan took the edge off his sadness at leaving his students.

Llana and Dan had been busy shopping for wedding clothes for Grey and Khan and making arrangements.

That night, under a starry sky, in a seaside garden with the Caribbean reflecting silvery moonlight, the nuptials by a priest commenced. Grey was gorgeous in a frothy Mexican wedding gown. and Khan magnificent in a silver-trimmed black suit. A violinist accompanied a marimba band. Llana cried, Dan beamed. In the most perfect moment of Grey's life, she and Khan were pronounced man and wife. Thank you, God, she thought as he kissed her to seal their vows, for making my life finally wonderful.

After a champagne wedding dinner, the newlyweds retreated to a flower-filled cottage. And it was as Khan had said—a night of a thousand delights. Afterward, while his new wife lay sleeping, he drank in her exquisite face and again swore nothing would ever harm her.

19

The airplane shook ferociously within a full-fledged storm over the East China Sea. In the darkened cabin, Khan slept. Grey gripped his hand, using the strength there to calm her. She thought of her last long journey—across Europe as Mrs. Fowler with her drunken husband, a pitied object of curiosity.

Now, as Mrs. Sun, she was again an object of curiosity, for very different reasons. From Mexico, via California, Hawaii, Wake Island, and Tokyo, Grey and Khan wended toward Taiwan. A more beautiful couple was not to be seen; their unique way of moving, lithe and strong, made them even more noticeable. Journeying eastward, the newlyweds seemed to grow taller when actually the people around them were ever shorter. By time they reached Japan, Khan's great height, plus Grey's bright hair and jade eyes, were beacons drawing enormous attention.

Now, from Osaka, Japan, they were on the last leg of the trip aboard a rickety China Airlines plane, without even a stewardess aboard, being terrifyingly buffeted by winds.

Grey released her hold on Khan's hand and clutched the seat arms, thinking the engines sounded tired pulling against the storm. Finding no comfort in hardwood, she grabbed his hand again as a major gust whipped the aircraft. She pushed fear away with thoughts of the future.

Khan was by now impatient with her continued questions about the martial arts nun. The last she had extracted from him between Wake Island and Tokyo: "The nun and her son are hidden against government edicts, training oppressed people," he stated matter-of-factly, leaving her more curious.

"How can a nun have a son?"

"I don't know. Scuttlebutt says a man is with her. Maybe she adopted him or was raped."

"Tell me about her psychic abilities."

"Her martial arts are beyond belief, she can heal, is a true clairvoyant and capable of great psychic feats." He reeled off the bizarre list of talents as if he knew the mystic figure, and sensing his irritation, she stopped her questions, wondering for the thousandth time, Could such a creature exist? Wasn't this a chase after the Loch Ness monster or the yeti? What does it matter? I'm with Khan. It will be a great adventure, she thought, within the miracle of her marriage, actually feeling a happy glow.

She thought again of what he had told her of Taiwan's two-class system. There were Mainlanders, descendants of Chiang Kai-shek's one million decadent Mandarins (including an army) chased from Mainland China, who had descended on Taiwan's thirteen million people and taken over. Mainlanders still ruled within a brutally enforced dictatorship.

And there were Taiwanese, descendants of those thirteen million who had been living for many generations on Formosa when the Mainlanders arrived to rule. Although the vast majority, Taiwanese were second-class citizens, needing special visas to travel, kept in check by the Mainlanders. There was an organization of protesters among the people known as T.I.M., whose members were hunted, often tortured, certainly killed when found.

Just then a horrendous sheet of lightning flashed at the plane's window, and she thought of Ralph Daniel's warnings. The lightning, however, was the storm's last hurrah. Abruptly the plane flew smoothly, and the engine sounded stronger. She tipped her head against the seat, slipping into an edgy twilight sleep.

After twenty-eight hours of traveling, they reached Taiwan bone weary, wanting hotel and bed. Instead they were embroiled in a fracas immediately after clearing customs when two cab drivers argued furiously over who would have them as fares in the almost deserted airport. All at once, one cabbie was surrounded by brown-uniformed men materializing as if from nowhere. They took the suddenly silent driver away.

"Not to mind, he was just a crazy escapee from Red China," said a gray-suited, ingratiating Chinese man with a wide smile and bad teeth who also materialized as if from nowhere, speaking broken English. The man, some sort of official, helped Grey and Khan into the remaining cab.

It was a long, desolate ride into Taipei, past factories, shacks, and barren, dusty countryside. She had expected the city to be a mysterious Oriental delight. Khan, ecstatic on the isle of his dreams, said little and sat forward in his seat, looking eagerly from the open window.

She was disappointed. The city teemed with people. There were no sidewalks. Pedestrians, bicycles, handcarts, buses, and trucks shared the same streets amid clamoring horns and enormous dust clouds.

When they reached the hotel, they learned their reservation was missing. Grey was glad to let Khan, who spoke a smattering of Mandarin, handle the situation. The Mandarin lessons she had studied the last two weeks meant nothing; everything sounded a babble.

Clad in jeans, canvas boots, and T-shirt, she sank wearily into a worn burgundy armchair in the stark lobby, stuck her feet out, and arched her body, trying to stretch and ease her aching back.

Feeling eyes on her, she looked up. She saw a few tourists, Americans mostly, conservatively dressed, she guessed from the Midwest. Most in the lobby were Oriental.

Oriental or not, they watched either Grey or Khan, who in jeans and jean shirt dwarfed everyone as he stood at the front desk. The clerk gaped openly at his war lock. Grey looked away from the curious eyes at her simple gold wedding band. *They probably think we're hippies.*

She was correct, for it took some time for Khan to complete business. Filling in a long questionnaire and making arrangements for a guide the next morning, he asked for the nearest martial arts school. The clerk's eyes flickered nervously about the lobby as he denied ever hearing of martial arts. "Gung fu?" Khan asked. The clerk only looked blank and seemed relieved when the big Eurasian left his station. In a plain room, the exhausted couple slept.

The next morning, after a hearty room-service breakfast, there was a barely discernible knock. Standing in the doorway was a painfully shy girl in a conservative skirt and blouse, white ankle socks, and flat shoes—their guide.

"*Ni hau a?*" Grey properly greeted her.

"*Hau. Ni hau a?*" the girl answered and raised a hand to cover her blushing face. "I do speak English," she added, to Grey's great relief. "My name is Su-wen and I am a student at the University of Taipei."

"Wonderful!" Grey exclaimed, causing Su-wen to jump like a doe ready to dart. Grey realized she'd shocked the timid girl with her enthusiasm and would have to be more subdued.

Hesitantly Su-wen ventured in, sat in a straight-backed chair, drew her knees primly together, and folded her hands in her lap. Grey and Khan sat on the rumpled bed, which disconcerted the guide, as did the smiling exotic foreign creatures. Su-wen attempted concealing her discomposure as she spoke. "Would you like first to visit the Lungsham Temple with its carved stone columns and ornate roof design?"

"Eventually," Khan said. "But first we wish to locate a martial arts sword master."

Su-wen was confused. "I have lived here my whole life and have never heard of such. But I will inquire. Now perhaps you would like to see the National Palace Museum, which houses the world's greatest Chinese art treasures."

Chiang Kai-shek's plunder, according to Khan, Grey thought, then saw the blighted hope on his face. "It's going to take awhile," she said, trying to ease his mind. "Why don't we do usual tourist things and keep asking questions? We'll find what we came for."

So Su-wen guided them about Taipei. During a boring morning trip to the National Martyr's Shrine, Grey felt the first waves of nausea. By afternoon, in Confucius Temple, the waves were a turbulent sea, and by the time they returned to the hotel, she was in full throes of traveler's sickness.

For the next three days, they were dragged through all of Taipei by their dauntless guide. Terribly sick, Grey ate no food, but for Khan's sake, hid her discomfort as much as possible. At his insistence, much to Su-wen's chagrin, they combed Taipei's back alleys and frequented a local tea house, where bitter herb tea was served in tiny cups while an old storyteller sat cross-legged on a wooden platform spinning ancient tales.

Khan was deeply frustrated. He was not here to see Presidential Square, nor Chiang Kai-shek's Memorial Hall. No one would speak to him about martial arts. Whenever he inquired, people looked askance or fearful. Grey's illness was not getting better. She was never far from a bathroom, rapidly dropping weight, and her usually glowing skin had taken on an ashen pallor.

The morning of their fourth day, waiting for Su-wen, Khan held Grey. "Maybe we should leave," he said. "I'm worried about you."

"We came halfway around the world to find your master and that's what we're going to do! I'll be fine," she said, realizing the enormous affirmation of love his offer represented.

It was dawn and they stood in front of their room's one window. Directly outside, the only English sign on the street "HAPPY V.D. CLINIC," blinked in bright red neon, its garish color playing across their faces. The absolute ridiculousness of the advertisement caused them to laugh, severing the tension until she raced for the bathroom with horrible stomach pains.

Everywhere they went, they were followed by crowds. She mistakenly thought they meant harm, but soon came to realize Taiwanese people were just curious. That made it no less upsetting. "Having hundreds of people follow you about is weird! I feel like the Pied Piper," she said when a particularly large crowd waited outside the teahouse.

"They call you '*Hwang*' ", Su-wen said, then could not find an English equivalent. They were later to learn that literally translated, *hwang* meant "wide," the Mandarin version of "far out."

Grey's flamboyant coloring, combined with sleeveless T-shirts, long cotton skirts, and flowered canvas flat-heeled boots—so unlike any outfit worn on the streets—attracted like a magnet, as did Khan's height, war lock, and mixed blood. Su-wen constantly explained Grey's shagged haircut to women on the street. One young woman sadly shook her head when Grey offered, through Su-wen, to show her how to cut her long black hair into layers.

"Oh, no," Su-wen said, consternation in her meek voice. "She can only look and admire. It is against the law to wear something different here, even a hairstyle. A girl was arrested just yesterday. The newspapers said her crime was wearing an Indian sari as a wedding gown. The marriage ceremony was interrupted and government men took her, still a maiden, to jail!"

"Why?" Grey asked, momentarily thankful for anything taking her mind off her stomach. "What's wrong with wearing something unusual to get married?"

"I will show you how it is," Su-wen said, guiding them to a large public school, where they waited for the noon bell and blue-uniformed children poured into the eighty-degree afternoon to eat brown-bagged lunches.

"You see," said Su-wen, "the children dress alike and have same haircuts. They must do so until tenth grade. Then they may wear their own things, but may not be too different."

"Why?" Grey asked, looking over a stone wall at youngsters looking like peas in pods, sitting in neat circles on the lawn, quietly eating.

"That is the way it is," answered Su-wen, shrugging exactly as she had when Grey had asked why men with machine guns took up posts each night after curfew, and why there was curfew when there was no crime.

That afternoon, Su-wen brought good news. "My uncle has informed me we have a distant cousin who is a member of the Chinese Boxing Association. He has arranged for you to have lunch tomorrow with an important master, Sao Ping."

Khan gave a war whoop, grabbed Su-wen, and kissed her cheek. The plain girl went into such spasms of shyness and purple blushing that he silently swore he'd never do that again.

Su-wen recovered from his kiss, the sort of thing a Chinese would never do, particularly a Mainlander like herself. The fact there was to be such a meeting surprised Su-wen, as did her uncle's interest in these tourists. Although they had no idea of good manners or proper dress, Su-wen was coming to like them very much. Her fascination with Grey's emerald eyes and long, swooping lashes invaded her dreams. And Khan, who scared her to death in a million ways, showed her pictures of himself in magazines from America, where he was a fighting champion. She was very impressed and told her uncle.

*   *   *

Sao Ping sucked a duck head one last time, then spat it into a gleaming black cloisonné bowl bearing a straw-colored Tang Grass design. He wiped grease from his double chin with a hand-embroidered Irish linen napkin as his calculating raisin eyes gazed interestedly at the informer before him. The miserable street creature was recounting the activities of the famous karate fighter and his woman. They constantly asked about martial arts and sword fighting, Mainlander privileges—taboo for Taiwanese. Sao Ping had heard much lately about the couple nicknamed *Hwang*. He knew all about them, including the exquisite woman's vast fortune.

Sao Ping was a martial arts impresario. As a young man he had excelled at "boxing" and had been a famous fighter himself. That period did not last long. Being a privileged class member, he easily became fat and rich. Now his youthful athletics were long forgotten, eating his most strenuous activity. Commissioner Sao Ping sat on the governing council and was a personal friend of the dictator himself.

It had become Ping's habit to gather fine fighters and pit them against others, even sending teams to foreign countries. He was not capable of training them himself, so the fighters were already skilled when he conscripted them. Still, he had built a reputation as a martial arts master. Enough of the charade left him believing his own reputation and he accumulated excellent fighters.

No, he thought, scratching his bald head, where there were spreading freckles, it would never do to have a foreigner of championship quality align with anyone else. Nor would it do for the couple to find a Taiwanese master. There were some who practiced illegally in the mountains, despite death threats.

Intermittently soldiers would find rebellious martial arts students, like the seventeen boys machine-gunned down last night in front of their village homes. The youths were suspected of belonging to T.I.M., and that suspicion alone brought swift death without trial or questioning. And so the village had been invaded while all slept, and the boys who studied martial arts outside government-monitored schools had been shot, their bodies left in the streets.

Sao Ping had ordered microphones activated in the couple's hotel room. The fidelity was quite good. He listened to tapes while eating breakfast of pork and twenty-year-buried quail eggs. It was a noisy bed. *In extremis* the woman yelled. Sao Ping enjoyed overhearing their lovemaking, but did not glean much information, since they spent most of their time outdoors. Making contact through their Mainlander guide's family, he had arranged a luncheon meeting. Such a fighter would be a feather in his cap.

Sao Ping dismissed the miserable stoolie with a wave of his ringed, pudgy fingers and, rising from his chair with surprising agility for one so rotund, went to his kitchen to spend the afternoon supervising and tasting in anticipation of the evening meal.

Khan noticed the extra attention paid them during guided tours. He was well aware that trained observers followed along with curious onlookers. This was what he wanted, knowing unusual inquiries would attract attention from higher-ups, hoping it would be those he sought. He said nothing to Grey, who was having problems enough with her sickness, of the surveillance. He fantasized in a thousand different ways the master he would meet on the morrow.

The next morning, a much thinner Grey awoke feeling better, but still not trusting her stomach to food. Su-wen arrived at 5 A.M. as planned and took them directly to Hyde Park for sunrise. Once there, Khan was pleased to see hundreds of men, women, and children also greeting the sun, practicing t'ai chi ch'uan. He gazed with admiration at an old man, easily in his eighties, moving through the dreamlike, slow motion of the oldest recorded Chinese martial art.

"This is health exercise most people do everyday before work," Su-wen said.

In a cab to Mandarin Hall, Grey was suddenly ravenously hungry. She was so hungry that she hid how insulted she was when Khan suggested she remain silent during lunch. She would instead concentrate on food.

Mandarin Worker's Hall was a one-story, plain wooden building surrounded by factories. Inside, long tables held thousands of factory workers at midday meal.

They were led to the only round table, boasting the only tablecloth, and a fine linen one, Grey noticed, set against a wooden screen. Six of nine chairs were already occupied by Sao Ping, his friend General Tszu, a thin, nervous man, and four tough-looking boxers, including Sao Ping's champion, known as the biggest person on the island until Khan had appeared. When they sat, Su-wen was flanked by Grey and Khan, who sat across from Sao Ping.

Immediately an overlarge, museum-quality porcelain bowl was placed in the center of the table. It steamed, wafting wonderful aromas. Ginger? Parsley? Grey sought to isolate the smells as waiters placed small hand-painted bowls of steaming rice and shiny orange chopsticks decorated with gold dragons before each person.

None of the seven men at the table spoke or looked at Su-wen and Grey. Nonentities we are, Grey thought, noting by the manner of the huge, shaven-headed champion, looking carved from granite, that he hated Khan, even as she reeled from the insult of not being introduced. Su-wen, nonplussed by the slight, sat with no expression on her broad face. None of the workers at nearby tables glanced their way, but only continued a steady rhythm with their chopsticks. Nor did the workers talk to each other.

Sao Ping was in heaven. Khan was beyond his dreams, and his champion, seated to his left, already was relegated to second class. And Sun's woman! Though no one acknowledged her presence, it was undeniable. Just as his friend, General Tszu, on his right, had said. Tszu, a member of the Defense Ministry's Intelligence Bureau, responsible for conducting what remained of the war with the Communists for possession of Mainland China, was a womanizer—and of key importance to Sao Ping's carefully orchestrated career.

I can feel his chi, Sao Ping thought, appraising Khan, planning the Eurasian's first fight—with the *president* himself as guest of honor.

He bit into a noodle, tasting the ginger flown from Jamaica especially for him. In 1977, America was considering normalizing relations with Mainland China. Taiwan was on a hook, desperately needing American goodwill, weapons, and protection. President Chiang would appreciate Sao Ping's new acquisition. What public relations—an American fighter! Sao Ping envisioned more money, perhaps a resident French chef. Like a vintage wine, he would add Khan to his cellar.

General Tszu planned also—how to get the woman! He had asked Sao Ping for today's invitation, having heard through his spy system of her presence in Taipei. Tszu's present eighteen-year-old mistress was considered the most beautiful woman on Taiwan. Half Korean, half Chinese, she caused near riots whenever Tszu paraded her through the Grand Hotel, the only place he could show her off to cohorts, since protocol demanded his wife be present for official functions. His mistress's beauty paled before Grey's.

Khan complimented his host on the savory noodles and slowly ventured into more complicated conversation requiring Su-wen's linguistic skills.

Sao Ping made sure to inform Khan that the Taiwanese people in the mountains had no culture, were childlike, and blessed that President Chiang looked after them. Pausing between noodles, Ping explained tales of monks and martial arts were hearsay. "The only true training is with me, right here in glorious Taipei. You are lucky to have found a true master. You may begin training with me tomorrow," Sao Ping said, closing the meeting. Then, with a move so nimble Grey dubbed him "Twinkle Toes," he sprang from his seat, pirouetted on his toes, and abruptly departed, his companions in close attendance. Khan, Su-wen, and Grey were left at the empty table in the now empty hall.

"Why didn't you just tell him you wouldn't be joining his school?" Grey asked when they were alone.

"Best to soothe the enemy when you're in his camp," Khan said, at the same time planning how to find a real master.

At five the next morning, Khan returned by himself to Hyde Park, where he saw t'ai chi practiced. Again he watched the ancient moving melody. Then he saw what he had returned for. Following one old man through the slow-motion exercise was a good-looking young man taller than most, wearing shorts. He was athletically fit with bulging calf muscles and a different haircut than the other, shorter men, more neatly trimmed.

"Play football?" Khan asked the man when he finished his t'ai chi, and Hyde Park was clearing of people on their way to work and school.

Delight played on the young man's chiseled face. Breaking into an engaging smile, he extended his hand. "English. Great to hear! Yeah, I play football. I'm Bob Chou, the football coach at the American School in Taipei. How did you know?"

Khan laughed as he towered over Chou. "Your calves are a dead giveaway."

"Holy mackerel. I know you, you're Khan!" the Chinese American said wonderingly.

That same morning, Grey toured the American School. As she walked the large campus with Su-wen, she saw only gray-haired, sixtyish women teachers. She was sure the students, most of them Army brats, were smoking marijuana. The pungent odor was in the air. Some of the kids were acting so bizarrely, she suspected they were on psychedelics. There were quite a few preteen and teen interracial couples, black and white, necking on the school grounds. They looked defiantly at her.

Inside the school's main building, she was thinking how bored she was, wondering what Khan was up to, when the familiar strains of "Lucy in the Sky With Diamonds" drifted from a room labeled "SPECIAL EDUCATION DEPARTMENT." She walked in and saw bare feet draped over the top of a couch, keeping time to the music. The feet were replaced by a woman's cheery, freckled face. "Hello," she said in English. That's how Grey met blue-eyed, brown-haired, twenty-two-year-old Trish Chou, who taught hearing handicapped children.

Later that morning, Grey and Khan rushed at each other, simultaneously exclaiming they had a luncheon date with someone who really knew about martial arts on Taiwan.

Bob Chou, of Chinese-Caucasian ancestry, had been born and raised in San Diego, where he had been a star athlete and zealous martial arts student since his teens. *Black Belt Magazine* was his bible. He had been reading about Khan for years, and to actually meet him was phenomenal. *Then*, to have his wife, Trish, meet Khan's wife at the same time and also make a luncheon date seemed karmic coincidence.

"I want to find the Chinese in myself," Bob had said to Trish, who was Irish Catholic, when he proposed marriage and Taiwan on the UCLA campus, where they had met as students. Finding jobs had been simple when they had come to Taiwan three years ago, for the American School desperately needed teachers. Bob became skilled in t'ai chi and was a Chinese history buff. Trish studied Chinese zither and ancient dance. Together they attended every cultural event and backpacked through the mountains on vacations. The young couple loved their life, but did miss things American, especially music. Khan and Grey's appearance was a major event.

Grey and Khan were equally excited as they awaited Bob and Trish's arrival in their hotel room. When they did come, Bob placed a finger across his lips after introductions and pointed to the ceiling. Khan understood immediately and suggested they all go for a walk.

"Every room is wired," Bob said in a low voice to Khan as they strolled the jammed streets on the way to a restaurant recommended by the Chous.

"How come there are drugs on your campus?" Grey asked when they were seated behind a wooden partition in a stark eating establishment. "I thought drugs meant a death sentence here." While she talked, little heads peeked around the partition, as the owner's children risked punishment to capture a close look at Hwang.

"They are," Trish said, her blue eyes serious. "But right now, with the present political situation, Americans can do no wrong. Chiang is terrified of a U.S. arms sales cutoff. Red China would march in here in a minute!"

Their conversation halted as Bob ordered in rapid Mandarin.

"Repeat what you told me about martial arts for Grey," Khan said to Bob when the restaurant owner left.

"Anyone with involvement outside government-sanctioned schools wouldn't speak of it, and would practice secretly in the mountains," Bob confided, lowering his voice. "In open schools, if a Taiwanese boy earns the equivalent of a Stateside black belt, they induct him into the Army and control him. Mainlanders are basically against Taiwanese learning martial arts, for they feel, and rightly so, they teach independence.

"But martial arts are too deeply ingrained in this culture to be eradicated, no matter how hard Mainlanders try. They leave t'ai chi alone, consider it without threat. Once I overheard some Taiwanese Olympic athletes saying a rogue *kwon* (martial arts school) had been found. Supposedly the *sifu* was shot and the students conscripted into the Army."

Bob and Trish explained Taiwan's spy systems, the most intricate between the bureaus deliberately created by President Chiang with ill-defined check-and-balance systems. "That way the bureaus keep dangerous eyes on each other, preventing any one from building too substantial a power base. This creates not only chaos, but one of the world's most intricate spy systems. The bureaus fight each other and for the president's favor. And here in the Republic of China," Bob said, raising a fine black eyebrow, "Americans are always watched. Especially mixed bloods like you and me," he said to Khan.

The Peking duck came then, dispelling a foreboding that suddenly overcame Grey. She ate happily, rolling slices of succulent duck meat, crisp duck skin, raw scallions, and hot plum sauce into thin pancakes eaten with the hands. Heartily she made up for days of no food.

Trish, watching Grey's hair swing in layered rows, asked, "Could you cut my hair like that?"

"I can try," Grey said, evaluating Trish's shoulder-length tresses.

Still later, back at the hotel, the two couples, feeling like old friends, listened to Khan's tape collection, and the sweet sounds of Earth, Wind, and Fire filled the downtown Taipei hotel room as Grey cut Trish's hair.

20

After a nap Mikel Anton finally scored a good supply of drugs and, knowing his remaining time on Oahu was short, he again made calls to escort services. It was only eleven and most of their phones didn't answer. The ones he did reach refused his requests.

He worked out for a couple of hours, push-ups, martial art forms, stopping every now and then to snort another line of coke, smoke another joint. He talked to himself, causing both of the people who monitored his sounds on the same floor to reflect on their relationship with Mikel Anton.

In Halehana's apartment, the boy, Yu, listened to the sounds Anton made on a tape machine. "Push-ups," he said in halting English, knowing positively what the black man was doing by the noises. Hadn't he watched for years? Didn't he know all the sounds the animal made? Hearing them now scared Yu. Even though he was no longer affected by Anton's will, no longer under his domination, the boy quaked inside remembering Taiwan.

Halehana looked at Yu trying to hide his fear as the voice of the man who had been his slave master filled their Waikiki condo. "It's gonna be over soon," the big man said, stripping and heading for the bathroom to take a shower. His body was massive, even more developed than Anton's and decorated with formidable scars. Passing the mirror, he glanced at himself, thought of the woman down the hall who watched Anton. Had a flash of respect for her, whoever she was. No, I will not bother her, let it go. No one will kill him before me. I wonder though if anyone could need to see him dead as much as me? He showered, then went back into the living room with a towel around his tight waist, and while Anton's sounds filled their living room, he made the boy throw punches. Holding up his huge hands, palms open, he directed Yu. "That's it, kid, punch harder, harder."

The boy, black silky hair flying, slammed his small fists into the big man's giant palms, feeling some of his fear recede, knowing that was the idea, to get rid of his terrifying anxiety.

Down the hall in the condo next to Anton's, the Nightwalker did not feel fear, but rather exhilaration as her time to kill the monster came closer. The sounds he made as he worked out also stimulated her. Get stronger, be more formidable. I will enjoy your death even more. "And so will you enjoy his death, Khan, my darling, my love," she spoke to the air as though he was there, and for a moment she felt as though he would soon come walking in the door as if none of the horrors had ever happened.

21

<hr>

Grey listened to Earth, Wind, and Fire. The tape was worn, fidelity faded. It had been almost five years since she and Khan had listened to that same tape with Bob and Trish Chou in Taipei. Were it not for Khan's solar-battery charger, they would have no music. I wonder what's popular in the U.S., she thought, then heard sounds, and saw the monk approaching through the trees. She turned up the volume, knowing he hated the music and was looking for her. Grabbing the blue cotton square that was never supposed to be off her head, she whipped it on. Then the monk that always scowled stood before her and pointed toward the monastery. Clicking off the music, she went in the direction he pointed. The monk fell and tripped behind her, making a noise as he did. She stifled a giggle. He often fell when he bedeviled her, as though a mischievous entity badgered the monk for badgering her.

She heard the monk scramble to his feet, then fall again. This time she could not contain herself and giggled behind her hand. For a moment the air also seemed to vibrate with mirth. When the monk got up, she walked, herded by him. With strains of Earth, Wind, and Fire lingering in her mind, she thought back to Bob and Trish years ago. The haircut she had given Trish. There were dire warnings from Bob about insulting Commissioner Sao Ping, how powerful Sao Ping was, how he would never forgive being rejected by Khan. That night Grey and Khan headed into the mountains.

How afraid she was—and thrilled—that velvet night, defying authority, perhaps endangering their lives by the audacious decision to leave Taipei and thumb their noses at Sao Ping. They walked silently for hours, the night sky making their shadows hard black as they trudged away from civilization, backpacking into the unknown.

But that had been years ago, and the changes in her life had been as cataclysmic as the changes in Taiwan's world position.

In December 1979, President Carter had made the historic announcement: the U.S. and the People's Republic of China would establish diplomatic relations. Carter had also announced that on January 1, the U.S. would end diplomatic relations with the Republic of China (Taiwan), and would cease to recognize the defense treaty of 1954.

Premier Hua of the People's Republic of China said, "The problem of Taiwan has not been resolved with the U.S. in the spirit of the Shanghai Communique. As for the way of bringing Taiwan back to the embrace of the Motherland and reunifying the country, it is entirely China's internal affair."

Political Taiwan boiled with the intrigue escalated by real fear of "Mother China" just across the China Strait and her reunification plans. Spy networks were beefed up, professional troop-training mercenaries were hired, and bordering waters were watched closely in an attempt to stop infiltration of Red Chinese agents.

All of this intrigue meant nothing to Grey, whose world, with Khan at its center, was a temple, a courtyard, a half mile of woods, and a waterfall. And now that center was to expand. The last thing on twenty-five-year-old Grey's mind was Taiwan's political situation. Long gone also were thoughts of her long-expired visa or the danger of what they had done in Taipei.

It had taken almost a month of exploring the lush mountain gorges, kaleidoscopes of natural beauty, going from village to village of terraced rice fields, before they had found this place. They had crossed the crooked bridges of Sun Moon Lake, built to thwart evil spirits that Chinese believe travel only in straight lines, and stared awestruck at Chiang Kai-shek's summer palace in all its majesty. People in the villages were wary of the foreign couple and offered no advice or food. Only the long-haired goats wandering everywhere were friendly.

Khan hunted and foraged, always providing. They

cooked over low fires and slept balmy nights under the stars. They made love by waterfalls and in steaming springs common in the mountains—healing mineral wells, bubbling, sometimes shooting into the air. They hid often from troops. She was very scared then, he noncommital, only waiting for the soldiers to pass so he could get on with the search.

One day, he shook her awake, pulling the long skirt she used for a cover from her. "I've found something wonderful!" he said, soaking wet, dripping water. She followed him to a steaming spring, bigger than any she had seen. The spring's steamy mist made a white wall he led her through, and they faced a waterfall making its own mist and a wild, rushing noise.

He guided her through the waterfall also, and they stood before a stone cliff, seemingly solid until he pointed to a black opening. "Is it a cave?" she shouted over the roaring waterfall. He tugged her into the opening and she saw a cave complete with bats hanging on its ceiling. She was terrified, feeling bat droppings under her bare feet. He kept her moving and suddenly they were again in sunlight, facing another waterfall. He led her through the second waterfall, making a rainbow with its spray, and they emerged into a yellow bamboo woods completely surrounded by high-peaked cliffs topped with white clouds. Sun glinted off the shiny yellow bamboo and its green leaves. "Like finding the Hidden Valley," she said wonderingly, standing in the pool at the base of the waterfall.

He had no time for fairy tales and pulled her into the woods. Several blue and red parrots flew up screaming at the disturbance. "Where are we going?" But he would not answer. Then she saw a stone wall. Drawing closer, she heard familiar noises: human straining and weapons clashing. Peering over the wall, she found herself looking at a martial arts movie come to life.

Within a giant courtyard was a stone temple with orange-tiled, fluted roofs. In the courtyard, half-clad men trained at martial arts. Supervising them were brown-robed monks with shaven heads. Then she saw, wonder of wonders, walking among men and monks the Master, who might have stepped from an ancient painting. "God, he's gorgeous," she said in awe.

Easily in his seventies, with a two-pronged white beard flowing to his chest, the Master wore a long blue robe that fluttered at its bottom as he walked. Slim and fit, he stood very straight, and even from their distance they could see his eyes shone with wisdom.

Transfixed, they stared over the wall. In the courtyard, a forge held a high fire, where two men with leather wristbands sweated and pounded steel. "They're making swords," Khan said in a reverent whisper.

Suddenly, as he expected, alerted by screaming parrots, the couple was surrounded by monks and students. Wielding ancient weapons, they herded Grey and Khan inside the monastery until the couple stood, barefoot and water-soaked, before the Master. She remembered her first feel of that cool stone floor beneath her feet, a floor she was to know well in the following years.

The Master spoke slowly, in a soft voice. "We know of your search, Hwang. You have insulted one high in government. Soldiers seek you. It does not matter here, we are dead if found. This temple is kept secret by the people, but times are changing. Torture is common. We could be discovered. You could leave now, be safe, go back to your country."

Khan bowed. His voice was low as he spoke in halting Mandarin, "I know and accept these things. I wish to know the ancient ways, to follow a spiritual path. Please."

The Master looked at the couple for a long time. The silence was filled with Khan's hope.

"There has never been a woman here. Men's ways are forbidden to women. Why would you wish your woman to learn them?"

"My woman stands by my side in all things, and I will train her myself."

The Master almost smiled and there was a discernible twinkle in his eyes as he spoke. "You are well named, my son, Hwang. It is very strange, but perhaps meant. Her way will be most difficult. She must prove her worth, labor, and keep to herself."

"My woman is strong and worthy," Khan said, his deep voice ringing with conviction.

The Master reached forward, laying a hand on Khan's forearm. "You shall stay with us."

Later, alone in their minuscule stone-floored room with only a pallet as furnishing, Grey asked, "What did he say about me?"

"You have to earn your way," Khan said in such a distracted manner she followed the direction of his gaze and saw what he stared so intently at. The clear red outline of the Master's fingertips were imprinted on his forearm.

"But he barely touched you," she whispered.

"I know," he said, home at last.

But it was not such a sweet home for her. While Khan immersed himself in studies, wielding a sword, working at the forge, practicing one-finger *kung*, absorbing wisdom at the Master's feet, Grey carried water in two buckets like an ox and scrubbed stone floors like the nuns at St. Anne's. Three times a day, when the men ate, she was their serving maid. She ate alone in the kitchen. No one but Khan spoke to her, not even her nemesis, the scowling monk. *Supervising me must be a punishment for something terrible he did,* she conjectured of the pinch-faced man overseeing her duties. Never making a sound, he only motioned or poked her, indicating what she was to do.

Yet life was wonderful. At the end of each hard day, she met Khan in a magical place, behind the waterfall's concealing spray. There was a green moss carpet, a quiet pool at the base of the waterfall, and best of all, always a shimmering rainbow. He said the place reminded him of Hawaii.

At first, before her muscles became accustomed to heavy labor, she ached painfully, and he massaged her by the waterfall. Then, when she strengthened to her daily duties, he trained her by the waterfall, once again her stern sensei. And also in that place they laughed and made love, playing naked like children in paradise. There, where sun and mist combined, making rainbows, she often had strange, unexplainable sensations of laughter in the air, a kind of chortling vibration. Like she experienced when the mean monk fell, nothing she actually heard, but a "feeling."

Once, when they had just finished making love, she

thought she saw a flash moving from the base of the waterfall into a tree and the "feeling" was particularly intense. Then it was gone and she felt foolish mentioning it to him. Perhaps it is my own happiness filling the air, she thought, a byproduct of my ecstasy.

After one year the Master allowed her to join the lessons in the courtyard. She was put at the very back of the beginning gung fu students and told she might pick a kung.

The men warmed up with one hundred one-legged squats, then switched to the other leg for another one hundred. It took her months to accomplish that. When she was training, the only thing she saw was the back of the man before her, never glimpsing Master or monks. It was up to her to dope out what to do—and at the end of the day Khan explained what she did not understand.

She considered which kung to choose. There was jumping kung: one began by standing in a shallow hole and jumping out. Every week the hole was dug deeper. There were students in the courtyard easily leaping from seven-foot holes. Khan practiced one-finger kung. For hours every day, he stood in front of an iron bar hanging from a rope, pointing his finger at it. Someday the iron bar would move.

She finally settled on balance kung, and late at night, when no one was in the courtyard, she practiced on an enormous woven straw basket, six feet around and filled with stones. She used a stool to step lightly onto the edge of the basket, then, delicately, exactingly, she walked around and around. Every week she removed one stone. Someday, when the kung was completed, she would walk an empty basket's rim.

Ah, she loved her kung. Walking the basket in rope-soled slippers under the stars became a peaceful meditation. Once, feeling very confident, remembering balance-beam days at St. Anne's, she attempted a handstand on the edge. She fell, hurting herself on the stones. The "feeling" engulfed her. Oscillating laughter seemed everywhere. She made a defiant face at nothing and stuck out her tongue. Then, thinking herself daft, she rubbed her bruises and returned to walking the basket's rim.

Being a woman, she was never to touch the golden

Buddha or the altar in the temple's sanctuary, not even to offer incense. But when scrubbing the stone floor, feeling the sanctuary's holiness, she thanked God for her life and Khan.

And so the years went—just like that. She became a skilled martial artist, proficient at karate, a student of gung fu, and at twenty-five, more lovely than ever, and ever more in love with her husband.

Now, the scowling monk on her heels, she entered the courtyard and saw Khan in a far corner, swinging his blade. He had changed in the years they had passed in the temple. His head was shaven and only his war lock remained. His body was more keenly defined, torso even more massive. But the greatest difference, most important of all, he was at peace. The Vietnam nightmares he had suffered in New York and always kept secret were no more.

His dream of finding the martial arts nun still existed (and he knew in his heart of hearts she existed), but had faded into the background. Grueling martial arts, sword making, hours of meditation, time spent with the Master and training Grey so filled his life that weeks had blended into months, then years. He had never left the hidden valley to search for the Wing Chun nun. They still discussed her, though, in their private place, where last month she had told him they were to have a baby.

Scooping his wife up, he carried her into the quiet pool, to the spot where the rainbow began. Bathed in misty colors, he held her in his arms and raised his face. "Oh God, bless us, for we are with child."

What sorrows she had experienced in the Taiwan years she carried secretly, and no one knew of the tears she shed and the hollow place that needed to be filled with loved ones. Did Llana have a baby? But now those sorrows would be gone. They decided they wanted their child born in America. So, in another month, when she would be four months pregnant, they planned to leave the temple and make their way to an American military base.

Content with her life, she went happily in the scowling monk's path to bury wooden medicine casks the Master brewed. She pushed the shovel with her foot into the section where the medicine would remain buried and gather potency for five years.

Across the courtyard, Khan rested his sword and took a dipper of water. He contemplated Grey, a single braid hanging under her blue scarf, as she dug the ground like a coolie. Her martial arts prowess was remarkable, and, on a whim turned serious, he had over the years trained her also as a commando. She had a mind like a sponge. He laughed to himself, thinking how much was in her pretty head, remembering her green eyes widening when he produced a small case and quickly assembled a MAC-10. "How did you carry that through all those airports?"

"That's your next lesson, pretty."

He made her take apart and put the gun together a million times. She could do it blindfolded. And by means of his drawings, she became familiar with many different weapons as well as electronic surveillance, rigging and wiring, building and defusing bombs, booby traps . . . He pumped all kinds of esoteric SEAL information into her. Through it all, he knew it was a game she played to please him, hardly cognizant of her own lethal potential.

Yesterday he had gone to their place before her and climbed into a low, concealing tree. He watched her come wearily to the waterfall, step from her blue cotton pajamas, and loosen her braid.

Years ago she had ceased attempts keeping up the intricate shag. Now her hair fell in a straight cascade to her waist, where the still-shagged edges spread like a fluted fan to the back of her thighs. Botticelli's *Birth of Venus*, he thought, letting out a quiet chuckle from his tree perch. No one seeing her would know she was a deadly weapon.

Just then the tree branch vibrated, almost knocking him off, and he quickly adjusted his balance, watching his wife step into the quiet water gazing at the rainbow. He could almost hear her thoughts. Sure enough, she walked through the shallow water until she stretched, reaching her arms high, and was bathed in color of the rainbow. He saw the beginning of changes in her. A slight thickening at the waist, a soft rounding of her belly, an added fullness to her breasts. Then still inside the rainbow, she sat in the water, her hands crossed over her stomach, contentment on her face.

God, I'm proud of her, he thought. He wanted her all the time, he always would.

He dropped from the tree, catching her by surprise, thoroughly chastised her for allowing him to sneak up on her like that, then loved her on the green moss carpet.

A plane flew overhead, breaking into Khan's thoughts. One of ours, he thought, noting its insignia. He had taught Grey the difference, how to signal with a mirror code should they ever need assistance.

But that was unlikely. When it came time to leave, he expected to make their way as they came, without incident. After all this time, Twinkle Toes should have long forgotten them. In the eighties, an official in Taiwan had more important things, like Red China, on his mind.

He took another dipper of water, watching her squat and place the wooden cask in the hole. He would miss the Master, the temple, but he was satiated with learning here. He no longer wanted to stay forever, but was planning the future. He would especially miss their rainbow haven with its unique energies, he mused, as she stood and began shoveling earth into the hole to cover the cask. The air had a magnetic zing there, making him think of a place he had read about, where the water ran uphill. Was it Ireland? Some kind of magnetic reversal? Yes, the rainbow place reminded him of that.

Once when he had been training her, being particularly hard on her, he had caught a terrific cramp in his butt, as though someone had kicked him. Must be the result of standing at the forge in one position for so many hours, he had thought. But at the same time, there seemed to be laughter in the air. Diabolical. Like he might hear in a fun house, except he couldn't really hear this, it was . . . He searched for a description . . . More like a vibratory sensation. Sometimes he wondered if a spirit visited the spot.

She placed a tiny marker on the dirt mound, identifying medicine she had just buried. The Master was a herbal healer whose brewed medicines were prized by people of villages even far away. Every now and then parrots screamed in the bamboo woods and it would be villagers needing medical attention. The Master set bones, laid on hands, prepared poultices. One way or the other, he fixed whatever need fixing. I have learned so much, Khan thought. Here he truly breathed the fresh air of martial arts and would love this Master always for what he shared.

And my sword! It had taken him two years to forge it. Ah, how he loved his blade. He looked at it, gleaming at his waist, hanging from a scabbard attached to the short leather swordsman's skirt he wore. Glancing about the busy courtyard at other men's swords, he knew there was none that could compare. His blade was the biggest, the heaviest. No other man besides the Master himself could handle such a blade. Grey was walking around the medicine plot, her monk on her heels. Khan laughed to himself. Who would have thought? We'll have the baby in New York. I need my family, he thought, wondering what would become of their lives. Then we will go and live in Hawaii. Of course! Why didn't I think of that sooner? Where else besides this hidden valley could he find such peace and continue a life of martial arts? Where else did waterfalls and rainbows meet? Hawaii. He could establish a gung fu temple. I'm ready to teach again. Sometime in the future when my sons are old enough, I will come back here. Search seriously for the nun. Yes, Hawaii. Grey could have Darkchild. He could have his dogs.

Khan Sun took up his mighty sword again, as across the courtyard, Grey began digging in another section, where the medicines were buried for twenty years.

Anton was banging on the wall. It was if he knew the Nightwalker was on the other side of it, working out now, preparing her body to break his in little bits, to watch him die slowly . . . Khan. Khan. Khan.

She knew now it had been Y Shin Sha deviling the mean monk in Taiwan. Y Shin Sha had always watched, making the rainbow place alive with his energies . . .

"Why didn't you stop it from happening? Where were you, Y Shin Sha, when it happened?" Her question was an hysterical whisper.

Anton's banging increased in intensity, as if he was drumming doom, the way he had doomed her happiness.

22

Grey crossed the courtyard basking in the sun's warmth. Logs piled in her arms were unwieldy and heavy, but she carried them deftly. As usual, no man looked at her, nor did she glance at them. She searched for Khan, and once in sight, her gaze never left him.

He worked diligently on a sword form, under the Master's direct tutelage. It was but days from their departure. Naked from the waist up, he swung his precious sword in beautiful arcs. He ran with sweat, gleaming in the sunlight, engendering in her thoughts of Dan's painting come to life.

She watched him, thinking about the baby and concentrating also on her belly. "I love you," she said softly to both him and the child. Was that an answering flutter she felt? Wasn't it too soon to feel the baby? she wondered as the first rifle shots resounded in the courtyard, cutting into her consciousness. She saw Khan's body jerking as bullets ripped into him and he dropped his sword. Men were falling around her. The Master fell.

Logs spilled from her arms as the courtyard filled with hard-eyed men in brown uniforms running and firing guns. She ran also—screaming amid the slaughter—toward Khan. She was grabbed by many men, threw some off, kicked others, gouged eyes, bit. A rifle butt slammed her head, and she felt her skull crush, blinding pain, clothes torn from her. They had her by the hair, by the arms, by the legs. They smashed her to the ground.

She felt the first man enter her, but her eyes never left Khan. He saw what was happening to her, tried to rise, couldn't, inched on his side toward her, blood pouring from his mouth. A huge black man appeared and plunged a bayonet into Khan's stomach. Her eyes were still riveted on Khan as the black man turned him over and plunged again with the bayonet, this time toward Khan's back. Her eyes remained on her husband's body when the second man entered her and she was screaming Khan's name. Only when the soldier atop her grabbed her hair and beat her head against the ground was Khan lost from sight.

And then a horrible pain, more than she could bear, took her. And she entered a place of such peace and beauty, she did not ever want to leave, but only be within opium-induced flower smelling visions. And there did she stay, incorporating those who cared for her into the dreams, until she awoke screaming to Lo Ling's sweet face.

The Nightwalker listened to Anton speaking on the phone. "Haleakala Crater, night after next," he said, hanging up the receiver.

Anton's long black fingers rested on the telephone as he paused in a moment of thoughtful contemplation. If someone had his phone wired, that suited him fine. However the motherfucker who was ripping him off got info didn't matter. The Haleakela Crater night after next was going to be a showdown Anton was looking forward to.

He decided to try for a couple of hours of sleep, then go searching toward evening for more coke. He dialed the front desk requesting a wake-up call in two hours, then dropped his huge frame onto the bed, and closed his eyes.

Next door, the Nightwalker made several phone calls. She booked the largest suite (with secretary at beck and call) of the Hyatt Regency at Kanapali, then into the Intercontinental in South Kehei and the Hana Ranch in Hana—all on Maui. Just in case he changed his plans at the last minute and didn't do his marijuana deal at the Haleakala Crater, there would be secure bases everywhere. "Yes, that's correct, Grey Coltrane, New York City," she said, making a last call, ordering electronic equipment put on a plane from L.A.

Should get some rest myself. Assuring herself all was quiet with Anton, pulling the living room curtains to block the bright sunlight, she stretched out on the flowered rattan sofa. Throwing one leg over its top, she stared at a picture of a hula girl, rattan framed, on the wall. "Oh, Khan, this is where we were to live," she whispered in a moment when anyone else would have cried. Swallowing the emotion the Nightwalker had vowed never to let grip her, she forced herself to sleep.

She dreamed. Mother the angel swooped the air with a white-winged, Adonis-like companion. What fun it would be for me and Khan to fly like that, she thought, watching the angels play in the sky. Then Grey missed Khan and was about to go and look for him, when, thank God, Khan was there, making love to her. The head of his big cock was just pushing her tingling pussy lips open, about to enter her when Y Shin Sha was watching and, terribly embarrassed, she started crying. Then creatures were trying to rape Mother. "No, don't rape her!" And Grey had to stop it, started fighting to kill Mother's attackers, but she didn't have to because Y Shin Sha kicked and punched them away, antennae flying. "Thank you, Y Shin Sha, for protecting Mother. Could you protect Khan, too?" Then she was holding her baby, sweet baby, ahahaha baaaaby, rocking it, so sweet, her baby.

"Aieeee." The Nightwalker was jarred awake by her own keening cry, and saw it was time for Anton's wake-up call.

Finally reaching the Vietnamese woman again, Mikel Anton argued on the phone with her. The woman again refused further service and berated him for his too-violent behavior. "Fuck off," the Merc yelled, banged the phone down, and exited, slamming the condo door with great force. This was his last planned night in Honolulu, and the Nightwalker surmised he was again headed for Hotel Street.

Unwinding her legs, the Nightwalker rose from the bathroom floor. "Soon, soon . . ." Pulling the listening device from the tile wall, she threw it inside the light frame over the bathroom mirror, quickly climbed into skimpy T-shirt and jean shorts, slipped her feet into thong sandals, and tied a bandana gypsy-style on her head, one long braid hanging from it. There were studios near Hotel Street—a stained glass shop, picture galleries, a handicraft shop—she looked like an artistic type and would blend in. It was early enough in the evening for other than whores to be in the area. Grabbing her sarong bag, she hurried out.

Hotel Street is the female prostitutes' main drag. Transvestites own Pauahi Street, one block over, parallel to Hotel. A street of two- and three-story houses, darkly lit, mostly deserted at night except for transvestites bunched on corners and near an empty lot in the middle. The transvestites plied their trade in short skirts and elastic tank tops they pulled down to expose their silicone breasts for potential customers cruising in cars.

The transvestites were tall, and no matter how long their wigs or enormous their phony breasts, it was obvious they were men. Sheer stockings covered legs too muscular and hips too square for any female body to support.

Pauahi Street was unequivocally theirs. No whore would dare try to make a buck on it. The transvestites were also deadly combatants known to beat up tricks refusing them. It was this street Mikel Anton chose to walk, spoiling for a fight.

He was furious at the motherfucker who had ripped him off and made an ass of him, plus he couldn't find any children to take to his condo. It seemed the Vietnamese woman absolutely controlled that aspect of whoredom and she had put out word on him. Only adult whores were left for him, and he, the great premature ejaculator, was scared to death of their scorn.

Now, loaded on coke and tequila, pissed off and horny as a randy dog in heat, he decided to get off by violence. Striding toward the first group of freaks, he laced his fingers together, cracking them one by one. It had been too long since he had had an aiki fight.

Anton had first seen aiki in Japan when he was a Marine. Always loving hand-to-hand combat, he was highly impressed with the dual art of control and joint breaking, but didn't have an opportunity to learn it. Then, by accident, he had run across aiki in New York a couple of years ago.

He had been in Manhattan, working for Larry, who owned an electronics business on Madison Avenue. Actually, Larry was a gun-runner, in cahoots with an old colonel who ran an anti-terrorist training camp. Anton had met Larry while at the camp looking for dirty work.

He got in with Larry, who hired him and brought him to New York. There Anton supervised arms shipments for a few months to American Indian reservations and guerrilla troops in South America—until Larry got busted by the FBI and Anton was again on the loose.

But while in New York, Anton attended a karate tournament at Madison Square Garden and to his surprise, saw a demonstration of aiki by an American master. Anton showed up at the Master's dojo the next day, impressing the Master, who was a real bedbug but lethal, by beating up his top students and then asking to learn aiki.

It was an interesting few months. The Master was really proficient and choked Anton into unconsciousness several times. No matter how powerfully Anton attacked, the older man avoided his onslaught and took him down with two fingers. With those two-finger grabs, Master could also break any joint in the body. One day Anton became so frustrated by the Master's unbeatable aiki he attacked him with a sword hanging on the wall. The Master grabbed Anton's pinky finger and, twisting it against Anton's skeletal structure, causing multiple levers, broke the huge black man's wrist, elbow, and shoulder. This was accomplished in one unruffled, two-fingered move. Anton was impressed. Though banished from the school and encased in plaster, he was happy, having learned enough to practice aiki himself.

Continuing to practice religiously, he had developed "aiki feel" and had used aiki a few times to kill people. It was wonderfully artistic, so many variables. He cracked his fingers again, excited now, wanting action. He got it.

"Wanna eat my pussy, handsome?" a six-foot freak with three pairs of false eyelashes looking like whisk brooms asked. "Whaddya say, black and beautiful?" The freak pulled up a Spandex skirt, flashing pubis. His cock and balls were tucked back between his legs.

Anton snapped a hand, seeming to lightly touch the transvestite's elbow. The freak began screaming, his arm dangling suddenly useless at his side. He kicked Anton with a spike-heeled, size-eleven shoe, and two of his friends who were standing with him on the corner leaped at Anton.

Anton laughed his way through the ensuing melee, kicking ass up and down the street. The huge black man made sure to only use aiki and really got off each time he felt a joint snap under his two-finger application or saw a body crumple from his chokes. There was one time, though, when he just couldn't resist planting a solid kick in the gut of one freak coming at him with wide-open arms, asking for a foot in his stomach. Anton left the street, melting into the night, when he heard police sirens.

The Nightwalker watched from the roof of a two-story building, her own hands tingling with chi as below her Anton did battle and mutilation, then fled. In two days she would face him and kill him with the aiki he so prided himself on. Police cars arrived. They lit the street with floodlights, and transvestites who were still mobile crowded the flabbergasted policeman, telling their stories.

She thought about her own aiki training. She had returned to America when she discovered Anton had studied aiki with the same master who had been Khan's teacher and gave her a memorable zen lesson. At the Georgia training camp, posing as a journalist, she obtained good information on Anton, but missed the fact he was hired by someone at the camp. By the time she found he was working in New York, where she resumed her life, Anton was long gone, unbelievably, into a job as a child's bodyguard! So it went, she living a covert life as Nightwalker, stalking her prey—but continually two steps behind him—as though it was ordained her fate to perpetually just miss him. Until now in Hawaii.

With her billions, she could have hired the world's best to get him, could have purchased him from any government he ever worked for. At his job in Chile at the gold mine, five hundred dollars would have bought his head on a stake. She chose to hunt him herself, to avenge Khan herself.

When her investigations had led her to the zen master and aiki, she reminisced. She had been terrified long ago with Khan that same master might give her an aiki lesson, never dreaming a time would come in her life when she would want that lesson. Pursuing Anton, she came across victims of his aiki several times. He had tortured women with it. T'was fitting he die by it, by her hand.

She presented herself to the Master. "You told me once a long time ago to come and study with you. Will you teach me?"

The Master accepted her, the first woman he had ever taught aiki. He knew some of her story. She had come back to New York amid much publicity. Her arrival at the American military base in Taiwan was leaked to the press that same day. The Master was deeply saddened by his favorite son's death. The martial arts community mourned Khan. Khan's black belts, who trained with the Master while awaiting Khan's return to America, were devastated.

Carol almost died herself, so overcome was she by the news of Khan's death. She was chief sensei of the school Khan had started, wife to Gary and mother of a son named Khan, now five. The first time Grey saw the child she almost lost control. She watched little Khan train, thinking, So graceful, young, full of hope for the future . . . Her only future was someone's death.

The zen master studied Grey carefully on that day she came to him. It had been years since he had last seen her, but he realized she was stoic neither from age nor experience. He perceived a flicker of insanity which, combined with her raving beauty, made her irresistible in his eyes. The Master trained her privately without putting her to any test, feeling life so far had tested her sufficiently. He simply instructed her in the aiki way. But she took to it so religiously, so perfectly, remaining so fanatically unruffled even under his chokes and levers, the Master's overactive curiosity finally got the best of him.

One day, with the ever-present towel draped about his neck, he looked at the black board, where Grey had earlier drawn all of the aiki breaking points, chokes, and multiple anti-levers correctly. *No one ever got them all right.* Now she was midway through a stint of one hundred fingertip push-ups, strengthening her for the "aiki feel," signaling the end of her private session with the Master. As he watched her, irritated by her absolute perfection, a group of fifteen men came onto the floor in gi, ready to train.

The zen master could not resist the temptation to see how stoic she would remain under intensified pressure. He called her from push-ups and announced a sparring session including her.

He would not soon forget what happened. She dealt

with each of the men, even the black belts, as though they were nothing. She didn't really hurt anyone, but rather embarrassed them. Each man tried without success to escape her devastating sweeps leaving him on the floor on his back, or to score on her body that was never there. After the fourth match, the Master saw a faint glow about her, but refused to acknowledge the sight, not willing to give credence to anything he could not explain. But he did give credence to the woman's fighting prowess, and after that he kept Grey from the others, only teaching aiki, delighting in her as a student. And so she became skilled.

Below, in the Honolulu night, an ambulance arrived. Watching the chaos Anton had created, she projected the Haleakala Crater on Maui across the screen of her mind. She saw him, tortured and broken at every joint, begging for his own death. "For you, Khan."

There had never been another man. There never would be. No one knew what had really happened on Taiwan. She told the military police her husband was killed by soldiers and that she had been wounded, suffered amnesia, and was cared for by villagers, she knew not where. She deleted any mention of Anton, the monastery, the camp of women, Mother, Y Shin Sha. When they attempted questioning her further before they flew her to America, she only looked blankly, as though just come from amnesia. She told no one about the rape, or the child she had lost, keeping those horrors to herself, bringing them forth to feed the fires of her hate for Anton. Only Llana knew about the baby. Something had made her tell Llana . . .

Two hours later, she boarded a plane for Maui.

23

Maui's magic unfolded below Halehana as he piloted a paramilitary McDonnell Douglas helicopter to Haleakala National Park, then flew directly over the crater. According to Hawaiian legend, demigod Maui stood on the crater rim and snared the sun from the sky, giving it its name, "House of Sun," or Haleakala.

"It's the world's largest dormant volcano," the big man yelled to the slight boy sitting in the copilot's seat over the rotary blades' *whop-whop*. It was exactly sunrise, and suddenly the floor and walls of the crater blazed with changing colors intensified by always present cloud layers. It was an astounding sight, what tourists came to see, pulling themselves from comfortable hotel beds at 4 A.M. to be at the summit observatory by six. "Nineteen square miles of volcano. The crater alone is seven-and-a-half miles long and twenty-one miles around and three thousand feet deep," he yelled.

Yu only looked ahead, not responding to the beauty below or the geography lesson. The boy never responded. The big man wondered if Anton's death might release his emotions, allow him to live as a youngster. Laugh and play. Probably not, he mused. The kid was too damaged. But, he thought, dipping the copter over the rim and into the crater, only time would tell. Anton was buying it tomorrow night.

I am through playing games, time to get it over. He kept close along a crater wall, evaluating the lava rock terrain, banks of cinders, and unusual volcanic cones, standing reminders of volcanic eruptions, the last of which had occurred about 1790. Like to drop an antipersonnel mine right *there*, he thought, sighting a niche that would neatly hide a surprise package. There were so many ways to get at Anton tomorrow night.

The sun rose higher. He transversed the crater's air space as strings of tourists on horseback at the rim headed for the crater floor, where it was already ninety degrees, though it was forty at the summit with thirty-mile-per-hour winds. If it weren't for the tourists, he'd mine the whole damn crater. What's one more big bang to a volcano? Sorry, Pele, he mentally apologized to the volcano goddess. But no need to think that way, dauntless tourists were always there.

Where would Anton make the exchange? After being ripped off so easily three times, he would be wary. Have good cover. At the summit, at eleven thousand feet? Too windy, too cold, he guessed. But then you never knew. He guided the helicopter through intricate figure-eights up and down a lava cliff, looking for possible hiding places, meeting sites. He sensed Yu's interest as the flying became tricky. They were dangerously close to the crater wall. He scanned with binoculars. At the rim, another group headed toward the depths. They had mules, tarp-covered loads. Supplies. Hmmmm. Planning on crater camping for the night? Some did. But usually they were hikers, backpackers, mostly hippies. He saw only men, big men. "Want to take her?" he yelled to Yu. "I want a closer look at that group with the mules."

A Papillion Tours helicopter bearing forty tourists flew over Haleakala National Park. Its pilot noted the small chopper inside the crater, fancily maneuvering close to the crater wall, and admired the pilot's prowess. In that copter, the man released his hold on the collective stick, leaning back in his seat, turning flight function over to the boy. As he did, Yu looked at his adopted father's hands. So large, the fingers so square at the tips. Hands that could be wonderfully gentle and incredibly strong. No one was stronger than his adopted father!

Yu knew this man wanted him to show feelings. The boy wanted to himself. Buddha, he had tried! But the wall built to hide his emotions was thick. The three years he had been free still wasn't enough time to tear it down.

Yu was terribly afraid his adopted father would misinterpret his seriousness and the fact he didn't call him "Father," addressing him by name instead. The boy had a real father, even though he could never see him again because of the shame . . .

So Yu didn't talk except when absolutely necessary and didn't smile or say "Father," but that didn't mean he didn't love the man who had adopted him. He did, desperately. The wall was just too dense. The boy worried.

As his adopted father directed him patiently, Yu manipulated the copter along the crater wall, closer to the tourists leading mules. The Chinese boy thought of how terrified he was that when the hunt was over and Anton was dead, this man would abandon him. That was the boy's biggest fear, that this relationship would end with Anton's death.

The boy maneuvered the copter even closer to the wall, nearer the objective. Suddenly the boy's back stiffened. His breath caught. The lead horseman was the commander, Mikel Anton. "Khan, Khan," he yelled. "It's him!" Yu did not have to see Anton's face to recognize him. That straight and massive back, set rigidly astride a horse, was part of a body Yu would never forget. A body he had dressed, watched for years—a body that had torturously invaded his . . . Yu's hands, one minus a pinky tip Anton had lopped off, froze on the controls.

The helicopter slapped the crater wall, breaking off a main rotor and a piece of tail. It careened crazily for a moment, then dropped like a stone.

"You're my son, with me for life, no matter what happens," Khan yelled in the only moment he had before they hit.

"Your New York messages," the highly efficient Japanese secretary in tailored skirt and blouse at the Hyatt Regency said, handing a paper to Grey. "Would you like me to make any calls for you?"

Grey looked over the long list. Many names were unfamiliar. Probably requests for money, marriage proposals, death threats. That's why Ralph Daniels, bless his old heart, had arranged this system of communication. Her New York phone rang at Fowler and Fowler. She got messages only on request, choosing never to answer a phone herself. Another piece in her jigsaw puzzle of isolation.

She frowned at one name. Anne Saxon. A free-lance reporter. Kept requesting interviews, came up to Grey on the street, at social functions, too. Grey thought a couple of times the young reporter was onto her double life. Continuing to scan the list, she smiled, spying Llana's name.

Llana was the mother of a boy and girl, and pregnant again. Llana knew something was different about Grey, having personally experienced Grey's heightened senses one day when she and her children had been in the park with Grey. Little Angelique, eighteen months old, fell, cracking her head against an iron monkey bar. She screamed and bled profusely. Grey got to her before Llana. She grabbed Angelique and placed a hand over the open wound. Llana *saw* Grey's hand glow. The bleeding stopped, the child quieted and returned to play as though nothing had happened.

Llana never spoke of the incident, but a look passed from her to Grey saying much more than thank you for healing my child.

Llana was also aware of a deadness in Grey. She had felt it the first time she hugged her when Grey came back, after everyone thought she was dead—missing all that time. "There was a baby . . . I almost had a baby," Grey said, looking directly into Llana's eyes with no display of emotion. There should be tears, Llana thought.

Llana left Khan's death, the blank years, all that had happened to Grey, with Grey. She never questioned her, but was a friend, there if needed. There was nothing else Llana could do. She knew when Grey disappeared for unexplained periods of time that something serious and scary was going on—and Llana really didn't want to know what it was about.

"Book me on the next available air tour of the Haleakala Crater," Grey said to the secretary, continuing to scan the list. Several charities had left messages, and she marked them to be called, having become an avid fund-raiser.

What will I do with myself when your murderer is dead, Khan? How will I fill the blankness then? There was her promise to Mother to teach. Her mind flashed to Y Shin Sha, as it often did. Every time she heard of resurgency on Taiwan, she wondered if it were his doing. Was he still there? Should she go back after Anton was dead and seek him?

"Ms. Coltrane," the secretary said, "I can get you on a helicopter in a half hour, leaving from the roof of this hotel. Is that all right?"

"Yes, fine. That's all for today. Thank you," she said, hustling the woman from the suite when she finished the booking. There was precious little time to make many arrangements.

As Grey reached for the phone, she again pictured Anton's brutal aiki devastation of the Honolulu transvestites. Like a black panther loose in a cage of monkeys, no contest. It would be a different story when she faced him tomorrow. She called forth Khan's image, Lo Ling's—blanked them out, raised the specter of Anton's face, and all but hatred left her mind.

Riding the lead horse inside the Haleakala Crater, Mikel Anton had been heading toward the crater floor when he spied the small helicopter bounce off the crater wall, then drop out of sight behind a lava bank. Great! Divert attention that might be coming my way, he speculated. Stupid bastard anyway to fly into this hellhole. Fuck, steaming hot and only morning! He opened another package of melted chocolate-covered macadamia nuts, ate them, threw the packet to the ground, licked melted chocolate off his fingers. Fucking heat reminds me of Taiwan. His mind flashed to the incident on the lip of a mountain gorge preceding his departure from Taiwan. One side of him truly believed he had encountered the weirdest of weird, his haunting nightmare come to life. Another side of him, the indomitable Marine, attempted rationalizing the experience. But the rationalizations never rang true. Despite the steaming heat, chills ran the black man's spine thinking of the laughing weirdo, how the air had vibrated until Anton thought his brain would burst. Like he met Joker, escaped from the *Batman* fantasy. He did not go back to the site after his broken bones healed to see if the apparition really existed. Fuck. I'll fight a herd of buffalo in the noonday sun—but a dream? He had been sick of Taiwan and the fucking gooks, anyway.

Christ, it was hot! The sun beat on his massive back, making his shirt stick with sweat. Fuck. Son of a bitch motherfucker making him go out of his way like this to avoid getting ripped off. Anton's tree-trunk thighs rubbed uncomfortably against the bulky Western saddle as the nag he rode did its best to negotiate the narrow path amid lava rock. He turned in the saddle, looking behind. Also on horses, four tank-size locals, all bearing shotguns, led four mules loaded with eight hundred pounds of Ritchie's primo marijuana—replacement for the last ripped-off load.

Anton turned forward again in the saddle, cursing the heat. He meant to ride the circumference of the crater until he felt like making radio contact with the people who were to get the grass. Anton had suddenly changed the rendezvous to today, notifying the people by pay phone in the wee hours of this morning—making sure he wasn't followed to the payphone—of the change in tactics.

Anton had changed his M.O. completely, taking every precaution now after deciding he wanted to keep his job too much to risk going for revenge while taking care of business. He knew if he lost another load, it would end this gig.

He conceived this last-minute plan—broad daylight in the middle of the fucking Haleakala Crater with tourists inside, helicopters overhead, rangers . . .

Tomorrow night, after safely transferring this load, he promised himself to take care of his smartass friend, whoever he was. Yeah, set the motherfucker up good, have some fun. Right now he felt confident about making the exchange, especially with that small copter down. Deciding to make the meet not too far from where the damaged helicopter must have hit, he put a walkie-talkie to his mouth, broadcasting to those who waited.

She peered through the tour copter's window with state-of-the-art West German Steinger Optik binoculars, examining Haleakala's terrain, thinking she had until tomorrow night to plan things perfectly. She knew where Anton was headquartered—in Pukalanai, downcountry from the crater—in a simple cabin with a simple phone system. As soon as she had arrived on Maui, where a rental car awaited, she had scouted the site, dropping an infinity transmitter (ordered from California, waiting at the airport for her) in his phone receiver. But he hadn't used the phone—that bothered her. She was sure he would continue announcing his every move, flapping his big mouth over the phone as he had in Honolulu.

She calculated the crater's logistics: the vast bowl, result of centuries of erosion, containing lava cliffs, volcanic cones like small mountains, terrain that could hide anything, tourists on horses, hikers on foot. Over a loudspeaker the helicopter's pilot described the silver sword enclosure at the summit protecting "an endangered species of surrealistic-appearing plants with a silver glow, hence their name."

As the pilot continued lecturing and cruising the big A-Star 350D Papillion back and forth over the crater, she spied more people on horseback and zoned in with her high-powered binoculars. Three women led by a young man. She activated a microscope zoom and read the young man's T-shirt: "PONY EXPRESS TOURS."

I'm glad I've got the dogs, she thought. There had been a gorgeous pair of rented rottweilers waiting in her suite at the Hyatt. "Track anything from here to Samoa," promised the trainer who brought them. "And eat it alive if you want them to," he said, grinning, holding the deep-chested, black-and-tan rottweilers by thick leather leads. He demonstrated the hand signals that prompted the dogs and taught her verbal commands. Yes, she was glad for the dogs, for she might well need them to track Anton in this crater. The rottweilers were already familiar with his scent. She had left them with a stolen undershirt of his for company after thrusting her own nose into it.

Confronted with the crater's terrain, not knowing where he would make his meet, she was also forced to consider she might miss him. Three years to this pinnacle. Had she blown her chance by being too picky, too theatrical? Should she just have waited in his condo in Honolulu? Killed him there? Not to worry, she chided herself. I know where he is all the time now. I can always find him. That thought was not comforting. She was primed and ready. She had waited long enough.

Just then the big helicopter banked inside the crater's rim and she spied a strange caravan of horses and mules, men bigger than normal. Zoning in, she gasped, seeing Anton at its lead, tarps covering what must be marijuana. As she went to highest power on the binoculars, Anton's bulk came close. The Nightwalker scanned his body astride the horse, muscular thighs pushing at soft, washed-out jeans, massive chest straining against a sweat-soaked white shirt. She thought of how he had looked in tiny shorts at the International Club in Honolulu. She shivered with delight, realizing he had changed his plans. Not to another location as she had thought he might, but to an earlier date. But daylight? Would he dare, or would he wait until nightfall? Yes, he would dare. The Nightwalker admired Anton's audacity while blessing the quirk of fate placing her overhead of her prey. *I must get into that crater!* Rising from her seat in the forty-passenger helicopter, she put on her most vivacious smile and headed for the cockpit.

Khan pulled himself from a tangle of console panel parts and windshield, wiped blood from his eye, and felt the sting of an open cut in his brow. Looking at Yu, he saw his eyes were closed. Khan reached a hand to the boy's neck to feel his pulse. Slowly extracting himself from the wreckage of the chopper, checking to be sure he had no broken bones, he made his way around the other side. The door was caved in. He ripped it off as though it were paper and carefully pulled Yu from the wreckage. *Got to get away from here,* he thought, *somebody probably saw us go down.* The giant Eurasian grabbed a bulging canvas bag from the cockpit, shouldered it, threw the still unconscious Yu over his other shoulder, and hurried in the direction he figured Anton would come if he continued following the crater's circumference trail.

After gaining a half-mile's distance from the wrecked chopper, Khan took cover in a lava fissure, laying the boy gently down. He took off Yu's shoes and began strongly massaging his feet, then switched to his hands. He kept this up, alternating hands and feet, until the boy's eyes opened. "You're gonna be okay, son, you're gonna be okay," Khan repeated in a soothing voice, like the one he had used years ago when he had found Yu hidden in a deserted Taiwan mountain camp and coaxed the boy into coming with him.

"*Ni hau a?*" Yu said in a barely audible whisper, looking at the blood over Khan's eye.

"*Hau.* I'm fine. Speak English," Khan said with a grin. "You stay here, it's cool. You're well hidden. I'm going to see if I can find him. I'll be back for you."

"I want to go with you," the boy said.

"No," Khan said emphatically. He picked up the canvas bag and strode off. As he came out of the shade of the fissure, the blazing sun glinted off his cleanly shaven head.

Yu lay back in the shaded place, hand going to his belt checking to make sure *it* was there. Yes. The slight Chinese boy found and caressed a leather sheath holding the U.S. Marine Raider stiletto. The commander's favorite blade and souvenir of Yu's hell. It was the only thing the boy had taken from Taiwan, a macabre reminder of his former master, that stiletto had cut off his fingertip and Yu had seen Anton kill with it. Khan had admired the stiletto, never knowing it belonged to his most hated enemy. "My son, no matter what," Yu whispered, repeating Khan's last words to him before they had crashed. Yu prayed.

The pilot/owner of Papillion Air circled the Haleakala Crater, feeling every now and then at the packet of money in his lapel pocket. Ten grand in hundred-dollar bills! What luck! He hadn't believed it at first, thought the gorgeous woman in the white linen suit with the fancy binoculars was kidding about giving him ten grand to cut short the tour and hire out to her. She made a quick believer of him, though, by handing him a thousand dollars right then and there. Happily he dropped her on the roof of the Hyatt, refunded the other passengers' money, dropped them, then returned for her.

The pilot checked her in his mirror. She looked like a different person now, fastened to a window with binoculars. The woman and two devil dogs, the kind they used in horror movies, were the cabin's only occupants. She was no less beautiful than in her white suit, but now she was scary as hell!

The woman had appeared crazed to him from the moment he returned and saw her waiting on the Hyatt roof, attired in khaki T-shirt, combat boots, and camouflage pants. A military cap covered her unforgettable hair. The pilot sensed those deep fatigue pockets bulged with things lethal and that the too-silent dogs on thick leather leashes were also weapons. He felt again at the packet of hundred-dollar bills and hoped he could just drop her off and get away without becoming involved in whatever she was about.

In the helicopter's cabin, two hours after first seeing him, the Nightwalker breathed with relief as she again spotted Anton on the circumference trail. She instructed the scared pilot to hover, then languidly examined the Merc. He wore a straw cowboy hat fending off the sun, but frequently he removed it to fan his face and she drank in the gleaming blackness of him. The Nightwalker examined the men in his retinue, their size, their shotguns . . . I should let him do his deal. He's got to give the grass to somebody, somewhere. Once he's rid of it, I can get him alone. She saw how slowly the mules plodded under their heavy loads in the heat. I could keep up with him easily on foot. But where will he deal? How? She saw from the air that Anton's caravan kept to the narrow trail, and she guessed he would have to in order to protect the animal's hooves from sharp lava rock and cinder. She knew it for sure when the pilot flew over the trail Anton had already covered and saw fairly equally spaced candy wrapper litter. Four of them. He was eating one per hour, she calculated. I have to keep surveillance until he dumps the marijuana.

The pilot was genuinely relieved to say good-bye to the hell-bent-for-leather woman and dogs at the summit observatory parking lot, where she had instructed him to drop her. He also thanked his lucky stars she made no mention of picking her up later. I'm glad she's not mad at me, the pilot thought, hopping the copter back into the gale winds, watching her retreating form jog toward the crater, a rottweiler on either side of her.

The Nightwalker trotted the observatory road with the dogs. The wind blew great gusts and it was only thirty-five degrees. Neither she nor the dogs paid the weather any mind.

Reaching the rim of the crater, she jumped in, continued running, digging in her heels to avoid slipping, so steep and treacherous was the trail she choose. The Nightwalker felt the big dogs' chi on either side of her. A male and a female, keeping exact pace with her. My bookends, she thought, feeling good. Alive! It was 10 A.M.

24

Khan strode from the fissure behind the lava cliffs where he had left Yu, mentally cataloguing his weaponry. The sniping equipment to be used tomorrow night was not with him. He had not planned to be stuck via a downed copter in this crater!

Pulling off his khaki safari shirt, he tied it over his head for protection against the blazing sun and checked his watch. Ten. Walking, he pulled parts of a field-stripped MK Arms MK760 9mm. carbine from the canvas bag. In a few seconds he reassembled the sleek 760 with its handy folding skeleton stock. They called it a new weapon, but that was hedging. It was in fact an almost screw-for-screw copy of the Smith & Wesson 76 9mm. submachine gun discontinued a few years ago. Good weapon, but he would have to get closer to Anton than he intended. No, life doesn't always give us what we plan, Khan thought, reliving his last sight of Grey:

Shot, almost dead, he had crawled in the dirt of the courtyard towards her, saw Mikel Anton suddenly standing over him with a poised bayonet. Khan used the only survival technique left—feigned death—and took the bayonet's gut-slicing thrust. Still aware when Anton turned him over, awaiting a last bayonet thrust that never came, he blacked out.

He awoke to silence, his own pain. Through bloody blurs that were his eyes, he saw dead bodies everywhere. Grey! Not far. Fingers clawing the earth, gripping and pulling, pulling, until he reached her naked, bloody body, touching the carotid artery at her neck. Nothing! A last look, then Khan pulled at the earth as his shot and stabbed body permitted, inching away from what had been his wife.

Now, moving quickly along the crater trail, Khan laid

the assembled 760 along his leg, took a nylon covering case from the canvas bag, concealed the carbine, and Velcroed it to his leg. Little pistol caliber semi-automatic. Not what he would have wished for—a long-range sniper weapon would be preferable. Redundant fool, you got what you got. He rummaged the canvas bag. Ah, a scope. A short-tube 4X rifle scope. He could use it on its own. Better than nothing. His binoculars had been smashed in the crash. He realized he was thinking trivia in order to wipe the picture of Grey from his mind.

Amazingly, he had survived. Buddha meant it to be, perhaps so he could save the boy. Moving ever closer to Anton, Khan thought of how he had doctored himself with nothing but mud until he was found by trusted villagers bringing supplies to the monastery. Those villagers were appalled to find the monastery a graveyard— the giant foreigner loved by the Master in the woods near death. The terrified villagers risked their lives to hide and heal him. He left on his own as soon as he was able.

Khan retreated for almost two years, then returned to Taiwan, seeking Anton. His inquiries led him to a deserted camp in the mountains. The soldiers were gone, Anton gone, only the boy Yu, living like a jungle rat, afraid of everyone and everything.

Khan took Yu back to Hawaii and the Valley of the Temples, Khan's home now, where his father had left him as a boy. The zen monks allowed Khan to live among them, and when he came back with Yu, they accepted the boy also. And Khan followed Anton's mercenary trail, always just missing him, until by Buddha's humor, Anton surfaced as a central figure in Hawaii's uppermost echelons of marijuana dealing. And in Hawaii, Khan bedeviled the black man, taking his loads of marijuana, causing Anton the worst kind of embarrassment before his employers, showing Yu how to make his enemy lose face before killing him.

So now, he would wipe Mikel Anton from the face of the earth. He and Yu could get on with life. Suddenly the big Eurasian pictured New York—so many loved ones who thought him dead. He thought about the amount of noise the 760 would make. How he might quickly conceal it and Anton's body, get back to Yu, out of the crater.

Khan's thoughts were broken by the sight of two men

on horseback approaching the crater floor. He scrutinized them. Preppy, pressed, plaid shirts, loafers? One of them had a walkie-talkie. *They had come to meet Anton.*

Sitting by the side of the trail as though resting from the sun, Khan waited until the two horsemen passed him, thinking how inexperienced at survival the men were not to pay attention to him at all. When they were almost out of sight, he again took to the trail.

25

It was eleven when Anton saw the two men approaching. He could tell they were Ritchie's friends. Assholes. Gentlemen pot dealers. The huge black man thought how lucky Ritchie was to have his services and was forced to surpress his laughter at their outfits as the two men rode closer. Gringos. Extremely uncomfortable on horseback, the men got a lot more uncomfortable when they saw Anton, his local helpmates, and their shotguns. So now face reality, assholes, Anton thought.

"Here's your product," Anton said, nodding his head at the loaded mules, when they were close enough to talk, near where a lava cliff began. The two men looked at the mules as though they were creatures from another planet.

"How-how are we going to get it out of here?" the blond one said, squinting in the sun without hat or sunglasses, having labored under the misconception they were meeting Anton to set up an exchange point.

"I'll send my men with you."

"Well, I don't know," the blond man said, obviously out of his element, thinking of being killed for the marijuana, cursing the idea that had them doing this personally for secrecy, in case it was one of their underlings masterminding the rip-offs. This was Ritchie's replacement for that which was taken. Ritchie swore Anton was trustworthy and would guarantee this load's delivery. Never in their wildest dreams had they imagined being confronted with four mules bearing eight hundred pounds of marijuana in the middle of a volcanic crater.

Fuck! Anton felt a headache worsening in the heat. He reached for his last candy packet, swearing tonight he would sleep. These *stupidos* were going to be a pain in the ass until they were out of the crater. "Don't worry, my *moks*," he said, using the most disparaging term possible, referring to the oversize Hawaiian men behind him, "are scared to death of me. They won't mess with you or the product." He shrugged. "Then again, take the mules and go. Radio me where you leave them." Anton watched them spook at that suggestion, too. They were fucking spooked by everything, especially him. Anton knew his reputation among this group—he enjoyed the hell out of their fear.

By rights his job ended here. But these assholes were good customers, and this was the first time they had entered the scenario themselves. Anton had never seen them before. Their hirelings had physically handled the pakalolo—before the ripoffs. The Merc was enjoying the buyers' discomfort and would have fucked with their minds longer if not for his headache. He decided under the circumstances, scoring brownie points with Ritchie's crowd couldn't hurt.

"Tell you what," he said magnanimously, "Lead where you will. My men will follow with the mules. I'll bring up the rear, make sure everything's okay. Just get your show on the road."

The assholes agreed, although still obviously jittery, and Anton's smiling demeanor did nothing to ease their trepidation. As the group commenced traveling, Anton made them yet more jittery by allowing the buyers and the caravan of mules and men to be out of sight for periods of time, during which he smoked pot. Then the black man would kick the shit out of the plug he rode and gallop to the caravan. His helter-skelter approach eased the buyers' minds and scared the piss out of them at the same time.

Anton was tiring of the game, just fanning himself with his hat, wondering by which trail the buyers would finally exit, when he saw the soldier and the dogs scrambling a steep lava cliff. Badass dogs. He admired the powerful rottweilers. Must be Canine Corps, he surmised, seeing the trainer's khaki and camouflage attire. Yeah, probably Marine. Tough terrain. Good teamwork! Hawaii was loaded with military training everywhere. Then he saw the dog trainer pause for a moment, stand, twist his torso. It was not a man, but a full-breasted, small-waisted woman—exactly the lushly mature sort Mikel Anton detested. His curiosity aroused, he kept an eye on the sensuous body atop the cliff until he rode out of sight.

The Nightwalker knew who and what was within the five-miles-square radius she surveyed from her position on a lava cliff. She deduced Anton was giving safe passage to the Harvard types who had come for the marijuana. She had first spied the unlikely pot dealers from the helicopter. They had had a camper in the summit parking lot. There also was activity in an area concealed from the trail by volcanic cones. A helicopter down there, attracting air rangers, who hovered it a few times. She guessed there soon would be horse rangers come to examine it. A slow-moving group, four tourists and a guide on horses, were about three miles behind Anton. A tall man on foot with a bad leg walked the trail about a half mile from Anton. He was unusual, she kept her glass on him. A shirt was tied over his head, his torso was bare. She traveled the limping man's big body with state-of-the-art binoculars. Scarred chest and belly. Examining his head, she saw the long sleeves of the khaki shirt twisted into bands, creating a neatly tied and tucked headdress. Lawrence of Arabia. Sensible in his circumstance, she thought, saving himself from the sun. But why is he out here without a shirt, on foot, alone? She spied a canvas bag slung over the limping man's shoulder, checked out the big figure's stiff leg again. Swinging her glasses to the downed chopper on the cliff's other side, between it and the lava wall, she realized: *the man had come from the copter.*

Playing the binoculars on the man's head, she strived to see his face. It was concealed by the headdress's shadow. She dropped her sights. His body was incredibly developed —lithe, even with a stiff leg. Khan had been . . . Her thoughts were horribly interrupted as the big man on the trail uncovered a semi-automatic strapped to his leg, took it off his leg, and became suddenly agile. He began loping, gun in hand, in Anton's direction. He was after Anton!

"No," she yelled, "you can't have him. He's mine!" She broke into a run, scrambling, a dog on either side of her, down the treacherous lava cliff.

*   *   *

Yu scurried up and into the lava rock. The slight boy had never before disobeyed his adopted father, but now his fear of losing him drove Yu from where Khan left him. At least I will be able to see, he thought, picking his way through cinder rock, circumventing the trail Khan had taken.

Anton was at the bottom of a trail to the rim. Finally he was watching the buyers, men, and mules ride up it. The two buyers had their heads together. Anton imagined they plotted how to get rid of the locals before the men saw their vehicle and its license plate. Anton was wishing they would just get it the fuck over with so he could get out of this hellhole himself when the woman Marine or whatever the fuck she was appeared above him on the sheer crater wall.

Nobody could negotiate that wall, let alone a woman. Before he could further ponder, the woman jumped from the height, landing directly in front of his horse, and pulled off her military cap. Blazing reddish hair streaked with gold spilled from it, framing a ravishingly beautiful face punctuated with exotic green eyes. Before the incredulous Anton she opened her arms as though to embrace him. Her full breasts thrust against her khaki T-shirt. "I love you," she stage-whispered, then began laughing.

A fucking lunatic! He felt his horse spook as the nut's laughter increased in intensity. He kicked the nag to run her over, but the horse reared instead. Motherfucker! Why did he have to run into this screwball? He had a brand-new Colt 10mm. automatic and was dying to try the handgun out, but the downed copter was not far away. A gunshot now could bring the wrong sort of attention. The marijuana was not out of the crater yet, he thought, the caravan would still be below the rim. The mercenary looked around for the rottweilers, for they were all that prevented him from dismounting.

"Don't worry about the dogs," she said, halting her insane laughter. "They're making sure we're alone. Just you and me." Her voice was throaty, teasing. She batted her eyelashes.

"Fucking cunt. I'll kill you."

"Come and play with me, handsome," she said, her jade eyes gleaming.

Then, to Anton's astonishment, she began snapping her hands in a manner he recognized all too clearly from those Taiwanese nightmares that had so haunted him, and he would never forget. Wild-eyed, she resumed laughing, and this time, to Anton's horror, her laughter assumed a reverberating quality. He leapt from his horse.

Khan came around a bend and saw a large rottweiler standing in the trail. Anton's? He didn't remember seeing a dog. He took a few steps nearer. The dog growled, but remained in position. He moved off the trail into lava rock, which seemed to appease the rottweiler, who watched him walk away, but continued guarding the trail. Khan climbed.

As soon as he gained height enough, he peered ahead with his scope. In the small field it provided he saw Anton dismounted, seemingly intent on something before him, his bulk blocking whatever it was. Khan swung the scope. The caravan was not in near view. Have to go up and over, he thought, spotting another rottweiler a little along the trail. He moved quickly, hurrying to get close enough to Anton to take him out while no others were in the area. Attaining enough altitude to be out of the dogs' vision, Khan came upon a trail and headed down it, toward the crater floor and Anton's location. That's when he ran head-on into the caravan. The two preppies at its lead saw the gun he carried, remembered seeing him before on the trail below, and panicked. The four locals leading the loaded mules took another attitude. Suddenly four shotguns were pointed at him.

Anton reached for her throat. She smiled and broke his thumb. His eyes widened in disbelief. He looked at his broken thumb as if it were on someone's else's body, then lunged for her again. The Nightwalker broke his forefinger, then leapt lightly to a lava rock, and stuck up her own thumb. "This little piggy is for Lo Ling." She put up her forefinger. "And this little piggy is for my baby," she crooned in a sing song. "And this little piggy," she screamed, coming off the rock at him, suddenly a flying fury with aiki claws, "is for Khan!" and hooked his jugular.

*   *   *

Khan's mind was a machine gun. The four men with shotguns ringed him. "Drop da gun, Bhra," one said. Khan hit the ground and rolled. It was impossible for any of the men to fire as they were facing each other, and Khan's sudden movements spooked the horses and mules. The animals reared, snorted, backed up, circled. In the confusion, Khan rolled and fired with perfect accuracy, blasting two shotguns from their holders' hands, wounding their fingers. The preppies galloped from sight, scared out of their minds.

Another local dropped his shotgun as his horse bucked. Khan rolled, grabbed the 20-gauge, tossed it into a lava fissure. As the spooked mules ran, another man, his arm hooked into their reins, was pulled from his saddle and hit the rocks hard. He's out of it, Khan calculated, rolling still, evaluating the last man left. He saw him jump from his horse and scurry behind a rock, wanting no part of Khan's deadly accurate bullets.

Got to get out of here myself, Khan thought, realizing gunshots might have been heard by the wrong ears. Scrambling to his feet, he ran at the two men whose fingers he had shot bloody and, whirling in a spinning crescent kick so rapid his leg was a blur, he knocked both men cleanly out and scrambled once again in Anton's direction.

In the instant of contact, the Nightwalker bent a hooking thumb properly around and behind Anton's jugular and closed her clawed fingers, gagging him. With her legs wound around the huge black man's body, she rode him like a lioness atop running prey. His thick, engorged jugular pulsed life in her hand. I could kill him now, she thought, even visualizing sinking her teeth into his blood-filled jugular and ripping out his throat, but it was too soon. He had not yet suffered properly. Letting his jugular snap back into place, she two-finger-hooked into a cluster of nerves just above his collarbone and applied aiki pressure. The black man yelled in pain. It was such a sweet sound to the Nightwalker that she hesitated a second to appreciate it, breaking a rule of her kind.

No matter. He reeled with pain. Broken fingers or no, well trained or not, this was a bitch and no bitch could best Mikel Anton! The huge black man smashed an elbow deep into the hellcat's solar plexus.

His elbow struck true. She hit rocks and rolled, bruising back, hip, and elbow, and lay gasping.

Thinking her stunned, he lunged again. Struggling for breath, the Nightwalker rolled closer to his legs as he came, feeling rocks cut her body. It was the opposite direction he expected her to take and caught him by surprise.

Taking advantage of the moment, still gasping air, she grasped his foot by toe and heel, twisted to an anti-lever, and gave a strong wrench, fracturing his ankle and metatarsal. The bones gave forth crunching sounds as they broke.

He felt the third and fourth bones break, took it, stood on his good leg, realizing through the excruciating pain he had to kill her immediately before she killed him. It took four broken bones for him to admit the bitch was aiki lethal! On one leg he lunged for her yet again, his good hand forward, racing adrenaline driving him despite his agony.

"I'm Mrs. Khan Sun," she yelled, leaping out of his reach and in another instant to his side. He turned towards her, his hand with broken fingers nearest. In a flash she had the hand, anti-levered, broke that wrist and elbow. "I'm Mrs. Khan Sun!" She looked into his face, searching for realization, needing him to know who killed him, why he was slowly dying by her hand. "Mrs. Khan Sun!" she screamed.

Those words Khan heard. He raced toward them, recognizing the voice, believing, not believing. "Grey, Grey," he screamed at the top of his lungs, coming over a volcanic cone.

She was frozen to the spot by the voice yelling her name, a voice she had never expected to hear again.

Despite the incredible pain he suffered, the mercenary took advantage of the instant when the woman's eyes were glued over his shoulder as though seeing a ghost. With his unbroken hand Anton grabbed her throat.

She saw Khan! The man with the headdress was Khan! In that moment, her neck in Anton's iron grip, when thousands of thoughts became one, among them the realization that Y Shin Sha had known Khan lived, by all rights she should have lost her life in Anton's bone-crushing choke.

But it did not happen that way. His hand let loose its mighty grip, not because of a bullet Khan fired, although his sights were on Anton. For in his incredulous recognition of Grey, Khan saw with horror if he fired, he would shoot her too. Nor was it the dogs who saved Grey's life. Those well-trained rottweilers kept their positions on the trail.

It was a slight, battered sixteen-year-old Chinese boy coming from a fissure behind the cliff who caused Anton to loosen his stranglehold on her throat.

For, at that instant when Anton dangled her by her throat, Yu thrust the U.S. Marine Raider stiletto, Anton's own weapon, up from the ground into Anton's gonads. But Yu was not a knife fighter. The boy trembled and missed. So it was not the commander's balls Yu sliced with the deadly sharp stiletto, but Anton's femoral artery, which set up a lovely gusher of blood. Anton dropped Grey as his life blood spurted into the air. For a flashing second Anton looked beneath him, saw Yu, saw the stiletto, recognized both.

With a burst of survival instinct, Anton clapped a hand over his spouting artery and tried to remount his horse with the other. But he could only dangle from the pommel. The horse, already spooked, smelling Anton's blood, bolted, plunging frantically around the lava cone. Anton dragged for a bit, over the rocks, past Khan Sun, then fell into a fissure.

And there he lay, having time, as his life blood left him, to consider the three faces peering at him from above. He now positively recognized each: the fighting champion Anton thought he had killed in Taiwan, his woman, also surmised dead, who had bested him at aiki, he appreciated that, a macabre humor having hold of him now; the boy he had ripped from his mother and enslaved, killing him with his own stiletto . . . Then Anton, who had never believed in fate or karma, acknowledged both. Two of the faces watching him disappeared, but the boy remained. And as Mikel Anton finished bleeding away his wretched life, Yu's face was his last sight.

It was near noon in the Haleakala Crater when a group of tourists on horses came over a rise and were greeted by a strange sight. They rode by, wondering why two of the most beautiful people they had ever seen were hugging each other and crying while a blood-spattered, skinny Chinese boy stood watching and grinning.

So the boy who would never smile, smiled; and the woman sworn never to cry, cried; and the man sworn to celibacy was again a romantic lover.

Holding Grey, seeing Yu's smiles, Khan thought, praise Buddha, we are a family.

And then, to better drink her in, he moved her to arm's length and saw his magnificent wife had a glow about her. He looked up, out of the magic place, Haleakala, House of the Sun, at the clear Hawaiian sky and thought how interesting life was going to be.